"Miss Sloane, I assure you that the thought hadn't crossed my mind. Granted, you have, er, unusual ideas for a female. But I...I..."

"I am joking, sir," said Olivia. "I couldn't resist. You always look so serious. So solemn."

"Do I?"

John smiled, and as a spark from the torchiere caught on its curl, Olivia felt a shiver of fire dance down her spine. She wondered what it would be like to be kissed by him. Would it be a mere perfunctory brushing of lips? Somehow that firm, sensual mouth seemed to whisper silent promises of stronger passions.

Oh, what moonlight madness has taken hold of me? Olivia was ruefully aware of needing a steel corset to cage the longings that all of a sudden were hammering against her ribs.

"Indeed," she said, mustering a show of outward calm. "You have a countenance made for teasing, Lord Wrexham." Her gaze moved back to the ballroom. "We ought to be going in, sir."

And you *have a countenance made for kissing.* The thought leapt unbidden into his head as John offered his arm to Olivia.

Acclaim for the
Hellions of High Street Series

Scandalously Yours

"Excellent!...witty and fun...an entertaining Regency romance."

—DreysLibrary.com

"A promising start to a new series. It's an easy, undemanding read, the characters are likable, and the writing is intelligent and often humorous."

—All About Romance (LikesBooks.com)

"Delightful...What a beginning!...a must-read...Ms. Elliott has done a wonderful job of mixing romance with politics and passion. Well done indeed!"

—MyBookAddictionReviews.com

Passionately Yours

"A classic example of romance, adventure, and fun! Only Cara Elliott could balance all these elements and keep them equally interesting...Carolina Sloane is such a fantastic character!"

—RamblingsfromthisChick.blogspot.com

"Entertaining...She writes with a very engaging and funny style."

—SweptAwaybyRomance.com

"Engaging characters and an intriguing storyline will keep you up all night turning pages...a very enjoyable read!"
—MyBookAddictionReviews.com

Sinfully Yours

"A pleasant and enjoyable read."
—HarlequinJunkie.com

"Fun and well-written."
—RedHotBooks.com

"Sinfully fantastic!...I enjoyed this story immensely, would recommend and re-read!"
—RamblingsfromthisChick.blogspot.com

Acclaim for the Lords of Midnight Series

Too Dangerous to Desire

"What a wonderful storyteller and a wonderful way to end a trilogy. A must-read."
—MyBookAddictionReviews.com

"The well-paced storyline, brimming with several nail-biting escapades, keeps readers glued to the pages as much as the love story. Quite simply, this fast, sexy read is a pleasure."
—*RT Book Reviews*

"What a fun, little guilty pleasure read this turned out to be. I ate this book up like a fine dessert...A romance that should be on everyone's keeper shelf."
—GraceBooksofLove.com

Too Tempting to Resist

"Elliott provides readers with a treat to savor in this fun, sexy, delicious tale. With smart, sassy characters, a charming plot, and an erotic bad boy/good girl duo, this fast-paced story will keep readers' attention."
—*RT Book Reviews*

"Nothing is more sensuous than a delicious meal, and Cara Elliott's food-inspired sex scenes are, quite literally, *Too Tempting to Resist*...likable characters, a fast-moving plot, and unique, engaging sex scenes that are deliciously tempting."
—HeroesandHeartbreakers.com

"Haddan and Eliza's charming wit and banter will absolutely capture the reader from their first meeting...[It] can easily be read as a stand-alone, though most readers will want to rush out and find a copy of the first book to get more of Cara Elliott's Hellhounds. A real page-turner, readers will not be able to put this book down."
—RomRevToday.com

Too Wicked to Wed

"Elliott packs the first Lords of Midnight Regency romance with plenty of steamy sex and sly innuendo...As

Alexa and Connor flee London to escape vengeful criminals, their mutual attraction sizzles beneath delightful banter. Regency fans will especially appreciate the authentic feel of the historical setting."

—*Publishers Weekly*

"A surprisingly resourceful heroine and a sinfully sexy hero, a compelling and danger-spiced plot, lushly sensual love scenes, and lively writing work together perfectly to get Elliott's new Regency-set Lords of Midnight series off to a delightfully entertaining start."

—*Booklist*

"The romance, adventure, and sensuality readers expect from Elliott are here, along with an unforgettable hoyden heroine and an enigmatic hero. She takes them on a marvelous ride from gambling hells to ballrooms, country estates, and London's underworld."

—*RT Book Reviews*

Praise for the
Circle of Sin Trilogy

To Tempt a Rake

"From the first page of this sequel…Elliott sweeps her readers up in a scintillating and sexy romance."

—*Publishers Weekly*

"An engaging cast of characters...Readers who thrive on empowered women, sexy and dangerous men, and their wild adventures will savor Elliott's latest."

—*RT Book Reviews*

"Elliott expertly sifts a generous measure of dangerous intrigue into the plot of her latest impeccably crafted Regency historical, which should prove all too tempting to readers with a craving for deliciously clever, wickedly sexy romances."

—*Booklist*

To Surrender to a Rogue

"4 stars! Elliott's ability to merge adventure, romance, and an intriguing historical backdrop will captivate her readers and earn their accolades."

—*RT Book Reviews*

"With mystery, intrigue, laughter, and hot, steamy passion...what more could any reader want?"

—TheRomanceReadersConnection.com

"Another fantastic read from Cara Elliott. Can't wait until the next book."

—SingleTitles.com

To Sin with a Scoundrel

"HOT...Charming characters demonstrate her strong storytelling gift."

—*RT Book Reviews*

ALSO BY CARA ELLIOTT

Circle of Sin Series

To Sin with a Scoundrel
To Surrender to a Rogue
To Tempt a Rake

Lords of Midnight Series

Too Wicked to Wed
Too Tempting to Resist
Too Dangerous to Desire

Hellions of High Street Series

Sinfully Yours
Passionately Yours
Scandalously Yours

Scandalously Yours

CARA ELLIOTT

FOREVER

NEW YORK   BOSTON

Forever
Hachette Book Group
1290 Avenue of the Americas
New York, NY 10104
forever-romance.com

Printed in the United States of America

Originally published as an ebook by Forever in January 2014
First mass market edition: March 2015
10 9 8 7 6 5 4 3 2 1

OPM

Forever is an imprint of Grand Central Publishing.
The Forever name and logo are trademarks of Hachette Book Group, Inc.

The Hachette Speakers Bureau provides a wide range of authors for speaking events. To find out more, go to www.hachettespeakersbureau.com or call (866) 376-6591.

The publisher is not responsible for websites (or their content) that are not owned by the publisher.

For my Perfect Hero
You know who you are

Scandalously Yours

Chapter One

$\mathcal{A}$ soft flutter of air stirred the emerald-dark leaves, releasing the faint scent of oranges. Drawing a deep breath, the Earl of Wrexham slid back a step deeper into the shadows of the large potted trees. He closed his eyes for an instant, pretending he was back in the steamy plains of Portugal rather than the gilded confines of a Mayfair ballroom. The caress of sticky-warm humidity against his cheeks was much the same, though here it was due to the blaze of dancing couples in their peacock finery, not the bright rays of the Mediterranean sun...

"Ah, there you are, John." The leaves rustled again, loud as cannon fire to his ear, and the earl felt a glass of chilled champagne thrust into his hand. "Your sister sent me to inquire why the devil you are cowering in the bushes when you should be dancing with one of the dazzling array of eligible young beauties." His brother-in-law gave an apologetic grimace. "Those are her words, by the by, not mine."

"Tell her I've a pebble in my shoe," muttered John after quaffing a long swallow of the wine. Its effervescence did little to wash the slightly sour taste from his mouth. "And that I'm simply making a strategic retreat to one of the side salons to remove the offending nuisance."

Speaking of removal, he thought to himself, *perhaps there is a side door leading out to the gardens close by, through which I can escape from the overloud music, the overbrittle laughter, the overzealous mamas with marriageable daughters.*

"Pebble," repeated his brother-in-law. "In the shoe. Right-ho. Quite impossible to dance under those conditions." Henry cocked a small salute with his glass. "If you turn right at the end of the corridor," he added in a lower voice, "you'll find a small study filled with exotic board games from the Orient. Our host keeps a large humidor there, filled with a lovely selection of cheroots and cigars from the Ottoman Empire." A sigh. "I'd join you, but I had better remain here and try to keep Cecilia distracted."

"Thank you." John gave a tiny tug to the faultlessly tied knot of his cravat, feeling its hangman's hold on his neck loosen ever so slightly. "For that I owe you a box of the best Spanish *cigarras* from Robert Lewis's shop."

"Trust me, I shall earn it," replied Henry, darting a baleful glance through the ornamental trees at his wife. "Your sister means well, but when she gets the bit between her teeth—"

"She is harder to stop than a charging cavalry regiment of French Grenadier Guards," finished John. He handed Henry his now-empty glass. "Yes, I know."

In truth, he was exceedingly fond of his older sister. She was wise, funny, and compassionate and usually served as a trusted confidant—though in retrospect it might have been a tactical mistake to mention to her that he was thinking of remarrying.

My skills at soldiering have apparently turned a trifle dull since I resigned from the army and returned to England, he thought wryly. Bold strategy, careful planning, fearless attack—his reputation for calm, confident command under enemy fire had earned him a chestful of medals.

The Perfect Hero. Some damnable newspaper had coined the phrase and somehow it had stuck.

So why do I feel like a perfect fool?

It should be a simple mission to choose a wife, but here in London he felt paralyzed. Uncertain. Indecisive. In contrast to his firm resolve and fearless initiative on the field of battle. He tightened his jaw. It made no sense—when countless lives were at stake, everything seemed so clear. And yet, faced with what should be an easy task, he was acting like a craven coward.

Henry seemed to read his thoughts. "It has been nearly two years since Meredith passed away, John. You can't grieve forever," he murmured. "Both you and Prescott need a lady's presence to, er, soften the shadows of Wrexham Manor."

"I take it those are also my sister's words, not yours," replied the earl tightly, finding that the mention of his young son only served to exacerbate his prickly mood.

His brother-in-law had the grace to flush.

"I appreciate your concern," John added. "And hers. However, I would ask both of you to remember that I am a seasoned military officer, a veteran of the Peninsular War, and as such, I prefer to wage my own campaign to woo a new wife."

He paused deliberately, once again sweeping a baleful gaze over the glittering crush of silks and satins. A giggle punctuated the music as one of the dancing couples spun by and the flaring skirt snagged for an instant in the greenery.

Ye gods, was every eligible young lady in the room a silly, simpering featherhead?

"Assuming I decide to do so," he growled.

Why was it, he wondered, that Society did not encourage them to think for themselves? His wartime experiences had taught him that imagination was important. And yet, they were schooled to be anything but original...

John felt a small frown pinch at his mouth. His military duties might be over, but he had no intention of living the leisurely life of a rich aristocrat. He wished to be useful, and politics, with all the intellectual challenges of governance, appealed to his sense of responsibility. As a battlefield leader, he had fought for noble principles in defending his country's liberties. He felt he had made a difference in the lives of his fellow citizens, so he intended to take his duties in the House of Lords just as seriously... which was why the idea that the only talk at the breakfast table might be naught but an endless chattering about fashion or the latest Town gossip made his stomach a little queasy.

"Point taken," replied Henry. "I—" His gaze suddenly narrowed. "I suggest you decamp without delay. It seems that Lady Houghton has spotted us, and I can't say that I like the martial gleam in her eye."

Taking John's arm, he spun him in a half-turn. "She has not one but two daughters on the Marriage Mart. Twins."

"Bloody hell," swore the earl under his breath as he cut a quick retreat between two of the decorative urns.

Civilized London was proving to be filled with far more rapacious predators than the wolf-infested mountains of northern Spain.

"Bloody hell," swore Olivia Sloane as she eased the door shut behind her. "If I had to endure another moment of that mindless cacophony, that superficial chatter, I might...I might..."

Do something shocking? Like climb atop one of the flower pedestals and dance one of the shimmying, swaying tribal rituals that her father had described in his scholarly papers for the Royal Society?

Olivia considered the thought for a moment, and then dismissed it with a sardonic smile. *No, probably not.* She was already considered an outspoken, opinionated hellion by Society. And with no beauty and no dowry to her name, it was best not to draw *too* much attention to her eccentricities. Not that she would ever blend into the woodwork. However, there were her two younger sisters and their future prospects to think about.

"Still, it would be fun to shock the look of smug complacency off all those overfed faces," she murmured softly. But she quickly reminded herself that she was doing that already in more meaningful ways.

Looking around, Olivia saw that the room in which she had taken refuge was a small study decorated in an exotic Indian motif of slubbed silks, dark wood, and burnished brass. As her eyes adjusted to the low light, she realized that it was a distinctly masculine retreat, a refuge designed to keep bored gentlemen amused. The flame of the single wall sconce showed a large painted cork bull's-eye bristling with feathered darts hung on one wall. In the opposite corner, grouped to one side of the hearth, were several brass and teakwood game tables. *Cards, dice, an intricately inlaid board with stone markers that she recognized as a backgammon set...*

And chess.

A sudden pang of longing squeezed the breath from her lungs. Her father had taught her to play when she was a child, and over the years they had engaged in countless matches.

Chess sharpens your mind, poppet—it teaches you to be logical, to be daring, to attack a problem from unexpected angles.

Skirting around a pair of leather armchairs, Olivia made her way into the shadowed recess and took a seat behind the double row of ivory figures, which stood waiting to march into battle against the opposing ebony force. *Black and white.* And yet, like life, the game was not quite so simple. One had to make subtle feints and oblique moves, one had to be clever at deception. And most of all one had to be willing to make sacrifices to achieve the ultimate goal.

No wonder I'm very good at it, thought Olivia as she fingered the polished king...

"Oh!" It shifted slightly under her touch and a flicker of moonlight from the narrow leaded glass window illuminated the ornate carving. Olivia leaned down for a closer look. "Interesting."

Like the rest of the room's decorations, the chess set had an exotic Eastern flair. Instead of the traditional European figures, the pieces were far more fanciful. The

Knights were mounted on snarling tigers, the Castles were carried by tusked elephants, and all the human figures, including the Kings and Queens, were...stark naked.

Not only that, observed Olivia. The men were, to put it mildly, all highly aroused.

"Interesting," she repeated. The sight of a penis wasn't at all shocking. She had seen plenty of them before—though mostly in drawings or statues such as these, not in the flesh. Her father, a noted scholar of primitive cultures, had written extensively on tribal rituals for the Royal Society. His notebooks had been filled with graphic sketches, and he had not hesitated to explain his research to his three daughters. Men, he had lectured, held an unfair advantage by keeping women ignorant of the ways of the world. So he was determined that his girls learn about Life.

Much to the chagrin of his far more conventional wife. Who had nearly had a fit of apoplexy when, several years ago, Olivia had enthusiastically agreed to accompany her father to Crete for a season and serve as his expedition secretary.

Thank you for such a priceless gift, Papa...though leaving us with a few more material assets would have made our current situation a trifle less worrisome.

But for the moment, Olivia decided to put her practical anxieties aside. She nudged the naked pawn—whose monstrous erection looked more like a battle sword than a fleshly appendage—forward two squares, then reached for the opposing ebony pieces. Playing a solitary game against herself was always an intriguing challenge and would help pass the tedious minutes until it was time to take leave of the ball.

A second nudge moved the black pawn over the checkered tiles.

The game had begun.

Lost in thought, Olivia was not aware that someone else had entered the study until she heard a sudden whooshing exhale, followed by satisfied sigh.

"A room free of simpering ladies. Thank God."

She froze as a pale puff of scented smoke swirled in the shadows. Flint scraped against steel and a candle flame flared to life.

"*Lord Almighty*," intoned the same deep masculine voice, though this time he didn't sound quite so pleased with the Heavenly Being.

Slowly releasing her hold on the ivory Queen's voluptuous breasts, Olivia looked up and squinted into the silvery vapor. For an instant there was naught but an amorphous blur. Then, as the gentleman took another step closer, the flickering light brought his features into sharper focus.

For an instant, she couldn't blink. She couldn't breathe. Sharp lines, chiseled angles—an aura of strength seemed to pulse from every pore of his face, holding her in thrall.

But then, willing herself to break the strange spell, Olivia quickly regained control of her wits.

"Have you never seen chess played before, sir?" she asked calmly, ignoring his gimlet gaze. Honestly, one would think that a man would not look so shocked at seeing a graphic depiction of the male sex organ. Granted there were rather a lot of them, but still...

"Actually, I am very familiar with the game." As he lifted his gaze from the checkered board, the undulating flame lit a momentary spark in his dark eyes. They were, noted Olivia, an unusual shade of toffee-flecked brown.

A powerfully mesmerizing mix of gold-flecked sparks and burnt sugar swirls that seemed to draw her into a deep, deep vortex of shadowed spice...

She made herself look away.

"However," he went on, "I have always been under the impression that it is not an activity that appeals to ladies."

"Then you think wrong." Olivia moved the ebony knight, putting both the ivory bishop—who in this set was depicted as a wild-eyed whirling dervish—and a pawn in danger.

The gentleman didn't answer. Drawing in another mouthful of smoke from his glowing cheroot, he studied the arrangement of the remaining pieces for several long moments.

His reaction was a little unnerving, as was his aura of calm concentration. Olivia wasn't quite sure why, but her fingertips began to tingle.

"Which one will you save?" he asked gruffly.

"The pawn, of course," she replied.

A look of surprise shaded his face. Looking up through her lashes, Olivia watched as the low, licking light accentuated the chiseled cheekbones, the long nose, the sun-bronzed skin. It was an interesting face, made even more intriguing by his oddly expressive mouth.

Sensuous. That was the word that popped to mind.

And like the sinuous coiling of a serpent, her ribs suddenly contracted, squeezing the air from her lungs.

With an inward frown, she shook off the unwelcome sensation and quickly shifted the pawn out of danger. "It's easy to see why if you look three moves ahead."

"Strategy," murmured the gentleman. "You seem to have"—a tiny cough—"a good grasp of the game's strategy," he went on as she picked up the whirling dervish bishop by its phallus and placed it aside.

"Do you think that ladies are incapable of conceiving a plan of attack that requires thinking three or four steps ahead?" She knew the answer, of course. Most men were predictable in their prejudices, assuming the fairer sex had naught but feathers for brains.

Which made his reply all the more unexpected.

"I have a sister," he said slowly. "So I am acutely aware of how sharp the female mind can be." A rumbled chuckle softened his solemn expression for just an instant. "Indeed, their skill at riding roughshod over an enemy's defenses put the efficiency of many of my fellow officers to blush."

He is a military man?

That explained the ramrod straightness of his spine, the hint of muscled hardness beneath the finely tailored evening clothes, the tiny scar on the cleft of his chin.

The unmistakable impression of steely strength.

She made herself shift her gaze from the intriguing little nick. "So, you are a soldier, sir?"

"A former soldier," he corrected. "Duties here at home made it imperative for me to resign my commission in Wellington's forces and come back to England from the Peninsula."

Olivia returned her attention to the chessboard, but not before muttering under her breath, "There are plenty of important battles to be fought on our own soil."

"I beg your pardon?"

She repeated what she had said in a louder voice.

His eyes narrowed—in censure, no doubt.

That was hardly a surprise, thought Olivia bitterly. Ladies weren't supposed to have opinions about anything meaningful. Especially if they were one of the three poor-as-a-churchmouse Sloane sisters.

Of course that did not stop her from saying what she thought. It didn't matter that Society dismissed her as a rag-mannered hellion, tolerated only because of the beauty and charm of her younger sister. She could take a measure of inward satisfaction in knowing there were far more effective ways of being heard...

Clearing her throat with an exaggerated cough, she added, "If you must blow a cloud, sir, might you do it on the other side of the room?" She had come here for the express reason of avoiding the other guests. With any luck, he would take the hint and go away.

"I beg your pardon," he repeated, quickly stubbing out the offending cheroot. "Had I known there was a lady present, I would not have been so ill-mannered as to indulge in a smoke."

Olivia gave a brusque wave without looking up. "Apology accepted, sir." Hoping that silence would help to encourage a quick retreat, she propped her elbows on the table and continued to study the position of the remaining chess pieces.

The gentleman didn't budge.

Repressing a huff of impatience, Olivia pushed the last ivory pawn forward with a touch more force than was necessary. It slid over the smooth marble tiles and collided head-on with its ebony counterpart. With a soft *snick*, the two erections hit up against each other.

A glint of emotion seemed to hang for an instant on the

fire-sparked tips of his dark lashes. But surely she must be mistaken—it was only a quirk of the candlelight that made it appear to be amusement.

In her experience, military officers were not wont to display any sense of humor.

"Madam," he murmured, after another moment of regarding the board with a hooded stare.

"Miss," she corrected.

A frown flitted across his face, but after a tiny hesitation he continued, "I concede that you seem conversant in the concept of chess. But this evening, perhaps, er, playing cards would be a more appropriate choice of entertainment."

"I loathe cards," said Olivia. "They require such little mental effort. Chess is far more cerebral."

"Indeed. However, in this particular case, it is the, er, *physical* aspect of the game that is cause for concern—"

"Why?" she interrupted. "Seeing as chess is considered by many to be a metaphor for war, it seems singularly appropriate that male figures display their swords." A pause. "Sword is a euphemism that you gentlemen use to refer to your sex organ, is it not?"

His bronzed face seemed to turn distinctly redder in the uncertain candlelight.

Good—I've truly shocked him.

Now perhaps he would go away, thought Olivia, quickly moving one of her pawns to another square. She had been deliberately outrageous in hopes of scaring him off. His presence—that tall, quiet pillar of unflinching steel—was having a strangely unsettling effect on her concentration.

"You might want to reconsider that particular strategy." To her dismay, the gentleman slid into the seat across from her and took charge of the ebony army.

The faint scent of his spicy cologne floated across the narrow space between them, and as he leaned forward for a closer survey of the board, the candle flame flickered, its red-gold fire catching for an instant on the tips of his dark lashes.

Breathe, she told herself. It was the exotic smoke that was making her a little woozy.

"If I move here," he pointed out, "you are in danger."

His words stirred a prickling sensation at the nape of her neck, as if daggerpoints were teasing against her flesh.

In and out, in and out. Olivia forced her lungs to obey her silent order as she studied the positions of the pieces. The blood was thrumming in her ears, and for one, mad, mercurial moment, she feared she might swoon.

No—only feather-brained gooseberries swooned. And of all the derogatory comments she had heard whispered behind her back, nobody had ever called her an idiot.

"True," she replied to him.

The sudden scuffling of approaching footsteps in the corridor prevented him from making a reply.

Damnation. Fisting her skirts, Olivia shot up from the table, belatedly realizing that she had put herself on the razor's edge of ruin.

Damn, damn, damn.

The rules of Society strictly forbid an unmarried lady from being alone in a room with a gentleman. Her name would be blackened, her reputation would be ripped beyond repair.

Ye gods, if I am to be sunk in scandal, at least let it be for the right reason, she thought, quickly whirling around and moving for the narrow connecting portal set in the recessed alcove.

Clicking open the latch, she darted into the welcoming darkness of the adjoining room.

John watched as the lady flitted away in a swirling of shadows, smoke, and indigo silk.

Who the devil is she?

It had been too dark, too hazy for him to make out more than a vague impression of her face. *Arched brows. Slanted cheekbones. A full mouth.* And an errant curl of unruly hair—it looked dark as a raven-wing, but he couldn't be sure of the exact color—teasing against the curve of her jaw.

The lady's voice had been the only distinctive feature. Slightly husky, slightly rough, the sound of it had rubbed against his skin with a heat-sparked friction.

He frowned, feeling a lick of fire skate down his spine and spiral toward his . . . sword.

Good Lord, had the lady really uttered such an outrageous observation? He wasn't sure whether he felt indignant or intrigued by her outspoken candor.

"No, no, definitely not intrigued," muttered John aloud. He shifted in his seat, willing his body to unclench.

Everyone—including himself—knew that the Earl of Wrexham was, if not a perfect hero, a perfect gentleman. He respected rules and regulations. There were good reasons for them—they provided the basis for order and stability within Polite Society.

Don't think. Don't wonder. Don't speculate.

No matter that the blaze of fierce intelligence in her eyes had lit his curiosity.

Granted, she might be clever, he conceded. But a lady who flaunted convention was his exact opposite. And like oil and water, opposites never mixed well.

"John? John?"

It was his sister calling. The muted echo of his name was followed by a tentative rapping on the study's oak-paneled door. "Are you in there?"

Women.

At the moment, he would rather be pursued by Attila the Hun and his savage horde of warriors.

The latch clicked.

Deciding that he had had enough uncomfortable encounters with the opposite sex for one night, the earl hesitated, and then, like the mysterious Mistress of the Exotic Chessboard, he spun around and made a hasty retreat.

Chapter Two

So, Mr. Simmonds, you just write up a detailed description of what you are looking for?"

"Aye, it's pretty much that simple."

"And then you just send it to the newspaper? And it's published for a great many people to see?"

The innkeeper smiled at his interrogator. "Well, yes, that's the whole point, lad. The more people who read it, the more likely you are to find exactly what it is that you want."

"See, I *told* you that's how it worked, Scottie." From her perch on the keg of ale, a girl in a sprigged muslin dress fixed her friend with a supercilious smile. "Only you wouldn't believe me."

"That's because you always think you know everything, just because you are a year older than I am. And you don't—you were wrong about the acrobats at Astley's."

"Well, in *this* case I was right." Lucy Simmonds gave a toss of her braids. "You owe me three purple ribbons and a packet of horehound drops."

Her father was quick to interrupt the exchange. "Why the sudden interest in newspapers, milord? I do hope you aren't thinking of putting an ad in the *Shropshire Bugle* for a matched pair of high steppers or a pack of prime foxhounds." Much amused by the notion, Simmonds burst into laughter.

Viscount Linsley, scion of privilege, heir to the Wrexham earldom—and all of ten years old—gave a rather weak smile. "Ha, ha, ha."

"Ha, ha, ha," echoed Lucy.

"In any case, I doubt your pin money would cover the cost of a racehorse or fancy curricle. So don't be getting any ideas. Ha, ha, ha." Still chuckling at his own joke, Lucy's father finished inspecting a tray of pewter tankards. "Your father wouldn't like it above half. High stickler, the earl is. As is quite proper for a gentleman of his exalted position. Let's not give him any reason to regret your friendship with Lucy."

Setting an earthenware jug on the counter, he poured each child a glass of lemonade. "So, you best be heading back to the manor after you finish this, else we'll be having Withers rattling his saber in our faces."

"Your father's valet *is* a bit of an ogre, Scottie," remarked Lucy.

Simmonds smiled. "Off ye go, lad," he said, and then stepped outside to await the arrival of the Tunbridge Wells mail coach.

"Jem says Withers is always scowling, as if he had a bayonet sticking up...where the sun doesn't shine," added Lucy, once she was sure her father was out of earshot. She made a face. "Wherever *that* is."

"Dunno," said Prescott. "But don't expect me to ask

my tutor to explain it. Last time I repeated one of Jem's sayings to him, I couldn't sit down for two days." He blew out his breath. "Withers is not a bad sort, I suppose. Father says it's because he's used to ordering soldiers around that he sounds so gruff."

Lucy exaggerated a snarling growl.

"Between him and my tutor, I can't *ever* step out of line. Not that they are cruel," added Prescott. "Just... strict." His sigh ended in a bit of a sniff. "At least I have you to talk to. Even though you can be a real nit at times."

Abandoning her earlier smugness, Lucy bit her lip. The occasional brangling aside, the two of them were best friends. "You still miss her a lot, don't you?"

Both Prescott and Lucy had lost their mothers within several months of each other. The Countess of Wrexham had fallen victim to the influenza epidemic, while Mrs. Simmonds had, along with her newborn infant son, succumbed to complications of childbirth.

"Yes. I miss her awfully." Prescott swiped his sleeve across his eyes. "And Father never laughs anymore, and the Manor is always so quiet. I overheard the housekeeper say that we need a lady's touch to add cheer to our lives. Mayhap she's right, but..." He blew out his breath. "But I have to prevent Father from making a Big Mistake."

"You know, you may end up in the suds if you go through with this plan," warned Lucy. "If Wilkins the Wasp finds out about it, he'll probably birch your backside so hard you won't be able to sit down for a fortnight."

"I know. And yet it's worth a try." Slanting a sidelong look, he asked, "Are you still willing to help? You might end up in trouble as well."

Her eyes narrowed. "Oh, right. I'm naught but a silly

girl, who can't be counted on in a pinch. Let me ask you—did I squeal over who took Mr. Bowdon's apples? Did I quail at putting the frog in Miss Haverstock's sewing basket? Did I refuse to climb to the top of the elm tree to rescue your stupid cat?"

Prescott grinned.

After wiping her fingers on her skirts, Lucy held out her hand. "Did you bring it?"

Without a word, he reached into his pocket and brought out a neatly folded sheet of paper, properly sealed and franked.

"Excellent." After examining the note, Lucy gave a nod of approval and slipped it into her sleeve. "Let's go."

"Y-you are sure you can do it?"

She rolled her eyes. "Come on, you silly goose, we have to hurry. There isn't much time."

"What do you make of this?" The ink-stained clerk made a face and passed over a letter.

Mr. Josiah Hurley, the owner and editor of the *Mayfair Gazette*, took a moment to read it. After adjusting his spectacles, he read it again.

"Hmmph." The paper fell to the desktop.

"No doubt it's a hoax, sir," murmured the clerk. "Or some tulip of the *ton* engaged in a silly wager." After cracking his knuckles, he reached out to take it and toss it into the waste bin. "Good Lord, you would think that Town gentlemen would have better things to do with their time than compose such blatantly ridiculous ads."

Hurley quickly caught hold of the letter. "Not so fast, George."

His assistant's brows shot up in question.

"You think this silly?"

The question only caused the other man to look more confused. "Well, sir, to be, er, truthful..."

"Since when did truth have anything to do with selling newspapers?" Hurley's face split into a wide grin as he read over the letter for a third time. "I don't doubt that it's a hoax. Doesn't matter. With the right headline and intro, the reading public is going to lap this up like a cat loose in a creamery." He picked up his pen and began to scribble on a scrap of foolscap.

A tentative grin began to form on the clerk's face.

"Well, don't just sit there, laddie. Tell Grimes to pull out a fresh case of type."

Chapter Three

You have a spot of jam on your chin." John dropped his voice to a discreet murmur as he passed a cup of tea to Prescott.

His son feigned a look of surprise, then fumbled with his napkin, causing the rest of the raspberry tart to ooze over his shirtfront. "Oh! Sorry."

Ignoring the tightening of the earl's jaw, Prescott ran his sticky fingers through his hair, leaving streaks of red among the golden curls. "Sorry," he repeated, flashing a brilliant smile at the person seated across from him—a smile that revealed every single one of the seeds lodged between his teeth.

The lady did not smile back.

"I see you are an indulgent parent, Wrexham," she said primly. "I, too, am of the opinion that a young person should be allowed to make an occasional appearance in adult company. Assuming, of course, that he is capable of proper manners."

"I assure you that Prescott is not usually quite so

clumsy, Lady Serena." Letting out a harried sigh, John turned back to his son. "Scottie, I am sure you wish to make a handsome apology to our guest."

His son did just that. But not before cramming a blueberry scone into his mouth.

"You are excused," said John, in a tone that warned of an impending discussion on etiquette once they were alone.

Head bowed, Prescott slipped from his chair and bolted for the door, letting it fall shut with a thump.

Curling a rueful grimace, John expelled a sigh. "Let me add my apology to that of my son, Lady Serena. I assure you, he does not normally behave like a heathen savage."

Lady Serena Wells nodded. "I am sure you make every effort to see that he receives the proper instruction and discipline. However, the young man might benefit from a more structured regimen to assure he is not exposed to undesirable influences." She paused. "I must say, I have noticed him on several occasions in the vicinity of The Bull and Bear."

"There is no need for concern." His chagrin softened somewhat. "Scottie is merely visiting the innkeeper's daughter, Lucy. They are close in age and are good friends."

"Good friends with the daughter of an innkeeper?" Her brows arched. "You think such an attachment...wise?"

John considered the question for a moment, suddenly a little uncertain about his own judgment. "I see no harm in it. Simmonds is a solid, respectable fellow. I trust him to see that the children don't get into any mischief." After a sip of his tea, he added, "Surely you do not think he is introducing Scotty to the vices of spirits or dice?"

"No, but as to the sort of coarse manners and rough speech that are generally associated with a tavern..." Her words trailed off as she patted her napkin to her lips. "But naturally, you are the best judge as to what is correct for your son."

Am I?

The Oolong tea suddenly tasted bitter on his tongue. This wasn't the first time he had wondered whether he was doing a credible job in raising Prescott. Although his military service had afforded plenty of experience in training soldiers, he often felt baffled—nay, intimidated!—by the task of raising a ten-year-old boy by himself.

His fingers tightened on his cup.

What sense of loss must his son be suffering? A stab of pain—or was it guilt—knifed through his own insides. His late wife had been a wonderful mother, choosing to spend much of her time with their son rather than delegate his raising to a retinue of servants. Mother and son had formed a special bond while he was away at war...perhaps because Meredith herself had retained a certain childlike innocence and exuberance.

It could not be easy for Prescott, living in the shadows and silence of the Hall, with naught but a moody father and a host of adult retainers. And yet, he had thought that the two of them had managed together tolerably well.

But of late...

"Forgive me, Wrexham, if I have spoken out of turn."

"No, no." Looking up from the dregs of his tea, John took pains to force a smile. "I would appreciate any advice you have to offer."

"Well, then, perhaps you might try to find the young

viscount a more suitable playmate than the daughter of a country innkeeper."

He shook his head. "You are acquainted with the gentry in the surrounding area. There are no children near his age. And what with estate duties and my Parliamentary responsibilities in Town, I am often away. I daresay the lad gets lonely."

"Only if he is idle, Wrexham." Lady Serena straightened the pleats of her skirts. "I believe a well-organized routine is the best thing for a child. After his daily lessons are done, you might engage the vicar to provide spiritual instruction, and then, if there are additional free hours, I don't doubt that there a great many educational books or games in the schoolroom to occupy his time."

"He is only ten—"

"I see you are an indulgent father," she replied before he could go on. "And it is all to your credit. But it doesn't do to spoil a child. Indeed, my father has always held that is never too early for a young gentleman to learn the responsibilities of his station in life." A small smile softened her criticism. "Good heavens, I am not suggesting you put young Prescott on bread and water. I am merely saying that you may want to ensure that he keeps occupied with more appropriate activities. And company."

"Yes, yes. No doubt you are right."

Yet John couldn't quite dampen the niggling suspicion that Lady Serena would not consider splashing about in a rowboat appropriate behavior for a future earl. His late wife had found nothing wrong in coming home soaked to the bone from catching frogs, or in voicing laughter rather than reproaches as her young son and half a dozen puppies tracked mud across the expensive carpets.

But he forced himself to swallow such thoughts. It was grossly unfair to make comparisons.

Lady Serena Wells might lack Meredith's natural exuberance and warmth, but she had a good many admirable qualities of her own. *Poised. Polished. Pretty.* John began composing a mental checklist. More importantly, she was sensible enough to converse on more than the latest fashions and gossip.

Repressing a shudder, John recalled all the simpering young things who had been pushed his way during his last visit to London.

So, he assured himself, he was fortunate to have made the acquaintance of his neighbor's cousin, who had arrived several weeks ago for an extended visit. The daughter of a marquess, Lady Serena possessed a peerless pedigree to go with her faultless manners. That her dowry left something to be desired, due to the gaming habits of her father, was unimportant. He didn't need to remarry for money. And if her demeanor tended to mirror the cool marble smoothness of her profile, that was perfectly well and good. At the advanced age of thirty-four, John was the first to acknowledge that he was also rather set in his ways.

Lightning didn't strike twice.

Which might be all for the best, he reflected, as another twinge of guilt stirred deep within his chest. After the first blaze of attraction had burned down to the comfortable glowing coals of everyday life, he had come to wonder whether he and his late wife would ever share more than a sunny but superficial marriage. Meredith had cared naught for serious subjects like politics or philosophy, which had left him feeling...

Unhappy wasn't precisely the word. It was a far more complicated emotion than that.

But John shook off his brooding, deciding it was best to delve no deeper into such thoughts. It was unrealistic to dream of a perfect partner. He was older and wiser and had learned to temper his expectations. So while there was no real spark of passion between him and Lady Serena, he had come to the conclusion that what they had in common augured well for an excellent match.

It was time to put memories and recriminations aside and think of the future.

Lady Serena would make a perfect countess, bringing order and companionship to his life, and a much-needed female figure of authority for Prescott.

John sighed again. From the atrocious display of behavior he had just witnessed, it was none too soon for the latter.

"Are you all right, Wrexham?"

John turned his exhale into a slight cough. "Er, just something caught in my throat."

"Ah." The look of concern smoothed from her brow. "Thank you for tea. I ought to be returning to the Close, for I know Aunt Clara is anxious to have the embroidery thread I purchased in the village." She set aside her cup and made to rise. "Will you be attending Squire Tresham's gathering next week? Or does the upcoming debate in the House of Lords require your presence in Town?"

"I may have to run up to London for several days, but will make a point of returning so that I may have the honor of a waltz with you. I trust you will save me the first one."

Her lashes lowered demurely. "It would be my pleasure, sir."

"And mine, I assure you."

Lady Serena accepted his arm, resting her hand upon his sleeve with just the proper amount of pressure. As he escorted her and her maid to the waiting carriage, John congratulated himself on having come to a tentative decision about the future. Sensible, steady—the two of them were really a perfect match in that they were each in complete command of their emotions.

We rub together without creating any friction.

Unlike a certain other recent encounter.

For an instant, the unbidden memory of a smoke-swirled room and a sultry mouth voicing highly improper innuendos flared up, its spark leaving a trail of tingling heat on his skin...

Shaking off the unsettling sensation, he assured himself that once the current political battle in Parliament was settled, he would begin his courtship in earnest.

Lady Serena and I rub together without creating any friction, he repeated to himself.

Unfortunately, he had a feeling the same could not be said for the coming encounter with his son.

"Have you heard about the advertisement?"

"For what?" Olivia looked up as her younger sister sat down beside her in one of the side alcoves of Lady Mountjoy's drawing room. "The latest potion to remove freckles? Or is there some new hoax?" Expelling a sardonic sigh, she resumed reading the book she had hidden in her lap.

"Put that away," warned Anna. "Mama will have a fit

of vapors when we return home if she spots you ignoring the other guests. You are supposed to be making an effort to converse with the Misses Kincaid." Her sister's murmur took on a wry note. "Their older brother is a viscount, you know, and possesses an income of ten thousand a year."

"Oh, bollocks," muttered Olivia. "It hardly matters if I am spotted sneaking a peek at my book. Mama will only find fault with some other aspect of my behavior. And as for the viscount..." She brushed an unruly curl from her cheek. "Neither he nor his blunt are likely to attach themselves to an aging bluestocking." However, after one last, longing peek at the page, she tucked the offending volume under her shawl.

Anna had to bite her lip to keep from laughing. "You are only three years older than I am, so it's not as if you are tottering into a permanent decline." Her gaze dropped from Olivia's scowl to the flounce of frilly lace bunched around the prim neckline of her gown. "And you know, if you would show even a passing interest in fashion, you would attract more than your share of admirers. Your looks are striking, but that particular shade of pink clashes horribly with your auburn hair."

Olivia responded with an even more unladylike word than "bollocks."

"Just as if you would make even a passing attempt at social pleasantries, you would find both Mama and the bucks of the *beau monde* a bit more tolerant of your intellectual interests."

"Right," said Olivia. "But I have neither your delicate beauty nor your sweet disposition." Lowering her voice, she added, "Like the heroine in your current novel, you have a knack for making yourself agreeable to everyone you meet, while I have exactly the opposite effect—"

"That's not true!" protested Anna. However, as honesty also numbered among her sterling attributes, she was compelled to add, "Er, well, not exactly. If you would but try—"

She fell discreetly silent at the approach of the dowager Countess of Frampton and her two granddaughters. The three ladies settled themselves on the facing sofa and began discussing the latest style of bonnets, signaling an end to any further sisterly exchanges.

While Anna smiled and was quick to join in the conversation, Olivia sat back, somehow refraining from caustic comment on the decorative merits of cherries versus roses. Having absolutely no interest in the subject, she quickly found her attention wandering.

Her fingers curled around the spine of the hidden book. These tedious rounds of morning visits were, to her mind, a pernicious waste of time that could be spent in far more interesting pursuits. Unfortunately she was not very skilled in disguising her disinterest, while Anna...

Olivia expelled another sigh. Unlike herself, who all too often wasn't smart enough to hide her rebellion against Society's rules, Anna was blessed with both beauty *and* brains. Her sister's manners were charming, her temperament sweet, and her appearance angelic. No one would ever guess that such a demure, dainty figure was, in fact, the author of the wildly popular racy novels featuring the intrepid English orphan Emmalina Smythe and Count Alessandro Crispini, an Italian Lothario whose exploits put Giacomo Casanova to the blush.

The sigh now turned to more of a snort. The only paper

and ink associated with Anna were the odes composed by her admirers. More than one besotted swain had been inspired to write poetry in praise of her ethereal looks.

Exceedingly bad poetry, amended Olivia with an inward wince. Their youngest sister, Caro—who was *exceedingly* good at composing verse—had rightly remarked that the gentlemen in question ought to take up shovels rather than quills, and be made to clear away the steaming piles of ma-mangled English they had put down on paper.

Her mouth thinned in a self-mocking grimace. She, on the other hand, inspired naught but muttered criticisms among the *beau monde* for her outspoken views on politics and social reform. Society frowned on females who dared to be different.

And Olivia didn't give a fig about offending their sensibilities.

It was an attitude that drove their mother to distraction—and sometimes to her bed, a bottle of hartshorn in hand and bitter complaints on her lips at having to put up with such an unnatural child.

Lady Trumbull's only consolation was that Anna seemed sure of making a magnificent match, despite a modest title and paltry dowry. Even having an unconventional, unmarried older sister had not proved a major impediment. The Season was hardly under way and already an earl, a viscount, and the younger son of a duke had shown a marked interest in Anna's company. The baroness was sure that one of them would soon come up to scratch.

Thank God that Anna possesses uncommonly good sense to go along with all her other stellar attributes, thought Olivia. For all her show of sweetness, she would not let their managing Mama bully her into marrying for power or position rather than...

"...Yes, we were just discussing it, too, weren't we?" A nudge from Anna cut short Olivia's musings.

"Er, yes," she replied, having no idea what her sister was talking about.

"I vow, it is so *romantic*," gushed Lady Catherine.

"I see I shall have to curtail your reading of those Minerva Press novels," remarked the dowager countess with a slight sniff. "Young ladies these days are much too impressionable—"

"But Grandmama, everyone is talking about it!" chirped in Lady Mary. "And even so high a stickler as Lady Gooding allows that it is quite a darling missive. She says that Arabella may respond."

"Hmmph. Well, I suppose if Lady Gooding does not object..."

Lady Catherine pounced on her chaperone's indecision. "I mean to write a reply, of course. Everyone I have talked to does!"

"A reply to what?" asked Olivia.

"Why, the advertisement in the *Mayfair Gazette*!" chorused the other set of sisters.

"I was just starting to tell you," murmured Anna. "It's asking for applicants—"

"Applicants?" Olivia wasn't sure she had heard correctly. "The belles of the *beau monde* are being allowed to apply for a...job?"

"La—I wouldn't call it that precisely," tittered Lady Catherine.

"No, not at all," giggled Lady Mary.

"The ad is looking for applicants to be a mother," explained Anna. "A stepmother," she hastened to add, on seeing the dowager's eyes begin to flare in alarm.

"No experience necessary," said Lady Catherine.

Olivia blinked. "You are joking."

The tiny quirk of Anna's mouth indicated that she, too, found the matter bordering on the absurd. "I assure you, all the young ladies of the *ton* are talking of nothing else."

"And no doubt sounding even sillier than usual," observed Olivia under her breath.

A quick cautioning look from Anna caused her to swallow any further sarcasm.

Ah, well, she thought. At least the topic was a good deal more original that those usually discussed in the drawing rooms. Curious to hear more, she asked, "What, exactly, does the advertisement seek in an applicant?"

"Oh, a fairytale princess," was the dreamy reply from Lady Catherine.

Olivia arched her brows. "Does that mean you are required to kiss a frog?"

While Anna struggled to maintain a straight face, the dowager's other granddaughter gave a rather uncertain laugh. "La, what Cat means is, the writer is seeking a lady who is both—"

Olivia had no doubt that the description would have proved highly diverting, but much to her disappointment, the arrival of her mother interrupted the young lady before she had a chance to continue.

"Ah, here you are, Anna. Come, we had better take our leave if you are to be ready for a promenade in the park later this afternoon." Flashing a brilliant smile at the dowager, Lady Trumbull made a point of adding,

"Lord Davies has asked Anna to accompany him on a drive through the park, and it wouldn't do to keep such an important personage or his prime team of grays waiting for even an instant."

For an instant, Olivia was tempted to remain seated, to see if her mother would notice the absence of her eldest daughter. But as she was anxious to escape the stuffy drawing room, she gathered her reticule, slid her book inside it, and followed along.

"Are you going to birch me?" asked Prescott.

Nonplussed, John frowned. "Birch you? Don't wax melodramatic, Scottie. Since when have I ever used the rod on you?"

His son's eyes remained locked on the tips of his boots. "Maybe not *you*. But..."

He felt a frisson of alarm run down his spine. Was he so blind that he hadn't seen that his son was being mistreated? "Are you saying that someone in this household resorts to such tactics?"

Prescott kicked at the fringe of the carpet.

"Scottie, a gentleman—even if he is only ten years old—is expected to answer a direct question." The sharpness in his voice had been meant more for himself than his son. Belatedly aware of its edge, he added, "I should hope you know you can always come to me if there is a problem."

Prescott lifted his chin. "Wilkins says a gentleman— even if he is ten years old—is expected to accept punishment for his transgressions with a s-s-stiff upper lip."

The earl knew that the gruff Scotsman was not in any way a cruel man. But in retrospect, perhaps it had not been such a wise idea to assign a former drill sergeant the duties of playing nanny to a lad.

"I shall have a word with him," he said softly.

Prescott's face remained scrunched.

"Is something else amiss?"

"Everything is amiss!" blurted out his son. "Wilkins the Wasp whacks my backside whenever I step the slightest bit out of line. Taylor the Tyrant gives lessons that are dull as ditchwater. And you—you never laugh anymore." The lad gave a watery sniff. "It wasn't at all like this when Mama was here."

John was aware of a painful clenching in his chest, but he marshaled his expression to a stony stare. Giving voice to his own uncertainties would only exacerbate his son's misery. So, not knowing what else to do, he fell back on his military training. "Well, your Mama is *not* here, and you must to learn to live with that fact."

"Just as long as I don't have to learn to live with that Other Lady."

"Prescott..." began the earl.

"She's *horrid*!" Ignoring the warning, his son made a face. "Wrexham, do have a care—your son is tracking a bit of mud on the Aubusson carpet," he went, giving a frightfully accurate imitation of Lady Serena's prim tone. "Why, Lucy says if Lady Serena's corset were laced any tighter, the whale bones would crack! She probably has them made out of steel."

"That is quite enough!" It was the desktop that was in danger of splitting as John's fist thumped down upon the blotter. "Such a show of disrespect toward your elders will not be tolerated in this house, do you hear? Perhaps Lady Serena is right to imply I have been remiss as a father by allowing you to run wild with a rag-mannered hoyden."

"Lucy isn't a hoyden. Sh-she is my friend. The only one I've got." Blinking back tears, the lad squared his shoulders. "I don't want the Steel Corset for my new mother. And if you wish to have Withers birch me for saying so, go right ahead."

Torn between the desire to hug his son and the feeling that discipline dictated a show of restraint, John un-clenched his hand and raked it through his hair. "Look, I know it is difficult, Scottie, but you must make an effort to keep an open mind. Lady Serena possesses many ad-mirable qualities, if you would but give her a chance to display them."

"Yes, sir."

Had he ordered his son to down a bottle of castor oil in one gulp, the level of enthusiasm would have been greater. Overlooking the mulish scowl, the earl essayed a smile. "In the meantime, I will speak with Wilkins and Taylor about being a little less rigid."

"Yes, sir."

The hollowness of Prescott's voice left the earl with a void in the pit of his stomach. Heaving a sigh, he added, "And I—I shall endeavor to see that we have a bit more...play in our lives." He managed a forced laugh. "How about on the morrow, we take the afternoon to go fishing, and get covered in mud from head to toe?"

Looking utterly miserable, Prescott gave a slight shrug. "If that is all, may I be dismissed, sir?"

Had he turned to naught but a martinet in his son's eyes?

The notion cut to the quick. He wanted desperately to

do the right thing, but perhaps, after so long away on the battlefields of Spain, he had lost all sense of how to be a good father.

He drew a deep breath, but as he could think of nothing else to say that might ease the lad's hurt—or his own—John gave a curt nod.

As the door slammed shut, he reached for his pen and a fresh sheet of foolscap.

Chapter Four

*I*t wasn't until several hours later that Anna had a moment to poke her head into the family's library.

"Here, I thought you might find it amusing to read this yourself." She dropped a snippet of paper on Olivia's desk.

"Mmmm." Olivia didn't look up from her writing.

"What is it?" asked Caro, the youngest Sloane sister. "The latest sonnet from Brackleburn?" She set aside her own studies for the moment. "How that gentleman managed to stumble through four years at Oxford without tripping over a rudimentary understanding of rhyming meter is beyond me."

"I think your lecture on iambic pentameter was sufficiently scathing to scare him off any more literary endeavors." Anna smiled, then tapped Olivia on the shoulder to get her attention. "It's not a poem, it's the newspaper advertisement I was telling you about. And speaking of style, I think you will find it highly original."

"Mmmm," repeated Olivia. But seeing that her sister

had nudged the paper under her nose, she gave a martyred sigh. "Oh, very well. I'll take a look."

Glancing at the tall case clock in the corner of the room, Anna gathered her skirts. "I must run, lest it be Mama, not Lord Davies's prime horses, who kicks up a dust."

"Would that *I* ever got to go anywhere interesting," groused Caro. "Or do anything exciting."

"Driving through Hyde Park at a sedate speed does not qualify as exciting," said Anna. "Next Season, when you are old enough to make your come-out in Society, you will see how mundane these entertainments really are."

"But they sound so awfully intriguing in your books."

"Artistic license," quipped Anna. "Like poets, we novelists must often exaggerate emotion for dramatic effect."

"Drat," muttered Olivia, scratching a thick black line through the sentence she had just written.

Anna turned for the door. "The ad, Livvie," she reminded. "Do have a look."

With a resigned shrug, Olivia put down her pen and skimmed over the short newsprint paragraph.

"Good Lord."

She read it again.

Then, pulling a face, she tossed the clipping aside. "Ye gods, that is the most absurd thing I ever heard of," she muttered, before turning her attention back to her work.

Pulling a face, John tossed the newspaper clipping aside. "Ye gods, that is the most absurd thing I ever heard of," he muttered, before turning his attention back to the letter on his desk blotter.

It was odd how his sister—an eminently sensible female in most every regard—was always *au courant* with the latest Town gossip. Even odder was the fact that she thought he might be entertained by this latest show of silliness. His lips pursed as he reread the first page of her missive. Under normal circumstances, he might have enjoyed a laugh or two at her pithy observations. But at the moment he had far too serious matters on his mind to find such a juvenile prank amusing.

"Absurd," John muttered again, glancing at the crumpled newsprint before turning the letter over. There, to his relief, he found a lengthy response to his uncertainties concerning Prescott.

Patience. Perseverance. And a sense of humor in the face of adversity. That part of Cecilia's advice had a strangely familiar ring to it. As a colonel in the Royal Regiment of Horse Guards, he had learned the importance of just such mental attributes in warfare. However, his sister went on to say that unlike in the military, life did not often march along according to carefully mapped-out plans. Rather than stand firm, she counseled, it was imperative to improvise. When confronting young people, taking an entrenched position was only inviting ignominious defeat.

The earl shifted uneasily in his chair. *Am I digging myself into a hole with my son?* On the battlefield he had intuitively known how to react, no matter how thick the choking smoke or heavy the enemy fire.

But now?

Aware of an uncomfortable tightening in his chest, the earl rose and poured himself a stiff brandy. *Henry is right—the Manor definitely needs a woman's touch.* Duty, both to his son and to his position in Society, demanded that he take a new countess. So the sooner he made up his mind on the matter of remarrying, the better, he reflected, downing the fiery spirits in one gulp.

Ah, but he *had* made a choice, John reminded himself. And Lady Serena Wells was a perfectly good one.

So why am I so strangely indecisive?

Resuming his seat, John stared bleakly at the banked fire. The perfect match—or was it? It would, by his own admission, be a marriage of politeness without passion—

"Be damned with passion," he growled. Passion was dangerous. It fuzzed the brain and made people do rash, reckless things. Discipline, detachment had served him well in war and would serve him well in civilian life. Like a colonel, an earl had a grave responsibility for the well-being of a great many lives.

The hide-and-seek light seemed to stir a ghostly flutter from the portrait of his late wife that hung above the mantel. *And what of Scottie's life?* The unspoken question floated for an interminable instant in the dark space between the painted canvas and his chair. *Surely you see that he yearns for light and laughter to once again brighten the hallways and hearths of Wrexham Manor...*

As if in echo of his pensive mood, a log crackled and a tiny flame flared up from the red-gold sparks.

"Scottie will come to appreciate Lady Serena's good points," murmured John aloud.

With her guinea gold hair and highly polished manners, she would certainly bring a welcome shine to the Manor. And if her glow was more reflective—like light bouncing off ice rather than lit by its own inner spark— well, he was sure that relations between her and his son would thaw to a mutual respect over time. After all, a proper lady was supposed to keep all show of emotion tightly hidden beneath a layer of cool reserve.

Toying with the buttons of his waistcoat, John suddenly recalled Scottie's comment about steel corsets and found himself chuckling aloud. His son, at least, had found a female in whom he could confide. Lucy Simmonds was actually a very sharp little girl, wise beyond her tender years. True, Lady Serena did have a bit of a strait-laced manner—

Stifling his amusement in a brusque cough, he reminded himself that a retired army officer and newly appointed leader in the House of Lords should be much too mature to find such impertinent observations laughable.

Laughter. Strange, he was suddenly aware of how little laughter there was in his life. Even in the military there had been chuckles and guffaws, as well as the occasional thunderous hilarity that could bring tears to the eyes. But perhaps now that he had grown older, if not wiser, it was only natural for things to have changed. No doubt his late wife would have grown more subdued as well, her high spirits slowly tempering to fit into the proper mold.

The proper manners, the proper deportment...

Clearing his throat, the earl forced a frown. Lady Serena was absolutely right. He must think again about whether it was wise to allow Scottie to run tame at the inn. A gentleman of his rank was expected to maintain an appearance of rigid dignity and self-discipline—

Discipline.

Right-ho, he reminded himself. From now on, he would keep his thoughts marching in a straight line.

* * *

"Did you enjoy your drive?" asked Olivia.

"Yes, actually it was very pleasant," answered Anna, her cheeks still a touch rosy from the outdoors.

At least, Olivia had assumed it was the wind that had caused the two spots of color. But as her sister continued, she realized that the flush might be due to some other force of nature.

"Unlike a great many other gentlemen, Lord Davies is capable of conversing on subjects other than himself, or his hunters and hounds," explained Anna. "We had quite an interesting discussion on books. He said that he was rather surprised to learn the author of *Pride and Prejudice* is a lady."

"Given the keenness of its perception and the honesty of its observation, that does not surprise *me* in the least." The scratch of Olivia's pen stilled for a moment, and she slanted a quick glance upward. "So, what else did you talk about?"

"Oh, I don't know—any number of things." Anna began to toy with the piece of crumpled foolscap that had been batted to the far end of the desk. "I—I don't really recall the specifics."

"You don't sound like a feather-brained peagoose very often," remarked Olivia dryly. She rubbed at her nose, leaving a smudge of peacock blue ink. "But this is one of them. I trust that over the course of an hour, you managed more than a few chirping noises."

"I don't think that I appeared completely bird-witted."

A high-pitched clucking sound floated up from the overstuffed leather armchair by the hearth.

"Oh, *do* put a cork in it, Caro. Little sisters aren't supposed to eavesdrop," groused Anna. But after a moment, she, too, flashed a grin. "He did say he found the ostrich feathers of my new shako quite fetching."

Caro snapped her book shut. "So you like him?"

"He is nice," said Anna after a slight hesitation. "And in truth, it is refreshing to be spoken to as if my brain were not the least important part of my anatomy."

"Ah." Olivia decided to refrain from any further teasing concerning Lord Davies.

"Mmmm." Apparently just as happy to let the subject drop, Anna started to smooth the crinkles from the discarded paper. "What's this?"

"Oh, er—nothing."

"Clearly it is something, seeing that both the front and back are covered with your distinctive scrawl." Anna peered closer. "Oh, good heavens! You didn't...this isn't..." Reading rapidly, her sister flipped to the other side.

"Oh, I couldn't resist," muttered Olivia as Anna began to laugh. "Lady Catherine and her sister were so earnestly serious in their intention of writing a reply to the ad, the prospect for parody was simply too wickedly tempting to resist."

"It's really quite funny," wheezed her sister. "What are you going to do with it?"

Olivia shrugged. "Consign it to the flames—what else?"

"Ah." Anna casually folded the paper. "By the by, are you make any headway on your essay for Mr. Hurley?"

"A bit."

"Isn't it due the day after tomorrow?" demanded Caro. She nodded.

"Well, you had better stop dawdling and get on with

it," warned the youngest Sloane. "Especially as you have to attend Lady Battell's ball this evening."

"Drat. I forgot all about that," grumbled Olivia. "I wish you could go in my stead."

"So do I," replied Caro. "It's cursedly boring being stuck in the schoolroom while you two have all the fun in Town."

"It's *not* fun," said Olivia.

"Well, neither is being treated like a child. How can I write decent poetry if I never get out and experience... *Life*!"

Olivia repressed a wry smile. With her penchant for drama, Caro would discover for herself when she made her debut into Society that Life was not always as wildly exciting as she imagined it was. So often it was more a muddle of compromises. But knowing it was pointless to try to explain that, she merely heaved a disgruntled sigh.

"Speaking of writing, I really need to make another trip to Hatchards first thing in the morning. The newly published collection of Hingham's political writings that I ordered from the University at St. Andrews has arrived and I really need to double-check a certain reference before I can finish this dratted essay..."

Intent on explaining the problem to her sisters, she didn't notice Anna slip the discarded paper into her reticule.

Chapter Five

Stop looking like you're standing before a firing squad," murmured the earl's sister as she fluttered a cheery wave at a pair of turbaned matrons by the punch bowl.

"If I appear terrified, it is because your elbow is a lethal weapon," grunted John, rubbing at the sore spot on his ribs. "I can't believe that I allowed you to maneuver me into coming to yet another cursed ball."

Cecilia rolled her eyes. "Someone needs to take charge of your social engagements. You cannot live the rest of your life as a hermit. For Scottie's sake, as well as your own."

"I am aware of my duties," he muttered.

"Duties be damned, John," she retorted. "I am talking about having a little fun."

"Right. Fun." He looked around the crowded ballroom and made a pained face. "Don't bother with the firing squad. I'll simply step out onto the balcony and hang myself from the balustrades."

The comment earned him another sharp poke. "Now that you are here, why not try to relax and enjoy yourself?"

And pigs might fly.

"I have someone I wish for you to meet," went on his sister.

John shot a baleful glance at a gaggle of young ladies whispering among each other. "I assure you, I've no interest in simpering chits fresh from the schoolroom—"

"Give me a little credit, John." She tugged on his sleeve. "Ah, there she is now."

He followed Cecilia's gaze to a dark recess within the decorative colonnade. A figure nearly as tall and slender as the fluted marble was standing among the shadowed stone. She turned her head slightly and arched a sardonic brow as she surveyed the crowded room...

Good God. Unless his eyes were playing tricks on him, it was *her*. The Mistress of the Exotic Chessboard.

"The lady doesn't look interested in making any new acquaintance—" began John.

"Shhhh!" Squeezing him to silence, Cecilia started to make her way around the perimeter of the dance floor. Seeing as there was no way to dig his heels into the polished parquet, John reluctantly fell in step beside her.

"Who is she?" he demanded.

"Miss Olivia Sloane, eldest daughter of the late Baron Trumbull."

"What makes you think that Miss Sloane and I have anything in common?" John angled another quick glance at the lady in question. "Save for a desire to be somewhere else."

"Miss Sloane is...interesting. I've met her at the

Royal Historical Society lectures, where she asks some very intelligent questions. She seems very reform-minded."

"A radical female?" He chuffed a harried sigh. "I need *that* like I need the plague."

"You would rather expire from sheer boredom?" countered his sister without missing a stride.

"That's unfair," he protested. "The fact is, I have recently met someone who..."

Ignoring his retort, Cecilia ducked around a dancing couple and tugged him into the alcove. "Miss Sloane, how nice to see you here tonight."

The lady spun around with an odd little herky-jerky step. John blinked. *Was that a pencil and paper she had just jammed into her reticule?*

"What a crush," went on Cecilia brightly. "How clever of you to find a spot where one can catch a breath of air. I hope you don't mind if we join you for a moment? Oh, and this is my brother, Lord Wrexham, who has just come up to Town for several days."

Miss Sloane seemed flustered by the sudden intrusion. She jerked her head up, the abrupt motion loosening one of the pins holding her upswept tresses. John stared in fascination as a curl sprang free and slowly tumbled across her cheek. Her hair was dark, but not quite as dark as it had appeared in the hazy shadows of the game room. He saw now that it wasn't black but rather a deep auburn flecked with sparks of red-gold from the hide-and-seek flicker of the wall sconces.

"Y-yes, of course, Lady Silliman." Olivia turned to meet his gaze. "Milord."

John felt his throat tighten. She was by no means a

conventional beauty, but there was something about the molten intensity of her jade green eyes that rendered him momentarily speechless. Aswirl in their smoky hue was a hint of fierce intelligence, along with a rippling of other emotions he couldn't quite fathom.

"Wrexham," murmured his sister, flicking him an exasperated look.

Though still tongue-tied, he forced himself to speak. "Miss Sloane. You...you have lost one of your hairpins. And another appears in imminent danger of coming free."

Her hand flew her face, which was fast turning a shade redder. Embarrassment pinched at her mouth. "Yes, well, that happens more often than not, milord," she said, quickly tucking the errant strand behind her ear. "As you see, there is a good reason the tabbies call me the Hellion of High Street."

"Do you not care about fashion?" he inquired, distracted by the graceful, shell-pink curve. He had never before thought of an ear as erotic, but there was something strangely sensual about hers.

"Not as much as I care about other things," she replied, her husky voice holding a faint note of challenge.

What things? he wondered. *Other than chess.* But aware of how stilted his comments were sounding, John remained silent.

The awkwardness stretched for several moments before his sister edged back a step. "Oh look, there is Lady Repton. If you will excuse me, I must have a word with her before she disappears for good into the card room." said Cecilia. "Wrexham, the musicians are striking up a waltz. I am sure that Miss Sloane would like to dance."

"His Lordship need not trouble himself—" began Olivia.

"Oh, it's not trouble at all," said Cecilia breezily. "Indeed, my brother *adores* dancing."

John mechanically held out his hand.

One, two, three. One, two, three…

Olivia could swear she heard him counting under his breath. Ticking off the seconds, no doubt, until he could escape the embarrassment of having to partner an ape leader.

A *clumsy* ape leader, she amended as she missed a beat and trod on his toes.

"Sorry," intoned John.

His hold on her tightened. He had big hands, yet their touch was surprising gentle. And warm. Olivia was suddenly aware of a tingling heat spreading across the small of her back.

Perhaps dancing isn't so odious after all, she mused, acutely aware of his long legs and corded thighs scant inches from her body. The thought took her by surprise. Up until now, the experience had left her cold, but there was something about the earl that set him apart from other gentlemen of the *ton*.

His evening clothes, for one thing, observed Olivia. Unlike many of the puffed-up popinjays present tonight, he was dressed in unrelenting black, save for the brilliant white hue of his simply-tied cravat and low-cut shirt-points.

And in contrast to the soft, fleshy figures dancing close by, the earl was as solid as chiseled steel. Beneath her gloved hand, she could feel the flex of hard, lithe, muscle.

Military muscle.

She had, of course, recognized the Earl of Wrexham at once as the soldier from the smoke-shrouded game room. That he seemed oblivious to her identity was probably all for the best—it had been an odd encounter, to say the least, and one that was best forgotten.

As they spun beneath one of the ornate crystal chandeliers, she ventured a look up through her lashes, curious to have a better look at his face in the bright light. Up close, his sun-bronzed features had the same austere lines and sculpted strength as wind-carved granite. Save for his mouth, which once again struck her as having...a sinuous sensuality.

Good Lord, thought Olivia with a self-mocking smile. *I must remember to pass that description on to Anna for the next scene in her novel.*

Shifting her gaze, she watched the thick strands of his ebony-dark hair dance against his collar. He wore it unfashionably long, and the silky texture softened the sharp line of his jaw. The earl, she decided, wasn't precisely handsome, he was...interesting.

"What were you writing?" he asked abruptly.

So, he had been observant enough to see that.

"Oh, er, nothing of any interest, sir."

"A secret *billet doux* to one of your admirers?" John cracked a smile for the first time. "Ho, ho," he added, his joviality sounding a bit too forced. "Have no fear, Miss Sloane. You may count on me not to say a word about it."

Olivia bristled. How like a man to assume that a lady was capable of writing naught but love notes. Ashamed of herself for imagining, even for a scant moment, that he was different from the other tulips of the *ton*, she replied tartly, "You know sir, not all females are brainless widgeons."

His brows shot up in confusion. "I didn't say that."

"Oh, yes," she replied sweetly. "You did."

"I—"

"Perhaps not in so many words. But the insinuation was there."

He frowned.

Olivia lifted her chin, refusing to be intimidated.

They twirled in silence through a spin. This time it was he who put his foot in the wrong place.

"*So* sorry," he said through gritted teeth.

So sorry that he was stuck with her until the music ended. She closed her eyes for an instant. *Oh, what did it matter that he thought her odd and ungainly?* If she were to be ridiculed, it might as well be for her true self.

"Actually, sir, if you really wish to know, I was jotting down some ideas on a political essay that I had just read. On the subject of social justice." Olivia took grim delight in seeing his eyes widen.

Ah, once again I have shocked him.

"It's a very interesting subject," she went on. "Especially given the difference in philosophies held by democracies and absolute monarchies."

John made an odd little sound in his throat. Apparently she had rendered him speechless.

"Oh, but then, I see you are like most gentlemen and think females incapable of rational thought." She paused for a fraction. "Would you rather discuss the weather?"

"I…"

The final flourishing crescendo of the music saved the earl from having to answer.

"Thank you for the delightful dance, sir," she finished. "No need to escort me back to my wall niche. My sister is there by the potted palms and I need to have a word with her."

Releasing her hand and stepping back, John inclined a stiff bow.

Damn. He watched her move off, unsure whether to feel relieved or annoyed. *Hellion, indeed.* No wonder she had been hiding in the shadows. If his two encounters were any indication, Miss Sloane had probably insulted and offended most of the gentlemen in the room with her outspoken opinions. Taking a glass of champagne from a passing waiter, he gave a mental toast to his quick escape.

There would *not* be a third encounter, he decided as he quaffed it in one gulp.

Yet somehow the wine's effervescence left a strange burn on his tongue.

His attempt at humor had, perhaps, been a trifle cowhanded, but it had been unfair of her to assume he had a low opinion of the female intellect. As for defending himself, her unexpected attack had taken him by surprise. And apparently his military skills—not to speak of his chess skills—were indeed sadly rusted, for he hadn't reacted quickly enough to regroup.

The thought was galling, and yet another reason why he intended to march straight out of this overheated room, with its overloud laughter, overbright lights, and overpowering perfumes.

"To the Devil with dancing," he muttered under his breath as he snagged a fresh glass of wine. But as he turned for the archway, he hesitated. *An experienced army*

officer leaving the field of battle in ignominious defeat?
That was even harder to stomach than his rusty reactions.

Out of the corner of his eye, John saw Olivia take leave
of her sister and head back for the colonnaded alcove.
Veering sharply, he caught up with her just as she circled
around one of the decorative flower urns.

"A moment, Miss Sloane."

She stumbled. Clearly he had caught her off-guard.

Good—it was time to take the offensive for a change.

"Allow me to correct your earlier misassumptions," he
said softly. "For a skilled chess player, you seem a little
quick to jump to conclusions."

Olivia drew in a sharp breath. "So, you did recognize
me after all."

"Your face was mostly hidden in shadow during our
previous encounter, but nighttime reconnaissance mis-
sions teach a soldier to have a sixth sense about that sort
of thing."

"Ah. I see."

"Be that as it may," went on John, "It is this evening's
exchange that I wish to speak about."

Her silence seemed a signal to continue.

"First of all, I have absolutely no interest in discussing
the weather. Second of all, I have no preconceived prejudices about the powers of the female mind." He paused.
"But then again, after your display of haughty high-
mindedness, perhaps I ought to reconsider."

A momentary flare of outrage lit in her eyes. She
scowled—and then curled a wry smile. "Touché, sir. Most
gentlemen aren't willing to listen to a lady's opinion."

"Most ladies aren't willing to offer one."

"Can't you blame us?" asked Olivia. "Society doesn't

exactly encourage creative thinking in the fairer sex. We are meant to be seen and not heard."

"Um, yes, well, I…" John flushed, realizing that his gaze had slid down to her bodice. Beneath the overblown ruffles, it appeared that she had a shapely swell of bosom. "I—I also wanted to apologize for trampling on your toes."

Her laugh, like her voice, was very intriguing. Low, lush, and a little rough around the edges, it reminded him of an evening breeze ruffling through shadowed leaves.

"Good heavens, don't look so stricken, sir," she said. "The fault was all mine, I'm afraid. I can never seem to keep the dance steps straight." Another laugh. "What a pity we can't just ignore the rigid patterns and simply follow the rhythm of the music."

"Like wild savages, dancing around a bonfire to the sound of a beating drum?" he said slowly.

"Haven't you ever lifted your face to the moonlight and spun in circles to the dusky song of the nightingales and—" Olivia shook her head. "No, of course not. What a ridiculous question to ask." The errant curl had come loose again and was inching close to her nose.

"Your hair, Miss Sloane," he murmured.

"Has decided to dance to its own tune tonight," she said tartly, brushing it back with impatient fingers. "As you see, I seem to have no control over my body's primitive urges."

John almost let loose a very unlordly chortle. But quickly recalling his glittering surroundings, he managed to smother it in a cough. A peer of the realm did not chortle in public.

"Perhaps…" A dangerous glint lit in her eyes. "Perhaps I should give in to impulse, strip off my clothing, and waltz naked across the dance floor."

He tried not to picture her lithe body without a stitch on. *Discipline, discipline.* A gentleman must be ruled by reason, not primal urges.

Clearing his mind with another cough, he quickly changed the subject. "Just what sort of social essay were you reading, Miss Sloane?"

Her mouth quirked. "Horatio Edderley's most recent work on how a country should care for its disabled veterans."

Veterans! His brows shot up in surprise. There seemed to be no end of unexpected statements from Olivia. Why, that was exactly the social issue that he had decided to focus on.

"And what did you think of it?" he inquired.

"Well, I cannot agree with all his points," she began. "Hingham's ideas are much more in line with my own thinking. I am very much looking forward to reading his new essays."

"Hingham's new essays are not yet available in England," pointed out John.

"Actually, they are. Hatchards has one copy on order, and it's scheduled to arrive tomorrow."

"By Jove, I mean to purchase it," he said, more to himself than her.

"I'm afraid that won't be possible, Lord Wrexham. It's reserved," said Olivia. "For me."

"But—"

"Ah, there you are, John! Why are you skulking behind the flowers?" Cecilia rounded the massive display of lilacs and ivy at a fast clip.

"I am not skulking," he replied with a scowl. "I am conversing with Miss Sloane."

"In a manner of speaking," murmured Olivia. "In truth, I think I am shocking His Lordship."

Cecilia regarded them both thoughtfully for a moment before saying, "Good! He needs to have his cage rattled, so to speak."

John narrowed his eyes in warning.

"Now, if you will forgive me, I must take my brother away. The dowager Duchess of Needham, a dear friend of our mother, is demanding that he come make his greetings while he is in Town. And since he is haring back to Shropshire in the morning, it must be now."

"Of course," said Olivia, crooking a tiny smile. "I hope you have pleasant weather for your journey home, sir."

"Pleasant weather?" repeated Cecilia, once they had moved out of earshot. "Somehow I doubt that Miss Sloane was bringing that odd look to your face with talk of whether tomorrow will bring rain or shine."

John didn't reply, hoping she might drop the subject.

"In my experience, she always has something interesting to say." A pause. "So, what were you discussing?"

Sensing that this was a battle he would not win, John surrendered with a chuffed sigh. "Dancing."

His sister fixed him with a skeptical stare.

"Truly," he added before she could add a caustic comment. "Miss Sloane was explaining how..." Feeling his sister needed to have her own cage rattled just bit, he decided not to blunt the thrust of Olivia's sentiments. "...How she thought dancing would be far more enjoyable if we all just ignored the choreographed steps of the waltz and instead simply stripped off our clothing and shimmied to the natural rhythm of the music."

Rather than appear rattled, Cecilia merely nodded thoughtfully. "Well, I suppose that makes some sense, given her upbringing."

"What the devil does that mean?" growled John. "Is she a Polynesian princess in disguise?"

A small laugh slipped from his sister's lips. "Not exactly. However, her father was a noted scholar of primitive cultures, and his work is very highly regarded by the leading members of the Royal Society. Native ritual was one of his specialties." She paused for just a fraction. "Unfortunately, he succumbed to a tropical fever a year or two ago while on a research expedition to the South Sea Islands."

He darted an involuntary look at the decorative colonnade, but Olivia had disappeared.

"Lord Trumbull was, by all accounts, a very interesting, erudite gentleman. Which I've heard drove his wife to distraction. Apparently he had no head for finances and left his family with barely a feather to fly with."

When John didn't respond, she went on. "It's a pity. Miss Sloane and her sister, Miss Anna, are presently out in Society, and Lady Trumbull is aggressively angling to attract a rich husband for one of them, preferably one with a title to go along with the money. But without a dowry, her daughters will have a hard time attracting any suitors."

"It's Miss Sloane's tongue, not her purse, that will likely scare off potential husbands," muttered John. "She has some very...unusual ideas."

"I have no idea why gentlemen seem to prefer ladies

who are naught but patterncards of propriety over someone with a spark of individuality," remarked Cecilia. "I
swear, most of the prospects on the Marriage Mart might
as well be fashioned from pasteboard instead of flesh and
blood."

The thought of Olivia's lithe body, bared in all its
fleshly glory, dancing naked in the moonlight made
John's blood begin to thrum.

"Speaking of propriety," he said through gritted teeth.
"I was not jesting when I said that I have met a very nice
young lady in Shropshire."

His sister slowed her steps as they passed beneath the
overhanging fronds of the potted palms. "Go on."

"She is a relative of my neighbor, and is from a very
proper but impoverished family. So like Miss Sloane, she
has no dowry to speak of. But then, I have no need to
marry for money."

Obscured by the slanting shadows, Cecilia's expression had turned inscrutable. "No," she said slowly, "you
are fortunate enough to be able to marry for love, John."

He avoided her gaze. "We are well suited. The lady
in question has poise, polish, and a steady temperament.
And she can converse intelligently on a number of topics
that interest me." Aware that he was sounding a little de-
fensive, he quickly added, "All in all, I think she will
make a perfect countess."

"Then why do I see a shadow of doubt in your eyes?"

"Because," admitted John, "there is one slight problem. Scottie doesn't like her."

"A definite problem," agreed his sister.

"But I'm sure he'll come around once he gets to know
her better."

Her silence was far more eloquent than any words.

Damnation. He had been hoping that she would agree with his assessment. "It will just take him a little time to get used to the idea. I am hoping that in a few weeks he will be more comfortable with the idea of a courtship."

"So, you haven't made a formal proposal yet?"

"No," confessed John. "I—I plan to, just as soon as Parliament finishes the debate and votes on the bill concerning pensions for returning soldiers."

"I would think that passion would override practical matters such as politics," murmured Cecilia. "Assuming, of course, that she stirs a passion in your heart."

"We rub together well," he answered.

"And yet, it seems the contact sets off nary a spark."

"Fire and friction aren't necessarily good in a marriage."

"Neither are ice and a piece of marble so perfectly polished that it's lost any hint of individuality."

John expelled a low oath. "That's unfair. You haven't even met the lady yet."

"So it is," said Cecilia. She slipped her hand into the crook of his arm. "My apologies. I promise that I shall keep an open mind."

"Thank you."

"I just want to see you happy, you know."

"Ye gods, you think that at my advanced age I don't know what will make me happy?"

His sister answered with an enigmatic smile. "I shall reserve judgment on that, too. Now come, the dowager is waiting."

Chapter Six

*Y*ou didn't really say that," exclaimed Caro.

"Oh, but I did," replied Olivia. Setting down the coffee she had brought in from the breakfast room, she closed the door to the study.

Anna looked concerned, but Caro giggled. "Oh, Lud. I wish I could have seen the earl's face."

"He looked...well, I'm not precisely sure how to describe his expression. It was odd."

"Dancing naked across the ballroom." Anna tapped a pen to the tip of her chin. "Hmmm, come to think of it, that could make for an interesting scene in Count Rudolpho's castle. My story has been getting a little boring since Emmalina escaped from the Barbary pirates. I need something titillating to liven up this next chapter."

"Or I could use it as inspiration for a dark and dangerous poem." Caro quickly got in the spirit of things. *"Her pale flesh glistened in the firelight, a spectral beauty moving in rhythm with the jungle drums..."* She paused. "I know, I'll call it 'The Hottentot of High Street.'"

Anna groaned. "Don't you dare. Olivia is skirting on the edge of scandal as it is." Fixing her eldest sister with a quizzing stare, she added, "You really shouldn't have gone out of your way to be rude to the Earl of Wrexham. I've heard that the Perfect Hero is a real stickler for propriety."

"Starchy?" asked Caro.

"His shirtpoints probably stand up by themselves," quipped Anna.

"Pffft. What a bore."

Olivia pursed her lips. "Actually, I think he has a sense of humor, though he doesn't wish to show it."

"It won't be remotely funny if he makes any disparaging comments about your conduct," pointed out Anna.

"Afraid that your eccentric sisters might scare Lord Davies away?" asked Caro with a sly smile.

Two hot spots of color flared on Anna's cheeks. "Of course not! That would be rather like the pot calling the kettle black." She sighed. "I'm simply saying that it might be wise for Olivia to temper her tongue the next time she meets him."

Olivia shrugged and went back to rearranging her notes. "Don't worry, I'm not likely to engage in any intimate conversation with him again. The only reason we were together was because his sister forced him to ask me to dance. Given his druthers, I expect he'll avoid me like the plague."

For some reason the thought stirred a small frisson of disappointment deep within her chest. It had been rather fun crossing swords—verbal swords!—with the earl. He had been quick with his own retorts, and his attitude toward women was more enlightened than those of his fellow peers.

As for his smile...

Snapping her portfolio shut, Olivia looked up. "Oh, by the by, Anna, I thought of a phrase that might come in handy for your next chapter."

Anna paused with her pen hovering over the inkwell. "I am always looking for artistic inspiration," she said dryly. "Do tell me."

"You could," she said, "describe your hero's mouth as possessing a sinuous sensuality."

"Oooo, I like that," piped up Caro as she surreptitiously scribbled something in the margin of the poetry book she was perusing.

"Might I inquire what sparked that thought?" asked Anna, once she, too, had written it down.

"You know how phrases are," answered Olivia evasively. "On occasion they just pop to mind."

"On occasion, they do," agreed Anna, though the speculative gleam in her eye warned that the matter would not be forgotten.

After checking the clock on the mantel, Olivia gathered up several pencils, along with a small notebook, and jammed them into her reticule. "Hatchards will open in a quarter hour. Does either of you wish to accompany me?"

"Yeeech."

Prescott looked up as Lucy creased the piece of paper into a series of elaborate folds and launched it into the air. After several lazy spins, it dipped sharply and landed splat in the dregs of their morning chocolate.

"That one was the worst reply yet," she announced.

"Even worse than Lady Serena?" he asked.

"Lady Serena doesn't threaten to smother the darling

little cherub who wrote the advertisement with hugs and kisses, does she?"

Prescott's glass thumped down on the tavern table. "I'm doomed," he announced, once he had choked down the last swallow of his lemonade.

A rip cut through the gloomy silence as Lucy tore open another letter. "Come on, show some bottom, Scottie. We're not even halfway through the first pile." She pointed to the two mail sacks lying at their feet. "And then there are all the rest of these to plough through. Surely there has to be one lady worth considering."

"Ha!" Prescott gave a morose kick to the weather-stained canvas. "And pigs may fly."

"Don't be cynical," she said primly, tossing yet another letter into the hearth.

"What's that?" he demanded.

"I'm not precisely sure." Lucy started skimming the next missive. "But when Mr. Phipps says it, it means that you aren't supposed to say something negative, even if it is true." She made a face, and the paper quickly joined the growing pile of ashes. "Keep digging. That is—unless you would rather resign yourself to having the Steel Corset as your surrogate mother."

Repressing a shudder, Prescott snatched up a handful of the letters from London and fell to breaking the seals.

Despite the added urgency, their energy was beginning to wane, along with the afternoon light, when Lucy suddenly straightened in her chair and reread the note in her hands.

"*Eureka*," she announced.

"I hope that's not her name," mumbled Prescott. "It's sounds like you've just spotted a dead mouse."

"No, silly—Papa says it is a foreign word, and it means something very good," explained Lucy. "Like when he discovers a gold coin wedged beneath the dross and sawdust of the taproom floorboards." She handed over the paper and waited for several moments. "Well?"

Prescott grinned. "*Eureka.*"

Olivia pushed open the shop's door, setting off a muted chiming from the cluster of tiny brass bells hung above the molding. A puff of dust motes swirled up from the ancient counter, quicksilver specks of reflected sunlight dancing against the jumbled shadows.

"Ah, good day, Miss Sloane." The proprietor peeked out from behind a pile of pasteboard boxes and set aside the ledger he had been reading. "How nice to see you. It has been a long time since your last visit."

"As I just come to look, rather than make any purchase, I do not like to impose on your good will, Mr. Tyler," she replied. "However, the new chess sets in your window look so intriguing, I couldn't resist the temptation to stop in and have a closer look."

"They are rather lovely, aren't they? I just received them as part of a special shipment from Persia, along with some elaborately painted playing cards." He smiled. "And you are always welcome here, regardless of whether you spend any blunt or not. Your father and I shared many happy hours discussing the game and its nuances." A brusque cough. "I miss his friendship."

"As do I," she murmured. She glanced at the display nook above his desk. "I see you still have the ivory and amber set from Russia."

"Aye, it's a very unusual design—not to speak of very

expensive—so it will take a discerning buyer to recognize its worth."

Olivia repressed a sigh of longing. "I hope it goes to a good home."

"Aye." Tyler gestured to the rear of the shop. "You'll find a display of the other sets in the alcove behind the bookshelves. Please feel free to spend as long as you like with them."

"Thank you." Olivia wasn't quite sure what had moved her to cut through the quiet side street rather than take a more direct route home from her trip to the bookstore. Perhaps, she mused, it was because last evening's encounter with the Earl of Wrexham had reminded her of the subtle thrusts and parries that played out over the checkered board.

He was an interesting opponent—the fact that she couldn't read his mind made a match much more challenging.

The earl is not an opponent, she reminded herself. *He's not*... Her boot snagged for an instant on the uneven floorboards. *He's not anyone who ought to be distracting my thoughts.*

She shifted the wrapped book in her arms as she walked down the narrow corridor. "Especially when I have an essay to finish," she added in a chiding whisper.

That said, she decided that a quarter hour spent admiring the Persian sets would not mean the end of the world. Slipping into the cozy display space, she put her package down on one of the small tables and began to examine the different chess pieces.

The first grouping was made of Persian turquoise, with one side carved out of a soft shade of sky blue stone while the other was a deep green-gray hue. The workmanship was superb, with detailings of rich burnished gold highlighting the smoothly polished surface. She picked up the lighter Queen for a closer inspection, only half aware of the faint tinkling of brass floating down from the front of the store.

Steps followed—a masculine tread of boots over the waxed wood—then paused at the alcove displaying the playing cards.

Breathing a sigh of relief, for she wasn't in the mood for company, Olivia returned her attention to the chess figure in her hand.

"More games, Miss Sloane?"

Silent as a stalking tiger, the earl had moved up behind her.

"Or should I say, contemplating new and exotic ways to slay your opponent?"

The sound of his voice, low and edged with a hint of humor, had the oddest effect on her insides—her stomach gave a sudden little lurch, and her heart jumped and thudded hard against her ribcage. Flummoxed by her own unaccountable reaction, she drew a steadying breath and took a fraction of a second to regain her composure before turning.

"Contrary to what you might think, Lord Wrexham, I am not a bloodthirsty creature."

"No, but you do like to win," he murmured.

"I don't imagine that most people like to lose," countered Olivia. "Do you?"

"A fair point," replied John, though he didn't respond to her question. After a whisper of silence, he picked up the dark turquoise knight. "This is unusual. And exquisite."

"Mr. Tyler always has a wonderful selection of sets." A pause, and then she couldn't help but add, "None of the figures are stark naked, so your sensibilities won't be shocked."

"How fortunate," he replied, allowing the same sliver of silence to pass. "Seeing as I left my smelling salts at home."

Good heavens, the man *did* have a sense of humor. And an impish one at that.

"Do you come here often?" he asked.

Olivia shook her head. "Not anymore." Placing the Queen back on its square, she moved to the next table. "But my father used to be a regular patron, so I'm very familiar with its offerings."

"Ah." Strangely enough, John followed her.

"And what brings you here, sir?" she asked, reaching abruptly for a pawn made of color-swirled Murano glass.

The earl apparently had the same impulse for their hands, entangled, knocked the figure to the floor. He held her fingers for just an instant, but in the fleeting touch, Olivia was aware of a skittering of different sensations.

Calloused fingertips, strong grip, pulsing warmth.

She pulled away as if singed.

"Sorry," murmured John, bending to retrieve the pawn. The flex of muscle rippled the finely tailored wool of his coat as he searched through the shadows.

"No harm done," he announced a moment later, straightening and setting it back in place.

The same could not be said for her own peace of mind. Feeling a little unsettled by the brush of his bare skin, Olivia quickly edged away to the next display.

Again, he moved with her, his big body now looming only scant inches from hers.

The air between them seemed to spark and thrum.

John, however, appeared unaffected by any unseen currents. His voice betrayed not a hint of a tremor. "In answer to your question, I thought I would purchase a chess set for my sister, as thanks for her hospitality. She and her husband have been more than kind in hosting me during my frequent visits to Town while Parliament is in session." He made a quick survey of the room. "And perhaps a miniature traveling set as well, to replace one I lost in transit from Lisbon to London."

"Well then, you have come to the right place." Olivia tried to shake off the odd tingling that was radiating through her limbs. "Mr. Tyler has a very discerning eye and offers a wide range of lovely choices. I am sure you will find something that catches your fancy."

John didn't answer right away. Lifting a whimsical papier-maché rook from the nearby board, he slowly twirled it between his fingers. "This is rather charming. Do you think my sister might like it?"

"I—I don't know her tastes well enough to offer an opinion."

"Then let me ask—what do *you* think of it, Miss Sloane? The painted details are magnificent, are they not?" He angled it to catch the light filtering in through the narrow diamond-paned window. A wash of gold limned his face, accentuating the strong lines and chiseled features.

The Perfect Hero—a perfect moniker. At that moment, she thought he looked just like one of the classical Greek warriors depicted in Lord Elgin's marbles.

"And aren't the pastel hues just the sort of colors that appeal to a lady?" he went on.

Olivia blinked and forced her attention back to his question. "I am the wrong person to ask, for as you have no doubt noticed, my tastes rarely coincide with popular opinion. The fact is, I find pastel shades rather vapid. I much prefer bolder, stronger colors," she said. "So although the artist has rendered a lovely work of art, the set would not be my first choice."

"No?" John put it down. "What materials do you favor? Wood? Stone? Precious metal? Or some other exotic substance?" A subtle smile played on his lips. "Spun sugar? Molten moonbeams?"

She felt a tiny tickle of amusement tease at the back of her throat. "So that one could eat any mistake?" For a gentleman whose expression was normally so solemn, he was showing a very serendipitous sense of humor this morning. "Or only sit down to a game at midnight?"

The smile became more pronounced. "That could be an impediment. One never knows when one will be in a playful mood."

Don't look at his mouth. Wrenching her gaze away, Olivia quickly crossed to the other side of the display table and feigned an interest in an elaborate set of burnished gold warriors, one side with shields made of garnets, one side with shields made of peridots.

"I would not have guessed that glitter and sparkle would appeal to your sensibility," he murmured.

Hell's bells. The alcove was small and she was running out of space to retreat.

"I can admire the craftsmanship without yearning to possess them," she replied tightly.

John surveyed the tables. "All jesting aside, what is your favorite material?"

He would probably think her half-mad if she tried to explain.

But most people think me eccentric, so what does it matter?

In answer, Olivia picked up a jade knight. "Shut your eyes and hold out your hand, sir. Palm up, if you please."

John hesitated for a fraction and then did as she asked.

"Describe what you feel," she said, circling the stone in the center of his hand.

"A rock," he quipped.

"Oh, never mind," she muttered, stopping in mid-stroke. "You are making sport of me."

"No, wait. Please do it once more."

Olivia warily touched the jade to his skin.

"Hard. Cold," he announced. "Smooth."

"How about this?" She took up an ebony King and ran it across his fingertips.

His mouth pursed in thought.

She waited, and as she watched his face, a strangely intimate awareness suddenly stirred inside her head. *John. His given name is John.* Olivia decided it fit him. There was a strong, steadfast, sensible ring to the sound.

John cleared his throat, interrupting her musing. "It somehow feels...more alive."

The answer took her by surprise. She hadn't really expected a hardened soldier to have such a sensitive touch.

"That's very good, Lord Wrexham." *I must not think of him as John.* "Wood was once a living, growing organism, so for me it has more soul than stone."

"An interesting observation," he replied. "By the by, may I open my eyes now?"

"Not just yet." Olivia took a moment to gather a turquoise and a jade pawn. "Can you tell the difference between these two?" She drew first one and then the other down the length of his hand.

John's face furrowed in a thoughtful frown. "Both are stone and both are polished, yet the first one felt slightly rougher."

"Yes, there are subtle differences in texture. Look— you may open your eyes now. See how the turquoise has pebbled veins swirling through it while the jade possesses a translucent smoothness."

He nodded. "Yes. It's somehow warmer, too, as if it was formed by a hotter fire."

"Y-you..." blurted out Olivia, then let her voice trail off.

"What?" he asked, looking slightly quizzical. "Did I say something wrong?"

"On the contrary. You have an excellent feel for nuances. I confess, I didn't expect it."

"Soldiering is not all about slashing sabers and cavalry charges, Miss Sloane. Indeed, careful observation and attention to detail often ensure that victory can be achieved without the senseless loss of life."

"I—I see." A sudden shivering sensation—*A sliver of ice? A tongue of flame?*—licked through her limbs as John reached out and took the two pawns from her hand. But then, her emotions were always at a fever pitch when working to the crescendo of an essay.

Speaking of which...

"I really must be going, sir," said Olivia. "I've lingered here too long and I've tasks that await me at home."

He shifted back a step but remained blocking her path to the corridor. "A moment more, if you please. Might I ask you to help me select a set for my sister before you go?"

"You don't need my help, Lord Wrexham. Besides, one can't go wrong with any of Mr. Tyler's offerings."

"Nonetheless, I should like your opinion."

Olivia's face took on an odd sort of pinch in reaction to his question, and John recalled that she had once remarked on how Society frowned on any lady who dared to express an opinion.

I should not like having to constantly bite my tongue, he thought. That he was free to give voice to his ideas, no matter how roughcut and unpolished, simply because of his sex, was indeed unfair.

Intelligence was not simply a matter of a person's intimate...plumbing.

Clearing his throat, John forced away all thoughts of her body—however intriguing they were—and quickly added, "To begin with, I assume you would recommend a set made of wood instead of stone."

That stirred a fleeting smile. "Not necessarily. Yes, I know I said that I prefer materials with soul. But there are other factors that come into play."

"Such as?"

"I'm also affected by the visual form of the chess figures—I love fanciful creations like centaurs and basilisks. And I respond to bold colors as well." Olivia pressed her palms together. "It is hard to describe in words, but the essence of a set's attraction is how it feels against my fingertips."

"You've been very eloquent, Miss Sloane." Her face was equally expressive, he noted. It spoke volumes on the hidden passions that swirled within her.

She is a very interesting and unusual individual—if she were a man, we would be likely be good friends...

But Miss Olivia Sloane was *not* a man, he reminded himself. So however intriguing she was, he must be careful to keep a distance between them.

"And I think I understand what you are saying." John made a slow circuit around the tables, taking in all the sets on display. *A look, a touch, a tweak.* None of them felt quite right.

As if sensing his thoughts, she murmured, "There are several others atop the storage cabinet in the far corner."

He moved to the spot she had indicated. On one side sat a delicately carved set made out of a rich, fine-grained rosewood and a buttery ivory that was the exact color of Devonshire cream. The figures, John noted, were whimsical birds—light owls and dark ravens.

"Cecilia will adore this," he murmured. "She has a great fondness for feathered creatures."

Olivia nodded. "I think it will suit your sister very well."

His gaze strayed to the other end of the cabinet top, where a quartet of miniature sets were aligned side by side. Crouching down, he saw they were all embellished with exquisitely rendered details. But one in particular caught his eye on account of the colors.

Carnelian—a deep shade of red-orange that glowed in the shadows like a glowing coal. *Malachite*—a sinuous swirl of smoky green hues.

"And I think this shall do very well for me," he announced, running his hand lightly over the figures. They felt good against his bare skin. "I have missed having a traveling chess set. It will provide a welcome distraction during the tedious hours of being cooped up in a carriage."

Olivia's eyes were hidden by her lowered lashes. He couldn't tell whether she approved or disapproved of the choice.

Not that it should matter.

"Enjoy your purchases, sir." She turned abruptly, pausing only for an instant to scoop up a package from the table by the alcove opening before disappearing into the corridor.

Damnation—the book! John had forgotten that she had planned to pick up the volume of Hingham's essays from the bookstore this morning.

"Miss Sloane!" he called, hoping to press his plea to borrow it sooner rather than later. However, by the time he sidestepped the chess displays and reached the passageway, the tiny bells above the doorway were already sounding a parting chime.

"Damn, damn, damn."

He was leaving for Shropshire in the morning, and wasn't due to be back in London for at least a week. There were duties to attend to at home—including escorting Lady Serena Wells to the County Militia's annual ball.

Order and precision. Logic and discipline. Not fanciful musings about wood possessing a soul or stones having an inner fire.

Reason would rule.

Which, of course, was as it should be.

But as he gathered up his intended purchases, John found his thoughts were straying from smoothly polished marble to a substance that possessed a slightly rougher and more interesting texture.

Chapter Seven

The swirl of scarlet silk, a vivid reminder of a foot soldier's regimental coat, turned the earl's thoughts from the capering figures of the country dance to the upcoming debates in the House of Lords. It was, he thought grimly, going to be one hell of a battle. The issues concerning the welfare of returning veterans were complex, and it would take a good bit of adroit maneuvering to broach his reforms without stepping on toes...

"Wrexham?"

The staccato notes of the violins suddenly ceased sounding like the whine of bullets to his ears. "Forgive me," he murmured, ruefully aware that one of his wandering feet had nearly crushed Lady Serena's dainty slipper. Once again he found himself on the dance floor. And once again, he was making a hash of it. "I fear that what few skills I have at these sorts of maneuvers are a trifle rusty."

"On the contrary, sir, your movements are quite precise," replied Lady Serena. "You just need a bit of practice."

"Like drills on the parade ground?"

"Exactly. Indeed, if you break the figures into individual elements and perfect each one, you will find it easy to avoid a making a mistake."

"Ah." His breath came out in a sigh. *Was a misstep truly important if one was caught up in the spirit of the music?* Recalling Olivia's outrageous words, he nearly smiled. Somehow, she was under the impression that dancing was meant to be more than an exercise in regimented moves. Indeed, the Hellion of High Street had cheerfully acknowledged her disapproval of strict rules in general...

"Wrexham?"

John quickly corrected his errant step. "So sorry."

"Would you rather sit out the rest of the set, sir?" asked Lady Serena. "You appear to be thinking of things other than the intricacies of a gavotte."

"Perhaps we had better, in order to avoid grievous injury to your toes," he admitted with a rueful grimace. "I am afraid I have been allowing my thoughts to stray a bit." Then, realizing how churlish his words might sound to a lady, he hastened to add, "An unforgivable offense, given the present company."

"Oh, you have no need to apologize, milord, for I am aware that you have every reason to be preoccupied. Uncle Justin says that you are very concerned about the upcoming debate in the House of Lords over the treatment of our war veterans. And from what he has given me to understand, you will among the leaders in pushing for serious reforms. Do you mean to forward the idea of a pension?"

"Well, as to that..." As John began an earnest explanation of his positions, the clench of his muscles slowly loosened. Lady Serena's questions were informed and intelligent. And she seemed truly interested in his answers.

Looking around the crowded ballroom, he found himself feeling both relieved and reassured. Indeed, the more he considered it, the more the lady by his side seemed the perfect choice for a countess.

"...what is more, a soldier certainly brings a laudable discipline to any task he is assigned," finished Lady Serena.

John had lost track of which reform she was commenting on, but the reference to discipline suddenly brought to mind a topic closer to home. After a moment of hesitation, he decided to broach the subject.

"Perhaps too much so."

Her brow quirked in question.

As the dance ended, he steered their steps out to the garden terrace while explaining about his choice of a drill sergeant as tutor for Prescott.

An evening breeze swirled lightly through the ornamental shrubbery and set the torches by the stone balustrades to dancing along with the echo of the music. In the softly shifting patterns of light and shadows, it was impossible to make out any nuance of Lady Serena's expression.

Nor were her first words any more revealing. "I see," she murmured.

"See what?" he probed.

"In truth, I see nothing wrong with your decision, milord. In my opinion, it is better to err on being a trifle too strict rather than too lenient. As your heir, young Prescott must learn about duty and discipline. It is never too early for a young gentleman to understand his responsibilities in life."

It was, to be sure, an eminently rational response, but John felt his brow furrow.

"You do not agree with me?" asked Lady Serena.

"In principle I do. And yet, surely there is an alternative to the rigid application of rules and rods. I . . ."

He drew in a deep breath. Bloody hell, if he intended to speak out on important issues, he would have to do a better job at articulating his feelings than he was doing now.

" . . . I wish that you might try to be a bit more friendly with Scottie," he said in a rush, deciding that blunt honesty was the best tactic.

"I appreciate your candor, my lord," she replied slowly. "Just as I believe you would prefer me to answer with equal forthrightness. I shall never be Prescott's friend—the differences between an adult and child are simply too great to think otherwise. I would, however, hope that I might win his respect and some degree of affection."

Respect and some degree of affection.

She had certainly won *his*, he told himself.

And what more could he ask for than such a firm foundation on which to build a new life? Scottie would learn to appreciate that in time . . .

Still, on offering the lady his arm, the earl could not quite shake the feeling that the brick and mortar of his future was slightly askew.

"The morning post, milord."

"Thank you, Whitney." Without looking up, John motioned for the silver tray to be placed to the side of his plate. Nothing among the assortment of mail promised to be half so interesting as the essay he was reading. Bold, witty, imaginative, it voiced a fresh perspective to the very Parliamentary issues that were weighing on his own mind.

Indeed, he must remember to jot down several of the phrases...

As he reached for his coffee, he caught sight of his sister's distinctive script atop the unopened stack of letters.

Duty before pleasure, he reminded himself. This week's feature by the *Morning Gazette*'s clever political columnist could wait for a few minutes while he attended to family matters.

John set the newspaper aside. Not that he didn't enjoy Cecilia's pithy commentaries or words of wisdom. However, he had an unsettling feeling that she had not given up the battle to maneuver him back into the ballrooms of Mayfair.

Not a snowball's chance in hell, he vowed, ignoring the tickling little daggerpoints of heat dancing down his spine as he suddenly recalled Miss Olivia Sloane's molten green eyes and her interesting opinions.

He couldn't afford any distractions in his life at the moment.

Prescott's entrance was a welcome enough diversion that John did not comment on his son's tardiness or the smudge of dirt on his cheek.

"I've a letter here from your Aunt Cecilia. She sends her love, and says to tell you that she has found a lovely book on sailing ships that she thinks you will enjoy," he murmured, skimming over the first few paragraphs.

So far, so good. Perhaps he had been exaggerating the danger.

"And your cousin Schuyler suffered a broken finger while playing cricket at Eton." He looked up with a smile, only to find his son fixing him with a rather fishy stare.

"Hmmm. Life in London appears be a trifle dull, despite the Season being in full swing." Refolding the missive, John reached for his newspaper.

"Speaking of letters, Father..." A much-creased sheet of stationery slid across the polished mahogany. "Try this one. I think you will find it vastly more entertaining."

The shirred eggs did a queasy little lurch in his stomach. "Where did that come from?" he asked.

"Just read it, Father," insisted Prescott. "Please."

John rang for a fresh pot of coffee before gingerly picking up the paper.

"Who the devil is Lady Loose Screw?" he finally demanded, once he had read over it twice.

"My new mother," blurted out Prescott.

John nearly dropped a cup of the scalding brew in his lap.

"Of all the applicants, she is the only one who measured up."

Undaunted by the earl's oath, the boy went on in a rush, "As you see, she likes books and philosophy, she knows how to cast a fly and ride astride, she doesn't mind frogs and mud. And she is really quite funny. In a word, she's perfect, Father."

Mother. Applicants. Replies. The words stirred a dire foreboding.

"Do you mean to tell me it was *you* who placed the advertisement in the *Morning Gazette*?" John spoke softly, trying to keep his outrage from boiling over.

"Yes." The tilt of his son's chin was no doubt a mirror image of his own tightly clenched jaw.

"Perhaps I was wrong in telling Withers to relax the rules governing your behavior."

"Just listen to what she says regarding rules!" Prescott reached across the table to snatch back the paper. "*Rules may be the screws that keep the gears of Society spinning,*" he read. "*But if on occasion a screw loosens, and a few squeaks ensue, my experience has indicated that the machine doesn't fall apart.*" He looked up expectantly. "She sounds like just the sort of lady we are looking for."

"Lady Loose Screw indeed—she sounds like a complete rattlehead!"

"Well, at least she is not as rigid as the Steel Corset!" retorted Prescott. "I think she would make a perfect wife."

Aghast at the suggestion, the earl drew in a deep breath. And let it out in a shout. "Well, then perhaps in another ten or fifteen years, *you* may consider making her an offer. In the meantime—"

"But Father—"

"In the meantime, you are going to march to the schoolroom this instant and write an apology to the editor of the paper, along with an immediate retraction of that ridiculous ad." Embarrassment added an extra edge to his outrage. The idea of becoming the butt of ridicule, especially at such a sensitive political time, was unthinkable.

At least, he prayed that would be the case.

"By the grace of God," he growled. "If we act quickly to squelch any more newspaper stories, we may manage to scrape through this farce without anyone connecting it to the Wrexham name."

"You—you mean you won't at least consent to meet with her?"

"Absolutely not!"

"But—"

"Not another word! That's the end of this matter—do you hear me, Scottie?"

John found he was not the only one capable of stinging sarcasm. "Loud and clear, sir," came the reply.

For a moment, father and son eyed each other with mutual loathing.

"Then I suggest you sharpen your pen and get to work on composing a suitably contrite admission of your transgressions," snapped the earl. "You will have ample time in which to hone your choice of words, seeing as you are confined to your quarters for the rest of the day."

Prescott said nothing, but the glitter of tears was eloquent in its resentment. Kicking back his chair, he rose and fled from the room.

John fisted the offending letter into a tight wad and chucked it into the fire. *To the Devil with Lady Loose Screw*. He took a rather childish satisfaction in watching the flames lick up and consume the crumpled paper.

Ha! If only it were half so easy to reduce the rest of his problems to naught but ashes.

Retreating back behind the pages of the newspaper, he sought solace in the clear-headed thinking of the political essay. But the fight with his son had left him too drained, too distracted to concentrate. Fed up, John abandoned his breakfast and stalked off to his study.

Now that his initial outrage had worn off, he found himself shocked at the ferocity of his son's reaction. *And his own*. Raking his hands through his hair, he stared glumly at the crossed cavalry sabers hung on the wall.

Women! Let them set pen to paper, and all hell broke loose.

Slapping a fresh sheet of foolscap upon the blotter, he, too, began to write. First a note to his sister, then one to Lady Serena, informing them of his abrupt decision to return to London several days earlier than originally planned. The newspaper essay—and his own stuttering reply to Scottie's latest misbehavior—had roused him to action.

To have any hope of winning both the battle for military reforms and the fight to keep his son from coming to hate him, he would need better ammunition than his own roughcut thoughts. Words were a powerful weapon, and to marshal them into an effective fighting force, he would need help from an experienced general.

Cecilia, Serena, Olivia, and now this Loose Screw. Wrexham repressed a slight shiver. Their names seemed to slither across his skin, like the damn serpent from the Garden of Eden.

After being bedeviled by females, he needed to talk to a kindred spirit. It would be a breath of fresh air to seek counsel from another gentleman as savvy and wise as "The Beacon."

"All good things must come to an end."

Josiah Hurley stepped back from the type case to see what had provoked the mournful announcement.

"It looks as though we shall have to come up with a new farrididdle—er, that is, feature—to keep the public's interest. It's a pity. Circulation is bound to drop off." His assistant chuffed a sigh. "At least we had a good run."

"Not so fast." After a quick glance over his clerk's shoulder, Hurley relaxed.

"But—but you see for yourself that our anonymous author admits to a hoax and withdraws the ad."

"You have a good deal to learn about the newspaper business, George." Hurley picked up the second sheet of paper that had fallen from the packet. "A story does not lose its momentum until we cease giving it legs...so to speak." Tapping an ink-stained finger to his chin, he contemplated the schoolboy scrawl. "Sometimes, when the original path seems to be fading away, you simply have to find a new slant."

Chapter Eight

Don't slouch. And don't squint." Lady Trumbull's eyes narrowed to mere slits. "Reading and writing are such *unnatural* occupations for a young lady. It is no wonder you have an odd kick to your gait."

Olivia's slipper grazed the delicate Chinoise curio table, nearly knocking several porcelain figurines to the floor. "Anna has enough grace for two, Mama. You need not worry that she will follow my lead."

"Hmmph!"

A reproachful glance from her sister caused her to leave off the subtle teasing. Not that her silence would do anything to soften her mother's scowl. It was only the sight of her middle daughter, looking resplendent in a gown of ivory sarcenet trimmed in daffodil yellow, that fashioned a look of budding triumph on the baroness's face.

"Indeed, Anna, you are looking in the first bloom of beauty tonight. I have no doubt you will have every eligible gentleman buzzing around you." Lady Trumbull slanted a glowering glance at Olivia. "Unlike *some*, who make no effort to display a sweet disposition. Lady Knowlton mentioned to me this morning that she overheard you contradicting Lord Howell over some detail of parliamentary procedure."

"He had his facts wrong," she replied calmly. Her mother's criticism had long since lost its sting. "On several points."

"That has *nothing* to do with the matter," exclaimed the baroness. "A lady is expected to offer compliments, not corrections, when a gentleman offers his opinion."

"Even when he is a pompous ass?" muttered Olivia under her breath. It was a good thing her mother had not heard of her spirited exchange with Lord Wrexham the other evening. It would have required a sea of smelling salts to bring her back to life.

From behind the baroness's back, Anna twitched another quick warning sign.

Olivia tweaked a brow, but refrained from further comment.

"You are sure you do not wish to change your mind and come along?" asked Anna.

"No, no. I think I shall just sit by the fire for a bit and catch up on some correspondence before turning in for an early night." Though in truth, her candle would likely be burning until well into the wee hours of morning. The book from St. Andrews had clarified the main problem in her essay, but if she didn't—as Caro put it—stop dawdling, she would be in danger of missing tomorrow's deadline. And seeing how Mr. Hurley was most pleased with the attention his new columnist was attracting, she did not wish to disappoint him.

"Anna, do step away from your sister before you catch a sniffle. It would never do for your admirers to see you with a red nose."

"Yes, go," urged Olivia before edging back into the shadows of the little parlor.

"A lady is expected to be prompt," began the baroness as she gathered her shawl and hustled Anna toward the foyer. "A lady is expected to be charming. A lady is expected to be…"

A lady is expected to be an utter bore, mouthed Olivia. Which was why she was quite content to be an aging bluestocking rather than a belle of the ball. At least there were two thoughts to rub together inside her head…even if the friction sometimes set off sparks.

Without the fire of ideas, life would seem awfully cold.

After stirring the coals in the hearth to a cheery blaze, she sat down at her desk and opened her portfolio of papers. Neatly folded atop her notes was the latest edition of the *Morning Gazette*.

"Hell's bells," she muttered, after finishing the column that Anna had carefully circled in red.

A lady is expected to have more sense than to pen a parody and leave it lying around where her sister might find the dratted thing.

No matter that it was her sister who ought to have a peal rung over her head, Olivia could not help feeling a twinge of guilt at the part she had played in fanning the flames of the farce.

Apparently now, with this new twist, it was hot enough to make the front page news.

The formal retraction, had it appeared on its own, would have put an end to the nonsense once and for all.

But Mr. Hurley, who possessed the nose of a bloodhound when it came to scenting a good story, had seen fit to publish an addendum.

"Hell," she echoed, on reading over the fine print. "And damnation." Perhaps it was merely a clever joke, penned by a skilled writer. She, of all people, should know how language could be manipulated to create an infinite range of emotion.

And yet, there was something so poignantly raw and real about the short paragraph that Olivia didn't doubt it was written from the heart. She might be an adult now, but she still recalled with painful clarity what it was like as a child to feel alone and vulnerable.

As for the prospect of a cold, unfeeling mother, a "Steel Corset" who held rules and regulations in such high regard...

She expelled a sigh, thinking of her late father, and how wonderfully free of constraint he had been in encouraging his daughters to explore the world.

Oh yes, I know what it is like to lose a beloved parent.

Uncapping her inkwell, Olivia set to composing a second response to the unknown young gentleman.

"Stop fussing! You are the one who told me to show some bottom," pointed out Prescott.

"Yes—but I didn't mean for you to risk having it paddled from here to Hades." Lucy grimaced. "This isn't a good idea, Scottie."

"Neither is having the Steel Corset for a mother," he retorted.

Unable to think of a reply, she looked away and began to twist at the end of her braids.

"I need to go to London." Prescott waved the letter under her nose. "Look, she's given me a time and a place to meet if I am in Town. And she says if I ever need advice I may always feel free to contact her by sending a note to this address."

His friend took a moment to read it. "So you mean to show up for this meeting?"

He nodded.

"Then what?"

"Well..." He folded the slip of paper and tucked it back in his pocket. "I thought I would invite her to visit Wrexham Manor. I am sure if Father meets her, he will like her very much."

"That's your plan?" The waggle of her brows mimicked the note of skepticism.

It was Prescott's turn to remain silent.

"Ha! It has more holes than a sieve." Sliding down from the bale of hay, Lucy started to pace in circles. "You'll be sunk before you even get out of the stable-yard."

"Not if you'll help." His lip quivered ever so slightly. "There may be a few leaks, but it's not as if I have to make it to Cathay...just the Painted Pony in St. Albans Street."

"Stowing away on the mail coach isn't the problem. In the boot, there is a small space where they keep extra spokes. If we work quickly while they are changing the team, and I retie the canvas..."

"You are a real brick, Lucy."

"Hold your horses. I haven't said yes yet." She fixed him with a searching look. "What if she is not at home, or you lose your way, or something else goes wrong?

It's one thing to sneak into Squire Dimworthy's apple orchard, but quite another to venture into London all by yourself."

She blew out her cheeks. "You may be a real goose at times, but...but I should never forgive myself if you ended up roasted."

"It's not so very dangerous." Prescott moved quickly to counter her concerns. "You see, I won't be on my own. My Aunt Cecilia lives in Mayfair, and she is always inviting me to visit her. The point is, I have to move fast. I heard Father telling Withers that he is changing his plans and returning to London several days early. Once he leaves, it will be too late. I'll be doomed."

"Hmmm..."

"You are right. Maybe it is better if you don't get involved. I'll find another way. I'll go—"

"You'll go to the Devil," she muttered. "The only way you have a prayer of this working is if I lend a hand." She cracked her knuckles. "Have you any money for emergencies?"

Prescott checked his pockets. "Two shillings, tuppence."

A low snort expressed her opinion of the piddling amount. "Take this." She slapped a guinea into his palm. "And you'll need a packet of food for the journey. Maybe a blanket as well."

"Lucy, you are a—"

"I am an idiot." She grinned. "But I am also your friend. Come on, we haven't much time."

The galloping thud of the hooves matched the pounding of John's own racing heart.

Dear God, if anything were to happen to Scottie...

It was only by an act of providence that Withers had stopped by the inn for a pint of ale. When he had casually asked about Prescott's whereabouts Lucy had looked a little guilty. Further questioning had elicited the truth, and his former batman had come pelting back to the manor with the news.

Hurry, hurry. Horrible things could happen to a lone child in London. There were dastards who hung around the coaching inns, snatching young girls and boys for thieving rings and brothels...

Wrenching back on the reins, John slowed his speeding curricle as it swung into the turn, managing by a hair's breadth to keep the wheels from skidding out of control. The near miss forced his attention back to the road. He had been enough of a ham-fisted clutch of late, without compounding his clumsiness by driving into a ditch.

Regaining his grip on his careening emotions, John steadied the horses to a more measured pace.

If only his luck would hold. He had made excellent time, despite the darkness and intermittent drizzle. At his last stop, the ostler had said the mail coach was no more than a half hour ahead. Given the weather and his much lighter vehicle, he ought to catch up by the next scheduled stop in Westerly.

An hour, he estimated. *Maybe an hour and a half.*

But it seemed like an eternity before a glimmer of light up ahead pierced through the fog. With a last, desperate flick of the whip, John urged one more burst of speed from his tired team and turned into the muddy stable-yard. Before the wheels had stopped rolling, he was off his perch and sprinting past the startled post boys.

"Scottie!" His fingers, stiff with cold and fear, fumbled with the knots of the canvas covering the boot of the mail coach.

"F-father!"

Near dizzy with relief, John yanked the cording free and pulled his shivering son into his arms.

"I'm sorry, I'm sorry," gulped Prescott, his voice sounding very small within the folds of the earl's great-coat.

"It's all right, it's all right." Hugging the boy tighter to his chest, he tried to stop his hands from shaking.

"Y-you can birch me until my bum is black and blue, but please don't take me back to the Manor, Father," begged Prescott. "I *must* go to London. I have a very important m-meeting with Lady Loose Screw, and a gentleman m-must always keep his appointments, isn't that so?"

John felt a lump form in his throat. Until now, he hadn't truly fathomed the depths of his son's despair. No doubt, Lady Serena would counsel a firm hand and a firm rod, but at the sound of snuffling against the wet wool he couldn't harden his heart to the appeal.

A seasoned soldier knew that sometimes it was neces-sary to make a strategic retreat before regrouping for the final victory charge.

"What say you to this, Scottie? We'll both continue on to London tonight. I was planning to return this week in any case, and now, with you with me, we'll have a chance to spend some time together, visiting the sights, seeing the acrobats at Astley's—"

"And keeping my meeting for tomorrow in the gardens of Portman Square?"

John drew in a long breath. "I shall make a bargain with you, Scottie. I shall agree to meet your Lady Loose Screw if you will agree to give Lady Serena a fresh start to win your regard. For whatever reason, I fear you have taken an unreasonable dislike to her. Give her a fair chance."

Prescott raised a tear-stained face. "Will you give Lady Loose Screw a fair chance as well?"

He relaxed. It was an easy enough promise to make. That Scottie's anonymous letter writer could hold a candle to the poised and polished Lady Serena was absurd. "Yes, you have my word that I shall meet her with an open mind." He smoothed his hand over Scottie's damp curls. "So, do we have a bargain?"

His son nodded solemnly. "Yes, we have a bargain."

Chapter Nine

Unlatching the side gate, Olivia slipped inside the high-fenced gardens. Thick twines of ivy hung heavy on the wrought iron, obscuring the winding paths and leafy shrubbery from the street. The square was quiet at this time of day, and aside from a harried maid walking a pair of lively pugs, the graveled walkways were deserted.

A fool's errand, she chided herself. She must have bats in her belfry to continue this odd correspondence with a child. Her other writing was far more important.

The letter crackled her hand. *Or was it?* She knew all too well what it felt like to be subject to a cold, uncaring parent. If she could offer a few words of counsel, well, perhaps she could help ease his pain.

Hell, the boy's father must be an uncaring wretch, to have so little concern for his son.

Rounding a bend, she saw that she was not the only resident of Mayfair, aside from the servants and dogs, out for a morning stroll. Up ahead, two figures, one tall, one short, were coming from the east entrance and their path was about to cross with hers.

Bloody hell. Olivia hastily tucked the letter into her glove as she recognized Lord Wrexham.

The earl stopped in his tracks, a look of surprise—or was it annoyance—flitting across his face. "Miss Sloane," he said stiffly, touching a hand to the brim of his high-crown beaver hat.

"Milord," she replied. His position prevented her from moving on.

"You are, er, out awfully early."

"Yes, I am an early riser and like to begin the day with a brisk walk," she replied. "And you, sir?"

He shifted uncomfortably from foot to foot. "My son and I arrived in Town late last night, and he was anxious to, er, get out and see the sights."

"Yes, well, I can hardly blame him. London certainly has a great many things to attract a young man's interest."

Though the earl looked reluctant, good manners dictated that he go through the ritual of introductions before moving on. "Miss Sloane, allow me to present my son, Prescott, Viscount Linsley." The boy, she noted, appeared far more interested in surveying the surrounding shrubbery than in meeting an adult. It took a discreet nudge from his father to get his attention.

"Scottie," murmured John, "make your bow to Miss Sloane."

"How nice to meet you, Lord Linsley," murmured Olivia in reply. Anxious to cut the meeting short, she was about to excuse herself when the boy looked up, revealing a large purpling bruise around his left eye. "My, that is *quite* a gruesome shiner you have," she said admiringly. "I imagine there's a corking good story to it."

Prescott flashed a shy grin. "I hit my head on a bundle of wheel spokes when the Tunbridge Wells mail coach ran over a very large rut in the road. I was in the boot, you see, and it was pitch dark, on account of it being close to midnight—"

"Scottie," warned the earl, in a tightly coiled voice. To her, he added, "Forgive us, Miss Sloane. I am sure you are *not* interested in my son's misadventures."

Actually she was. That the Perfect Hero had a boy prone to mischief was intriguing. However, the look of solemn reserve on his face made clear he did not wish his son to talk about it. "I am sure there is a very exciting story to why you were in the boot of the mail coach," she murmured. "And while I would no doubt enjoy hearing it—"

"I stowed away," blurted out Prescott.

Out of the corner of her eye, Olivia saw John's mouth thin to a grim line as his son hurried on with his explanation.

"My best friend Lucy helped me. Her father owns the inn in our village."

"How very intrepid of you. I imagine you wanted a grand adventure." Olivia smiled, recalling one of her own youthful escapades. "I once snuck into our neighbor's farm cart on market day, thinking it would be quite an exciting lark to journey to Dover." She chuckled at the memory. "But it wasn't at all what I expected. The truth is, it was horrible! I ended up cold, starving, and smelling like turnips for the next week."

"I didn't like it very much, either," admitted Prescott. "It was wet as a witch's tit—"

"*SCOTTIE!*" exclaimed John.

Olivia had to bite her lip to hold back a peal of laughter.

The boy scrunched his face in confusion. "What? Wilkins says that all the time and you never bellow at him."

"It is not a word that ought *ever* be said in front of a lady," explained John tightly.

"Sorry," said Prescott in a small voice.

Olivia dismissed it with an airy wave. "Oh, pffft. I've heard a good many worse sayings than that," she confided.

Prescott responded with a grateful smile. "Lucy knows a lot of colorful words, too. She's eleven, so she has more experience in life than I do."

Leaning down, Olivia gave a conspiratorial wink. "Yes, well, we older women are wise in the ways of the world."

The boy giggled.

As for John, he was watching her with a hooded gaze that was far less revealing of his feelings. *Disapproving?* It was hard to tell. His dark, thick-fringed lashes formed an impenetrable curtain over his dark eyes.

Olivia pulled herself back from pondering what emotions the earl might be hiding. At the moment, it was quite obvious from his fidgeting that his primary wish was to be rid of her company.

After her "dancing-naked-in-the-ballroom" comment and strange ritual of stroking wood and stone chess pieces, he must think her the Hellion from Hades.

"Well, do enjoy your stay in London, Lord Linsley," she said, becoming a bit edgy herself. She didn't relish having to explain the real reason for own her presence in the gardens. "I am sure you will find Town more interesting than...wherever it was you were going on your Adventure."

"Actually I was on my way here to Town," replied the boy, darting a defiant look at the earl. "On account of having a very important meeting arranged."

Olivia felt her skin begin to prickle. *Oh, no. No. Impossible.*

"Father did not approve," he went on. "But an honorable gentleman does not back out of his commitments, so I was forced to—"

"As I said before," interrupted the earl. "Miss Sloane is *not* interested in hearing any more childish tales of woe."

"I'm sure your father has only your best interest at heart." *Impossible*, she repeated to herself. Trying to shake off her sneaking suspicions, she essayed a joke. "I do hope you weren't dashing off to Gretna Green to be married over the anvil."

"It's not *me* who is thinking of getting married," blurted out Prescott. "It is Father."

"*Scottie.*"

Ignoring the ominous rumble emanating from his father, the boy added, "To the Steel Corset."

Oh, *merde*, thought Olivia, recognizing the unflattering epithet at once. Seeing as it appeared several times in the letter she had hidden away in her glove—underscored with bold black lines—she could no longer deny the terrible truth.

Swallowing a far more colorful curse, Olivia gave a cluck of commiseration. "Oh, dear, that sounds rather... unyielding."

John looked distinctly uncomfortable. "There is no formal agreement between us," he growled to Scottie.

"*Yet*," intoned the boy.

Olivia didn't need to hear any more. Deciding her only option was to beat a hasty retreat, she shifted her reticule, hoping her face wasn't as red as it felt. "Well, much as I am enjoying our tête-à-tête, I really must be going, Lord Wrexham."

To his son she added, "It was a pleasure to meet you, Lord Linsley. I hope that your visit to London meets all your expectations."

The boy had stepped away from John and was turning in a slow circle. "Are you sure this is the right place, Father? I—I don't see her."

"Mayhap she has more sense that I gave her credit for," replied the earl with a harried sigh.

"Or mayhap she has a very good reason for missing the appointment." As Olivia started to walk away, she caught Prescott's eye and softly added, "Ladies, too, have a sense of honor. They do not leave someone in the lurch except under extreme duress."

John let out his breath as Olivia walked away, thanking the heavens that Prescott's Lady Loose Screw had not yet made her appearance. Eris, the Greek goddess of Chaos, had wrought enough mischief in his life as it was.

Why, he thought to himself, *it is no surprise that the ancient Greeks chose a woman to embody Strife and Mayhem.*

"I don't see her," repeated Prescott, returning from a hurried check of the surrounding shrubbery.

Seeing his son's crestfallen face, the earl refrained

from caustic comment. "As Miss Sloane pointed out," he said gently, "a last-minute emergency must have occurred to prevent her coming."

Prescott nodded, manfully blinking back tears. "Miss Sloane is awfully nice," he declared after a moment. "I wager you that *she* doesn't wear a steel corset."

"'Corset' is another word that a gentlemen never, ever mentions in the presence of a lady," said John through gritted teeth. Especially as mention of the word stirred an unwilling mental picture of sylph-like Miss Sloane wearing nothing at all.

A naked Nereid, dancing across a moon-dappled meadow.

Bloody hell, the mad dash through the rain and fog must have brought on a brain fever. How else to explain the strange shivers of heat pulsing through his body.

Keeping his eyes averted from the provocative sway of Olivia's fast-retreating hips, the earl pursed his lips. "It seems I've been sadly neglecting your lessons on proper manners, Scottie. Lady Serena was right to point out my shortcoming."

"To the Devil with manners," mumbled his son. "And to the Devil with the Steel Corset."

John pretended not to hear the last few words. He couldn't blame his son for thinking Miss Sloane was nice. In fact, she had been more than nice. She had been kind and funny. And not at all condescending. Unlike some, she seemed to know intuitively just the right thing to say to a ten-year-old boy.

Ashamed of himself, he quickly quelled such disloyal thoughts.

"Come, we have just enough time to stop at Gunter's

Tea Shop for strawberry ices before I leave you with Aunt Cecilia for an afternoon of sightseeing."

"I swear, this is becoming more absurd than a Minerva Press novel," exclaimed Anna, as soon as Olivia finished giving her sisters a detailed account of the morning encounter.

"I know, I know," she said glumly. "But honestly, it's half your fault. If you hadn't shown me that newspaper clipping, if you hadn't mailed that dratted letter—"

"There's no point in moaning over spilled milk," pointed out Caro. "The question is, what are you going to do about it?"

"Nothing, I hope," interjected Anna. "You've done enough already to make the poor boy think that this marriage can be avoided. I'm not sure it's right to encourage false hopes. It might just be better for him to accept his father's decision, and learn to live with his new stepmother."

Caro made a face. "That's not very romantic."

"Neither is the earl," quipped Olivia. And yet, she wasn't so sure that was true. Seen in a certain angle of light, his eyes had an impish spark that was intriguingly at odds with his oh-so-solemn expression.

"There, you see? That's what I mean." Anna took a moment to sharpen one of her quills. "Er, by the by, do you mind if I use this little incident as part of the plot for my next chapter?"

"Oh, I am *so* glad that my travails can serve as inspiration for Emmalina and her *amours*." Olivia sank into one of the armchairs by the hearth and took her head in her hands. "Drat. I should be smart enough to come up with a clever solution. I can't very well arrange another face-to-face meeting between Lady Loose Screw and Lord Wrexham's son, now that he knows my real identity. But there has to be another alternative. Despite what you say, Anna, I feel like a wretch leaving the boy in the lurch."

A thoughtful silence came over the study, punctuated only by the crackling coals and the scratch of Anna's pen.

"I have it!" Caro suddenly snapped her fingers. "We can kidnap the Steel Corset and sell her to a ring of white slavers." She chortled. "Just like in Lord Byron's poem, *The Corsair*."

"I'm not sure we'll find any pirates cruising along Piccadilly Street," said Olivia dryly.

"Thank God," murmured Anna. "My book earnings would not be near enough to bail both of you out of Old Bailey."

Undeterred by her sister's sarcasm, Caro began pacing the length of the bowfront window, her face scrunched in thought.

Olivia sighed and picked up the newly purchased book of Hingham's essays.

"I have it!" Caro suddenly stopped in her tracks. "You can't meet the boy, but I can! Seeing as I'm not allowed to attend any balls or parties yet, none of the *ton* is familiar with my face. Even if Lord Wrexham happened to spot me, he wouldn't have a clue as to who I am."

Olivia reminded herself that the road to Hell was paved with good intentions. And yet, knowing how much Caro was yearning for an Adventure in London, she couldn't bring herself to dismiss it out of hand.

"Hmmm," she murmured. "And just how would we arrange this meeting without his father knowing of it? I doubt we could simply send a letter to the earl's town-house with provoking suspicion."

Caro thought for a few moments. "Easy. You send a nice picture book to the boy, with a note attached to the cover saying that you hope his eye has healed. Lord Wrexham will of course read it, but there's nothing to stir his suspicions, right?" She paused. "But *inside* the book, where the earl won't see it, you put another note, say-ing that Lady Loose Screw had observed this morning's meeting and was afraid to show herself and reveal her true identity with you there. However, because she didn't want Prescott to feel she had abandoned him, she had this book secretly delivered to your house, along with a note to you explaining the circumstances."

"Caro—" began Olivia. But her youngest sister quickly waved her to silence.

"No, let me finish! You see, she, um, knows you from one of your political societies, and so feels she can trust you to pass it on to Prescott discreetly. I will write a sec-ond note to put inside the book, this one from Lady Loose Screw, setting a rendezvous with the boy in the gardens of Grosvenor Square. I'm sure he is clever enough to think of an excuse to walk there. After all, it's right outside his father's door."

"Lud, you have a Machiavellian mind," murmured Anna. "You've even thought of the little details, like mak-ing sure the handwriting on the two notes is not the same."

"It must come from reading your novels," said her youngest sister, with an evil grin.

"Ha! No wonder we novelists are blamed for corrupt-ing the young and the innocent." Anna rolled her eyes, and then looked at Olivia. "That said, Caro is showing a budding talent for plotting. Her plan just might work."

Caro dropped an exaggerated curtsy.

"Which begs the next question," drawled Anna. "What in the name of Hades do you intend to have Caro tell the boy?"

"Short of suggesting that he sell the odious 'Steel Corset' into a pasha's harem," added Caro.

"I'm not exactly sure yet," answered Olivia. "But I'm sure I'll think of something."

Quickening his steps, John turned the corner and crossed the street. A bell tinkled as he entered the door to the shop, setting off a flurry of whispers among the ink-stained clerks.

One of them rose from his stool and ushered the earl into a private office. "I'll tell the guv that you are here again, milord."

John removed his hat and began to peruse a series of colorful broadsides hung on the far wall.

"So sorry, milord!"

The earl turned at the sound of the booming voice.

"I apologize for keeping you waiting," went on Josiah Hurley as he paused in the open doorway and straightened his rumpled waistcoat. "Do have a seat, sir. How may I help you today?"

Distracted for a moment by the fleeting glimpse of a cloaked figure exiting the shop, Wrexham didn't answer for an instant. Taking the proferred chair, he furrowed his brow. "Why, that was Miss Olivia Sloane who just left here, was it not?"

"Was it?" Hurley rubbed at his jaw, leaving a smudge

of linseed oil. "To tell the truth, I didn't ask the lady her name."

How very odd, mused the earl. Young ladies did not usually go out of their way to visit a printing shop.

"What did she want?" he asked after a moment's hesitation.

Hurley shrugged. "You would have to ask my assistant, sir. She may have come to fetch a missing newspaper for her family. Ladies sometimes do that when the daily delivery goes astray."

"Ah." Reminding himself that he was here on more important business than Miss Sloane's peregrinations, John leaned forward and placed a hand on the newspaperman's desk. "Any word yet? Have you been able to arrange a meeting with your columnist? I am most anxious to have a talk with him at his earliest convenience."

"Er, well, as to that, sir." Hurley shifted in his seat. "I'm afraid I've disappointing news. As I warned you, 'The Beacon' is a very private person and turned me down flat."

"Perhaps if you give me the fellow's name and address name, I could appeal to him directly."

Hurley shook his head. "Oh, er, the gentleman doesn't reside here in London."

"Then where?" pressed the earl.

"Forgive me, milord, but 'The Beacon' is a recluse. I've sworn to keep the name and address a secret."

"Damn," muttered John. "It's imperative that I contact him. A very important debate is coming up in Parliament, and I wish to ask his advice on the issues." To punctuate the sense of urgency, he began to drum his fingers on the desktop.

The newspaperman remained unmoved. "I wish I could help you, milord. But a promise is a promise."

John opened his mouth to argue, but Hurley quickly quashed any possible protest.

"As a gentleman, you surely understand."

"Well, may I leave a note, then?"

After a hitch of hesitation, Hurley agreed. "Aye, I suppose that would be fine."

"And you'll see to it that it gets to delivered to 'The Beacon' without fail?" demanded John.

Signing a cross over his heart, Hurley gave a solemn nod. "You have my word on it, milord."

Rising, the earl took a muttered leave of the newspaperman and returned to the street. It was a less than satisfactory arrangement. However, he had no choice but to accept it.

For now.

However, he hadn't won a chestful of medals in the Peninsular campaign by sitting on his bum. If he didn't hear anything soon, he would have to switch tactics and take the offensive.

In war, as in chess, there were a number of different strategies for achieving victory.

The Beacon was proving adept at making elusive moves. But the battle—or was it a game?—was just beginning.

Chapter Ten

Thank you, Miss Anna." As the music ended, Lord Davies brought his twirl to a graceful stop in front of Olivia and smiled. "Your sister is a splendid dancer, Miss Sloane. She moves like…"

"Spun sugar?" suggested Olivia, eyeing Anna's white silk gown with a glint of amusement.

Their mother had insisted on adding a confection of tiny pink taffeta roses along the scooped neckline, nearly ruining the elegant simplicity of the design. But with naught but the simple strand of pearls at her neck, and a sprig of snowy Baby's Breath twined in her honey-gold hair, Anna was still a vision of ethereal, elfin beauty.

"Lud, you make me sound like a sweet nothing," replied her sister with a mock grimace. "I hope I have more substance than that."

Davies looked a trifle uncertain of how to respond. "Be assured, Miss Anna, you are…"

"Absolutely delicious?" suggested a half-mocking voice from behind Olivia's back.

She turned to see a gentleman step out from the shadows. His long, dark hair was carelessly combed, and he wore his tailored evening clothes with a nonchalance that bordered on insolence.

"Ah, Lord Davenport," murmured Olivia. "What a surprise to see you here tonight." The marquess was reputed to be a ruthless rake and rarely made an appearance in the ballrooms of Mayfair. His favored haunts were said to be in the more dangerous, disreputable parts of Town, where the drinking was deep, the gambling was outrageous, and the women were unfettered by the rules of Polite Society.

His mouth curled up at the corners. "Oh, on occasion, I can behave in a civilized manner."

"Yes, but one wouldn't expect that an occasion like this would bring out your better nature," she replied.

He laughed. "It hasn't. I'm only here because I'm looking for a rich heiress."

Olivia bit back a smile. Despite his awful reputation, she rather liked The Devil Davenport and the way he flaunted his utter disregard for what people thought of him. "Alas, sir, I'm afraid you've come to the wrong corner of the room."

Davies frowned a warning at the marquess and hastily changed the subject. "Have you two ladies read the latest novel from Sir Sharpe Quill? My sisters say it's highly diverting."

Olivia slanted a sidelong glance at Anna, who didn't turn a hair.

"Though I suppose you are both far too sensible to read such silly scribbling," added Davies with a smile.

"On the contrary," replied Olivia. "I enjoyed it."

"As did I," said Davenport.

"Seeing as my sisters were making such a fuss about the book, I felt compelled to read it as well," explained Davies. "I confess, it was amusing. But absurd."

"Of course it's absurd," drawled Davenport. "That's the point. But unlike most of the other books of its type, it's clever and very well written." He turned to Anna. "And you, Miss Anna, have you read it?"

"Yes," she said rather curtly.

Davenport raised an inquiring brow. "*And?*"

"I see things that could be improved."

The marquess flicked a wrinkle from his sleeve. "Such as?"

Before Anna could answer, Lady Trumbull appeared, and began clucking in agitated alarm, like a mother hen herding her chicks away from the jaws of a stalking fox. "Come, girls, I must speak to you for a moment." Glowering at Davenport, she added, "In private, if you please."

Inclining a sardonic bow, the marquess sauntered away.

Catching Lord Davies's eye, she quickly softened her scowl. "*You*, sir, are of course most welcome to return and escort Anna in to supper. I shan't be long with her."

"My pleasure, madam," replied Davies, discreetly backing away in the crowd.

"Pray, do *not* encourage such a scoundrel as Lord Davenport, Olivia," scolded her mother. "Do you wish to scare off all the eligible suitors for your sister's hand?"

"It wasn't Olivia's fault that the man joined our group," said Anna. "The Devil dances to his own tune."

"Hmmph!" Lady Trumbull swatted one of her turban's drooping feathers away from her face. "Don't contradict me, my dear. It's not ladylike. And don't speak to that rogue again."

"Yes, Mama," replied Anna sweetly.

Mollified, their mother returned to the group of basilisk-eyed chaperones sitting near the refreshment table.

"Perhaps we should have mentioned that last time you came to a ball, you danced with the Earl of Wrexham," mused Anna as she watched the bobbing ostrich plumes slowly recede from view. "That would have spiked her guns, so to speak."

"As you well know, Mama needs no real reason to fire away at me," muttered Olivia.

"That's because you make yourself an easy target," pointed out Anna. She surveyed the room over the top of her fan. "Speaking of Wrexham, I wonder if he is here tonight?"

"It doesn't matter if he is. Trust me, the earl won't willingly seek out my company."

"Oh?" Her sister's voice held the tiniest note of smugness. "And yet, I saw him follow you behind the potted dahlias at Lady Battell's ball."

"Only because he was intent on having the last word in our argument. This morning, he couldn't get away from me fast enough." Olivia stared at the tips of her slippers. "By the by, they were lilac branches, not dahlias. I though a novelist was supposed to be observant."

"I'm interested in *human* nature, not plant life. And from what I observed, I wouldn't be so sure that Lord Wrexham won't ask you for another waltz."

"Don't be absurd," muttered Olivia, trying to still the little butterfly beating its wings inside her chest. The thought of dancing with him again shouldn't stir such flutters. The man was all but engaged.

To the Steel Corset, she reminded herself.

So despite his intriguing smile, his sly sense of humor, and big, warm body, Wrexham must be, at heart, a rather cold prig who preferred a life caged by convention.

"Davies is coming," murmured Anna out of the corner of her mouth. "Will you be all right if I leave you alone?"

"Of course," she whispered back. "I couldn't be happier—I've pencil and paper to partner me through the rest of this tedious evening. I'll find my usual spot in the shadows." She would, however, avoid sneaking off to private rooms, no matter how intriguing the games it contained. Her run-in with Wrexham had shown that the risks of a midnight encounter with a man, however accidental, were too high.

They exchanged sisterly smiles, and then Olivia edged away from the milling couples. The one dance she had mastered was retreating from the crowd without drawing any notice. It required an intricate set of steps and just the right timing. Not too fast, not too slow...

"Miss Sloane?"

She started, and nearly tripped over her skirts.

John caught her by the elbow. "Sorry. Did I startle you?"

"No, of course not," she replied. "I was just going to..." Loath to admit that she was going to assume her place as permanent wallflower of the *beau monde*, she looked around and spotted the French doors leading out to the balcony. "I was just going to get a breath of fresh air."

He offered his arm. "Allow me to escort you."

"It's not at all necessary," she said rather ungraciously.

"Nonetheless, it would give me great pleasure."

She walked with him for several steps before casting a sidelong glance at his profile. "Then why, sir, do you look as if you've just eaten a piece of bad fish?"

"You don't ever mince words, do you, Miss Sloane?"

"You should know the answer to that by now," she countered. "And why should I bother? Most gentlemen can't digest what I say, no matter how I slice things."

He chuckled. "I have a feeling your tongue could cut a fellow into tiny pieces if he weren't careful."

Olivia wasn't quite sure how to answer. Passing through the doors, she lifted her face to catch the evening breeze. The cool air felt good on her overheated skin. "I have a feeling you haven't invited me out here to discuss cooking, sir."

John turned and carefully folded his hands behind his back. Silhouetted in the shimmering firelight of the torchieres, his dark-clad shoulders looked even bigger than she recalled, their solid, sloping breadth accentuating the tapered waist and long, lean lines of his legs.

"A sharp guess," he said dryly. The hint of humor didn't quite cover his embarrassment. "I, er, wasn't planning on coming here at all. However, I was hoping to find you in attendance, so that we might have a word about this morning."

"Your son is a very engaging boy," she said quietly. "I enjoyed meeting him."

"Thank you. I appreciate your patience. And kindness. Lads of that age and, er, liveliness, can be trying."

"On the contrary. I think spirit and exuberance ought to be encouraged in children. They should have some freedom to explore and discover the world on their own terms."

The scudding shadows hid the earl's expression, but Olivia heard him expel a long breath.

"I fear that Prescott may be a tad *too* exuberant. The tale he told you..." Another chuff of air as he shifted his stance to stare out over the garden. Pale gold glimmers of torchlight threaded through his windblown hair, softening the chiseled lines of his profile. "I was hoping...that is, I would be grateful if you would not mention it around Town."

"I assure you, Lord Wrexham, I am not wont to gossip about people and their private lives."

"Thank you." His relief was palpable.

"There is no need for thanks. I am merely doing what any honorable person should do." She paused and then impishly added, "But then again, given my odd notions of ladylike propriety, perhaps you question my honor?"

"Miss Sloane, I assure you that the thought hadn't crossed my mind. Granted, you have, er, unusual ideas for a female. But I...I..."

"I am joking, sir," said Olivia. "I couldn't resist. You always look so serious. So solemn."

"Do I?"

He smiled, and as a spark from the torchiere caught on its curl, Olivia felt a shiver of fire dance down her spine. Just for an instant, she wondered what it would be like to be kissed by him. Would it be a mere, perfunctory brushing of lips? Somehow that firm, sensual mouth seemed to whisper silent promises of stronger passions.

John turned a fraction, breaking the enchantment. The flare of light died as shadows swallowed his face.

Oh, what moonlight madness has taken hold of me? Olivia was ruefully aware of needing a steel corset to cage the longings that all of a sudden were hammering against her ribs.

"Indeed," she said, mustering a show of outward calm. "You have a countenance made for teasing, Lord Wrexham." Her gaze moved back to the ballroom's blur of colorful silks and sparkling crystal. "We ought to be going in, sir."

And you have a countenance made for kissing. The thought leapt unbidden into his head as John offered his arm to Olivia.

Don't, he warned himself. *Don't* find her molten jade eyes so intriguing. *Don't* find her inner spark so fascinating. Hell, it was dangerous to play with fire. Flames could so easily flare out of control.

Clearing his throat, he asked, "Have you started to read Hingham's new essays?"

"Yes," she replied. "And I find them extremely interesting. He has some very thought-provoking ideas on what a government owes all its citizens, regardless of their wealth or rank."

"I stopped at Hatchards. Unfortunately you were right and the only copy in London is currently in your possession. I ordered one for myself, but it will take several weeks to arrive."

He paused as they passed through the open doors, unwilling to end the conversation just yet. Keeping hold of her hand, he sidestepped behind the marble statue of Terpsichore, the Greek goddess of dance. "Which is a pity. You see, I am preparing a speech for the upcoming debate in the House of Lords on caring for our veteran soldiers and had hoped to become familiar with his theories on social justice."

"Some of them are quite radical." Her voice seemed to hold a slight note of challenge.

"I like to think I am open-minded enough to consider all points of view before I make up my mind on an issue, Miss Sloane."

"Then you are very different from most of your lordly peers," she answered. "Whose primary concern is to preserve their own privilege and position regardless of the cost."

"Change is frightening to most people," he agreed. "Yet the world is changing all around us, and those in power have a duty not to turn a blind eye to it."

Her expression underwent an odd little transformation, though John could not describe it in words.

"You surprise me, sir. I would have expected a former military officer to be more rigid in his thinking."

"And I would have expected a lady who takes pride in her keen intellect to be less rigid in her assumptions."

Olivia flushed, turning her skin a delicious shade of pink. For one mad moment, Wrexham was tempted to touch his tongue to the pulse point at her throat. The tiny tremoring of flesh was intensely erotic.

"I stand corrected," she said in a husky murmur. "If you would like, I would be happy to loan you my copy."

"I would be exceedingly grateful. Might I call on you tomorrow and pick it up?"

"Oh, er..." Her eyes flared in alarm. "I'm afraid I need it for another day or two, and then I will be most happy to pass it on. As for fetching it in person, I don't think that would be wise, Lord Wrexham. It would be better for you to send a footman, rather than come yourself. I would rather that my mother not see you."

"Have I grown scales or spots?" he inquired dryly. "Or some other malady that might render my person abhorrent to her?"

Olivia shook her head. "On the contrary. She might get the wrong idea and actually think you were interested in *me*, not my book. And I assure you, sir, that wouldn't be very pleasant for you. If she scents a whiff of interest, my mother is more dogged than a foxhound in pursuing a title." Her mouth quirked a sardonic smile. "Especially if it's attached to a plump purse."

"Thank you for the warning, Miss Sloane. But I've survived hand-to-hand combat with Napoleon's most fearsome Hussars."

She made a face. "You haven't met my mother."

He smiled. "I'll take my chances."

"Frankly, it's not just you I am concerned about, sir. Mama has all but given up hope of my ever attaching an eligible gentleman, so she leaves me in peace. If she thinks—mistakenly, of course—that you have any interest in me, she'll begin pestering me to death about my appearance and my need to behave with ladylike manners."

"Which are, I take it, not high on your list of priorities."

"No, Lord Wrexham, they are not." Her chin took on a pugnacious tilt, as if she were defying him to disagree. "The truth is, I don't give a whit if people think me a handmaiden of Medusa."

"Speaking of Medusa," he murmured, watching an unruly curl slither over her cheek. "Your hair has snaked free."

"Oh, drat."

But before she could fix the loosened pin, he reached out and brushed it back.

Olivia recoiled as if singed.

"Sorry," apologized John, though he itched to peel off his gloved and twine his fingers through the red-sparked auburn strands. They looked soft as spun thistledown.

Touching her face, she inched away. "Is your betrothed not in London, sir?"

"My…" Still entranced by the sinuous sight, he needed a moment to puzzle out her meaning. "My son is mistaken. I have no agreement with the lady in question."

"Ah." For someone who professed little interest in ballroom frivolities, Olivia suddenly appeared enthralled by the figures of a lively country gavotte. Eyes locked on the dance floor, she added, "Your son will be greatly relieved to hear that you aren't going to be marrying the Steel Corset."

John wasn't quite sure how he had slipped onto such dangerous terrain. The parquet seemed to have shifted into a quagmire of quicksand, and he felt himself slowly sinking.

"I—I didn't say that." He shuffled his feet. "Not precisely."

"Well, either you are or you aren't," she said dryly. "It doesn't seem that there's any middle ground. Unless, of course, you mean to make her your *cher amie*."

He stood speechless, telling himself he ought to be shocked beyond words. She was utterly outrageous. Instead, he had to choke down the ungentlemanly urge to laugh. The truth was, he found her company…provocative. He had never met a lady as interesting or knowledgeable about so many different topics.

Including ones with which she ought *not* be familiar.

"Miss Sloane," he wheezed, trying to look stern. "A gently bred female is not supposed to know—"

"Is not supposed to know anything interesting," she finished for him. "Yes, I am aware of that." Her lashes fluttered in annoyance, setting off a winking of golden sparks. "Ye gods, is it any wonder that men seek out mistresses, seeing as the highborn ladies they are compelled to take as wives have been trained from the cradle to be bland and boring as boiled oats?"

"I'm not sure this is a conversation we ought to be having," John murmured.

"Of course it isn't," shot back Olivia. "We might actually engage in a meaningful exchange of ideas. I'd actually be curious to hear your reasons for having a ladybird."

"I don't..." John realized he was blushing. "I don't intend to discuss such a singularly inappropriate topic with you."

She muttered something under her breath. Something that sounded suspiciously close to "prig."

They stood for a moment in awkward silence, watching the glitter of diamond-bright light play over the swirl of colorful silks. John couldn't help feeling his own inner thoughts were spinning in the same confusing, conflicting blur of patterns.

Bloody hell.

The music finally came to end, and the couples began to move away from the dance floor.

"If you'll excuse me, sir. I see my sister beckoning." Without waiting for a response, Olivia turned on her heel and stalked off.

Chapter Eleven

 $\mathcal{A}$ n intriguing pair of sisters, don't you think?"

John looked around to see Lord Davenport leaning against one of the stone columns, one hand toying with the tails of his carelessly tied cravat.

"They certainly stand apart from the crowd of color-less chits being paraded on the Marriage Mart," continued the marquess. "A pity they haven't a feather to fly with."

John grunted in reply.

"Ah, but then, you don't have to marry for money."

"No," he said curtly. "I don't."

"Lucky you," drawled Davenport. Straightening from a slouch, he took a long swallow of his champagne. "But surely you aren't naïve enough to marry for love."

"God perish the thought." Signaling to a nearby foot-man for a glass of wine, John assumed a sullen silence, hoping the other man would take the hint and go away. He was in no mood for company.

But by some perverse stroke of luck, his wave caught

the attention of two gentlemen who had just emerged from the card room.

"Ah, there you are, Wrexham." The earl recognized the taller of the pair as the Duke of Sommers, whose holdings included several vast estates in Lincolnshire and Durham. "Lumley and I have been looking for you."

"I can't imagine why," he murmured somewhat ungraciously. Hell, he hardly knew the fellows.

"Actually, we have a common interest," said the duke smoothly. "One that draws all gentlemen of superior rank and intellect together in these tumultuous times."

"A common interest *and* a common cause," added Viscount Lumley. "We understand you intend to give a speech on the upcoming reform bill."

"Yes," said John, regretting his show of rudeness. "I am glad to hear that you agree with me on the principles involved. We members of the House of Lords have a responsibility to act for the good of the country. It is a very important issue."

"Indeed, it is," agreed Sommers.

"Which is why we are sure that you will want to reconsider your position, once you understand the fundamental error of your thinking," said Lumley. "You see, you have it all wrong."

"Pray, do go on," he said quietly. "I am anxious to hear how I have got it all wrong."

Lumley smiled broadly, seemingly oblivious to the note of irony in the earl's voice. "The fact is, coddling our returning soldiers would be a horrendous mistake! Good God, Wrexham—surely you see that. A pension will only encourage laziness. A man should have to earn his bread with an honest day's work."

John regarded Lumley's overfed face, battling to keep his temper in check. The man had likely never lifted a finger, save to summon a servant. "And if there is no work to be had?" he asked. "Or if a man has lost an arm or leg in fighting for his country and is no longer fit for able-bodied labor?"

Seeing Lumley's blank stare, the duke quickly interceded. "That's not the issue—"

"That's *precisely* the issue," retorted John. "By the by, how many returning veterans do you employ, Sommers?"

"I couldn't tell you," said the duke with a small sniff.

"Well, I can. As well as figures for some of our other lordly landholders." Wrexham rattled off a list of numbers. "If you read some of The Beacon's columns in the *Morning Gazette*, you will see some very articulate and intelligent arguments for passing this bill."

"The Beacon ought to have his wick snuffed," exclaimed Lumley. "He's a dangerous radical. A rabble-rouser. No responsible man should listen to such drivel."

Sommers adopted a more conciliatory tone. "What we mean is that you, with your credentials as a distinguished military officer, will have a very influential voice in the upcoming debate, Wrexham. Your peers will listen to you and be swayed by your opinion."

"Then I have even more of a duty to study the issue carefully and say the right thing."

"Idealism is all very well in theory," murmured Sommers. "But really, one has to be practical."

"What you mean is, you wish for me to vote for preserving the privileges of the rich, no matter the cost to the rest of society."

"You would rather be a traitor to your class?" demanded Lumley.

Fury welled up in his chest, and it was all John could do to keep from smashing a fist into the viscount's wine-flushed nose. "Don't speak to me of treason. I fought in the Peninsula, as did so many of those brave men whom you so casually denigrate. It is because of their sacrifices that Napoleon is not dining on Lobster Thermidor in Piccadilly Street."

"Yet you defend radical republican philosophy—"

Davenport interrupted the heated exchange with a pained sigh. "Christ Almighty, must you three keep nattering on about abstract ideas? They give me a headache."

"So do French brandy and Scottish whisky, yet you seem to embrace each with equal enthusiasm," sneered Lumley.

Davenport finished off his champagne in one gulp. "That's because drinking doesn't take any mental effort." Lifting the empty glass to the light, he added, "But then, you know that as well as I do."

The marquess might be a sardonic sot, but at least he made no pretenses about who or what he was, thought John. And to his credit, he possessed a rather sharp wit.

"Arse," replied Lumley, his nostrils flaring in anger. "Someday soon, someone is going to cut out that insolent tongue of yours and hand it to you on a platter."

"Quite likely." A quicksilver smile flickered in the shadows. "But it won't be you."

Sommers took his friend by the arm and drew him back from the marquess. "I advise you to think carefully about what we have said, Wrexham. We, too, are not without influence. And I daresay ours is a good deal more powerful than yours."

"Is that a threat, Your Grace?" asked John, matching the duke's mild tone.

Sommers's mouth curled up at the corners. "Merely a friendly word of warning."

"You appear to be in danger of making some very unpleasant enemies," observed Davenport as the other two men walked away.

"They are sadly mistaken if they think that I can be intimidated into going against what I believe is right."

"A conscience is such a cursed nuisance," drawled Davenport, flicking a mote of dust from his sleeve. "That's why I don't bother having one."

"Go to the Devil," growled John.

"Actually, I'm on my way to a delightful gaming hell and brothel named Satan's Sanctuary. Care to join me?"

"Thank you, but no. I've been roasted over the coals enough for one evening."

"Drat." Olivia yanked out a snarled hairpin and dropped it on her dressing table. "Damn," she added as several more flew free and bounced off the polished pearwood.

"Alice is a sweetheart, but she's all thumbs when it comes to arranging hair," commented Caro from the doorway. "Give me a corkscrew and a carving knife and I'd do a better job of it."

"Shouldn't you be in bed?" replied Olivia rather crossly. The evening's entertainment had left her in a black humor. "I—*ouch*!"

Caro hurried over and unknotted the offending ribbon. "Why are you in such a vile mood? Don't tell me that Sir Sidney showed you another one of his sonnets to Anna?"

"Nothing so dire as that." She grimaced in the looking glass. "I'm simply tired of being forced to smile and simper to a crowd of cabbageheads."

"Ha!" Caro crinkled her nose. "I doubt that you could 'simper' if you tried."

"Poetic license." Olivia slipped on her wrapper and shook out her hair. "Honestly, it's a colossal waste of time."

"Especially for someone who has once again left finishing her weekly essay until the last moment."

"Did you have to remind me?" she asked glumly. "As if my night wasn't bad enough already."

Caro took a cross-legged seat on the bed. "It couldn't have been worse than wandering around an empty house, wondering what sort of experiences you and Anna are having."

"Don't get carried away with your fantasies, Caro. Balls can be dreadfully dull."

"I suppose." But her sister didn't sound convinced.

"I'm sorry you're feeling bored." Olivia sighed, wishing not for the first time that she could trade places with her more exuberant youngest sister. Caro craved Excitement and Emotion, while she, the stick-in the-mud rationalist of the family, was content with just the opposite. "Did you at least get some writing done?"

Caro flashed a mischievous grin. "Actually, that's why I wanted to see you." She took a piece of paper from her sleeve and held it out with a flourish. "It's one of my better compositions, if I say so myself."

Olivia read it over and laughed. "You have a flair for

the dramatic, that's for sure. I'm sure this missive will find an appreciative audience in young Prescott."

"I purchased the perfect book for him at Hatchards," went on Caro. "I'll just slip the letter inside it. Now all you have to do is write a note to the earl, and the explanatory note to Prescott. Then we'll have Freddie deliver it first thing in the morning." Rolling onto her back, she clasped a pillow to her chest. "Oohh, what fun. This is even more romantic than Anna's latest chapter on Count Alessandro's secret meetings with Princess Miranda."

"You know…" As Olivia watched the scudding moonlight play over Caro's dreamy expression, she felt a slight twinge of foreboding. "I have to confess, I am having second thoughts about this scheme. What if something goes wrong?"

Her sister's face fell. "What could possibly go wrong? The worst that could happen is that Lord Wrexham goes ahead and marries the stiff-rumped Steel Corset. And, according to Prescott, that's already a certainty unless we help save the earl from himself." The squeezed pillow emitted a feathery sigh. "Look at it this way—we are doing a good deed."

"I'm not sure that the earl would agree." However, she didn't have the heart to quash Caro's hopes of having a small adventure here in London. "Quite likely I shall regret this."

"No you won't," assured Caro.

Gathering up her scattered hairpins, Olivia dropped them one by one into their silver box.

"Oh, hell. Bring me a pen and paper."

"That's the spirit!" said her youngest sister.

"Neither spirit nor imagination is anything the three

of us lack," she murmured, as her youngest sister hurried away to fetch the requested items. "It is restraint over our creative impulses that we all might exercise a little more often." A sigh momentarily fogged the looking glass. "But in for a penny, in for a pound, I suppose." Caro was right—there seemed to be little harm in setting up one more meeting with the earl's son. He had looked so vulnerable in the park, looking for Lady Loose Screw to show up.

I can't very well leave him in the lurch.

Olivia quickly scribbled off the two short notes when Caro returned, and handed it over before she could change her mind.

"But remember," she cautioned, "your mission with Prescott is going to be to explain, albeit gently, that for compelling personal reasons, Lady Loose Screw can no longer be considered a candidate for marriage. And then to offer some counsel on how he might try to give the Steel—er, that is, the lady in question—a second chance."

Caro made a face. "I still say we should sell her to white slavers. She doesn't sound very nice."

"No, she doesn't, but that does not give us the right to interfere," replied Olivia. "Our agreement is that you will pass on my advice to the lad without your own embellishments, or..." She held out her hand. "... You can return my note and the plan is off."

"No, no, I'll do as you ask." Caro hastily tucked the paper up her sleeve. "But I still say we ought to come up with something more romantic than that."

"Enough of romance," she muttered. "I need to turn my thoughts to more practical matters—like finishing my essay."

Caro made a sympathetic sound as she turned for the door. "I'll leave you the pen and ink. Along with some peace and quiet."

"Thank you."

But the ensuing silence, lit by the soft, soundless flickering of the candles, did not quite calm the agitated whisper of thoughts in her head.

Mistresses. What imp of Satan had compelled her to bring up such a subject with the earl?

"Even for me, that was beyond the pale," she said to herself.

That he was planning a speech on the very issue that was so near and dear to her heart ought to have provoked something other than a deliberately tart comment on courtesans. It was as if she wished him to find her company repulsive.

Which I do, I suppose.

Olivia took pride in being forthright and honest, especially with herself. So honesty compelled her to admit that she found the earl intriguing. Attractive. Intelligent.

He was also all but engaged to be married.

She was willing to take intellectual risks—Good heavens, it would stir a swirl of scandal throughout the *beau monde* if it became know that the radical political essays in the *Mayfair Gazette* were penned by a woman—because the reward of stirring Society's collective conscience to action made it worthwhile.

However, there seemed little chance that an emotional risk would bring anything other than disappointment. The oh-so-proper Earl of Wrexham and the oh-so-outrageous Hellion of High Street? *Ha!* And it was not only their temperaments that were diametrically opposed. He was rich as Croesus and she was poor as a churchmouse.

Enough of indulging in mindless fantasies. The Beacon had real work to do.

Clearing a spot on her dressing table for a blank sheet of paper, Olivia dipped her pen in the inkwell and began to write.

Chapter Twelve

"The morning post, madam." Lady Silliman's footman set a silver tray down on the breakfast room table.

Cecilia thumbed through the letters and paused at a small parcel. "This is for you, John. And Scottie."

John broke the seal and skimmed over the note inside the wrapping. "Hmmph." He looked up. "It's from Miss Sloane. She hopes your eye is on the mend."

"The purple has turned to green and yellow," said his son. "I wish Lucy could see how hideous it looks."

"Perhaps we could invite her to come visit for a week," suggested Cecilia. "It's a pleasure for me to have children around, and I'm sure Lucy would enjoy seeing the city. John?"

"Whatever you wish," he answered absently, his attention still riveted on Olivia's note. Most female handwriting was light and frilly as lace. Hers, on the other hand, was strong, distinctive script. Bold, forceful, with a slight slant that added an exotic touch.

Rather like the lady herself, John mused, after slowly rereading the missive.

"Miss Sloane thought you might enjoy this picture book on coaches and carriages," he announced. After tracing a finger over the brightly striped wrapping paper, John slid it across the table. "For the next time you plan an overnight adventure."

"How very nice of her," murmured Cecilia.

"She's a great gun," agreed Prescott, eagerly reaching for the gift. "I like her laugh."

"Oh?"

Ignoring his sister's uplifted brows, John picked up the newspaper and opened it with a snap. "The less said about the incident, the better, Scottie. In the future, I would ask that you not speak of our private family matters with strangers."

"Yes, sir," muttered his son.

"What sort of matters?" pressed Cecilia.

"Father's impending engagement to the Steel Corset," answered Prescott in a funereal voice.

The newsprint slapped down against the polished wood. "The Devil take it, I have *not* asked the lady for her hand."

"Well, are you or aren't you?" countered Prescott.

Cecilia set down her teacup and waited expectantly.

"I haven't decided yet," he muttered through clenched teeth.

"Since you appear to be seriously contemplating marriage, John, I should like to hear a little more about this young lady."

Swearing an inward oath, John speared a large slice of gammon from his plate and began to chew, hoping against hope to delay or distract her.

Unfortunately, she was more relentless than a troop of Soult's cavalry in pursuing information that interested her. When he didn't answer, she turned to Prescott. "Does she have a name? Other than the, er…"

"The Steel Corset," repeated his son as he began tearing open the wrapping around the book. "Though I'm not supposed to say it aloud. That's what Lucy and I call her, on account of how she walks and talks." Sucking in his cheeks, he stiffened his face into a hideous grimace. "Wrexham, fetch my smelling salts! Your son has a spot of jam on his chin."

John choked down the lump of meat as Cecilia dissolved into laughter.

"That is *not* funny."

"Forgive me," said Cecilia, biting her lip. "Naturally, marriage is a very serious subject."

"Who in the hellfire name of Lucifer said anything about marriage!" he snapped.

"Your father is never at his best this early in the morning, Scottie," counseled Cecilia after a short stretch of stony silence. "Let us not badger him on the subject." To John, she added, "I shall not say another word on the subject."

His sister silent on matters of the heart? *Ha—and pigs might fly.*

"If you will excuse me, I have a great deal to do to prepare for the upcoming debate in Parliament." John scraped back his chair. "I shall be gone for most of the day."

"Oh, don't worry about us. Scottie and I have plans to tour the British Museum. And then we shall do a bit of shopping at bookstores and toy emporiums off Bond

Street." His sister shooed him off with a cheerful wave. "But remember, all work and no play makes for a very dull existence, John. Do try to relax and have some fun while you are in London."

Tactics and strategy. John drew in a calming breath. Both called for a cool head and dispassionate judgment, he reminded himself.

Pulling his hat down lower, he shifted his stance, trying to avoid the worst of the mud pooled within the sliver of alleyway. He had managed to put the uncomfortable breakfast interlude out of his head, but in truth he was still seething inside from last night's encounter with the duke and his crony.

However, any seasoned soldier knew that uncontrolled emotion was dangerous.

Right made might. He intended to use logic and rhetoric as weapons in his fight against the forces of greed and self-interest.

Assuming he could ever manage to meet the elusive thinker known as The Beacon.

The fellow was proving perversely difficult to track down. Yet another of his notes had gone ignored. So this morning he was determined to gird on his sword, so to speak, and take action. A talk with one of the clerks had elicited several key bits of information. The newspaper's weekly essays were always due on this day. And The Beacon was notoriously late, waiting until the very last moment to deliver the finished piece.

Shifting deeper into the shadows cast by the overhanging eaves, John tried to still his impatience. He had been watching from his hidden vantage point all morning, but aside from a delivery of linseed oil and lamp black for ink, the printing shop had received no visitors.

Damn. Surely he couldn't have missed the dratted fellow. And yet, a quick glance at his pocketwatch showed that there were only a few minutes left until the place shut down for the midday meal.

Baffled, he frowned and tried to figure out where he had gone wrong. The plan had been perfectly reasonable...

At the sound of hurried footsteps scuffing over the cobblestones, he flattened himself against the grimy brick and edged to the corner of the building. An angled look across the street showed Hurley himself opening the door and admitting the cloaked figure.

Bloody hell. What was Miss Olivia Sloane doing here again? The delivery boy for her newspaper must be the laziest imp alive. Or else...

No. Impossible.

His head said one thing, but war had taught him to listen very carefully to his gut feelings. And at the moment, their shouts were drowning out the voice of reason.

Of course, if he were wrong, he would appear a bloody idiot.

A short while later, Olivia emerged, head down, from the shop and began briskly retracing her steps. John waited until she had rounded the corner before slipping out from the alleyway and following at a discreet distance.

To his surprise, she didn't head back toward High Street, but instead turned in the opposite direction. After winding through several small side streets, she glanced over her shoulder before darting down a narrow cartway that cut between the walled gardens of two brick townhouses.

John counted to ten and then did the same.

Halfway down the shadowed path, Olivia paused and fumbled with the lock of a thick wooden gate. The hinges creaked as it swung open for a moment, and then fell shut behind her.

He hesitated, suddenly embarrassed that he might have trailed her to a lover's assignation. *Retreat*, he told himself. Reason called for a tactical retreat. And yet some strange force impelled him to move forward. Moving lightly, he silently crossed the rutted ground.

The latch had not quite caught, and he was able to ease the weathered oak open without making a sound. Through the narrow crack, he spied a jungle of thick bushes, their dark, glossy leaves shading the narrow gravel path that wove in and out of the dappled sunlight. Thick vines of ivy hung heavy on the brick wall behind them, adding to the play of shadows.

Squinting into the glare, John needed a moment to pick out Olivia's cloaked figure among the muted colors of the ornamental grasses and shrubs. Her back was to him, and as he watched, she suddenly stopped short and punched a fist in the air.

"Look into your heart, I say, and ask yourself what you see." A rustling whispered through the branches as her voice rose to a near shout. "Is it an oppressive black cloud, heavy with the weight of the past? Or is it a gleam of pale, pure light?"

He stayed very still, waiting for a reply. But no other voice sounded from the shrubbery.

"This is no time for slinking in the shadows of self-interest. We must rise..." Her palms slapped together, the sudden gesture causing her cloak to slip off her shoulders.

Kicking it aside, Olivia continued, "Rise *high* and reach for our better nature."

A sparrow chirped.

"Yes, you're right," she said loudly. "That's laying it on a bit thick. Let me think for a moment." Clasping her hands behind her back, she began pacing back and forth.

Any lingering doubts disappeared as it became obvious that she was alone. John pressed his lips into a tight smile. *Ha.* The Beacon's light was no longer hidden under the proverbial bush.

Shouldering his way into the garden, he swiftly cut a path across the mossy verge.

"We must rise up…no, *look* up." Olivia shook her head. "Drat, perhaps that would have been better…"

John was now close behind her. Close enough to see the tiny tendrils of dark auburn hair curling at the nape of her neck.

"Actually, I think you got it right the first time," he said.

She whirled around, mouth open in a perfect "O" of shock.

"The issue is such an important one that it demands a little drama, don't you think?" he finished.

Fisting her hands, she fell back a step, her face turning pale as parchment. "W-what in the name of God are *you* doing here, sir?" Her voice, though barely more than a whisper, betrayed a tiny tremor of fear beneath her outrage.

Her secret could spell ruin for her family, conceded John. But right now he was thinking only of the moment. "I followed you from Hurley's shop."

Her eyes widened, and he was acutely aware of the

fierce intelligence alight in the glittering green. At that instant, however, the hottest sparks burned from fear to blazing anger.

Actually, she was more than angry. She was furious.

And come to think of it, so was he. Perhaps the reaction was triggered by primitive male instinct—piqued pride, piqued pego—but John suddenly felt a surge of ire that he had been played for a fool.

"How *dare* you spy on me, sir!" demanded Olivia, once she had mastered her emotions enough to speak.

He fixed her with a commanding stare, the one that had set many a seasoned soldiers to quaking in their boots. "I would not have had to resort to such tactics if you had shown me the courtesy of answering my letters."

Olivia refused to be intimidated. Lifting her chin, she scowled back at him. "I did answer them."

"With a single word—no."

"And what," she asked with excruciating politeness, "did you not understand about such a simple syllable?"

John couldn't help but admire her grit. It took courage and resourcefulness to play in a man's world. *And she played well*, he conceded.

Expelling a harried sigh, he felt his anger dissipate just as quickly as it had come. She had no choice but to guard her secret very carefully. "Look, at least hear me out, Miss Sloane. Tracking down The Beacon has led me on a merry dance throughout Town."

Olivia paled at the mention of the *nom de plume*. Turning abruptly, she plunged off the path and darted around a tangle of holly.

"Wait!" John ducked under the prickly branches, losing his hat in the process.

"Go away!" Her voice was muffled by the overhanging leaves.

"Not until we talk!"

"I've nothing to say to you."

The Devil take it. All but a last little flutter of her skirts disappeared behind a shaggy yew hedge. Swearing under his breath, John cut through a patch of lavender. He hadn't come this far to be rebuffed. She would damn well listen. Or else...

Several long strides brought him within arm's reach of her. "Confound it, Miss Sloane, stop and listen," he called, lunging for her sleeve.

As his fingers seized the fabric, his boot snagged on a twist of morning glory. Pitched off-balance, he stumbled and fell, taking her with him. Tangled together, they hit the ground hard, their momentum rolling them into a patch of pachysandra.

"Ooof!" Olivia's flailing kick caught him square in the shin.

Flat on his back, John got a momentary glimpse of Olivia's irrepressible curls dancing in the breeze before another half turn landed him on his stomach. Burning with embarrassment, he tried to right himself, only to find that she was sprawled across his...posterior.

Bloody hell, he had never felt like a bigger arse in all his life.

They both started wriggling at the same time. He managed to twist faceup just as she slipped on the glossy leaves and fell back down atop him.

"Miss Sloane," he gasped.

"Lord Wrexham," wheezed Olivia, an odd little burr roughening her already throaty voice.

For an instant, he feared she was going to burst into tears.

Instead, she began to laugh.

And laugh.

Scottie was right. It was a delightful sound, its top notes shaded with a rich, sensual echo that seemed to stroke over his skin like a moon-dappled midnight breeze.

A twitch tugged at his lips. His dignity—as well as his coat—was in tatters, his pride was bruised, and though he should not find it at all funny, John felt a rumble vibrate deep in his throat.

Olivia tried to get up again, but her limbs were too weak with mirth. "Good Lord, what a ridiculous picture we must make!" she wheezed in between burbles of laughter.

"Here, let me help you." Levering to his feet, John lifted her up and as she seemed a bit shaky, he kept his hands on her waist.

"Well, it's not every day I take a tumble in the hay with an earl," she quipped.

"Please don't think that I make a habit of ruining a young lady's reputation," he answered.

Her cheeks, already pink from the breeze, turned a lusher shade of red as she looked up and wet her lips.

John felt his body clench. His legendary sangfroid began to bubble...His steely self-control went up in smoke...

Olivia flinched as his mouth possessed hers. She was like summer rain against his tongue. *So soft, so sweet.*

Her hands came up around his neck.

Hell, it would serve him right if she throttled him on the spot.

But then, all of a sudden, she was kissing him back.

In a daze, John twisted around and braced her back against the ivy-covered wall, the glossy leaves crackling under the crush of silk. He was dimly aware of a roaring like cannonfire in his ears, and as his hands slid down to cup her breasts he realized it was the pounding of his own heart.

Knocking all reason to flinders.

A gust of air ruffled his hair, stirring wild, wicked thoughts of her waltzing naked through the trees. In response, his own privy parts began dancing to their own drummer. *Thump. Thump. Thump.* His pulse was pounding a military tattoo, commanding all soldiers to stand erect.

And Dear God, his Major Organ was responding with unabashed enthusiasm.

Olivia didn't seem disgusted by his display of primitive lust. With a tiny moan, she tightened her hold and hitched her hips into him.

Lud, it felt good. No, better than good.

Exquisite.

He thrust himself against her thighs, reveling in the softness of her skin-warmed silks against his growing arousal. With a rough groan, he deepened his kisses, mindless of his crushed cravat and the fact that his shirt-tail had somehow pulled free of his trousers.

Olivia swayed as heat licked through her limbs. Her body felt so strange, as if it belonged to someone else. And perhaps it did, she thought hazily. She certainly didn't recognize the woman who had taken possession of her skin. The real Olivia Sloane was a spinster bluestocking, not a wanton jade.

And yet, the Earl of Wrexham didn't seem to be experiencing any reservations.

Nor was she.

His kisses had ignited a sudden spark of longing somewhere deep inside her. And while its flame burned hot, she meant to seize the chance to experience passion.

God only knew when it would come again.

Emboldened, she let her hands explore his big body. Slabbed shoulders, chiseled ribs, a hard torso tapering to a lean waist. His contours were utterly foreign.

Utterly fascinating. No gently rounded curves or feminine softness. He was all hard angles and unyielding muscle.

And his scent. He smelled of bay rum and burnished leather. It was earthy—dark and distinctly masculine. Burying her nose in his loosened cravat, Olivia sucked in a deep, deep breath, filling her lungs with the intoxicating fragrance.

"Miss Sloane," said John raggedly, his whisper hot on her skin as he broke off a torrid kiss. "Forgive me. I—I cannot explain my egregious lapse of gentlemanly honor."

"Then don't," she replied, nibbling at his lower lip. Oh, he tasted delicious. Faintly sweet, with some mysterious hint of spice that she couldn't quite put a name to.

"Don't," he echoed.

She froze.

"Don't stop," rasped John, his mouth covering hers again in a hard and hungry kiss.

Melting into his embrace, Olivia slid her hands down the side of his hips. Casting caution to the wind, she let them creep around, tracing the shape of his bum. Beneath the fine tailoring of his trousers, she could feel the taut thrum of flesh. There was something very primitive and powerful in his body. He reminded her of a sleek predator, all coiled strength and lethal grace.

Dangerous.

The word slowly seeped through the heated vapor clouding her brain.

Dangerous.

The echo reverberated against her skull, cooling her wild ardor.

What madness has possessed me?

"Dear God," she whispered. "You must forgive me, Lord Wrexham. The effort of finishing an essay stirs a certain fire inside. It—it takes a bit of time for it to burn itself out."

"Is that why you come here?" he asked.

"Yes," she said. "I find that ranting at the roses and rhododendrons helps release all the pent-up emotion." Her gaze strayed to the tangle of dark leaves and silvery vines. "And Hurley's garden never hurls back an unkind word."

"I know what you mean. My blood is still boiling from an encounter last night with two pompous, narrow-minded gentlemen." A wry smile tugged at his lips. "I suppose that explains what just happened here. Fire is a very volatile substance."

"Very," agreed Olivia, grateful for his trying to soften the sheer stupidity of her actions. "You, at least, can have the physical satisfaction of punching someone in the nose. My only weapons are my words."

"And powerful weapons they are," he said. "You have an extraordinary skill, Miss Sloane, and believe passionately in the need for social reform. So why have you avoided me?"

"Why do you think, sir?"

John made a face. "Right. An idiotic question."

"Writing as The Beacon, I can reach a great number of people," she explained. "Hurley goes along with it because I make money for him. But you, sir..." She plucked a furled rose from one of the bushes and slowly peeled back the velvety petals. "Revealing my true identity was too great a risk. If word got out that The Beacon was a female, no essay of mine would ever again see the light of day."

The earl ran a palm along the line of his jaw. He had, she noted, beautiful hands, strong and capable. The sight of his long, tapered fingers sent a queer little shiver through her limbs.

"You can trust me with your secret," he said.

Olivia couldn't help wondering just what he would say if he knew she was also the infamous "Lady Loose Screw."

On second thought, she decided that she didn't want to know.

Ever.

"I don't really have a choice but to count on your honor, sir."

A slight flush crept to his face at the word "honor." "I can hardly betray your identity without exposing myself to censure." One of his dark brows quirked up. "If it makes you feel any better, one word from you about what happened here would put me in a very awkward position."

She felt her jaw drop. "Surely... surely you don't think... Good God, the very last thing in the world I would wish to do is put you in *that* sort of awkward position."

The brow arched a touch higher. "Ah. I'm that unappealing?"

Flustered, Olivia quickly added, "It's not you in particular, sir. It's the concept."

"Of coercion?" A hint of humor glinted in his dark eyes. "Or of matrimony?"

"As far as I am concerned, they are one in the same," she muttered. "Women have no rights in a marriage. It's terribly unfair."

"I happen to agree with you," he said softly. "The Beacon ought to attack that issue, too." He paused. "However, having some experience in warfare, I would advise you that it would be best to fight one battle at a time."

"I know, I know." Frowning, she crossed her arms. "So what are you suggesting, sir?"

"That we become allies," he replied. "I would like for you to look at the rough draft of my speech and give me your suggestions. I need help in polishing both the ideas and the language."

"I have already promised you Hingham's book."

"I want more than Hingham. I want you."

Olivia tried to steady the erratic thump of her heart.

"Together we can beat these selfish, narrow-minded prigs who stand in the way of progress," finished Wrexham.

"You do not appear lacking in eloquence, sir," she said softly.

"With your help, I can do better," he said.

The idea was oh-so tempting. She cared passionately about the passage of this bill, and here she was, being offered a chance to shape a speech to the House of Lords.

How could she, in good conscience, refuse?

"Well...oh, blast—very well, Lord Wrexham. Send me your scribbles and I'll have a look at them."

"Thank you." He walked over to retrieve his hat.

"However, there are certain conditions," added Olivia.

His expression as he looked up was unreadable. "Which are?"

"*This* won't happen again." Repressing a shiver, she looked away. "I am The Beacon, a respected thinker, and you are the earl, a distinguished aristocrat...who happens to be engaged to the Steel Corset."

John carefully smoothed a hand over the bent brim. "I am not engaged," he corrected.

"Perhaps not literally," she said. "But be that as it may, it would be unwise for any number of reasons. And I should like to think that neither of us is lacking a brain."

"Fine. Anything else?"

"Not that I can think of at the moment."

"Excellent." He set his hat back on his head. "Then we have an agreement, Miss Sloane."

"We do, sir. But let us hope that neither of us comes to regret it," murmured Olivia.

Chapter Thirteen

This was not entirely my fault. You two bear part of the blame." Olivia carefully untwined a tiny twist of ivy from the cuff of her gown, praying there were no other telltale bits of the garden clinging to her clothing. "But seeing I ought to practice what I preach, I accept full responsibility for my fall from sanity."

Her sisters did not look terribly repentant. Indeed, Caro was doing a very poor job at repressing a fit of giggles.

"I am trying to picture exactly how *this* all happened," said Anna, slowly sketching a diagram of odd little loops in the air. "You...him...a tumble into the greenery... Could you kindly describe it again?"

"Put that pen down," snapped Olivia. "And no, I would rather not run through my egregious lapse in judgment."

More chortling from her youngest sister, which she silenced with a glare. "I am usually *very* careful about locking the garden gate."

"In Anna's version, Count Alessandro will no doubt

strip off all of Emmalina's clothing," said Caro. "And then his own, whereupon he would make passionate love to her in the garden."

"What do you know about making passionate love?" demanded Anna. "I hope you have not been snooping through my reference books again—"

"Not much, I trust," interjected Olivia, before the discussion could take a dangerous turn. Caro was already too knowledgeable about...a great many things.

"Not as much as I would like," countered her youngest sister. "I'm nearly eighteen, and it's time you two stopped treating me like a child."

Anna and Olivia exchanged uncomfortable looks.

"Of course I've read your novels, and know from Papa's lectures the basics of, er, how men and women join together."

True, their father had been a firm believer that ladies ought not be ignorant in the ways of the world, much to the dismay of their mother. Such unconventional ideas had been a sore point between them. As had the subject of money. So, mused Olivia, Lady Trumbull's obsession with propriety and marrying at least one of her daughters off to a man with a plump purse was understandable.

"But as for the specific details, I am a little fuzzy on certain things," continued Caro. "For example, you said that you could feel the earl was, um, fully aroused when he pressed up against you, Livvie. What, exactly, did you mean by that?"

Drat. Olivia instantly rued letting her tongue have free rein. In her own defense, she had been somewhat agitated when she had recounted the details of the garden confrontation.

"Well, er, . . ." she stammered, unsure how to go on.

"Oh, Caro is right," announced Anna. "As she pointed out, she already knows the basics about male anatomy from Papa and the sketches in his scientific notebooks. We might as well explain more fully what happens when carnal desire starts to heat a man's blood."

"Very well." Olivia drew a deep breath. "Er, perhaps you ought to do it. After all, you have the most expertise in describing how men and women arouse each other's passions."

"If you wish." Anna set down her pen. "Now pay attention, Caro. What Olivia meant was that the earl's pizzle had become larger. It expands when a man becomes sexually aroused, so she was aware of it pressing against her."

"Could you be more explicit?" asked Caro.

Anna rolled her eyes. "Let me put it this way—his manhood was like a length of hard steel beneath his clothing."

"That doesn't sound very comfortable."

"I don't think it is," said Anna. "That's why men are always in such a hurry to unbutton their breeches when they are in that particular condition."

Caro frowned. "I'm not sure I follow you."

"I'm not sure you should," murmured Olivia. "But do go on, Anna."

Anna looked around and spotted a branch of unlit candles. "Allow me to demonstrate." She took one of them in hand and placed it tip up flat against her belly. "As a man's organ swells, it rises, rather like hot air balloon. The flap of his breeches hold it in position like so."

Caro scratched a few notes in the margin of the poetry book she had been reading.

"When a man undoes the fastenings of his trousers or breeches, his shaft springs free, like so." The candle dropped to jut straight out.

Olivia raised a brow. "Perhaps we could make extra pin money by putting on a private show for prospective brides in one of the dressing rooms of Madame Tessin's dressmaking shop. We could call it 'The Wedding Night—A Primer to Pizzles and Other Monstrosities.'"

Before Anna could elaborate any further on the mysteries of sex, Lady Trumbull interrupted the lecture by throwing open the study door. "Now girls, it's extremely unladylike to giggle. I trust you will not indulge in…" As she looked around the room, her gaze came to rest on Anna. "What are you doing with that candle?"

"Oh, I was just explaining how to make the wick last longer," replied Anna without batting an eye. "A lady should know all the ins and outs of managing domestic affairs."

Lady Trumbull hesitated, and then nodded sagely. "Quite right, my dear, quite right. A firm hand on housekeeping is very important. Men appreciate such attention to the tiny details."

"Olivia has also been giving some very helpful hints on how to make the flame burn brighter," piped up Caro.

Olivia made a warning face. Her youngest sister had a tendency to allow exuberant emotion to overrule common sense. And while it was a laudable quality for a poet to have, it often landed her in trouble at home.

Their mother gave an audible sniff, as if scenting that something was amiss. But as Anna flashed her most innocent smile, she seemed mollified. "Listen to your sister, and mayhap the two of you will learn enough to attract your share of highborn suitors." Wagging a finger, she added, "Do remember that we are attending Mrs. Shelborne's musical recital tonight, Anna. Lord Chittenden is very fond of the pianoforte and is sure to be there."

"Yes, Mama," responded Anna.

"Olivia, you need not come tonight," went on Lady Trumbull. "It's an informal gathering, so protocol does not require your presence. And seeing as you make no effort to engage an eligible gentleman, it is not as if anyone will notice your absence."

Such comments had long since lost their sting. But Olivia saw Anna's nostrils flare in anger.

"Actually, Mama, Olivia has been attracting her share of notice these days. The Earl of Wrexham has been particularly interested in discussing politics with her."

Their mother turned so fast that she nearly snagged a slipper in the carpet fringe. "Wrexham! Well, I declare…" Raising her quizzing glass, she peered in surprise at her eldest daughter.

As if she were a botanist who had just stumbled upon some new and exotic species of mushroom, thought Olivia wryly.

"An earl," exclaimed Lady Trumbull. "And a very rich earl at that. Oh, you sly puss—"

"Anna is joking, Mama," said Olivia quickly. "Lord Wrexham has no real interest in me. He simply wished to borrow a book."

"Borrow a book? How very odd."

"Yes, very odd," she echoed. *Just like me.*

Lady Trumbull narrowed her gaze, unsure if she was being teased, but after a blink she let the comment pass.

Turning back to Anna, she said, "Be sure to take a nap

this afternoon, my dear. It wouldn't do for you to have puffy eyes. Oh, and do be sure to wear your seafoam green gown. I have heard that Chittenden is an avid sailor."

"Perhaps," murmured Olivia, after the door had fallen shut, "if we put a bridle on you, we could take you to Tattersall's and sell you to the highest bidder at the next auction of brood mares."

Caro gave a snort.

"And much as I appreciate your support, you need not bother trying to temper Mama's cutting comments. To her I'm a hopeless hellion, who will only end up being a burden to her old age."

"If you would but try to—" began Anna.

Olivia was quick to cut her off. "You know very well that I have not your skill at appearing amiable."

"To hone a skill, one must be willing to practice."

"True." Caro propped her elbows on the work table. "It's rather like writing, I suppose. One really must work at it to be any good."

"Thank you for the lecture." Olivia tried not to sound too shrill. "However, I simply cannot round off the edges of my rough-cut opinions. It is a weakness, I know, but so be it."

"We all have our strengths and weaknesses," said Anna softly. "Some are more hidden than others. Perhaps you will surprise yourself."

A cryptic statement, but Olivia was in no frame of mind to puzzle out its meaning. "I've had enough surprises for one morning," she muttered. "If you'll excuse me, I think I shall retire to my bedchamber and finish reading Hingham's essays so that Wrexham may take the dratted book."

* * *

The Beacon. John pursed his lips as he turned the corner onto Piccadilly Street. *The Beacon was a lady.* The idea was still a little dizzying...

And so was the faint trace of Olivia's sweetness on his mouth.

Lord Almighty, did I really behave like a randy, ravenous wild beast? Closing his eyes for an instant, he recalled possessing her in a hard, hungry kiss. It was utterly unforgivable.

And utterly unforgettable.

A frisson of uncontrollable lust speared through his belly as he recalled the lush, liquid taste of her, the soft, sensuous curves—

"Wrexham!"

His eyes flew open.

"How f'rtuitous to run into you here."

John would have chosen a different adjective. Viscount Lumley looked as though he had already been drinking heavily, despite the fact that it was barely past noon. "Indeed?" he replied coolly. "Why is that?"

"Because I know a m'litary man will listen to reason." The viscount fell in step beside him. "You un'erstand the notions of duty and loyalty, and the importance of rigid dis'pline. Can't let the common ranks get out of control, right?"

John felt his jaw tighten.

"The vote on this damned bill f'r veterans looks like it will be closer than it should be. You, as a r'spected war hero, will have a great deal of influence on the undecided peers. Sommers and I wish to, shall we say, encourage you to say the right thing."

"I assure you, that is my wish, too." It took all of his considerable discipline to keep his temper in check. "Be assured that I am reading all I can about the issues and will make a thorough study of their complexities before I draft my speech."

Lumley made a rude sound. "To hell with reading and thi'nking about the issue, man. We intend to make it easy f'r you. Come out in favor of our side and we shall see you are generously rewarded. Sommers and I have friends among the East India Company governors who are willing to give you stock in the new diamond trading venture."

"You are offering me a *bribe*?" asked John softly.

Lumley winked. "Call it an exc'hange of favors between g'ntlemen. It's done all the time."

"Save your breath," he snapped. "My principles are not for sale."

"Principles?" Lumley's eyes widened for an instant in surprise, and then narrowed to a slitted stare. "What about the *principle* of siding with your own kind against the rabble, eh?"

"My own kind?" said John, anger causing him to quicken his stride. "You are mistaken—I've nothing in common with parasites who feed with self-satisfied smugness off the sweat and suffering of others."

"You're a God-benighted fool, Wrexham," snarled the viscount as he struggled to keep pace. "The stock we are offering is worth a very large sum of money."

"I don't need money."

"A *very* large sum of money," repeated Lumley.

"No amount of blunt is worth my self-respect."

"You are not only a fool but also a traitor to your class.

Mark my words, if you don't rec'nsider your position, you will be sorry."

John curled a contemptuous smile. "That's the second time you've threatened me, Lumley. Do it again and it is *you* who will be sorry."

Chapter Fourteen

After a few early spitting showers, the next morning turned clear and cloudless, giving reason to believe that the planned meeting with Wrexham's son should go as planned.

Olivia insisted on accompanying Caro to the rendezvous in Grosvenor Square, and Anna decided to join in, too.

"Seeing as I am the expert at choreographing clandestine meetings," she announced, "I had better come along to ensure that nothing goes amiss."

They arrived at the large, leafy gardens of Berkeley Square well before the appointed rendezvous and took up a position within the thick ornamental bushes clustered near the central fountain.

"You are sure that you remember exactly what you are to tell Prescott?" asked Olivia, feeling a twinge of nerves.

Caro nodded. "You've had me repeat it enough times."

"And you won't forget that you mustn't on any account mention that I am Lady Loose Screw?"

Caro made a face. "That's the fourth time you have re-minded me. I'm not a complete ninnyhammer, you know."

"Don't fret, Livvie," counseled Anna calmly. "Every-thing will go smoothly."

"What if he didn't find the note in the book?" Olivia suddenly had an even worse thought. "Or, God forbid, what if his father found it and appears instead?"

"Don't fret," echoed Caro. "We went over all this. Even if the earl does appear, he won't recognize me. I shall simply walk right past him and he'll have no idea that I am the one who set up the meeting."

Her sisters were right, admitted Olivia. There was little chance of anything going amiss. Still, she felt slightly seedy for having orchestrated this assignation behind Wrexham's back.

Especially now.

No good deed goes unpunished, she thought wryly. She had agreed to this plan because she couldn't in good conscience leave the boy to think had had been aban-doned by Lady Loose Screw. However, her new arrange-ment with the earl had added another twist to an already tangled situation.

Drat Anna for letting her diabolically clever imagina-tion at concocting convoluted romance plots get out of hand…

Caro ventured a peek through the leaves at the town-houses across the cobbled carriageway. "It must be nearly time."

"Another three minutes," said Anna after consulting their late father's pocketwatch. "You ought to start mak-ing your way out to the perimeter pathway. Slowly—remember, you are simply out for a stroll."

After a bit of fussing with her bonnet strings and skirts, Caro edged through the opening in the bushes and was momentarily lost from view.

"I don't like that dangerous glitter in her eyes," muttered Olivia. "I regret letting her get involved in this. Her poetic nature is already excitable enough without any extra encouragement."

"There is no use crying over spilled milk," said Anna with her usual pragmatism. "Besides, for all her swishing and swooning, Caro has a modicum of good sense. I don't think she'll get herself into any real trouble."

Olivia expelled a silent sigh. *Would that I could say the same about myself.* Given the events of yesterday, there was ample reason to question her own judgment.

"Is that the earl's son?" Anna's whisper interrupted her brooding.

"Yes, that's Prescott," she answered. As requested by the note, he was carrying the book on carriages, so Caro could identify him.

"So far, so good," said Anna after watching their sister casually approach the boy and strike up a conversation.

Caro, was, admitted Olivia, an excellent actress, with skill honed by the countless late-night theatrical readings the sisters had staged to keep themselves amused. She had done an excellent job of quietly shepherding Prescott to one of the benches and at the moment was engaged in turning the pages of his book and making a show of admiring the pictures.

The boy appeared to be listening in rapt attention.

Another twinge of guilt squeezed a bit of breath from her lungs. *Was I wrong to counsel him to accept Fate in the form of the Steel Corset?* She, of all people, knew what it was to live with a cold, critical mother. The earl clearly cared very deeply for his son—continued rebellion might make him reconsider his choice of a bride.

Choices, choices.

Olivia frowned. She didn't usually dither over decisions.

"I think she's finished," observed Anna.

Caro was indeed rising and taking her leave of Prescott. The boy appeared to be taking her words with good grace. If he was disappointed at the loss of Lady Loose Screw, he was hiding it well.

Perhaps I overestimated the effect of my words of wisdom. Which was a rather depressing thought, considering the effect she hoped to have on the readers of the *Mayfair Gazette* in the coming weeks.

"Come along," murmured Anna. "We should circle around to the opposite side of the square, and wait for Caro at Gunther's tea shop. She deserves one of their famous ices for her performance."

Their sister was quick to join them in the main salon. Her face flushed with excitement, she slipped into her seat with a barely concealed grin. "Perhaps I should offer my services to Whitehall as a clandestine agent," she whispered. "I thought that I did a rather good job of it, didn't I?"

"Better than good," agreed Anna. "Allow me to treat you to some ice cream."

"Bergamot," said Caro, after considering the choices. "It sounds so intriguing. Perhaps the taste will inspire a sonnet."

"If I were you, I would choose strawberry, which is one of Gunther's specialties," counseled Anna. "Or if you wish for something exotic, perhaps the pineapple sherbet would be more to your taste..."

Still feeling a little unsettled over her interference in the earl's life, Olivia found herself listening to the discussion of the shop's confectionary treats with only half an ear. Shifting her gaze to the large, leaded windows at the shop's entrance, she watched the procession of fancy carriages and stylish, high-perch phaetons pass by, hoping the swirl of colors and faces might help distract her from her brooding thoughts.

From now on, I shall be more careful about controlling my creative impulses, she vowed. A careless jest had gone awry, and the consequences had involved her in the personal life of a stranger...

Oh, damnation. She bit her lip. *Of all the bloody luck.*

An elegant barouche had come to halt just beyond the outdoor tables and a couple was descending. The gentleman was the Earl of Wrexham—his chiseled profile and broad-shouldered silhouette was all too familiar.

And the laughing lady whose hand was resting lightly on his arm?

Olivia felt as if an iron band were tightening around her chest. Surely that couldn't be the Steel Corset.

Could it?

After watching the young lady's lively face warm with spontaneous laughter, her embarrassment ratcheted up another notch. Prescott was naught but a boy of ten. That he had taken an unreasonable dislike to a lovely lady was something that no doubt would soon be rectified.

As for herself, she felt even more like an idiot. Angling the brim of her bonnet to a lower tilt, she clasped her hands together in her lap and offered up a silent prayer that the earl and his soon-to-be-bride were not in the mood for sweets.

"Well, well, speak of the devil," murmured Anna.

Olivia resigned herself to an unspeakably awkward encounter. After all, just yesterday she had been locked in a passionate kiss with the young lady's future husband. Her only consolation was that John would likely feel just as uncomfortable.

But then, men were used to such peccadilloes. He would probably take it in stride.

As the click of boot heels on the polished tiles grew louder, she made herself look up, unwilling to appear a coward.

"Miss Sloane," drawled a deep voice. "Miss Anna."

Thank God for small favors.

The tall, dark-haired gentleman approaching their table wasn't the earl, but rather the debauched, devil-may-care Lord Davenport.

Olivia felt a rush of relief—a quick glance out the window showed the earl and his companion had turned away from the shop and were entering the square's gardens.

"Alas, I am not acquainted with the third member of your party," went on the marquess.

Anna stiffened slightly at the sound of his low laugh.

"And here I thought that I knew every beautiful lady in London."

"Our sister Carolina is not yet out in Society," replied Olivia as he sauntered up to her chair and inclined a casual bow. She decided to make the formal introductions, though her mother would likely swoon in shock if she even heard about it.

Davenport smiled at her youngest sister. "Charmed,

Miss Carolina," he murmured, flashing a seductive wink.

No gentleman ought to have such long, luxurious lashes or such glittering sapphire eyes, thought Olivia. Especially when he was reputed to be Lucifer in Hessians.

Caro was staring in mute fascination.

As for Anna, she, too, was eyeing the marquess with a silent, strangely speculative look.

Perhaps she was considering him as a character in her current novel-in-progress, reflected Olivia. Her hero, Count Alessandro, was in need of a new adversary, and The Devil Davenport certainly presented the perfect model for a dangerous, dastardly villain.

"I would not have thought you enjoyed such innocent pleasures as eating ice cream, milord," she said, when it became apparent that neither of her sisters was going to speak.

"You are correct, Miss Sloane." His wicked smile stretched a touch wider. "Innocence is not at all to my taste. However, I happened to spot the three of you through the shop window as I was passing and decided to stop and pay my respects."

"I was under the impression that you don't 'respect' anything, much less conventional manners," murmured Anna.

"Correct again," replied Davenport. "However, in this case I do have an ulterior motive."

Anna ignored the bait and went back to eating her lemon ice.

Curiosity got the better of Caro. "Which is?" she asked in a conspiratorial whisper.

Olivia was surprised when in answer, Davenport looked at her. "You might wish to warn Lord Wrexham that he would do well to stay on guard, Miss Sloane. I happened to overhear a snatch of conversation last night that leads me to believe he has made some very unpleasant enemies."

"W-what makes you think that I have any contact with the earl?" she stammered.

"You were dancing with him the other evening. That seems to signify some sort of connection."

"You are mistaken," she said quickly. "The earl's sister insisted on bringing us together. As a gentleman, he had no choice but to ask me for a turn around the ballroom. It won't happen again."

"Ah." Davenport flicked a mote of dust from his sleeve. "Then I suppose that Wrexham will have to fend for himself."

"You could tell him yourself," pointed out Olivia.

"Unlike the earl, I don't consider myself bound by the strictures of gentlemanly honor. So I don't feel compelled to go out of my way to pass on the warning. I simply happened to see you here." Touching a hand to the brim of his hat, he turned away. "Good day, ladies."

"Oooo, what a thoroughly intriguing man," said Caro, sneaking a last peek as Davenport left the shop. "I have always wondered what a ruthless rake was like."

"He is not intriguing, he is insufferable," snapped Anna.

"What has he done to earn your dislike?" asked Olivia.

"Nothing." Anna set down her spoon and sighed. "Oh, if you must know, it's the fact that he seems to take great delight in irritating me. Every time I turn around at a rout or a ball, he is watching me with that supercilious smile of his. It is as if he means to tell me that he knows..."

"Knows what?" pressed Olivia when her sister did not go on.

The question hung for a long moment in the sugar-scented air—so long, in fact, that she was sure that her younger sister did not intend to answer.

The silence, however, gave way to a rustle of muslin as Anna shifted in her chair. "Knows that I am no different than he is. For you see, I, too, am a predator of sorts, who is on the hunt to marry for money."

"That's not true," began Caro.

Anna cut her off with a curt laugh. "Yes it is. Mama is desperate to match me with a rich husband. And in many ways, I can't blame her. Despite all her faults, she wishes to secure the family's future. Our finances are, as you both know, precarious."

"Still, I should hope that you would marry for love, not money," said Olivia softly.

"Be assured I won't accept the hand of someone I cannot respect. However, a fat purse will allow me to take care of us all. So—"

"I would rather live in poverty," interrupted Caro, "than see you sacrifice yourself on the Altar of Unhappiness."

Olivia had to repress a smile. Caro did have a knack for composing dramatic phrases. That one was sure to end up in one of her next poems.

"And I know Livvie feels the same way."

Anna ran a fingertip around the rim of her empty cup. "No one could have more supportive sisters. But you might feel differently if you were cold and hungry."

"Never," replied Caro, stoutly. "If need be, I could find work as a governess or a lady's companion."

"You would have little time to write," pointed out Olivia. "There is nothing romantic about having to earn your bread. Toiling in the service of others would keep you busy from morning until night."

Her youngest sister opened her mouth to reply but after a moment's hesitation slumped back in her seat.

"Don't look so stricken, Caro," counseled Anna. "It is the way of our world. For the *beau monde*, marriage is all about the bartering of assets—wealth, privilege, power, beauty. A love match rarely happens outside the pages of a novel."

"Lord Wrexham is here to see you, Miss Olivia." The lone footman of the house—for the family had no funds to employ a proper butler—cleared his throat. "I have put him in the drawing room."

"It is Miss *Sloane*, not Miss *Olivia*, as she is the eldest," clucked her mother. "I pray you don't make such a buffle-headed mistake in front of a peer of the realm, Freddie. He might think that we don't belong."

Olivia gave the young man a sympathetic smile. "Thank you, Freddie." She began rummaging among the piles of notes and newspapers on her desk. "I shall be there shortly."

Lady Trumbull's horrified response rose above the crackling of paper. "Oh, you must *not* keep the earl waiting."

"I told you, Mama, he has simply come to borrow a book, not to enjoy the pleasure of my company."

"Men are odd creatures, child," lectured her mother.

"One never knows what may catch their fancy. And a widower may not be so choosy. You could at least make an effort to flirt with him."

And donkeys might turn into unicorns.

"I doubt Lord Wrexham and I would suit."

"Hmmph. You never know until you try."

For all her grousing, her mother did on occasion make an astute observation, mused Olivia as she finally located her copy of Hingham's essays under a copy of the *Morning Gazette*. "That is, for the most part, very true, Mama." Leaving Lady Trumbull looking a little perplexed, she gathered up the book, along with another that she thought the earl might find of interest, and quickly left the room.

Chapter Fifteen

$\mathcal{J}$ohn turned from his study of the curio cabinet on hearing the drawing room door open and close.

"Your father collected an unusually intriguing variety of artifacts, Miss Sloane. He must have been a very interesting man."

Olivia ignored the observation. "I thought you were going to send a servant for the book, sir," said she, without preamble.

"It is very nice to see you, too," he murmured.

A flush rose up to ridge her cheekbones. "Please don't say I didn't warn you. My mother has now decided that a widower may not be as choosy as a tulip of the *ton*. So you may find yourself considered fair game for all her machinations."

He smiled. "As I've said, I've faced far more formidable adversaries than your mother. I shall survive."

Her expression turned a bit pinched. "Speaking of surviving, Lord Wrexham, Lord Davenport approached me and my sisters while we were having ices at Gunther's earlier today and asked me pass on a message to you. He overheard some talk at whatever haunt he was visiting last night, and said that you appear to have made some very nasty enemies. So you should take care to be on guard."

"That's surprising," mused John.

"Yes, I was surprised, too," said Olivia. "You don't strike me as a man who stirs up strong passions."

He wasn't sure whether to feel flattered or nettled. "What I meant was, I'm surprised Davenport bothered to mention it. From what I gather, he isn't known for his altruism."

"There is that as well," she agreed. "He claims that he spotted us inside the tea shop and stopped on a whim because he had seen the two of us dancing together." A pause. "I assured him that it was only because your sister forced you to ask me."

"You seem to have an exceedingly low opinion of my backbone, Miss Sloane."

"I—I did not mean...that is, I—I wasn't intending..."

Her eyes turned an interesting shade of molten green when she was flustered—a fiery jade, shaded with a hint of smoke. Intrigued, John watched the swirl of hues spark beneath her lashes.

"Forgive me," she finished in a rush. Shifting the books in her arms, she held out one of them. "Here is the Hingham, sir."

"Thank you."

"And this"—a smaller volume thumped atop the leatherbound Hingham—"is a collection of essays from America on the inalienable rights of its citizens that I thought you might also want to read."

"I appreciate both of these," he said. "But as you said, I could have sent a servant for books. I've come for you."

The flustered look was back. "I—I don't understand."

"I thought we might go for a drive in the park. It's the fashionable hour for promenading, so we won't attract any undue attention."

She stared as if he were speaking in Hindi.

"You know—horses," he murmured, sketching an outline of said animal in the air. "A carriage, two people sitting on the seat."

"I may be a bit of a recluse, sir, but I am familiar with what the everyday conveyances of London look like."

But not, apparently, with the experience of actually riding in one, observed John to himself.

"Excellent. Then I'm sure you also know to bring a shawl, for the breeze can turn a bit chilly at this time of day."

"I—I did not say that I would come, sir," began Olivia.

"Miss Sloane…" He moved a step closer to her and lowered his voice a notch. "I thought we might discuss some of basic issues embodied in the proposed bill, and how best to address them. And it seems that we would have more privacy for such a chat outdoors."

Her eyes narrowed at the word "outdoors."

Casting a meaningful look at the closed door, John added, "First of all, I imagine that your mother has summoned your sister to come serve as a chaperone. And secondly, I would be willing to wager that her ear is already glued to the keyhole."

Olivia's wary expression slowly relaxed, allowing the corners of her mouth to curl upward. "You are no doubt correct on both counts, sir."

She has a very nice smile, he decided.

"May I take that as a yes?"

Her lashes fluttered, the shadows not quite hiding the hesitation in her eyes. "I suppose so." She drew in a breath. "Just as long as we are clear that it is purely a professional meeting."

"But of course," replied John. "We made an agreement, Miss Sloane. You need not worry that I am going to ravish you in the middle of Polite Society's daily parade ritual."

"I should hope not, Lord Wrexham," replied Olivia tartly. "The lovely young lady you had hanging on your arm this morning—I assume she is the Steel Corset—would not be amused."

John had to think for a moment—and then let out a low laugh. "The lovely young lady hanging on my arm this morning was my *niece*, who has been in Town to visit her mother, my sister. We were enjoying a last carriage ride together, as her father is escorting her back to her home in Norfolk tomorrow."

The color ridging her cheekbones now spread to the rest of her face. "Perhaps you ought to choose someone else to assist you with parsing complex intellectual concepts, sir."

A frown pinched off his smile. "Why is that?"

"Because my wits don't appear to be functioning very well of late," replied Olivia.

"Given my son's flair for drama, it is completely understandable that you might assume...the worst. However, Lady Serena Wells—which, by the by, is her proper name—is not here in London. She is visiting her relatives in Shropshire."

"I am sure she is very pleasant," said Olivia stiffly. "No doubt Prescott will come to appreciate that in the near future."

"The chances would be better if that cursed Lady Loose Screw would stop writing him and...making him laugh."

"You don't wish your son to laugh?" she asked slowly.

John wasn't quite sure how the conversation had managed to take such an uncomfortable twist. With his own thoughts on the future so muddled, the last thing he wished to discuss with Olivia was his maybe—or maybe not—engagement.

"Well, yes, of course I do," he replied. "But Lady Serena believes that a parent must keep a certain distance and detachment, in order to remain a figure of authority."

"Oh, quite right," murmured Olivia softly—but not softly enough to hide the edge of irony. "Mustn't relax that firm hand of discipline. You know the old adage—spare the rod, spoil the child."

Hell and damnation.

He had the distinct feeling she was making fun of him, and it bothered him more than it should.

"I take it you have your own opinions on the subject," he replied. "And I imagine they are more in line with Lady Loose Screw's ideas."

Olivia turned abruptly. "I'll get my shawl, sir. It's getting late, and I can't afford to dawdle. I have a great deal of reading to do when I return in order to prepare my next essay."

He watched her hurry from the room, a little puzzled by her reaction. It seemed uncharacteristic for her to flee the field of battle without firing a verbal shot in reply.

But then, I don't really know her at all, he reminded himself.

The earl's hands were not only strong, noted Olivia, as he guided his phaeton through the Stanhope gate leading into Hyde Park. They were steady and capable, controlling the spirited team of matched grays with a quiet, confident ease.

Strange, she had never paid any attention to a man's hands before, but Olivia found herself mesmerized by their lithe grace. His snug-fitting York tan gloves accentuated his long tapered fingers—there was a graceful elegance to their movement, and yet it was not at all effeminate.

"Am I driving too fast for your taste?" he inquired politely, catching her eye. "You seem a trifle apprehensive."

"No, not at all." Olivia quickly forced her gaze to lock on some distant point straight ahead. "What do you wish to talk about, sir?"

"Ah, getting right down to business," he remarked.

"That is the whole point of this exercise, isn't it?" she replied.

"Most ladies would say that the point would also be to enjoy the experience."

"Yes, well, I rarely have the same views on things as most ladies."

"So I am learning."

Olivia found herself feeling unsettled by his relaxed manner. The solemn-faced, steel-spined earl was far easier to deal with—at least she knew what to expect.

"No doubt to your dismay," she muttered.

And yet, there was something liberating about this

newfound relationship. After all, he knew her more inti-
mately than any man, so she was free to be—

No, no, she chided herself. *Don't think about being
friends.* It was...

Terribly confusing.

A subtle pressure on the reins slowed the vehicle to a
leisurely trot. The thudding of the hooves and jangling of
the harness were the only sounds as he maneuvered the
phaeton through a narrow carriageway and turned onto
Rotten Row. An ancient "King's Road"—or *Rue de Roi*—
it was originally built to connect St. James's Palace with
Kensington Palace, but now served the *crème de la crème*
of society as the fashionable place to promenade each day
in the late afternoon.

"I can't help but wonder—is there a reason you go out
of the way to make yourself appear odd, Miss Sloane?"
asked John after guiding his horses around an elderly
dowager's lumbering landau.

"I *am* odd," said Olivia. *And ungainly*, she added to
herself. "I don't wish to mislead you as to who or what I
am, sir." Suddenly recalling her activities as Lady Loose
Screw, she hastily added, "That is to say, now that you
have discovered my secrets..."

Well, almost all of my secrets.

"...I would prefer that we have plain speaking between us."

"I see." His voice, like his hands, was calm and steady.
It gave nothing away.

Olivia told herself that was enough of an explanation.
And yet, for some *odd* reason she felt compelled to add,
"As for what most of Society thinks of me, I suppose that
like a hedgehog, I use a prickly exterior to deflect closer

scrutiny. As I said before, if it ever got out that The Beacon is a lady, my career as a newspaper columnist would be over."

The wheels jostled over a deep rut.

"And I care very passionately about my writing, sir. I should hate to give it up."

John shifted his long, muscled legs, and suddenly she felt very small and vulnerable on the narrow seat. His silence seemed to strip away the layers of her usual defenses, leaving her uncomfortable. Exposed.

This was a bad idea. For any number of reasons...

"Miss Sloane," murmured John as the phaeton pulled ahead into a less crowded stretch of the carriageway. "Rest assured that your secrets are safe with me." He turned his head and their eyes met. "I have nothing but the utmost respect for your ideas and your writings."

Ye gods, the man has beautiful eyes. She had always thought of brown as a rather dull color, but in the slanting sunlight the hue was alive with intriguing sparks of gold and amber.

"All the more so because of the many obstacles you face in making yourself heard, simply because you are a lady. It is..." He pursed his lips in thought for a moment. "It is unfair."

"There is much injustice around us, Lord Wrexham," replied Olivia softly. "Which is why I wish to wield my pen. My plight pales in comparison to what others suffer."

"You have exemplary courage and compassion," he replied.

Her cheeks turned uncomfortably warm. "I fear that you overestimate me, sir. I assure you, I have plenty of faults."

Another small stretch of silence. A sidelong glance at his profile revealed nothing. Whatever he was thinking, the earl hid his emotions well.

As for her own…She drew in a tiny gulp of air, hoping to steady her skittering pulse.

"We all have our faults," he finally murmured, his voice barely loud enough to be heard over the sounds of the thudding hooves. "Just as we all have secrets that we pray will never become public knowledge."

Olivia felt her chest constrict.

"It has occurred to me that perhaps you feel I now have an unfair advantage over you because I know you are The Beacon. I wish for us to be true partners in this endeavor to win passage of this bill. So I…"

John hesitated, and she saw his hands tighten on the reins.

"I shall tell you a secret regarding my own personal affairs—one that would cause me to be the laughingstock of London were it ever to be known by the *beau monde*."

"Sir, You need not—" she began.

He quickly cut her off. "On the contrary, I feel it important that from the very start of this campaign, we fight as equals."

"Lord Wrexham…" Now was the time to tell him about Lady Loose Screw, Olivia told herself. But this unexpected turn had taken her completely by surprise, and her tongue seemed tied in knots.

"No, no, please hear me out, Miss Sloane." John's voice held a note of quiet command. "I would imagine you are aware of the newspaper advertisement—the one concerning a mother—that is causing such a titter throughout the drawing rooms of Mayfair."

Olivia nodded mutely.

"Well, it was placed by my son."

"I...I see."

"Yes, well, I am sure you also see how horribly embarrassing it would be for me if that fact ever became public."

"You fear that the Perfect Hero would appear the Perfect Fool."

He chuffed a humorless laugh. "Yes, you've summed it up quite *perfectly*."

Olivia couldn't meet his eyes. "I have read the advertisement, sir. And it seems to me that Prescott should be applauded for caring so much about your happiness." She essayed a smile. "And indeed, he deserves a great deal of credit for conceiving of such a bold strategy. You have to admit, he is a *very* resourceful boy."

"Too bold." The earl's mouth gave a grudging twitch. "And definitely too resourceful."

A dappling of sunlight danced along the rueful curl of his smile.

Don't look. Don't feel...

It was guilt, she told herself, that was making her throat so painfully tight. Swallowing the sensation, Olivia reminded herself that she was The Beacon, a sharp-tongued intellectual, not a calf-eyed schoolgirl.

"There, you have had your say, sir, and now we both hold a weapon that can be wielded against the other." She lifted her face to the breeze, grateful for the cooling touch against her skin. "But let us move on to more important things and not waste any more precious time on personal talk. You have a speech to write—a speech that can have even more influence than my newspaper columns. As a noted war hero, your opinion on the upcoming bill in Parliament will carry a good deal of weight with your peers."

John nodded, but a flicker of his lashes seemed to darken his gaze for just an instant.

A sudden thought occurred to her. "Is that why Lord Davenport sent a warning about your having made some very unpleasant enemies?"

"There are some people who wish me to voice a certain opinion," he replied. "But you need not worry, Miss Sloane. I am not easily intimidated."

"I don't doubt that, sir. However—"

"As you said, we shouldn't waste time on trivial talk. I have just finished reading some of John Locke's works on social contracts, and I would like your opinion on a few points."

Olivia was not unhappy to shift the conversation to more familiar territory. Ideas were safe ground, while emotions were...

A slippery slope.

"Social contracts—ah, now we are getting to the heart of the issue," she said. We must, of course, talk about Thomas Paine as well."

"And Benjamin Franklin," interjected John. "The Americans have a number of interesting thoughts on the subject."

They began talking about political philosophies, and it wasn't until she looked up and saw the glimmering waters of the man-made lake up ahead that Olivia realized their meanderings had brought them far from Rotten Row.

"Oh, look—the Serpentine," she exclaimed.

"Sorry," murmured John. "I wasn't paying much attention to the pathways—"

"No need for apology, sir," she responded. "My father used to bring me here to feed the ducks. He loved to tell me all about the different species he had seen on his exotic travels." A wry smile tugged at her mouth. "And to explain their different mating rituals—much to the consternation of any adults who happened to be within earshot."

The earl reined his team to a halt. "Shall we take a stroll by the water's edge and toss them some bread-crumbs?"

"But we don't have any—"

"No matter." He had already vaulted down from his perch and was coming around to give her a hand down from the vehicle. "I am sure some kindly soul will consent to sell us some."

"But…"

John's firm grip on her glove cut off any further protest. "It won't take long." He signaled to one of the boys loitering near the bushes and tossed him a gold coin. "Walk my horses, lad."

There were still a number of people enjoying the sight of the ducks and their young paddling through the ripples of sunlight. The earl purchased a nearly full bag of bread-crumbs from an elderly man and guided her to the edge of the bank.

Olivia tossed a handful into the water and watched the downy chicks gobble them up.

Her throat suddenly tightened. *I miss you, Papa*, she thought. *And all the fun we had exploring new ideas.* He had taught her to think, to challenge, to keep an open mind.

John seemed to sense her pensive mood and remained

tactfully silent. He, too, threw a scattering of crumbs into the water and smiled at the antics of the quacking ducklings.

The bag was soon empty, and after a last lingering look at the scene, Olivia turned away. "We had better be getting back."

Stepping aside, he did not insist on taking her arm, but let her go on by herself.

Head down, her mind still lost in thought and old memories, Olivia started to cross the carriageway.

"Watch out, Miss!" bellowed the boy holding John's team.

She looked up to see an out-of-control curricle bouncing down the path. Cursing, the driver slashed with his whip at his skittish horse. The animal gave a sharp whinny and broke into a panicked gallop.

Dear God. Dear God. Everything seemed to be happening so fast. Dazed, Olivia couldn't seem to make herself move.

Then suddenly she felt herself lifted off her feet and swung out of the path of the charging horse. Shielding her body with his, John pivoted and planted his feet.

"Oiy!" Another cry from the boy as Olivia felt a jarring thud.

John grunted but kept his balance. She felt his muscles coil like steel springs and then release.

Twisting, he shot out a hand and grabbed the horse by the bridle. It tried to rear and shake him off, but he held firm and in a few strong strides, pulled the frightened animal to a halt.

"Easy now," he crooned, his steady voice quickly calming the foam-flecked snorts.

With the horse now under control, he turned his attention to the curricle's driver, a foppishly dressed young gentleman with a long-lashed whip clasped in his fist.

The braided leather arced through the air with another wild *snap*. "I say, unhand my bay!"

John regarded him with a level stare. "Put down that whip," he said in a quiet voice.

"Be damned, sir. That infernal beast needs a good thrashing to teach it to behave."

"Put down that whip," repeated John.

If anything, his tone was even softer, but Olivia felt a shiver run down her spine. The edge of command was like a saber cutting through the evening shadows.

"Or you will feel its lash on your own bumbling arse, you cow-handed clod," added the earl. "Only a bloody idiot would come into a crowded park without knowing how to drive properly."

The young man paled and swallowed hard. "It wasn't my fault. A cursed dog must have nipped at his hooves," he said sullenly, setting the whip on the curricle's seat.

"It's a driver's duty to know how to deal with such things," replied John. "Take some lessons on handling the ribbons before you come here again." Keeping firm hold of the bridle—and of her, noted Olivia—he carefully turned the vehicle around. "You will exit by the nearest gate. At a sedate walk. Do I make myself perfectly clear?"

Another swallow, followed by a nod.

"Excellent."

"You may put me down, Lord Wrexham," said Olivia as she watched the curricle move off at a snail's pace.

John ignored her. Shifting her weight, as if she were

naught but a feather in his arms, he turned and stalked toward his waiting phaeton. A rippling of applause ran through the throng of spectators who had gathered on the grassy verge.

"Lud, that was awfully brave, sir," said the boy who was holding the earl's team.

"And foolish," added Olivia. "You could have been killed."

"It wasn't as dangerous as it looked," he replied. "I'm a former cavalry officer, remember? I've plenty of experience with horses."

Before she could respond, he lifted her up and set her gently on the seat. "What about you, Miss Sloane?" Reaching for the lap robe, John carefully tucked it around her skirts. "Are you all right?"

"Yes," answered Olivia. "I am fine."

His brow arched. "Fine?"

"Perhaps a little shaken," she admitted. "But truly, no bruises or broken bones, thanks to you." She watched him climb a bit gingerly into the seat. "But you—you took a nasty blow from a flailing hoof."

"A mere bump," he said, gathering up the reins.

"I think you ought to summon a surgeon—"

"I assure you, I have suffered far worse, so let us not waste our breath on it." He urged his team into a trot, and as the breeze ruffled through his hair she saw a faint purpling on his cheekbone. No doubt there were other painful bruises beneath his show of nonchalance.

The Perfect Hero was also a Perfect Stoic.

"We've far more interesting things to talk about," he went on. "Indeed, getting back to your observations on Franklin's writing…"

John suddenly made a rueful sound as they rounded a turn and he saw that Rotten Row was almost deserted. "My apologies, Miss Sloane. I fear I've kept you out longer than I meant to."

"No apologies necessary, Lord Wrexham. It has been a *very* invigorating interlude." Olivia flashed a smile. "And yes, it has been an interesting conversation."

"It has been more than interesting—it has been extremely educational. You see so many things that I miss," replied John. "Blast it all, I wish that I had been able to write down some of your phrases. Perhaps..." He blew out his breath. "Perhaps next time we might meet where we could spread out our reference books, and have pen and paper to make notes."

She looked away, all thoughts of his recent heroics yielding to her usual wariness. "I cannot risk having you come to my family's residence for a work session. If my mother suspected that my writing is being published—and trust me, her basilisk eye misses very little when it's focused on a plump purse and fancy title—she would raise holy hell." Thinking of Anna's books as well, she added, "The consequences are simply too great."

"I understand." He thought for a moment. "It would be well within the bounds of propriety for you to pay a morning call on my sister, but I suppose that still presents the problem of possible discovery."

"Yes, it does," she answered. Much as the idea of continuing their intellectual exchange was appealing, Olivia didn't see how it could be managed. "I am sorry."

A flick of his hands turned the horses toward High Street. They rode in silence for several minutes. She liked that about the earl—most men seemed to feel the need to constantly natter on, but he was comfortable with his own thoughts.

"There is usually a way to conquer a conundrum, no matter how well fortified it may seem," he murmured as they left the park. "One simply has to attack it from an unexpected angle."

An astute observation. She had an inkling that the earl was a master of battlefield strategy.

"I take it you were a very good soldier, Lord Wrexham. Not just in terms of physical courage, which you've displayed in spades. But in mental sharpness as well."

"I did not take reckless risks with the lives of my men, but I wasn't afraid to improvise," he replied. "Even if it meant breaking some of the regimental rules."

Interesting. She was starting to realize that beneath the appearance of perfectly tailored propriety, the earl was a bit of a rebel.

Olivia wondered whether the Steel Corset knew that he wasn't laced quite as tightly as he seemed.

"So yes, I am not inclined to accept defeat quite so easily," went on John. He pursed his mouth in thought. "There must be an answer that will not compromise your secret."

A thought suddenly stirred from the depth of her thoughts. *A dangerous one*, she mused. And yet, the earl had just proved he was unafraid of stepping squarely into the path of danger.

"Well, perhaps..."

"Please go on."

Olivia cleared her throat. "There may be one possibility. Mr. Hurley owns a small cottage within the walled garden where you found me the other day. He uses it as a retreat for his own writing and has occasionally allowed me to make use of it when I've needed peace and quiet to finish up a last-minute revision on my column."

Another cough. "He's just as anxious as I am to see this bill pass, so I think he could be convinced to lend it to me—and guarantee absolute privacy—for some regular meetings over the next few weeks."

The breeze ruffled through his dark hair as John turned his head and their eyes met. "Would you ask him?"

Yes or no.

Olivia thought it over. She wasn't afraid of taking great risks intellectually, but in her day-to-day life, she had always erred on the side of caution.

He waited, silent and solemn.

However, in this particular case, she mused, the danger seemed minimal. After all, each of them had compelling reasons to make sure that nothing went awry.

"Very well," she replied slowly.

"Excellent, excellent." The angular planes of his face softened in the slanting sunlight. "When do you think we might begin?"

"Keep your powder dry, sir," said Olivia wryly. "It may take a day or two to arrange."

"I look forward to exploding the opposition's sense of puffed-up conceit and entitlement, so the sooner the better," he growled. "Mark my word, together we shall win this battle, Miss Sloane."

"Make no mistake, it will be a tough fight," she warned. "I am all too aware that passions are heated to a fever pitch on this issue. But I believe that if we marshal our arguments and then move carefully to counter the opposing side's view—"

"Like chess," he interjected. "We must simply study the board carefully and dare to be creative."

"Yes, like chess," agreed Olivia, feeling a tiny shiver slide down her spine at the recollection of their first smoke-shrouded encounter. "It's all about strategy. And with our two minds working together, I think we will prevail."

Chapter Sixteen

$\mathcal{H}$ow is your speech coming?" asked Cecilia as she added a dab of gooseberry jam to her buttered breakfast toast.

"Fairly well, I think," answered John. "There are still some rough edges, but I believe that I am making headway in smoothing them out."

"You are certainly dedicating a great deal of time to your research and writing," murmured his sister. "Perhaps you would care to take a break and join Prescott and me for a visit to the Tower menagerie?"

"Unfortunately. I have an appointment this afternoon. But if you could put it off until tomorrow, I would be happy to accompany you."

"Lucy is arriving tomorrow, Father," reminded Prescott. The boy's tutor was coming up from their country estate, and the earl had arranged with the girl's father to have her come to Town for a visit.

"Oh, quite right," said Cecilia. "We shall put off the visit until the following day, so she may enjoy the exotic animals, too."

"And don't forget Astley's!" exclaimed Prescott. "We must go again to see the riders and acrobats at Astley's Amphitheater, too. Lucy will like that very much."

"No visit to London would be complete without seeing such a spectacle," agreed his aunt. "So, we shall visit the Tower in the afternoon, and then we shall take in the evening performance of the acrobats." She looked to the earl. "Is that agreeable, John?"

"Hmmm?" The earl didn't look up from reading The Beacon's latest column in the newspaper. If anything Olivia's voice was getting stronger, surer, more nuanced. *By Jove, she was good.* "What?"

"I said"—Cecilia winked at Prescott—"we were thinking of hiring a pair of silver unicorns and flying to the moon to dine on green cheese for supper. Would you care to come?"

"Yes, yes, that will be fine."

His son started giggling.

Reluctantly setting the paper aside, he blew out a wry sigh. "Sorry. I have been a trifle preoccupied of late."

"Understandably so," replied Cecilia, her mirth softening to a sympathetic smile. "I know that you care a great deal about this issue concerning war veterans. And its importance is magnified by the fact that it is your first speech in the House of Lords."

He did care. *Passionately.* And so far, the three secret work sessions with Olivia had proved very helpful. She was a singular intellect—insightful, compassionate, and exceedingly clever with words. He would, he realized, miss her sharp mind, her pithy wit, her throaty laugh when their joint effort came to an end in another fortnight...

"And you must, of course, be missing your betrothed," went on his sister. "But personal sacrifices must be made for the higher good."

"Hmmm?" John blinked, trying to banish the thought of Olivia's unruly dark hair escaping her hairpins and curling across her cheek.

"Lady Serena Wells." Cecilia arched a questioning a brow. "Or have you forgotten her?"

Damnation. Snapping to attention, he quickly eyed the date on the newspaper. *Damn, damn, damn.* Somehow he had lost track of time and of any other commitments, save for his speech. He had promised to partner Lady Serena for the first waltz at the annual Militia Ball, but surely she would forgive his absence.

She, of all people, understood the notion of duty over pleasure.

"If you will excuse, I must pen a letter and send it off to Shropshire before I leave for my appointment."

"Yes, of course," murmured Cecilia, though she continued to eye him with a quizzical look. "But one last thing before you rush off. May we count on your escort to the Tower on the day after tomorrow? You need a respite from your work, and with Lucy here, I would be grateful for a hand in keeping two inquisitive young people from getting lost in the maze of courtyards and walkways."

"Yes, yes, you may count on me," replied John, feeling a pinch of guilt for having spent so little time with his son. "I promise that I shall schedule nothing to interfere with the outing."

"Are you sure these secret rendezvous are wise?" asked Anna.

"Not entirely," answered Olivia. "I realize that the risk for something going wrong grows greater with each meeting. But the earl is so...passionate in his feelings. I feel I can't let him down."

"Passionate!" Caro rolled her eyes. "He doesn't sound very passionate to me—save for the one time he kissed you in the garden. From what you have told us, the two of you talk of nothing but politics." Sighing, she lay back on Olivia's bed and clasped a feather pillow to her chest. "A walled garden, redolent with the perfume of roses, a secluded cottage, hidden from prying eyes...Ha! If you ask me, the man doesn't have a romantic bone in his body."

"Put a cork in it, Caro," said Anna. "When you have more experience in life, you will understand that romance comes in many guises, and not all of them involve fire and lightning."

"One wouldn't know that by reading your books," retorted Caro.

"Don't believe everything you read."

Olivia smiled into the looking glass as she listened to the exchange. "Whether the Earl of Wrexham possesses a romantic bone in his body is neither here nor there," she said, poking her last few hairpins into place. "I'm not looking for romance. Ours is a purely practical, pragmatic partnership. We are..." She thought for a moment. "We are like chess pieces of the same color, moving together across the checkered tiles to defeat the opposing army and achieve the ultimate victory."

Caro made a face. "I don't like chess. It's far too complicated and confusing."

"To each his own," murmured Olivia, snagging an errant curl and securing it with a hairpin. She threaded a narrow ribbon through her topknot. "The game requires focus, imagination, and a willingness to take risks. I like the challenge, for it keeps me mentally sharp."

"One small mistake can be the difference between victory and defeat," pointed out Anna. "Which is, of course, a metaphor for the game you are playing in real life."

"I'm well aware of that," replied Olivia, taking care to avoid the reflection of her sister's gaze in the looking glass. "Trust me, I am being exceedingly cautious with my own moves. In another two weeks this will all be over…"

Over, over, over.

"And Lord Wrexham and I will go our separate ways. So the worst of the danger has passed."

Their carefully choreographed strategy for entering and leaving the walled garden on their own had worked without a hitch. *We work well together*, she mused. *Strangely enough, despite all our differences, our strengths seem to complement one another.*

"Trust me, we are both extremely cautious. Unlike you two, the earl and I are ruled by cold logic, not fiery emotion."

"And yet, you can't deny that you've plenty of passion burning inside your breast," murmured Anna.

"That's different," replied Olivia quickly. "The fact is, it burns inside my head, not my breast—or any other part of my anatomy."

"Ha! Some hero will light a flame in your heart," said Caro. "After all, love is the most elemental of human emotions."

Anna choked down a burble of mirth.

"You've been reading too many of Anna's books." After spearing a last hairpin into place, Olivia glanced at the mantel clock. "Time to be off."

The long walk helped her gather her thoughts—for some reason they seemed to be straying far off the beaten path today. Using her key to unlock the garden gate, she slipped into the coolness of the shaded enclave and slid the bolt back in place. The fragrance of lavender and the grassy scents of the leafy foliage helped further calm her nerves.

Save for the twitter of a linnet, no sounds disturbed the stillness. Winding her way along the narrow pathway, she eased through an opening in the rhododendron bushes and entered the small cottage.

It had been the earl's turn to arrive early. He was seated at the desk in the far corner of the main sitting room and was already at work. Sunlight from the bank of diamond-paned leaded windows behind him played over his bent head. She could hear the *scratch-scratch* of his pen and the rustle of foolscap.

He had removed his coat and rolled up his shirtsleeves, for early on, they had agreed to shed the formal restrictions of Polite Society during these sessions. As Olivia unknotted her bonnet strings, she watched the rippling of his back muscles beneath the stretch of linen. Oddly enough, he seemed even bigger and broader…

With a small cough, she set her headcovering and gloves on the entrance table, followed by her shawl.

John turned around. "Sorry. I didn't hear you come in." A smudge of ink streaked his forehead just above his left eyebrow and several clumps of dark hair were standing up in spiky tufts.

Repressing a smile, Olivia replied, "Your concentration was on your work, which is all for the good."

Concentrate, concentrate.

He had also removed his cravat and unfastened the top two buttons beneath his collar. Swallowing hard, she forced herself not to look at the intriguing "V" of bronzed flesh peppered with coarse curls.

"How is the new section coming?" she asked brusquely.

"Slowly," he replied, raking impatient fingers through his hair. "I can't seem to get it right."

Moving to the work table in the middle of the room, Olivia perched a hip on the corner and began perusing one of the reference books that lay open on the blotter. "Have you looked at Jefferson's collection of essays?"

"Yes, and I have to say that I disagree with some of his points. And that's what's bedeviling me. I feel I should change my reasoning on several of the secondary issues. Let me explain why…"

The earl was growing more confident, she noted as they debated the merits of the American thinker's ideas.

"You have convinced me, Wrexham," she finally acknowledged. "I believe that all things considered, your point of view is better than the one I originally suggested."

"You do?" John looked a little surprised. "Truly?"

"Truly."

A boyish smile bloomed on his lips. "That is high praise indeed, seeing as The Beacon is an unwavering flame of Truth and Honesty."

Truth. Honesty.

Olivia felt her insides give a sickening lurch. *I must tell him about the Other Secret.*

"You, of all people, never prevaricate."

Oh, but not now. After the speech, she promised herself. She would confess to being Lady Loose Screw after their work was done. No doubt he would despise her, but by then it wouldn't matter.

For now, however, her own scruples must be sacrificed for the Higher Good.

"Never mind about me," she muttered. "We must focus on your speech. Read that last section aloud. It has to be perfect."

John did so.

"You're right about the concepts, but it needs to be stronger."

"How so?" he asked.

"It needs..." Olivia began to pace. "...More punch." Fisting her hands, she tapped them together. "The words must be tough, but lyrical."

He blew out his breath. "I'm afraid that lyrical doesn't come naturally to me."

"It's a matter of practice. You're very skilled with words, Wrexham, you just need more practice. Practice makes perfect."

Her steps quickened over the threadbare rug. "Lyrical, lyrical," she muttered.

Tap, tap. Her knuckles kept rapping a steady tattoo, as if the sound might conjure up inspiration from thin air.

As she reached the far end of the room, she suddenly pivoted on her heel and rattled off a few sentences.

John snatched up a pen and started writing.

"Lift your thoughts from self-interest! Raise your eyes from your estate ledgers and see the Higher Good..." The ideas were flowing fast and furious now.

"Blast!" exclaimed John as the pen point snagged in the paper. "Wait—I cannot copy that down quickly enough."

Expelling an impatient huff, Olivia made a face. "I

shall try to slow down, but words sometimes race out of reach if I don't keep up with them."

"Then keep going, keep going," he urged, grabbing a newly sharpened quill and a fresh sheet of paper. "I'll scribble as fast as I can. We can always go back and make corrections later."

Olivia was already rattling off a new sentence. For the next quarter hour, she criss-crossed the floor, shaping her ideas into heartfelt speech. When at last she was satisfied with her efforts, she paused and circled back to the work table, where John was just finishing the task of writing out the final words.

"Better?" she murmured, trying to read over his shoulder.

"It's brilliant," he answered. "Absolutely brilliant. The Beacon has never shone so brightly."

"You give me far too much credit, Wrexham," protested Olivia. "The core idea was yours, and without it the speech would fall flat, no matter how flowery the language."

"Hardly," he said, though she could see that her praise stirred a swirl of topaz-colored sparks in the chocolate-dark depths of his eyes. "Without your guidance I could never have done it. You've taught me to challenge myself, to question my assumptions, and to try to see things from more than one perspective."

She, too, felt a heady rush of exhilaration at his words of admiration.

"We make a good team," added John. "Though it is a pity you cannot receive the credit you deserve."

"That's not important. What matters is that the speech is a strong one," said Olivia. "It will sway the undecided votes."

"You think so?"

"I am sure of it!" she exclaimed. "With these words as your warriors, you will checkmate the opposition."

"As I said, I never could have done it without your inspiration," he replied warmly.

Feeling a tingling of heat spread over her cheeks, Olivia dropped her eyes. "Here, let me read over your notes, to see if I see any problems. I know there were spots where I was talking awfully fast."

He handed over the papers.

"Not, bad, not bad," she murmured, half to herself. "Only here, in last few lines, I think we should change 'ask' to 'demand' and 'rights' to 'inalienable rights.' "

"Yes," he agreed. "Much better."

She crossed out the originals and wrote out the new words. "There! I'm sure there will be a few other minor changes when you write out the final copy. But in essence, it's done!"

Smiling broadly, John rose and carefully tucked the papers inside his portfolio case, along with the drafts of the other sections.

"You should feel very proud of yourself, Wrexham. Most war heroes would be content to bask in the glow of their medals. That you care about fighting new battles is admirable." On impulse, Olivia circled her arms around his big shoulders and gave him a fierce hug. "More than admirable, in fact."

Taken by surprise, John couldn't react for a moment. Every muscle in his body felt as if it was held in thrall by some strange force.

Save for his heart, which was hammering helter-pelter against his ribs.

He inhaled slowly, filling his nostrils with the uniquely sensuous fragrance of her skin, her hair. *Verbena, neroli, and wild thyme*—slightly sweet, slightly salty, slightly exotic, it reminded him of sun-drenched Spanish hills and the Mediterranean Sea.

"Sorry," murmured Olivia.

"Don't be," he said.

She tipped up her chin, an uncertain smile quivering at the corners of her mouth. "As you know, the passion of words seems to release some primal, primitive emotion inside me. Society is right to call me the Hellion of High Street." She pulled back, the warmth of her body giving way to a lick of chill air. "So, you know yet another of my sordid little secrets."

"Your secrets," he replied slowly, "are safe with me."

"Yes—I don't doubt that I can trust you, sir." Her tone took on an odd note. "You are, after all, the Perfect Hero."

The hold on his body suddenly gave way to a different force as John felt himself seized by a fierce longing he couldn't explain. Couldn't control.

"Damnation—to the Devil with Perfection!" Impelled by the momentary madness, John caught hold of her shoulders, aware of the slide of silk against his calloused palms. "At this instant I'm not feeling very perfect." The fabric was soft. Sensuous. "Or very heroic."

Her eyes widened, and a blade of sunlight caught the swirling, spinning currents beneath the jade green hue.

"Damnation," he repeated, his voice dropping to a hoarse whisper. "I want...I want there to be no secrets between us." He leaned in a little closer, and suddenly he was plummeting, plummeting down into their depths.

Drowning. Unable to breathe.

"God help me," he rasped as his lips touched hers. His hands tightened, feeling the soft contour of her flesh, the firm slope of her shoulders. Hard and soft—a contrasting conundrum of textures and nuances.

Infinitely alluring, dangerously intriguing.

Retreat! The military part of his brain was commanding him to withdraw. But in the heat of battle, the word was naught but a fuzzed boom, echoing far, far away.

"Wrexham..." Olivia wrenched her mouth free. "Wrexham, th-this is madness."

His fingers brushed through the downy wisps of hair at the nape of her neck... found the fastenings of her gown...

Pulled the ties loose.

Heat thrummed against his skin as the finespun silk fabric slid down her arms.

Madness.

I am perfectly rational, perfectly honorable... and, apparently, perfectly mad.

"Is it?" His voice sounded drugged. Deranged. Whatever exotic substance was bubbling through his blood, it was potent as sin.

Olivia's laugh tickled against his cheek, light as a zephyr. "Utter madness," she whispered. And then kissed him full on the mouth.

The feel, the taste, the texture of her satin-soft lips on his snapped the last shred of sanity. His arms circled her waist and crushed her close, the rustle of lace petticoats entangling with the whisper of wool.

Her thighs touched his trouser front, her slow, swirling sway igniting a jolt of fire in his groin. He came to instant arousal, a groan rumbling deep in his throat.

"Miss Sloane—Olivia," he rasped.

In answer, she hitched her hips hard against him. And rubbed herself slowly against his steeled shaft.

John gasped, and with a wordless growl, lifted her into his arms.

Bed. There was a small bedchamber just off the main sitting room. Half-staggering, half-spinning, he somehow managed to navigate the short corridor. One of his hands twined in her silky tresses—he heard the *ping* of falling pins mark their progress along the rough-planked floor. The other was doing things no honorable gentleman ought to be doing to a respectable lady.

"Oh, please..." said Olivia in a fluttery whisper.

He stopped short in the doorway, suddenly, thoroughly, achingly ashamed of himself.

"...don't stop, Wrexham."

"It would be wrong of me to take advantage of the situation," he replied through gritted teeth. "I—"

"I ask you to rise above the petty prejudices and traditions of the past," she intoned, quoting a passage from the speech they had just created. "It's time to forge a new set of laws—a just set of laws—instead of letting ourselves be chained to the old way of thinking!"

Her eloquence was...erotic. The passionate words teased over his skin like a lover's caress.

"Make our own rules?"

"Yes, why not?" An errant curl brushed against his cheek as Olivia shifted and the scent of her sent another rush of heat through his body.

Its thrum was fast drowning out the argument from the Voice of Honor in the back of his head.

"I don't, as you know, feel bound by Society's rigid rules," she went on. "So..."

All thought of rules unraveled as Olivia pressed her palm against the top fastening of his shirt.

So, yes—to the Devil with rules! To the Devil with regulations and all the orderly thoughts that regimented his life.

"Then let us," he rasped, "cast them to the wind."

Chapter Seventeen

Olivia felt herself falling, falling, weightless and wondrous with the feel of his big, muscled body molding to hers. The bed shivered as their twined limbs thudded with an eager sigh atop the down coverlet. Fumbling, tugging, pulling—impatient hands sought ties and fastenings.

Yes. Yes. She arched upward, allowing John to strip off her gown.

Propelled by her palms, his trousers slithered down his thighs.

Her corset strings quickly yielded to his nimble fingers.

A boot thudded against the floor, then another.

"Yes. Yes." The words broke free from her lips as he cupped her breasts. And then speech was impossible as his mouth captured hers in a deep, delving kiss.

More clothing came away, baring their bodies. Flesh against heated flesh. Now the only thing between them was the thin scrim of her lacy cotton drawers.

Olivia was a little shocked by the sensations sizzling

through her core. Never had a man ignited such fire inside her. Not even that one time…

"Olivia," he rasped. "I shouldn't—"

"I'm not a virgin, John," she whispered, savoring the sound of his name on her tongue. "You are not stealing my virtue."

That had been lost several years ago, while on an expedition with her father to the isle of Crete. A handsome Frenchman had been part of the Royal Society's team of expert scholars. He had been interesting—no, *fascinating* was perhaps a more accurate word. By the end of the first month he had convinced her to agree to a secret engagement. In order, he said, not to cause any distraction or dissent within the group. By the end of the following week he had seduced her into anticipating the marriage vows.

Ah, yes, silver-tongued Pierre. He had talked of undying love, only to decide a short while later that the idea of a permanent legshackle did not appeal to his sense of free-spirited adventure. He lost little time in taking his leave of the expedition, shrugging off the affair with casual nonchalance.

Angry at herself for being so naïve, Olivia had never told her father the truth of what had happened.

Not even her sisters knew. Some things were simply too private, too painful to speak of.

Tightening her hold on John's sun-kissed body, she added, "If I wish to give myself to you, that should be my choice."

In answer, he gave a rough growl. "If you are sure…"

I should not sin again, she thought. But something of her father's radical ideas must have rubbed off on her after all, because somehow her body was responding to some primitive need pulsing deep within rather than listening to the Voice of Reason.

With a choked moan, she opened herself to his kiss. "I have never been more sure of anything."

Her words seemed to unravel the last shred of John's gentlemanly restraint. His palms slid up her thighs and eased them open.

Yes, yes. Then his long, lithe body, all hard muscle and heat-sparked desire, covered hers. Flesh on flesh— his weight and warmth felt unbearably wonderful. And yet, she wanted more.

More.

Arching up, Olivia wrapped her arms around his neck, tangled her hands in his hair. Its texture was like slubbed silk, rough and smooth, like John himself.

"John." The intimate whisper of his name felt so right on her lips. She said it again.

John's whole body shuddered in response, and the thudding of his heart quickened against her sweat-slickened skin.

"Olivia." Their zephyr-soft voices entangled, entwined like physical caresses.

She felt his hand slip between their bodies, felt his fingertips glide through her downy curls and probe deeper. She arched again, purring with pleasure as he found her hidden pearl and began a gentle stroking.

"Yes, yes." Urging him on with words, with touch, Olivia rocked her hips up, seeking more.

More.

As was he. A growl, deeply rough, deeply masculine, reverberated in her ear as John shifted and his arousal thrust into the honeyed slickness of her feminine folds. She heard herself cry out—a wordless plea that spoke clearly of her wanting, of her need.

John raised himself and thrust again. The head of his cock teased up against the entrance to her passageway. With a muffled groan, he eased back and then in one swift stroke he was inside her.

A pinch of pain. Her body clenched, taking a moment to adjust to him.

John went very still. "Am I hurting you?"

"No, no, it's good," replied Olivia. "It's glorious."

He kissed her slowly and softly, his lips feathering over hers as his hips resumed moving. Back and forth— ebb and flow—like the elemental rhythm of the oceans and the tides.

Olivia found herself submerged in a sea of indescribable sensations. His textures, his sounds, his scent swirled around her. Drowning, drowning, she gasped for breath, filling her lungs with a rush of cooling air. The rest of her was on fire, heat licking like a flame between her legs.

She clutched at his shoulders, palms sliding down the hard slope of contoured muscle. His hands were roving over the swell of her hips, the curve of her derriere. There was nothing languid or leisurely about their touching. A volatile eagerness seemed to have taken possession of them. A frenzied need.

"I want…I want…" The words broke free of their own volition. She wasn't quite sure what she wanted. All she knew was that a strange wave was cresting inside her, demanding release.

"I know what you want, sweetheart." John's voice was a little muzzy, as if he, too, were caught in some powerful current. "And the Devil take me, I want it as well." Quickening his strokes, he sheathed himself in her warm wetness again and again.

And again.

A cry—was it really hers?—shattered the surrounding stillness of the room as a brief burst of brilliant sparks outshone the sunlight. Olivia felt herself spinning, spinning in a shower of gold-flecked flickers of fire before floating back down to earth.

John covered her cry with his lips, the tremoring sound resonating down to his very core. Everything about Olivia seemed to thrum with passion—her eloquent words, her inspiring ideas, her beautiful body. Even her creamy soft skin seemed to radiate sparks.

Sparks that ignited some elemental longing.

She was exquisitely exciting. *Exhilarating.*

The mere scent of her, a beguiling mix of neroli and spice, had his emotions tumbling and turning topsy-turvy. And at that moment it seemed impossible to imagine being content with a coolly correct relationship. An arrangement of faultless manners, of easy expectations.

Being with Olivia was a constant challenge. She pushed him, prodded him, made him lose control. That was dangerous.

Dangerous. And a little frightening. But it also made him feel elementally alive.

He held her tightly as she came undone in his arms, her shudders sending a spurt of joy through his being. *So sweet, so sweet.* His own need was rising fast and faster, its fire burning through his blood.

His pulse was racing, his heart was pounding, his grip

on self-control was perilously close to snapping. By sheer force of will, he caught himself and withdrew just as his body convulsed.

With a ragged groan, John fell back upon the bed and pulled her close, their limbs tangling together in the rumpled sheets.

For a moment, he lay still, eyes closed, listening to the tandem echo of their breathing.

Two as one.

It was the last coherent thought he had before drifting into a dreamlike sleep.

Olivia was drowsily aware of floating in and out of wakefulness. How long, she wondered, had she been lingering in sweet oblivion? Time seemed awfully fuzzy, in contrast to her heightened perceptions of the physical surroundings. *The patterns of light on the whitewashed walls, the ruffling of a breeze through the garden hedge, the winsome melody of a linnet's song.*

They were matched by her acute awareness of her own body. *Languid limbs, pleasurable sense of peace...*

She felt John shift in a whisper of linen and prop himself up on one elbow. Turning slowly, Olivia gazed at him with a sleepy smile.

He smiled back, but she saw an odd sort of seriousness lurking at the corners of his mouth.

"You look pensive," she murmured.

"Do I?" His lips twitched slightly, which seemed to dispel the momentary illusion.

It must have been a mere quirk of the slanting light.

"I suppose," John went on, "that's because I have been thinking."

"Of what?" she asked, watching as a tiny gust from the open window set a lock of his dark hair to dancing along the curve of his jaw. It was, she decided, a very nice sight.

"Of what date we should set," replied John.

"But I thought the date of the speech was set weeks ago, when debate on the issue first began," murmured Olivia, still distracted by the beautiful shape and textures of his profile. "I can't imagine they will allow you to change the schedule at the last minute."

"Not the speech," he answered. "The wedding."

"What wedding?" He wasn't making any sense.

"Our wedding."

His words took a moment to sink in. And then...

She sat bolt upright. For just an instant, a pinch of pure, girlish longing squeezed at her heart, but she quickly slapped it away. "Don't be daft!" Practical, pragmatic— Olivia ruthlessly reminded herself that she was The Beacon, not some bacon-brained romantic schoolgirl. "You don't want to marry me."

"That is beside the point," he said softly. "There are rules governing Society. An honorable man must abide by them."

"For God's sake, Wrexham!" She no longer felt comfortable calling him John. "No one knows of this interlude. Nor will they."

"*I* know," he replied. "And I can't deny that knowledge."

Her chest felt as if an iron band were tightening around her ribs. "And neither can you deny that you are meant to marry the Steel Corset."

His face went rigid.

"She'll make a far better countess than I will," argued

Olivia, ignoring the painful squeeze. "I'd only embarrass you, sir. I'm outspoken, opinionated. And I don't take orders well." She forced a grim smile in hopes of defusing the tension between them. "You have to admit, that's not a good quality for the wife of a military officer *or* a member of the House of Lords."

John raked a hand through his sweat-damp hair. "After this, I can't, in good conscience, marry the Steel—Lady Serena Wells."

"Well, you can't marry me, either," retorted Olivia. "Because my answer is no!"

"I've compromised you, Miss Sloane. I've ruined your chances of ever making a respectable match."

"That is a moot point, sir, for I've told you from the beginning that I don't ever plan to marry."

A martial glint came to his eyes. "But honor demands—"

"Honor be damned!" she said hotly. "Men make women play by different rules, but in this case I absolutely refuse to jump through the hoops of conformity."

"You are being stubborn, Miss Sloane."

"And you are being tyrannical."

His teeth clenched—in another instant she fully expected to hear the molars crack.

"I told you I wasn't a virgin when we crossed the threshold of this room, if that's what you are worried about." She traced a fingertip along the hard line of his jaw. "My father had very radical notions about women and the fact that they ought to enjoy the same freedoms as men. So I was..." She hesitated. "...More adventurous than I should have been." Her hand stilled. "So unlike you, I am not perfect in any sense of the word. Which may repel you."

"Nobody is perfect," he growled. "Least of all me. However, I'm trying mightily to behave as a proper gentleman."

"Well, since I'm not a proper lady, there's no need to conform to the strictures of proper behavior."

Their eyes locked for an instant.

"And what of the cursed man who compromised you?" The sudden change in subject caught her by surprise. "Whoever the fellow might be, he's a damnable blackguard."

"He was French," replied Olivia, trying to make her voice light. "And we all know the Frogs have a different view of *amour*."

If anything, his expression turned darker.

"It happened in Crete, long enough ago that it really doesn't matter." She decided a certain amount of explanation might help ease his conscience. "My father had asked me to accompany his expedition and serve as his secretary. I was young, and giddy with excitement at being part of such a grand adventure. Pierre was one of the French scholars from the *Académie d'Histoire* who were invited to join the group for the summer. He was suave, sophisticated, and oozing with Gallic charm."

When he didn't react, she went on, "What happened is an age-old story. He courted me—in secret, which I suppose was part of the allure. In a fit of passion, I agreed to his plea that we not wait for our marriage vows to consummate our love."

John finally spoke. A muttered oath. In French.

She shrugged. "But once Pierre had gotten what he wanted, he suddenly saw no reason to be legshackled to a wife. We were both free spirits, he took pains to point out.

So why, he asked, should we conform to the petty tyranny of Society. I could hardly complain—it would have been a little like the pot calling the kettle black." A pause. "A week later, he left the island. I never saw him again."

"What did your father have to say about it?" he asked softly.

"He never knew about it."

"Miss Sloane—"

"It's ancient history, Wrexham," she quickly interjected. "What matters now is the present. And when you analyze the situation, it's really quite simple. You feel compelled to offer marriage for your honor. I feel compelled to say no for my independence. We both come away happy."

"I—"

She cut him off again. "You have offered, Wrexham. So honor is satisfied. Think of it as a duel—you gentlemen are often all afire to kill each other over some silly slight to your honor. And yet there is always a way to save face, is there not, if both parties are reasonable?"

He gave a curt nod.

"There, you see. No need to pull the trigger and kill off all chances of your future happiness."

Clutching the coverlet to cover her nakedness, she slid off the bed and hurriedly began gathering her garments. Behind her, she heard John's bare feet touch the floor, followed by the rustle of clothing.

"And you, Olivia?" he asked after several long moments.

The sound of her given name on his lips stirred an unwilling, unwanted longing. Emotion was all very well for romantics like Anna and Caro. But she was much happier with abstract ideas.

"What is it you have saved?"

"My sense of self, my independence," Olivia answered quickly. "I've fought so hard to win them, Wrexham, and at times the cost of battle has been very dear. You, as a soldier, should understand what I mean." She looked away to the shuttered window and the tiny blades of sunlight slicing in through the slatted wood. "I won't give them up."

She heard his breath release in a tightly measured sigh. "If that is what you wish..."

"It is," she said emphatically. Now dressed, Olivia turned to face him. "Good heavens," she added in a low voice. "According my father, many cultures consider virginity vastly overrated."

John carefully brushed a wrinkle from his coat. "But London Society is not one of them."

"Be that as it may, it is hard to respect any so-called code of honor made by people who, for the most part, are ruled by self-interest."

Silence.

"I refuse to be bound by their silly strictures."

He fixed her with a hooded gaze, his features unyielding, his expression unfathomable. "Very well. I cannot force your hand. So I shall have to accept your word on this."

She couldn't discern whether it was anger or relief in his tone.

"Thank you." Olivia ignored the new pinch of pain in her chest. "Now, let us put aside petty, personal concerns and get back to the far more important matter—the speech."

"Yes, the speech," he said slowly. "What do you have

in mind, Miss Sloane?" He turned his back. "I was under the impression that you were quite satisfied with our efforts."

For an instant, Olivia felt a hot, humiliating prickle against the back of her eyelids. Blinking back tears, she drew a steadying breath. "I am. But it is not simply the words, but how you say them that matters. So I think we ought to meet again for one last rehearsal."

"Here?"

"I see no other option. But I believe we can control our...passion for justice enough to ensure that there will be no further lapses in judgment."

"Your suggestion has merit." His voice was devoid of any emotion. "We must not overlook any detail that might give us an advantage over our opponents."

"It's just for one more time," she pointed out. "Then we both will move on. You will return to Shropshire, and I—I will find a new cause."

"An eloquent summation, as always."

Was he being sarcastic? Impossible to tell.

"Shall we set a time for tomorrow?" he went on.

Olivia shook her head. "I cannot. I have prior obligations. Indeed, the coming week is difficult. The only time I have free is the day after tomorrow. Shall we say in the late morning, around eleven o'clock?"

He hesitated for a fraction, and then gave a curt nod. "Fine. I will see you then."

Chapter Eighteen

No.

The word was still like a demon's red-hot pitchfork, its hellfire prongs jabbing at his consciousness no matter how many times over the last two days he had tried to banish it from his brain.

Frowning, John looked up from studying the notes for his speech and pinched at the bridge of his nose. The Beacon—that eloquent Master of Eloquent Rhetoric—had not bothered to embellish the sentiment when she had refused the offer of his hand.

She had given him naught but a single syllable.

No.

He should, by all accounts, be relieved. That a moment of madness would not chain him to an unmeditated marriage ought to be cause for rejoicing. And yet, his emotions were far from elated.

The truth was, he was feeling rather melancholy.

Miss Sloane—Olivia—had gotten under his skin in

ways he had never imagined. She was intelligent, she was witty, she was sensual, she was...

She was, in a word, exhilarating to be with.

"Exhilarating," he muttered aloud, with a grimace of self-disgust. "I sound like a puling schoolboy, not a battle-hardened soldier."

And that was the trouble—duty was at war with desire, and he wasn't quite sure which side he was on.

Did duty demand his allegiance to Lady Serena? He had made no formal offer, and while she was cordial and seemed to enjoy his company, there had been no sign that her affections were truly engaged.

Which was, John reminded himself, exactly as it should be among members of the *ton*. Most matches were made for practical reasons. Money, position, power—God perish the thought that such a mercurial emotion as love might swirl in like a North Sea gale and blow all such careful consideration to flinders.

"But who the devil said anything about love?" he growled, turning to a new page of his notes.

Olivia was most certainly not in love—she had made that clear as crystal. Nor did marriage hold any appeal. He could understand her intellectual opposition, for he was in agreement that as the laws were presently written, women had painfully few rights.

Yet he sensed that her fear was of a more personal nature. She had been seduced—oh, how his fingers itched to pound the slimy Frog to a pulp—and then jilted by a cad. Though she hid it well, he had caught a telltale glimpse in her eye and in her mannerisms that she felt herself unworthy.

Unattractive. Unwanted.

The damnable dilemma is that I see her worth...

"But she said no," John reminded himself. "So in fact, it's no dilemma at all."

Scowling, John forced his attention back to the notes.

Shuffling through the pages, he decided to recopy the section with Olivia's last corrections written in the margins. The rehearsal earlier that morning had gone well enough, though the tension between them had been thick enough to cut with a knife.

"Blast, where is my pen?" he grumbled, shifting a pile of old letters. The top one floated free and fell faceup on the blotter.

"Hmmph." John picked it up and made a face. It was the note Lady Loose Screw had sent to Prescott, giving directions to the garden meeting where she had failed to show up.

Thank God that embarrassment has disappeared from my life.

He was about to crumple the paper and toss it in the fire when the looping shape of an "S" caught his eye. A closer look, a quick comparison of the two examples of penmanship—and then, all at once, he felt his stomach tighten and twist into a knot.

"S" for her secrets.

"S" for his stupidity.

Balling a fist, John slammed it against the desktop, once, twice...

And then a third time.

Punctuating the last *thwock* with a fierce oath, he leaned back and rubbed his bruised knuckles. If ever he needed a reminder that reason ought to rule his life...

"Be damned with reason!" he roared.

Abandoning any pretense of cool, calm command, John rose and grabbed up his coat. "She bloody well owes me an explanation."

He shouldered open the study door and marched across the entrance hall, his boots beating a staccato tattoo on black and white marble tiles.

Chess—they reminded him of chess and their first encounter, where Olivia had blithely referred to chess as a metaphor for war.

"Oh, you want to cross swords, Miss Sloane?" John muttered, his mood growing more dangerous by the moment. "Well, be advised that you shall get your wish."

He was about throw open the front door when his sister burst in, clutching the hand of a disheveled Lucy Simmonds.

"John!" Tears had traced two salty trails down Cecilia's ashen cheeks. "Thank God you are here!"

He froze. "What's wrong?" As he spoke, he caught sight of the bruise darkening the little girl's brow. "Good Lord, Lucy is injured—"

"Oh, don't fret about me, sir," interrupted Lucy in a rush. "It's Scottie!" She paused to catch her breath.

"Scottie has been abducted!" finished his sister.

"It's wrong." Too agitated to remain seated at her desk, Olivia rose and began to pace the perimeter of the study. "I have to tell him."

Her late morning meeting with the earl to rehearse the speech had been a tense, awkward encounter—and not merely because of their sexual intimacies. Keeping mum about Lady Loose Screw had made her brusque and snappish, which in turn had made the earl stiff and tongue-tied. The more she thought about it, the more she felt guilty about keeping her other *nom de plume* a secret. She hadn't told him an outright lie, but neither had she been completely honest.

And somehow the oblique deception felt worse.

"I have to tell him," she repeated.

Anna remained silent, a pensive frown pursed on her lips.

Caro, however, was far more decisive. "Tell him you are Lady Loose Screw? Why? Isn't that asking for fireworks?"

Olivia gave an inward wince. Close as they all were, she had not yet told her sisters about the personal pyrotechnics between her and the earl. It still felt too new, too confusing.

"I think you should wait for exactly the right moment," went on Caro. "If I were you, I'd wait until he declared his undying love. Then I would burst into tears and say I've a dreadful secret to confess, which of course he'll forgive without batting an eye."

"Such a scenario may make for passionate poetry," replied Olivia. "But I'm afraid my real life conundrums are not going to be solved by a sonnet. To begin with, the Earl of Wrexham is *not* in love with me. We are ... well, I suppose we are best described as comrades-in-arms."

Because I can't think of a term that describes two rational people struck by temporary madness.

To Anna, she added, "I think we should consider putting Byron's works under lock and key until she's old enough to understand that melodrama has no place, save on the theatrical stage."

Caro made a face.

"Livvie has a point," murmured Anna.

"Ha! Sometimes real life can be far more dramatic than prose or poetry," retorted their younger sister. "You've said so yourself!"

"Be that as it may, a debate on artistic license is not helping Livvie at this moment." Anna turned her attention to Olivia. "I agree that Caro's suggestion errs on the side of excessive fantasy, but to be perfectly pragmatic, there are a number of good arguments for waiting until after the earl's speech. A distraction at this point might jeopardize all the good you have worked for."

"True," conceded Olivia. "I've been trying to convince myself of much the same thing. And yet, it somehow feels wrong. I—I can't explain why."

For a long moment, the only sound in the room was the *tap, tap* of Anna's pen point against a sheet of foolscap. "Then instead of trying to reason it out with your head, you must simply trust your heart."

Trust.

Olivia rose, the next move in this complex chess game of politics and secrets suddenly clear as crystal. "You're right. If I hurry, I can still pay a call at his sister's residence during the proper visiting hours."

"I'll come with you," offered Anna. "You'll want to request a private meeting with the earl, and my presence may help keep Lady Silliman from becoming too curious about the reason."

Grateful for the company, Olivia quickly accepted.

"Drat it all," groused Caro. "It's grossly unfair that I must always stay at home while you two are allowed to gallivant hither and yon having exceedingly exciting Adventures."

"Caro, we are walking to Berkeley Square, not Kubla Khan's fabled city of Xanadu," pointed out Olivia. "So I don't expect to encounter any adventure along the way. And 'exceedingly exciting' are not the adjectives I would use to describe the upcoming meeting."

Exceedingly uncomfortable was more accurate.

She had no idea how the earl was going to react to the revelation. But she doubted that he would be overjoyed.

"You've a role to play here," said Anna. "If Mama inquires where we have gone, you may tell her that we've taken a stroll to deliver a book to Lady Silliman. It's close enough to the truth without stirring any marriage machinations directed at the earl."

"Oh, very well. I shall—what is the military expression—hold the fort until you return."

Olivia blew out her cheeks. It did feel a little like she was marching into battle. "Thank you. It won't be for long."

"Abducted!" It took a heartbeat for the word to sink in. A stab of fear lanced through John's chest, but then all of his military training triggered to full alert, emotion giving way to iron-willed detachment.

"Tell me exactly what happened," he said calmly.

Steadied by his voice, Cecilia recounted what she had seen, with Lucy supplying the rest if the details.

"You are a *very* brave girl," he said when the story was done.

"I kicked the man hard and bit his hand," replied Lucy with a note of savage satisfaction. "But he wouldn't let go of Scottie. Then the other man hit me and I fell down."

John felt a clench of cold fury inside his chest. "You could not have shown more courage, sweetheart. Now I shall take command."

"W-will Scottie be all right?" asked Lucy, her bravado giving way to apprehension.

"Yes," said the earl emphatically. "I promise you, nothing is going to happen to him."

Lucy looked reassured, but Cecilia's eyes betrayed her own misgivings. "John, I fear that I and the guards saw little that might help identify—"

He silenced her with a quick wave. "I think you should take Lucy up for a hot bath and put her to bed while I map out a strategy for what to do next." That his sister had little in the way of clues to offer didn't matter—he fully expected a ransom note would be arriving at any moment.

And he had an inkling of what the price would be for the safe return of his son.

As Cecilia shepherded the little girl upstairs, John tried to keep his thoughts in the present and not the past. It was, he knew, a waste of time and focus to second-guess his decisions. Still, he could not help but feel a knifeblade of guilt prick against his conscience. If he hadn't let passion distract him from keeping a closer eye on his son... if he hadn't reneged on his promise to be part of the Tower outing...

"Yes, I have made mistakes, but all is not lost," he reminded himself. "As in chess, I must study the board and see how to move my pieces to regain the advantage."

The difference between victory and defeat often came to seeing a subtle opening and seizing the moment. Prescott's captors would demand an unconditional surrender. After all, they held the upper hand. But John had not survived the brutal Peninsular War without learning a few dirty tricks of his own.

Improvise—strike where they least expect it.

Fisting his hands, he returned to the study and found the small wooden chest where his brother-in-law kept a pair of deadly accurate Manton dueling pistols under lock and key.

No doubt the dastards would promise to free his son unharmed if he followed orders, but John didn't trust them to keep their word. During the war he had been involved in several hostage exchanges, all of which had ended badly. His son would have seen too much, heard too much for his captors to risk releasing him.

If Scottie is to survive, I shall have to rescue him myself.

But the question was how.

John closed the pistol case and began searching the cabinet for the box containing bullets and powder. He hadn't yet formulated a plan of attack. That would depend on the first message—but when it came, he would be ready to spring into action.

"What are you going to tell him?" asked Anna as they descended the townhouse steps and turned onto High Street.

"The truth," answered Olivia.

"The *whole* truth?" pressed her sister.

"In for a penny, in for a pound," she quipped. "But in answer to your question, yes, the whole truth. He is a man of integrity and principle—I think he deserves no less."

Anna was about to answer when her eyes suddenly

narrowed as a curricle came tooling around the corner. "Speaking of integrity, here comes a man who has none to speak of."

It appeared that the Devil Davenport was going to fly past them when all at once his vehicle skidded to a stop.

"Good day, ladies," he said, jumping down from his perch. "Might I stroll with you for a bit?"

"We are in a hurry, milord," said Olivia. "And in no mood to socialize."

"Neither am I." He drawled an order to his tiger to walk the horses and then quickened his steps to catch up. "Allow me to cut to the chase," he said, "an apt expression—seeing as Lord Wrexham's son has just been abducted from the grounds of the Tower menagerie."

"Abducted!" Much as Olivia itched to slap the supercilious smile from his handsome face, she kept her temper in check. "Why the devil are you dawdling here with us when you should be flying to Berkeley Square?" she demanded.

"Oh, don't bother quizzing him, Livvie," snapped Anna, her eyes sparking with ire. "Everyone knows the Devil doesn't exert himself unless he sees a profit in it for himself."

"I was, in fact, exerting myself far more than I usually do. If you'll notice, my team is in quite a lather."

Anna made a rude noise.

"However, there are complications. So when I spotted you two," he went on with infuriating sangfroid, "I saw the chance to solve several problems all at once." Moving with deceptive quickness, he slipped between Olivia and her sister and linked arms with them. "Do hear me out, ladies," he murmured, setting off at a brisk pace toward the east side of Berkeley Square.

"You had better have more to say than your usual sardonic quips, sir," said Olivia. "This is no laughing matter. We must alert the earl—"

"His sister is doing so as we speak," assured Davenport. "However, the information will be of little value to him, for she knows naught about the deed, save that the bantling has been snatched."

"And *you* know more?" demanded Anna.

"I do," he answered. "And if you will kindly refrain from interrupting, I shall explain."

Two hot spots of scarlet bloomed on Anna's cheeks, but to Olivia's relief, she kept her mouth shut.

"Please hurry, sir," urged Olivia, feeling her insides tangling into a tight knot.

Davenport's drawl steeled to a sharper edge. "I happened to be driving by the Tower grounds when I saw a little girl tussling with two grown men"—a darting glance at Anna—"and even an indolent wastrel like myself could not ignore the child's cries—she was, by the by, screeching loudly enough to wake the dead. However, just as I was about to leap down from my perch, the varlets pushed her down and fled to a waiting carriage. It was then that I saw they had a lad in their clutches."

"How do you know it was the earl's son—" began Olivia, but he waved her to silence.

"At that same moment, Lady Silliman came bolting out of the archway, followed by two of the Tower guards," he explained. "As she was very vocal in raising the alarm that her nephew had been abducted, I put two and two together..."

"The saving grace of a debauched gamester is the fact that he knows how to add," muttered Anna under her breath.

To his credit, noted Olivia, Davenport ignored the jibe. "Lady Silliman gathered up the girl, and I assumed that she would inform Wrexham of the situation just as quickly as I could. So I decided to follow the abductors."

"Oh, well done, sir!" she murmured.

"With all due modesty, I must say that my skill with the reins is not half shabby, so I managed to catch up with them just as they pulled to a halt in the coaching yard of The Dirty Duck Tavern. The boy—he was now trussed and gagged—was transferred to another vehicle."

"And no one tried to stop them when clearly something havey-cavey was going on?" burst out Anna.

"It is a rough part of Town, Miss Anna. People tend to mind their own business."

"Including you," she snapped in reply.

"Unlike the Earl of Wrexham, I am no hero," he shot back. "There were four men there, all armed. The noble sacrifice of my humble self seemed likely not only to ruin a rather expensive coat but also to prove useless in freeing the bantling."

Olivia was suddenly aware that as he had been talking, the marquess had quickened his pace and was now guiding them into the central gardens of Berkeley Square. Edging off the pathway and into the secluded shelter of a grouping of holly bushes, he drew to a halt.

"I have no time to linger, so listen carefully, ladies.

The important thing is that I recognized the waiting carriage. Though stripped of any identifying crest or decorative touches, it's familiar to me because Lord Lumley uses it for making the rounds of his carousing spots in the stews of Southwark."

"Lumley—he is one of the leaders of the faction opposing Lord Wrexham's reform bill," interjected Olivia.

"Correct. Not only that, I recognized the viscount himself as he took the boy from the original abductors, despite his wearing an oversized hat and driving cloak."

If Lumley were part of the plot, it was likely that the Duke of Sommers was also involved. Swallowing hard, she tried to keep the bitter taste of fear from tainting her tongue.

Ruthless—most men turn ruthless when their self-interest is threatened.

As Davenport gave them a detailed description of the carriage, he pulled a paper from his pocket. "And here's another bit of information that may prove useful. Lumley has a hunting lodge in the wilds of Dartmoor, southwest of Exeter, near Tavistock. Very few people among Polite Society know of its existence, for he uses it mainly to entertain his dissolute cronies. I would think it's a good bet that he will take the earl's son there."

"As a hostage?" said Olivia as she watched the marquess smooth the creases from a hand-drawn map.

"Yes. It stands to reason, don't you think? The viscount and his friends wish to silence Wrexham's voice in the upcoming Parliamentary debate, but the Perfect Hero cannot be bribed or bullied. So they must strike at the only spot where he is vulnerable."

To give the Devil his due, allowed Olivia, his smirking show of indolent boredom appeared to mask a sharp-witted mind.

"The dastards!" she exclaimed, sure that he was right. "It's imperative that the earl know all of this without delay! There is a good chance that he might catch up with the coach before it reaches the lodge." Freeing Prescott would be a good deal easier on the road.

"That," said Davenport, "is exactly why I stopped you two ladies. You see, it so happens that I have a very pressing engagement, and it would cause some rather unpleasant consequences if I were to be late."

"An amorous encounter, I presume," muttered her sister. "Or do you have several planned for the evening that depend on precise timing?"

"Presume what you wish, Miss Anna," he answered evenly. "Suffice it to say, you two will be doing both the earl and me a great favor if you would consent to serve as messengers in my stead." From inside his coat, the marquess withdrew a cylindrical package encased in a felt bag. "You might also give him these two items. One is a telescope fitted with special set of powerful lenses, and the other is a weapon that strikes silently but is just as effective as a pistol in putting an opponent out of action. Wrexham might find both of them useful in his pursuit of the villains. Stealth and the element of surprise can be a distinct advantage in the line of battle."

"Where did you get them?" asked Anna.

"Never mind," he replied. "They are a trifle complicated, so let me show you how they work."

"I accompanied my father on several of his expeditions," said Olivia. "I am well acquainted with scientific instruments like telescopes."

"Excellent." Davenport quickly explained how to maneuver the dials and levers.

"Yes," she murmured, "I understand. How ingenious."

"Thank God you are clever, Miss Sloane. But I had a feeling you would be."

"The weapon, however…" She stared at the hinged rods and the odd cording wrapped around them in consternation."

"It's not really as puzzling as it looks," he said, unfolding two metal arms upward from the center shaft to form a "Y."

Olivia was still mystified.

"Click these levers and rotate the bezel to lock the arms in place," he explained. "As you see, the cord is fastened securely to the arms, and then can be stretched, like so." He grasped the small leather square centered on its length and pulled it back. "There's a sack of steel balls inside the felt bag. You place one of them on the leather patch, then take aim and release." A sharp, snapping *thwang* rent the air. "It's nearly as effective as a bullet, but far more silent."

"Good Lord. It's a sling of sorts, but what is the cord made of? I've never seen anything like it."

"It's made from the sap of the *Hevea brasiliensis* tree, which grows in Brazil."

"And how—" began Anna.

"I don't have time to explain." Quickly rebagging the two items, he pressed them and the map into Olivia's hands. "Tell Wrexham that the instruments are borrowed, so he must return them when he is done, or else pay me the full value—which is bloody expensive." A jaunty salute. "And now, I really must be off."

"Wait, one last question—" she began.

But Davenport was already gone, his lanky, black-clad form moving like an Underworld wraith through the lengthening shadows of the bushes.

Chapter Nineteen

ℒord Wrexham is not at home," intoned the butler, cracking open the townhouse door barely wide enough to be civil.

Damnation. Biting back an audible oath, Olivia forced a smile. "Then would you be so kind as to inform Lady Silliman that Miss Sloane and her sister wish to have a word with her."

"I am afraid that Lady Silliman is not at home, either."

"It is a most urgent matter," she insisted, refusing to be brushed off. "Not at home" was the standard excuse when a member of the *beau monde* was not in the mood for visitors. Dropping her voice a notch, she added, "Concerning a private family trouble. I assure you, she will wish to hear what I have to say."

The butler hesitated, and then opened the door a bit wider. "Please come in. I shall see if she is available."

Olivia and Anna did not have to wait long. Cecilia appeared in the drawing room within minutes, her face looking pale and drawn. "Hawkins says you wish to speak to me," she said softly. "About a private matter?"

"Your nephew," said Olivia quickly. "And the fact that he's been snatched by the earl's political enemies."

"H-how did you—"

"The Devil Davenport witnessed it, and asked us to deliver some information that may help Lord Wrexham recover his son."

Cecilia sat down rather abruptly on the sofa.

Olivia gave a terse summary of the marquess's account. "I think he's right to suspect that Prescott has been taken to Dartmoor. And he has a very good idea of where." Paper crackled as she took the map from her pocket. "It's here, in the moors near Tavistock. However, there's a good chance that the earl can catch up with the coach before it arrives at its destination. But he will have to act quickly."

"Oh, Lud, John *must* have this information. The trouble is, he's left for Shropshire." Cecilia explained that a ransom note had arrived, and the earl had decided to return to his country estate in order to fetch his former batman and drill sergeant to help with the fight to regain his son.

"By the time he returns to London, it will be too late. Once the villains have Prescott locked away in the lodge, it will be far more difficult—and dangerous—to free him," exclaimed Olivia. "It's absolutely imperative that I find a way to alert Wrexham *now*."

"Oh, but John and I cannot expect you to involve yourself in such a risk," protested Cecilia.

"But I must! For Prescott's sake," answered Olivia. *Not to speak of my own sense of honor*, she added to herself. "You see, Davenport gave me a special telescope that may be useful for the earl, and he showed me how to work it. It's rather complicated—"

"Oh, dear," interrupted Cecilia. "I am all thumbs when it come to anything like that, so I'd be useless in trying to help."

"I'm quite skilled with maps as well," said Olivia. "So I may be able to serve as a surrogate for his batman."

"I admire your courage and your resourcefulness, Miss Sloane. But the ransom note warned of dire consequences should John tell anyone about Prescott's abduction. And even assuming the logistics could be worked out, such an arrangement would stir a storm of scandal if it became known—both for you and my brother." Cecilia expelled a ragged sigh. "I—I simply don't see how it is possible."

"Actually, I do," piped up Anna.

Olivia looked at her sister.

"You have a traveling coach, do you not, Lady Silliman?" said Anna.

Cecilia nodded.

"If *you* were to set out for Shropshire, it wouldn't stir a breath of scandal if Olivia goes with you. I could tell my mother that Lucy was taken ill and you asked her to accompany you to the country with the two children. That will explain her absence as well as that of Prescott. The *ton* won't think twice about accepting the story—it's known that the two of you are friends from the Royal Historical Society."

"So far, so good," said Olivia. "Go on."

"Lady Silliman will order her coachman to drive neck and leather—four horses should outpace Lord Wrexham's cabriolet," explained Anna. "Then, when you catch up with him, Olivia can transfer to his vehicle with no one in London being the wiser."

Cecilia blinked. "My goodness, you have quite a knack for plotting! I vow, that's nearly as good as one of Sir Sharpe Quill's novels."

"Yes, well, my sister is quite well acquainted with such tales." Olivia quirked a tiny smile before once again turning deadly serious. "She's right—it will work. And it makes sense that you return to Shropshire, where Wrexham's former soldiers can keep a close eye on you and Lucy. It will also help ensure that the public does not learn that Prescott has gone missing. Once we have him back," she added resolutely, "the earl can decide how to deal with the matter."

"I—" Cecilia hesitated, but only for a moment. "I think what you have suggested is a thumping good plan—but again I must ask you, are you sure you wish to take such a hellish risk?"

"Have your coachman ready the horses as quickly as possible. Then fetch Lucy," answered Olivia. "A hamper of provisions would be wise as well. And perhaps a valise of extra clothing for the earl. I shall need to borrow some garments as well, along with a traveling cloak. Wrexham and I will want to travel fast."

As Cecilia hurried away to make the arrangements, she turned to her sister. "Let us hope you are as convincing a storyteller with Mama."

"Leave it to me," assured Anna.

"One last thing," said Olivia. "If you put this in your novel, I shall throttle you."

* * *

The road twisted sharply and then dropped into a steep incline, forcing John to rein in his impatience and slow his lathered team to a more moderate speed.

Perseverance, he counseled himself grimly. *I must remain coldly calm and calculating.* Sliding into a ditch or breaking an axle would end any chance of catching up to the men who had Prescott in their clutches.

He was halfway down the hill when the sound of pounding hooves coming up behind him wrenched an oath from his lips.

"The damn devil is driving like a banshee! If he's not careful, he'll get us both killed." He ventured a look over his shoulder. It was a coach and four, coming on at a reckless pace.

John swore again, then was forced to turn his attention back to his own team. Few men were skilled enough to attempt such speed on this stretch of the road...

He darted another quick glance to the rear, confirming his sudden suspicion.

As the road flattened, he drew over, allowing his sister's coachman to rumble by him before drawing the larger vehicle to a skidding stop.

Scottie. His heart lurched against his ribs, and for a long moment John couldn't bring himself to breathe.

The coach door flew open and a cloaked figure scrambled down the iron rungs.

"Cecilia!" he called. "In God's name, what..."

It wasn't his sister, he realized, and yet the hooded garment was one he recognized as hers. Shading his eyes, he stared in mute consternation, wondering whether worry for his son was addling his wits.

"John!"

That was unmistakably his sister's voice, and sure enough, an instant later her face appeared in the open doorway. *Important news...change of plans...hurry*— gesturing wildly, she shouted out a jumbled explanation that was half-lost in the gusting wind.

As Cecilia tried to make herself heard, the cloaked figure hoisted a valise and hamper up to the storage nook beneath his front seat.

"What in the name of Hades..." The sound of feet climbing over the running boards caused him to wrench his gaze from the coach to his own cabriolet. "You!" he exclaimed as the hood slipped back, revealing a pair of molten jade green eyes.

"Yes, me," said Olivia. "I shall explain everything, but first let us turn around. We need to go back several miles and take the road for Exeter."

"*We* are not going anywhere, Miss Sloane."

"Oh, yes," she replied, "*we* are." Taking a sheet of paper and a felt bag from inside the cloak, she held them under his nose. "I've learned where the dastards are likely taking Prescott, sir. Here's a map. And I've some special instruments that may give you an advantage in planning a strategy for stopping them."

"Thank you," snapped John a little roughly, his anger with her still painfully raw. "You may hand them over and be gone."

"I fear that is impossible."

Damnation. She was right. He looked around to see the coach and four was already galloping on toward Shropshire.

"Besides, a second pair of eyes and hands will be helpful," she went on.

"I don't need your help," he said. "My batman—"

"You haven't time to fetch your batman, sir. There's a good chance we can catch up to villains—and by the by, it's Lord Lumley who is in charge—before they reach the place where they plan to imprison Prescott. But only if we fly without delay."

John hesitated, but only for a heartbeat. Circling his team, he urged them back up the hill. "You have a good deal of explaining to do," he growled, shifting his grip on the reins.

A slanted glance showed that beneath the wind-whipped highlights of color, her face had gone very pale. "Yes, I know. I'm aware that it's my fault Prescott was snatched. You were meant to escort them to the Tower but because of me, you changed your plans."

"It's not your fault," he said stiffly. "They were clearly watching and waiting for their opportunity. If not this morning, they would have found another way."

Olivia turned to face him, the sunlight catching the bruise-dark shadows under her eyes and in the hollows of her cheeks. He made himself look away.

"Still, you've every right to be angry with me," she went on, ignoring his attempt at reassurance. "However, let us put aside emotions and be practical, sir. Because of my father's work in the wilds, I am very good at reading maps, and possess a number of other skills that may prove useful. If need be, I even know how to load and fire a weapon."

Whatever her other faults, she had pluck, John conceded. Expelling a harried sigh, he muttered, "Let us hope it doesn't come to that."

"Quite right." Brushing a wind-snarled lock of hair

from her cheek, Olivia tersely explained about her encounter with Davenport, and the information he had passed on.

"What he surmises makes sense," said John, after thinking over what he had just heard. "Lumley will want to take Scottie somewhere secure from prying eyes. The hunting lodge is the most likely choice."

And if I am wrong?

No, he wouldn't think about that. The truth was, he had no other clues to pursue.

"Thank you," he added in a tight voice. To give her credit, she had reacted with remarkable composure in quickly putting together a plan to alert him of the marquess's news. Without those vital details, he would, at this moment, be blundering in the wrong direction. "I appreciate the risks you have taken to tell me this."

Ducking her head, she began fumbling with the strings of the bag in her lap. "In addition to the map, Lord Davenport gave me this spotting scope. He seems to feel its special lenses may prove very useful to you once we get close to the dastards. Let me explain—"

"I know how to use a damn military spyglass," snapped John, feeling torn between ire and admiration for her gritty resolve.

"Not this one," said Olivia. "It's awfully complicated." The strings finally loosened, allowing her to strip off the felt. "You see, there are a number of levers and screws."

The words triggered another fresh rush of anger. *Yes, you are very good with screws, aren't you?*

Her expression turned even more shadowed, as if she were reading his thoughts. "No doubt you would figure it out on your own, sir. The truth is, I wanted to be alone with you not only to apologize for unwittingly putting your son into danger, but also to make a confession."

The wind tugged at her bonnet ribbons, tangling them into knots. "I've interfered with your life—and Prescott's—more than you know. You see, I—I am Lady Loose Screw, whose clandestine correspondence has created such helter-pelter complications in your life."

"Actually," replied John, "I had just figured that out on my own."

"Ah." The wind nearly drowned out the sound. "No wonder you are furious. May I ask how?"

"Your handwriting. I happened to come across the letter you wrote to Scottie as I was working on notes for the speech." John kept his eyes on the road. "Why didn't you tell me earlier, instead of keeping it a damn secret?"

Though their bodies were not quite touching, he sensed her stiffen. "I have had to keep secrets for most of my life, Lord Wrexham," she replied in a low voice. "Men—and most of Society—give no quarter to a woman who dares to be different."

Assuring himself that he had every right to feel betrayed, John intended to snap a sarcastic reply. But the words seemed stick in his throat. "You lied to me," he muttered instead. "Or at least misled me."

"I did," agreed Olivia, making no effort to defend her actions. "And it was wrong of me." He heard the whisper of leather clenching leather as she knotted her gloved hands together. "I wanted to tell you after you learned that I was The Beacon, but I worried that it would distract you from the speech. And then... well, and then I became very confused."

She sat in silence for several moments. "I was tongued-tied, I suppose. And afraid of your scorn."

He released the pent-up air in his lungs. "Miss Sloane—"

"No, please let me finish," said Olivia. "It was never meant maliciously, sir. Indeed, it began as a harmless jest, but things went awry." She quickly explained about the reply she had written, and how Anna had sent it off on a whim. "We never expected anything to come of it." She lifted her chin. "What more can I say? I—I am very sorry."

"I suppose I should have guessed." All at once, John felt his anger ebb away. "After all, the chances of there being *two* women in all of England possessing such a cleverness with words are virtually nil." He looked around to catch the spasm of surprise flitting over her features. "I hate to admit it, but you were scathingly funny as Lady Loose Screw."

Olivia made an odd little sound in her throat.

A rueful grin crept to his lips. "Perhaps you should ask Hurley if you can pen a second column in the Gazette, giving advice on love and marriage."

"I think I might consign my pen to the Devil," came her ragged reply. "It seems to stir naught but trouble."

"On the contrary, it stirs fire and brimstone, which lights a much-needed flame under our country's complacency."

"Even though your bum feels a bit singed?"

He laughed. "My sister would probably say it was all for the good. She thinks I've become a trifle too stiff-rumped."

The cabriolet crested the hill and the horses quickened their pace over the flat ground.

"Be that as it may, sir, we had best put talk of our

own foibles aside and concentrate on the far more important matter at hand." Pulling another paper from inside her cloak, Olivia unfolded a large printed road map and smoothed it open in her lap. "Your sister's coachman gave me this, and I have been studying the routes that lead to Devonshire. We must turn at the next signpost, and that will take us to Guilford. From there we can make a beeline for Aldershot, which will allow us to pick up the main route into Andover."

She traced a finger over a long line stretching from London to the narrow finger of land to the west. "It seems logical that Lumley will want to travel as fast as possible and by the shortest route to Exeter. So my guess is that's the road he will take."

"Agreed," said John, as he assessed just how much farther he could push his tired animals before he would need to stop and change to a fresh team. "That you have a detailed description of the coach should allow us to know sooner rather than later whether we have made the right choice."

"He can't have gone north—there are no roads that would take him in the direction of Dartmoor. And while it's possible to cut south, through Salisbury and the Vale of Wardour, it makes no sense to do so when speed is of the essence."

"Assuming Davenport is correct in his information. Assuming they are intent on speed and not stealth."

"I think we are on the right track, sir," she said stoutly.

"I pray so, Miss Sloane." John urged an extra burst of speed from his lathered horses. "I pray so."

Chapter Twenty

Olivia drank down the last of the steaming tea, and handed the mug back to the stableboy. Drawing her cloak a little tighter around her shoulders, she sat back on the seat, grateful for the pleasant warmth that was now radiating out through her limbs. Despite the mildness of the early evening, the rising breeze and galloping pace had left her fingers and toes feeling chilled to the bone.

John appeared from behind a massive barouche that was having one of its rear wheels repaired, looking none too happy about his negotiations with the inn's ostler. "I managed to procure the last available team of horses," he grumbled. "Though the knave charged me an extra guinea." Perching a hip on the cabriolet's running board, he made a face. "I hope that my blunt will hold out. I expected to pick up additional funds when I reached Wrexham Manor."

A fat leather purse dropped onto the floorboard of the driver's box. "Your sister and I thought that might be the case," said Olivia. "So she sent this along with me."

He pursed his lips in a rueful smile. "If Whitehall were wise enough to hire ladies as quartermasters for our military forces, we would win the war within six months."

"Quite likely. We tend to think of the practical things." She handed him the other mug of tea she had ordered. "Here, drink this while it is still hot."

Their hands touched for a fleeting moment, sending a sweet curl of warmth through her tired body.

John downed it in several quick gulps. "Thank you," he murmured, stepping aside to let the stablehands harness the fresh horses to their vehicle. "I am sorry to ask you to continue on without a longer stop here. I am sure you must be tired and famished. However, I should like to reach Odiham before we stop for the night."

Olivia waited for the men to move away before replying. "First of all, sir, we need to establish some rules for this journey."

"You dislike rules," he quipped.

"Not when they serve a higher purpose," she retorted. "My likes and dislikes aren't important, Wrexham. Freeing Prescott is the only thing that matters. And so, if you wish to drive from here to Hades without pausing, you must do so without any thought to my creature comforts. Having accompanied my father on a very lengthy expedition into the wilds, I assure you that I am no stranger to traveling under primitive conditions."

He shifted his stance, his face unreadable.

"I asked to be part of this, knowing full well what to expect." That, Olivia admitted to herself, was perhaps not entirely true, but it was close enough. The earl's real feelings about her presence were still impossible to gauge.

"There is a hamper of food under the seat," she went on. "We can eat while we drive."

A final jangling of brass and leather announced that the harnessing of the new team was finished. The horses stomped and snorted, their breath forming pale puffs of vapor against the thickening shadows. The earl turned abruptly and swung a boot up to the foot rail—he, too, appeared impatient to be off.

"Very well, I shall take you at your word," he said, climbing up to his perch and gathering the reins. "But I warn you, the going may get a little rough."

Rough.

Hours later, as she gingerly climbed down from the cabriolet, Olivia had to admit that the ruts of the shortcut to the Andover toll road were worse than any she had experienced in Albania. Her bottom was bruised, her bones were aching, her joints were stiff...

John steadied her stumble, saving her from pitching headfirst into a rather foul-looking pile of horse droppings.

"Come," he murmured, taking a firm hold of her arm. "I shall rouse the proprietor and order up a hot meal."

She squinted at the darkened inn. "Never mind a meal. Let us hope they have an empty bed." In truth, she was willing to tussle with the tavern cats for a spot on the rag rug by the hearth. Anything, as long as it was softer than oak planking and marginally warm.

"It's important to eat," insisted John. "We must keep our strength up."

Too tired to argue, Olivia let herself be led to the front door.

Summoned by the earl's insistent knocking, the sleepy

innkeeper undid the locks and escorted them to a small private parlor adjacent to the empty tap room. John accompanied him back into the corridor, then reappeared several minutes later. "Despite the hour, he has agreed to serve us. It will be simple fare—a venison stew and day-old bread—but hot and hearty." He gave a rueful grimace. "Thank God for my sister's purse. However, no amount of coins could change the fact that there is only one bed-chamber available."

"Mmmm?" Eyes half-closed, she hitched her chair a little closer to the hearth and held her hands out to the freshly stirred coals. "Sounds delightful."

John raised a bemused brow.

"What?" mumbled Olivia, catching the tiny twitch.

"Nothing," he replied, moving to her side and adding a few logs to the fire. A few skillful jabs of the poker quickly raised a cheerful blaze.

The heat chased the numbness from her hands and toes. "Oh, how blissfully divine."

So was the hearty stew. Despite her assertions to the contrary, she quickly consumed a large helping, along with a glass of claret that John insisted she drink.

"Feeling better?"

"Much." Heaving a sigh of contentment, Olivia was aware of a mellow drowsiness stealing over her. It felt as if unseen hands were wrapping all the little aches and pains in cotton wool...

Somehow she found herself floating up the narrow flight of stairs. A latch clicked, a door opened and then closed. The flame of the earl's guttering candle illuminated a small room with a large featherbed, a narrow dressing table and washstand—with precious little space left over for the diminutive bureau wedged beside the dormer window.

"I apologize again for the accommodations—or lack thereof." John set the light down. "I shall, of course, sleep on the floor." Looking a little dubiously at what little there was of it, he added, "Or, if you prefer, I could seek a pallet of straw in the stable."

One bedchamber. Olivia shook off her muzziness as his earlier words suddenly took on a clearer echo in her head.

"D-don't be absurd," she replied. "The bed is large enough for the two of us to sleep comfortably."

He shook his head. "No, no, it would be awfully ungentlemanly to impose—"

Olivia cut him off with a chuffed sigh. "I appreciate your notions of nobility, Wrexham, but I thought we agreed to dispense with such things for the duration of this journey. You will be driving hard tomorrow, so it's imperative that you get some proper rest. If anyone should sleep on the floor it is I." She rubbed at the crick in her neck. "Although since I fully intend to spell you at the ribbons, I wouldn't mind something softer than a plank for a bed."

His mouth twitched.

A smile? She wasn't sure.

"You are pluck to the bone, Miss Sloane."

"Oh, please, don't mention the word 'bone,'" she muttered, wincing as she gingerly took a seat on the eiderdown coverlet. Even the softest of feathers felt horribly hard.

This time, his amusement was unmistakable. "I swear," he said with a low chuckle, "you are quite unlike any other lady I've ever met before."

"Much to your exasperation, I know..." Olivia's eyes flew open. "W-what are you doing?"

"Taking off your half boots," said John, who was already kneeling. "Stop squirming. The laces have tangled into knots."

It took him several long moments to ease the mud-spattered leather from her stockinged feet. After setting them by the washstand, he rose and moved—a little stiffly, she noted—around to the far side of the bed. "Our valises have been brought up. I shall blow out the candle, and if we both turn our backs to each other, we should be able to dress for sleep with a minimum of embarrassment."

"But of course, sir. That's a perfectly practical suggestion," replied Olivia, accepting the bag she had borrowed from Cecilia. "As you know, I'm not a dewy-eyed virgin, so I'm not about to fall into a maidenly swoon."

However, the soft rustling of fabric from across the darkened room did stir a fluttery little tingle along the length of her spine. She couldn't help but picture John's shirt sliding over his head, revealing the stretch of sun-bronzed muscle and the peppering of coarse curls on his chest—

Don't.

Olivia wriggled out of her garments and hastily assumed the heavy linen nightrail that the earl's sister had provided.

Don't think of his body, don't think of his kisses.

Only fools made the same mistake twice, and she prided herself on possessing a modicum of intelligence. Though that might be questionable, she admitted to herself, given her actions over the last few weeks.

Fishing a hairbrush out of the valise, Olivia edged over to the dressing table, grateful that the looking glass was naught but a dark blur within the moon-kissed shadows. Unpinning her locks, she ran the bristles through her windblown curls, hoping to smooth the worst of the snarls.

"You may turn around now, sir," she murmured, keeping her own back to the center of the room. "Even without the shroud of near darkness, modesty has been more than satisfied."

His steps stirred hardly a sound. There was something very intimate about the moment—the soundless shadows, the whisper of bare feet on the rag rug, the soft swoosh of her strokes.

Swoosh, swoosh.

John's touch was light as a zephyr—for an instant she thought it was merely a draft ruffling the loose linen of her nightrail. But then the pressure of his fingers deepened, their tips massaging at her taut muscles.

"Wrexham." Her voice wavered somewhere between question and a protest.

"Hush," he said, his palms stroking inward from the ridge of her shoulders to top of her spine.

Olivia wasn't sure that she was capable of further speech. Simply breathing was proving difficult.

"The travel was rough today," he added. The heat of him was soothingly warm. "And I fear it will likely get rougher."

His hands kept up their steady movement. *Strong, sure.* Yielding to his slow circling, the knots in her back began to melt away.

As for the lump in her throat...

Closing her eyes, she gave herself up to the sweet, sweet sensations of his touch. Heaven only knew if she would ever feel it again.

"You need not subject yourself to further discomforts," murmured John after another few minutes. "I have the map, the instruments. Come morning, you can stay here while I continue on. I can send a letter to Cecilia and she will come fetch you."

"Absolutely not," said Olivia, finally finding her voice. "I've come this far, and I've no intention of turning back and allowing you to face those dastards on your own."

"Miss Sloane, I've faced far worse odds on the battle-field."

"No doubt," she replied. "But you are forgetting that this is my fight, too. These men wish to silence *our* voice by threatening your son. I want to help you quash their nefarious plans—together we will free Prescott and see them defeated in Parliament."

A muffled sound, and a breath of air tickled against the nape of her neck. *A sigh? A laugh? Or perhaps a mixture of the two.*

"You," he murmured, "are far too determined—and too stubborn—for your own good."

"Yes, well, that is why the tabbies of the *ton* call me the Hellion of High Street. I have had to be tough as nails in order to follow my passions, sir. If that offends you, I am sorry. But I am not, and will never be, a demure demoiselle."

"It was not meant as a criticism," said John softly. Drawing his thumbs down either side of her spine, he set his hands on the small of her back. Their warmth sent a lick of heat spiraling through her core.

"Now come to bed, Miss Sloane. We had better get some rest. We need to keep up our strength so that when we catch up to these dastards, we can beat them to a pulp."

Bed. The memory of their passionate interlude in Hurley's sun-dappled cottage bed stirred an ache of longing. In watching the working of Society from the shadows of London's ballrooms, she had come to think that strong, solid men of integrity didn't exist in the flesh. And yet here was a paragon of masculine muscle who was kind and caring despite his brusque manner. He was...he was, in a word...

Perfect.

Olivia wasn't aware of having spoken, but somehow a sound must have slipped out, for he heard him chuckle.

"A lumpy mattress is hardly perfect," murmured John. "But I shall not complain. For all its faults, it's more comfortable than a hard slab of wind-chilled oak."

However, a sharp grunt as he rolled onto his side quickly belied his optimism.

"*Hmmph.* I wonder what the cursed fellow has stashed in the stuffing." He was no longer laughing. "My guess is turnips."

"Or perhaps chestnuts for the Christmas season celebrations," she suggested. "The lumps feel smaller than turnips."

The suggestion drew a low snort of amusement. But whatever the source, they were clearly making it hard for the earl to settle into sleep.

Without thinking, Olivia reached out and brushed the long, curling hair from the column of his neck. "Try to relax. Your muscles are bunched in knots. Let me see if I can help loosen them."

She took his silence as permission to continue. Deepening the pressure, she stroked her fingers over his flesh, moving up and down, from the base of his skull to the line of his spine.

"Better?"

"Much."

Emboldened, Olivia raised her other hand and went to work on his shoulders. The lone candle was still alight, its soft flicker playing over the thin cotton nightshirt, the dark contours of muscle. She had never touched a man like this before. There was a profound sense of connection to such a long, leisurely interlude of exploring his body. A warmth radiating from something far different, far deeper than sexual heat. The tingling against her skin transcended passion. The sensation was gentler, calmer—and yet no less powerful.

John grunted and she felt the tension start to ease from his body.

It was very sensuous to slide her hands over his spine, his shoulderblades, his muscles and feel the nuances of shape and textures—sharp and rounded, hard and soft. She found herself acutely aware of the broad stretch of shoulders, the curve of his rib cage, the lean tapered waist.

"A man," she mused aloud, "is really built quite differently from a woman."

The pillows muffled most of John's laugh. "It would be even more evident were I to turn over."

She rather wished he would.

He grunted again, a rougher rumble from somewhere deep in his throat.

"I'm not hurting you, am I?" she asked, realizing that

in her curiosity to learn all his subtle contours she had begun kneading his flesh with greater intensity.

"Mmmm, no, it feels good." He shifted slightly. "More than good, in fact. Divine."

"Your legs must be tired from bracing yourself on the box." Moving her hands downward, Olivia skimmed over the intriguing curve of his buttocks to the back of his thighs, taking secret pleasure in making his lean, lithe body respond to her touch.

"Lovely," he mumbled. "Lovely."

As she worked over his legs, her strokes settled into a smooth rhythm. A soothing rhythm that held a natural intimacy.

At the thought, Olivia stifled a laugh. This was, she realized, her very first night of sleeping with a man. How oddly ironic that there was nothing romantic about it.

But then, there was a closeness between them that few newlyweds had. More than lovers, they were friends. At least she hoped they were, despite all the tangled emotions.

A sound—a snore—interrupted her reveries. She kept up her rubbing until she was sure from his breathing that he had fallen asleep.

"Rest easy, Wrexham," she whispered. "Together we will find Prescott and bring him home safely."

Drawing the blanket higher, she carefully tucked it over his shoulders and smoothed a curling lock of hair from his jaw before blowing out the candle and slipping under the covers beside him.

Chapter Twenty-One

$\mathcal{B}$y the by, what did you tell our host to explain our odd traveling arrangements?" asked Olivia the next morning, after the innkeeper set down a breakfast tray and bustled out of the private parlor.

"Oh, as to that, I managed to cobble together a story worthy of Sir Sharpe Quill," replied John.

She choked on her swallow of tea.

"But likely you are far too serious to read those horrid novels." He took up a piece of buttered toast and downed it in two quick bites. "Cecilia seems to find them highly amusing—a fact which in this case proved very useful in spinning a colorful yarn." A steaming cup of coffee, dark as Hades, washed down the bread. "We are husband and wife, racing to reach your dying mother in Plymouth before she shuffles off her mortal coil. Our coach cracked an axle, so we had to leave it behind with our servants and hire the only vehicle available in Guildford—the cabriolet."

"Not bad," she murmured. "Though, I daresay Sir

Sharpe Quill would have added a few more embellishments."

The idea of Olivia curled up in an armchair with one of the wildly racy books brought a twitch of amusement to his lips. "So, you have actually read his stories?"

"Every one of them," replied Olivia.

John wasn't sure whether she was jesting, but other more important things pushed the topic from his thoughts. "Finish your tea, Miss Sloane. The cabriolet will be ready shortly and we mustn't waste a moment."

Dawn was just beginning to lighten the horizon as a flick of his whip set the horses into a steady trot. His muscles were a trifle sore from the pounding pace of yesterday, but he had suffered far worse conditions in Portugal. As for Olivia, he slanted a sidelong look at her profile. Head bent, she was studying the large road map supplied by his sister's coachman.

"Mr. Young says that if we take the left fork just past the village of Wheaton, it will cut over six miles off the distance to Andover." She looked up, her face already powdered with gritty dust. "It's a trifle narrow, he warns, and requires some driving skill. But the way is fairly flat and he's confident that we can gain time."

Pluck to the bone. Fatigue was etched at the corners of her lovely green eyes, and yet her spirit remained undaunted.

"Thank you," he said. "It won't be comfortable for you, but I cannot pass up the chance to gain ground on Scottie and his captors."

She snagged the flapping ribbons of her bonnet and tied them tighter. "Curse my comfort, Wrexham. Let your team fly."

The shortcut proved a testing route to negotiate, and the constant twists and jolts left his own insides feeling a little queasy. He could only imagine how his less battle-hardened companion was feeling. Her face, however, was a mask of stoic resolve.

I must be ruthless in pursuing every advantage, no matter how tenuous, John reminded himself. He couldn't afford any tender sentiment. Not with Prescott's life being used as a pawn in this dangerous game of check and checkmate.

Dangerous.

There was Olivia's reputation to think of as well. So far, they had been traveling on less frequented roads. Once they returned to the main toll road, the chances of being recognized grew greater.

That neither of them had sought to shine beneath the glittering chandeliers of Mayfair's ballrooms should be a point in their favor. However, John knew all too well how a chance encounter, a casual glance from some London acquaintance, could prove disastrous.

His brooding growing blacker by the moment, they made it to the outskirts of Andover an hour ahead of the expected time.

"I shall ask around among the stablehands about whether they've seen a vehicle resembling Lumley's coach," muttered John as he pulled into the yard of the first inn they came to. "If I have no luck here, we shall have to waste the precious time we have won in stopping at the others along the way."

"Patience," counseled Olivia. "It's important to learn how far ahead they are, so we can begin to plan a strategy."

"I'm well aware of that," he snapped, then swiped a

twist of brambles from the sleeve of his coat. "I'm sorry. My nerves are a bit on edge."

Olivia was already climbing down from the cabriolet. "I shall see about ordering some hot tea while you make your inquiries. Sometimes, the tavern wenches and scullery maids are more observant than the men who handle the horses."

No one, however, remembered a coach or tavern patron matching the descriptions that Davenport had given to them.

The same was true at the next two inns.

Fuming with frustration, John climbed down at the last possibility before the road skirted around a stretch of dense forest and led down into the center of Andover.

"If I were Lumley, I wouldn't choose to stop in the center of town," he muttered. "Too many eyes."

Olivia nodded in agreement. "Shall I go order more tea?" A pause. "Or perhaps you would prefer a mug of ale."

"If I drink any more liquid, I shall need a pisspot," growled John under his breath. Pulling out his fast-dwindling purse, he shook out a few coins. "That was unforgivably crude." His mood and now his gentlemanly manners were going to hell in a handbasket. "Here, take these and order some sustenance for yourself while I see if I can find the ostler and coax some useful information from him."

"Don't be discouraged, sir. They could very well have chosen to stop on the far side of town, figuring that travelers from London are more apt to halt here for rest and refreshments."

It was a reasonable point, but John wasn't feeling very

reasonable. "You need not coat the facts with spun sugar. The fact is, we are chasing naught but a hope and prayer. The dastards could be going anywhere." Fisting his hands, he tried not to think of his son, alone and frightened, being taken to God-Knows-Where. "Sommers has several estates in Yorkshire, so Davenport may have guessed wrong."

"Don't lose hope," said Olivia quietly.

"Are you always this damnably cheerful in the face of adversity?" he muttered.

"Not damnably cheerful, sir. Damnably stubborn, as you so rightly pointed out."

Her stalwart humor made him feel a little ashamed of himself. "You go have a rest while I make the inquiries out here," he said in a more measured tone. "If we have no luck, we shall do as you suggest and circle around the town and begin anew. Someone has to have seen them."

Placing the handful of coins in the pocket of her cloak, Olivia decided to stretch her legs near the paddocks rather than seek shelter and sustenance inside the inn. On further reflection, she had decided that Lumley would not likely show his face in a tavern.

"Think," she told herself, quickening her pace without looking up. Walking seemed to help stimulate her creative process, and if ever she needed an inspired idea it was now. "Is there something we are overlooking in our search?" she murmured to herself. "Some question we are not asking?" She felt in her heart that they were on the right track.

But my heart has been feeling odd things of late.

Olivia brushed that thought aside, forcing herself to

concentrate on the search for Prescott. The earl was doing
a heroic job of keeping his fears under rein, but she could
tell that his inner anguish was mounting.

We must not—we will not—fail.

"Oiy!"

A muffled grunt echoed the thud as she collided with
a grain barrel, knocking the postboy who was perched on
its top to the ground.

"I'm so sorry," she said, offering a hand to help him up.

Scowling, the lad rose on his own and made a show
of dusting off his grubby pantaloons. "Wimmen," he
scoffed.

Olivia bit back a smile. "Yes, we are silly creatures,
aren't we? I must have looked like a chicken, running
around without a head."

That drew a grudging grin.

"Here, allow me to make amends." She drew a bag of
horehound drops from her pocket and offered it to him.

The lad stared for a moment. "Yer giving me the whole
bag?"

"Why, yes. It's the least I can do to make up for making you take such a thumping tumble."

"Oiy, I take much worse ones from the horses," he
confided, after quickly stuffing the sweets into his jacket.
"Barrels don't kick."

"That must hurt like the very Devil," she murmured
sympathetically. Among their various duties, postboys
rode bareback on a hired team of horses to the next
changing inn, then brought them back. It was dirty and
often dangerous work for such small lads...

Her pulse kicked up a notch. "Unlike me, I daresay you
have to keep your eyes open at all times to avoid trouble."

"Oiy," he answered. "Ye got te have sharp peepers."

"I wonder…" Olivia lowered her voice. "By any chance did you see a black coach stop here recently?" She quickly described Lumley's vehicle. "The passengers might have been acting a little havey-cavey."

The lad's expression turned a touch wary. "I see a lot o' coaches. Why ye asking?"

She prayed that her instincts were correct—and that her skill at storytelling was half as good as Anna's. "Because my evil uncle has snatched my nephew, a lad about your age, from his parents. You see, he's squandered all of his own blunt on drink, and now he's threatening to sell Scottie to white slavers in Plymouth unless my sister and her husband pay a large ransom. But they haven't got the money."

"Oiy," breathed the lad. "And ye mean te stop them?" His tone didn't express much confidence in her abilities.

"Yes," said Olivia. "You see, my husband is a famous military hero, but he's traveling incognito."

"In-cog-neezo?" The lad looked a tad more impressed.

"In disguise," she explained. "So they don't know they're being followed." Her next words were a whisper. "My Hero has got some very special weapons in his possession and he knows how to use them. But first we must pick up my evil uncle's trail."

The lad looked around before answering. "Yer on the right track. I saw them here. The big, dark cove ye described paid the ostler a pair of sovereign te keep quiet about their stop."

"How long ago?"

"Late last night. Near dusk."

"Damnation," swore Olivia. There was still a daunting

gap between them. And if the coach had continued on all night . . .

"But I overheard them saying they were planning te stop in Weyhill fer a meal and lodging. The dark cove said that he knew the owner of the King's Arms."

"Thank you, er . . ."

"Will. My name's Will."

"I'm grateful, Will." She began fumbling in her cloak for the coins John had given her.

"That's not all I heard," added Will, his eyes narrowing. "They hit yer nephew when he tried to open the coach door. And then the dark cove's two friends started arguing with him."

Three captors—Wrexham will find that useful.

"The two others wanted to stay on the toll road leading te Exeter. But the dark cove said they will turn at Sparkford and take the back roads, on account of his knowing inns that will keep mum about what they see."

"Bless you," murmured Olivia as she tucked all the coins she had into his pocket. "That's all I can give you right now. But I shall see that you get a *pair* of gold sovereigns for your help."

"Oiy!"

"But for now, it's best to be quiet about this, Will," she counseled. "I'd rather not trust anyone, especially your ostler, until we free Scottie."

The lad nodded his understanding. "Is yer hero husband gonna thump the stuffing out of yer evil uncle?"

"Oh, yes. Be assured that the dark cove is going to be sorry that he ever declared war on the Perfect Hero."

Chapter Twenty-Two

*T*hree hours," announced John with savage satisfaction as he climbed back up to the driver's bench. A discreet bribe to one of the inn's stableboys had elicited the welcome news about their quarry. "Our breakneck efforts have paid off. Lumley is only three hours ahead of us."

"Then we should be in a position to confront them come tomorrow morning," said Olivia.

"Yes. If young Will's information remains correct, the viscount will be stopping for the night at The Hanged Man." He flexed his sore shoulders and took up the reins. They had traveled a day and night with only a brief respite since Olivia's fortuitous encounter with the postboy, and so far everything the lad told her had proved accurate.

"An apt name," went on John, "seeing as the bastard will wish he were already dead when I catch up to him."

"I'm assuming that you are not planning to stay at the same inn," said Olivia. "Given that lodgings are somewhat sparse along these back roads, it will likely mean we will snatch a few hours of sleep under the stars, so as to be ready to take them by surprise."

"Correct." He glanced at her profile. The poke of her bonnet cast her eyes in shadow, but the darkness couldn't quite hide the fact that her face was gray with fatigue. "I'm sorry. I know that I've pushed hard—"

"Don't be sorry. I have rather missed the madcap adventures of my youth, so this is an exhilarating change from my sedate London life," interrupted Olivia. "Remind me to tell you the details of the trek my father and I made in Crete," she added dryly. "One of his assistants had offended the tribal leader and we had to make a rather hasty departure from the mountains of Iraklio and journey to the port city of Zakros. And as the fellow was related to half the island, we had to avoid a good many of the villages."

"Most ladies would not think of that trip or this one as remotely exhilarating."

"True," she replied. "But by now, you know my way of thinking is vastly different from that of most ladies."

"True," echoed John. *For which I am profoundly grateful*, he added to himself.

She shot him a quizzical look. "That had an ominous inflection to it. I hope you are not regretting your decision to let me accompany you. I have done my best not to slow you down."

Not once, he reflected, had she voiced a complaint about being tired or cold, or hungry.

"I have tried to be useful," she added.

"You have been more than useful, Miss Sloane. And not just with Will. You've been an intrepid navigator in finding the shortest routes, a resourceful quartermaster in keeping us well-supplied with sustenance for the interminable hours of driving. Most of all, you've been a steadfast companion in trying to distract me from worrying about Scottie. I am not unaware that our long philosophical talks, and your entertaining tales of exotic travel have been designed with that in mind."

"Y-you give me too much credit for altruism, sir," replied Olivia. "I enjoy talking about abstract ideas. And you are one of the very few people of my acquaintance who cares to listen."

"I've learned more from you than I can recount."

"And I from you."

John must have betrayed his surprise, for she quickly went on to explain, "You have a steady calmness about you, Wrexham. You are careful and deliberate."

"I think perhaps I am too cautious," he countered. "Too regimented."

"Well, maybe on a few occasions." An impish smile, which curled up just a little higher at the right side of her mouth than it did on the left. He had come to recognize it as a sign that she was teasing him.

Instead of taking real umbrage he gave a mock grimace and growled. It was rather nice to be teased.

Olivia smothered a laugh. "Yes, I know it must come as a rude shock for the Perfect Hero to be told he is not without a teeny flaw."

"Good Lord, kindly refrain from reminding me of that ridiculous moniker. If I knew which journalist first penned it, I would cheerfully break every bone in his writing hand."

"It was actually very handy in impressing Will," she pointed out. "And besides, it would be rather churlish to inflict bodily harm on Mr. Hurley after all he has done to assist us with your speech."

"I might have known it was Hurley," groused John. "He would put his own grandmother in the boxing ring with Gentleman Jackson if he thought it would sell newspapers."

"Yes, and being a Hurley, she would probably knock the champion pugilist on his arse," said Olivia.

John let out a chuckle. "Probably."

"In all seriousness, sir, getting back to what I have learned from you..." She turned her head, just enough for the sunlight to spark the shadows from her eyes. "I tend to react emotionally to ideas. It has been a new experience for me to watch how you think things through so very coolly and logically. I am trying to emulate your restraint."

It took all the restraint he possessed not to lean forward and brush away the tiny smudge on her cheek.

With his tongue.

So much for cool logic.

The luminous green of her gaze was making him a little dizzy. Behind her, the fluttery leaves of the hedgerow swayed in shimmering shades of emerald and jade.

"Right," he said gruffly, fisting the reins and urging the horses to a faster pace. "Restraint."

The rutted road forced his eyes and his attention back to the task of driving. In response to the sudden jostling, Olivia shifted on the seat and slid a little closer to the side rail to steady herself.

"Have you thought up a plan of how to confront Lumley tomorrow?" she asked suddenly, the intimate connection between them giving way to the more pressing demands of the moment.

"I have," replied John, missing the warmth of her closeness more than he cared to admit. "We won't reach The Hanged Man until well after dark. I intend to drive on, and then choose a spot for us to pull off the road and rest until dawn. Davenport's telescope will allow me to pick a surveillance spot and watch the activities in the stable yard. I have an idea on how to stop them…"

He paused to draw an unhappy breath. "But it means that I must ask you to play a more active role than I would wish."

"I am more than ready to do so, Wrexham. I trust I have made that clear from the start," said Olivia.

"So you have. But that does not make it any easier for me to ask it of you. The risk is small, and yet it is there."

"What do you wish for me to do?" she asked without hesitation.

"I plan to enter the inn at first light, while Lumley and his cohorts are still sleeping. It seems likely that just one of the dastards will be with Scottie, while the two others share other quarters."

"You would need to be sure of the room, would you not, so as not to make a mistake and alert them to your presence?" she asked.

"Correct. The innkeeper will know, of course. But we have to assume he is friends with Lumley and would not willingly aid us."

"So a confrontation must be done carefully, and with no chance for him to raise the alarm," interjected Olivia.

"Yes." The next words did not come easy. "That is where I must ask your help. A lone female, appearing distraught and disheveled at the inn's door, is not likely to raise suspicions despite the early hour. My guess is the proprietor will unbolt the door to allow you entrance—"

She quickly took over the narrative for him. "At which point I shall fall faint into his arms and beg for a seat and a reviving cordial. He will have no choice but to assist me into a private parlor, leaving the door untended so that you may enter unobserved."

"I was thinking—"

Ignoring his attempt to speak, Olivia continued in a rush. "My histrionics will keep him distracted long enough for you to slip into the parlor." A tight smile. "At which point you will have the opportunity to persuade the man that it is in his best interests to cooperate with you."

John raised a brow. "You are frighteningly good at plotting this sort of thing."

"I have had ample experience," came the cryptic reply.

Yet another intriguing facet of Olivia Sloane.

"How—" he began.

"Never mind that now. What matters is that it's a good plan. I have every confidence that it will work."

"Let us pray so," he said softly.

"This seems a good spot." John drew the tired horses to a halt by an opening in the hedgerow. The scudding moonlight showed a faint cart path leading into a sloping meadow of tall grasses. And looming straight ahead, the dark silhouette of a granite outcropping rose out of the fescue, high enough to provide a vantage point over the road. "We are not more than a quarter mile past the inn, which puts us in perfect position for our plan."

Olivia nodded. Tired, hungry, bruised to the bone by the bumps and ruts, she wanted only to descend from the hellish perch and feel the solid earth beneath her feet. She had purchased provisions that morning so at least they had food and drink to fill their bellies. As for sleep—the thought stirred a longing for her soft feather-bed at home. But the truth was, her nerves were coiled too tightly to unwind into repose.

Time enough for rest when this ordeal was over.

A glance at John as he guided the team through the narrow opening showed fatigue etched on his face. His cheekbones were sharp as knifeblades, and the shadows under his eyes were black as burnt coals.

"Dare we light a fire?" she asked, once they had stopped and he had unhitched the horses. "I could toast some bread and cheese, as well as heat water for tea."

He looked to the thick copse of trees between them and the inn. "Yes, I see no harm in it. I noted a few farmhouses nearby, so a wisp of smoke won't attract any undue attention."

A pot and several primitive utensils had been added to their meager store of possessions. John set to gathering wood and kindling a flame while she unpacked the hamper. Sheltered within a niche of the wind-carved stone, the sticks were soon blazing with a welcome warmth.

They ate in companionable silence, the earl seemingly lost in his own thoughts.

Brooding no doubt about the coming day, thought Olivia, and all that could go wrong.

All will go right.

Looking up, she offered a silent prayer to the heavens.

Perhaps it was just her imagination, but the tendrils of mist seemed to skirl away, leaving the stars to shine with a sudden brighter brilliance—a sign that she chose to take as a good omen. Her father had held a great respect for primitive traditions and talismans...

Impelled by some powerful inner force, Olivia rose without a word and began to sway slowly back and forth in front of the undulating flames. After a few moments, she raised her arms, adding the rhythmic gestures she recalled from the tribal dances in Crete.

John looked up. He said nothing but beneath the curl of his dark lashes she saw the glimmer of a question.

He thinks me mad—and perhaps I am.

"My father wrote extensively about native rituals," she explained. *Sway, sway.* "Every culture has rituals for good luck—they are designed to align the local gods in their favor." *Sway, sway.* "Like my father, I am very open-minded about these things. I see no harm in appealing to all the deities in the universe." *Sway, sway.* She began to move her feet in soft, shuffling steps, tracing a wide circle around the fire.

The pale moonlight spun like silvery vapor around the brighter flickers of gold.

Caught up in her movements and the mesmerizing play of light against dark, Olivia didn't realize that she was not alone until a shadow fell across her face.

"I am willing to try anything," murmured John as he fell in step beside her and began mimicking her movements.

The flames seemed to lick up higher and she was suddenly hot all over. Unwinding her shawl from her shoulders, she let it trail away behind her.

Sway, sway.

And then an unexpected spin as John took hold of her and pulled her into his arms. Sparks flew up from the crackling logs, and somewhere in the nearby trees a pair of nightingales broke into a twittering song. Taking her hand, John slid into the figures of a waltz. He was humming, the soft notes in perfect harmony with the music of the night.

"That's lovely," she murmured after several bars. "What is it?"

"Beethoven's Sonata '*Quasi una fantasia.*'" A silver shimmer winked over his smile. "Which is more popularly known as the Moonlight Sonata."

Moonlight. Firelight.

The tangled glow traced over the planes of his face, the flame-tipped lashes, the stubbled whiskers, the lean jaw. Silhouetted against the iron gray stone he looked like a wild Druid warrior. *Dark. Dangerous.*

Olivia felt the breath shiver in her throat. This was not the civilized, straitlaced earl of a London ballroom, but a far more primitive male.

A little frightening, but undeniably alluring.

He released her and suddenly shucked off his coat. Beneath the white linen of his shirt, the shadowy contours of his muscles rippled as he raised his arms in martial salute to the moon.

The Perfect Hero, limned in the magic of midnight.

Spellbound by the sight, Olivia blurted out, "Oh, Anna and Caro would find this all terribly romantic. They enjoy…"

"They enjoy what?" he asked after a slow, spinning turn around the red-gold flames.

"Oh, er, you know—those wildly emotional scenes one reads about in novels and poetry."

John remained strangely silent. Rather than resume his

humming, he recaptured her hands, and for an interlude, the only sounds in the night were the crackling coals and their steps scuffing over the hardscrabble ground.

And the nightingales. The notes of a new song floated out from the dark, breeze-ruffled foliage of the trees.

"And you do not consider yourself romantic?" he finally asked.

Olivia shook her head. "Ye gods, no. I haven't a romantic bone in my body. My passions are purely pragmatic."

"I think you are very wrong. The essays you write are, at heart, powerfully romantic."

"Th-that's absurd. They—"

The touch of his fingertip stilled her lips. "They are romantic because they inspire us to think we can be better than we are. They give us hope that the future can be brighter."

The sudden warmth suffusing her cheeks was not from the burning branches, but rather from some inner glow.

They danced on. Olivia lost count of the steps and the minutes. Lost count of all the rational reasons to put an end to the whirling dervish dance of emotions inside her.

Stop. The inner word was lost in the echo of a myriad other longings. Throwing thought to the wind, she pulled away from John and peeled off her spencer jacket. It fell to the ground with a whispery sigh.

To her surprise, he laughed and suddenly stripped away his shirt and tossed it atop her crumpled spencer.

"You once said that waltzing was far too stilted and that we all ought to dance naked in the moonlight."

"I say a great many foolish things, Wrexham," said

Olivia, watching the light lap over his sun-bronzed skin. *I feel a great many foolish things.*

"But you say far more wise things," he murmured. He came close—too close. "And by the by, you called me John the last time we were alone in London. I should like for you to do so now."

"I—it doesn't seem right. That was when we were... friends."

"We aren't friends now?" he questioned.

I don't know what we are, she thought. Perhaps there wasn't a word to describe it.

When she didn't answer, he took another step, and once again, she was in his arms. "I should hope we are, Olivia. I feel a special bond with you that I don't have with anyone else."

She lay her cheek on his shoulder. "How strange, I feel quite the same way. I mean, I am very close to my sisters, but this feels... different."

A low chuckle. "I should hope so. I would be a little worried if you wished to kiss your sisters."

"I shouldn't wish to kiss you, either, Wrexham."

"John," he corrected. "Why not?"

"Because..." A wave of longing crested inside her. Tipping her head up, Olivia stared at the stars, hoping to hide the pearls of moisture clinging to her lashes. "Because of a great many reasons."

"Such as?" he pressed.

"Corsets, to begin with," quipped Olivia, though her throat was painfully tight.

"Ah. Corsets." John twirled the two of them in a tight circle. "I imagine they are deucedly uncomfortable things to wear."

If anything, his mood was even stranger than hers.

"Anything else?" he asked.

As if that wasn't enough? However, if he wished for more then she would humor him.

"Then let us move on to the rules of Polite Society. Do you wish a list of each and every one? As it is, we've already broken too many to enumerate."

"True." His voice was low and little rough around the edges. "But there are times when rules must yield to a more elemental force." And with that, he framed her face between his palms and possessed her mouth in a bruising kiss.

Chapter Twenty-Three

Madness.

The night before a battle, soldiers often felt a strange sort of spell bubble through their blood, thought John dimly as his lips moved hungrily over hers. A lust for life, perhaps. An affirmation that there was hope and joy in the world, not merely darkness and pain.

Olivia flinched and then softened. So sweetly, so sweetly.

And then suddenly he wasn't thinking anymore about abstractions.

Her warmth, her taste, her skin next to his—pure, primal need overwhelmed all else.

Their tongues twined, sparking a groan deep in his throat. Entangling his hands in her hair, John deepened the kiss, drinking in the intoxicating spice of her essence.

Silk on silk—his impatient fingers slid from her curls to the ties of her gown.

"Olivia," he growled, saying it over and over and over again.

In response, she found the fastenings of his trousers. One by one the buttons slipped free.

Their clothing came off, the *thump-thump* of shoe leather punctuating the soft sighs of cotton and wool.

The sounds gave way to his need-roughened rasps. Her breathing was coming in ragged little gasps.

"J-J-John."

"Say it," he demanded, sliding his palms over the swell of her hips. "Shout it."

Her cry reverberated against the surrounding stone, and he dared to believe that she wanted this just as much as he did. Swinging her up off the ground, he whirled round and round, his wild steps carrying them out to the very edge of the firelight. Spinning, spinning, their naked bodies gilded in gold and shadows.

Like two demented spirits sparked to life by some ancient alchemy.

Breathless, John slowed to a staggering stop. Olivia was laughing, and yet there were tears glistening on her lashes.

"Oh, I fear I've freed some impish inner demon in you," she whispered, her voice betraying a note of uncertainty. "And that come morning, you will regret it."

"Regret?"

"With all my unorthodox ideas and headstrong words, I've managed to turn your careful life topsy-turvy."

John held her very still. "For which I am profoundly grateful. Cecilia was right—I was in danger of becoming a stick-in-the-mud, stuck in conventional thinking. You have challenged me to see things from a different perspective."

"Yes, by knocking you flat on your arse in Mr. Hurley's garden," she quipped.

"But as I landed atop your luscious body, it was well worth the come-down."

"Ha! I'm not particularly well-padded," exclaimed Olivia. "I've none of the voluptuous curves that draw a man's attention."

"On many things, I am quite willing to defer to your intellect," he said softly, letting his hands add the emphasis. "This is not one of them."

"*John!*" Her eyes widened. "That is *very* naughty."

"So is this." He lowered his head and flicked a tongue over her bare nipple.

"However, there's naught but the forest foxes to witness my impish inner demon having his evil way with you."

Her laugh was back, a low throaty sound that had his body clenching with desire.

"You *are* going to let me have my evil way with you, aren't you?" asked John.

Yes.

"Yes," repeated Olivia, this time aloud. She touched his cheek. "Yes."

The blankets were already tucked in a shallow crevasse behind the fire. John eased her down on the flame-warmed wool.

They were both a little desperate—he to forget his fears, she supposed. And she to remember this last wild night of passion. It would, she knew, be her last lovemaking with him. This couldn't go on. She wasn't so foolish as to think a liaison was possible once they returned to London. Scandal would ruin both of them, along with her family.

But she wouldn't think of that now. Not the loneliness,

not the yearning, not the ache that would lodge in her heart.

Caro, ever the romantic, would wax poetic on doomed love.

But I can only be pragmatic and seize the moment, come what may in the future.

"Make love to me, John," she whispered. "I want you inside me." Connected in body and soul if only for a fleeting interlude. "I . . ." The word "love" almost slipped free.

I love you.

That, too, she wished to shout loud enough to be heard in the heavens. But it would be unfair to him. His fine-honed sense of honor was already cutting like a blade against his conscience. No matter her own pain, Olivia could not bear to sharpen its edge.

She had refused his offer—best to leave it at that.

"You what?" he prompted, pressing his lips to the pulsepoint at her throat.

"I . . . need you. Now." *And forever.* But that, she knew, was nothing more than a moonspun dream.

"And I need you," rasped John. "More than you can imagine."

"Then let us celebrate our bond, and offer up our spirit of friendship as an homage to the local deities," said Olivia. "So that they will favor us with good fortune on the morrow."

"I . . ." A hesitation hung for an instant on his lips. "I agree."

Perhaps it was the shadowy starlight or some unseen midnight magic casting a spell over their bodies, but their lovemaking was far softer and slower than their previous coupling.

The nighttime darkness wrapped them in velvet, smoothing their touch to a gossamer lightness. Olivia brushed her fingertips through the coarse curls of hair on his chest, vowing to memorize every nuanced shape of his skin, every chiseled contour of his ribs and muscle.

John inhaled sharply as she trailed her hand down over his flat belly and found his manhood. *Satin and steel. Hard and soft.* The pulsing of heat against the curl of her palm made her want to weep with joy for the present moment, and longing for...

No, I will not think of that.

Closing her eyes to the sting of salt, Olivia drew her caresses up and down his length, reveling in his masculine beauty. *The perfect hero.*

His breathing quickened, his body tightened in response to her touch. With a wordless groan, he seized her wrist, and then she was beneath him. Arching up, she opened herself to his gentle thrust.

Their rhythm had a desperate tenderness. No words, no sounds, save for the beating of their hearts.

She crested and came with a silent shout, and an instant later his essence spilled in a silvery pool on the folds of the blanket, its pale glimmer like liquid moonbeams.

The gentle crackling of the coals drew John out of a deep reverie. The flames had died down to naught but a mellow glow of red-gold gleaming through the dark ashes. And yet, a warmth still filled their small shelter within the stones.

Olivia stirred as well, and gave a feline stretch. "The Road to Perdition is a good deal more enjoyable to travel than the road to Exeter," she murmured. "Especially as I was damaged goods to begin with."

John rolled on his side and drew her close. "Enjoyable indeed. But you must not think of yourself as chipped or cracked by the ride. You are whole in every way that matters."

"That is very sweet of you. But the truth is, most people will think me a broken vessel." She made a wry face. "Ruined beyond repair."

John made a show of carefully examining her face from all angles. "Hmmm, everything seems perfectly formed to me."

The firelight accentuated the flush of pink now coloring her face. She ducked her head. "It is not a jesting matter, John."

His smile disappeared. "No," he said softly. "It is not."

"I don't care for myself," Olivia said softly. "But I must not do anything to hurt Anna or Caro's chances of making a good match." She blew out a breath, the pale plume of vapor curling up into the darkness. "I should be able to dodge a scandal over this because of your sister and the fact that she is willing to help cover up our travels with the excuse that I was her guest at Wrexham Manor while you were away. But once we return to London, I think it best that we don't see each other. It might stir unwanted gossip."

"On the contrary," he replied. "To be crass, Olivia, my dancing attendance on you would only raise interest in your sisters. The *ton* is easily influenced by the glitter of a title and money."

"You could make it fashionable for rich aristocrats to court penniless nobodies?"

"You are *not* a nobody, Olivia," he said a little angrily.

"It was a figure of speech," she replied. "Thank you, but I should not like to ask such a sacrifice of you."

She turned her head, and a tumble of auburn curls fell down to curtain her face.

Hide and seek. Questions and conundrums.

Sensing that Olivia was loath to say anything more for the moment, John lay back and looked up at the stars. Their light shimmered and winked like countless points of fire, and he found himself drifting into a reflective mood.

Were there answers to life's complex conundrums hidden within the random patterns?

As he regarded the glitter, he could trace out the word "No" in his mind's eye.

And "Yes."

Somehow, he would hone his skill with language to coax that syllable from her lips.

Practice. She had, early on in their work, advised him that practice made perfect. He shifted and after listening to her slumbering breath, he ever so gently ran the back of his knuckles along the line of her jaw.

There were a great many things he wished to practice with her.

Ideas, arguments, challenges, laughter.

Which brought him to the heart of his dilemma. Honor had always been a guiding force in his life. So, what was the most honorable thing to do? Olivia...Lady Serena—to whom did he owe honor?

There was no question of who possessed his heart.

As to the moral question, there were a myriad of philosophical essays on the subject, a myriad of ideas on how to parse right and wrong. But perhaps this was a case where reason ought not overpower a more elemental emotion.

Love.

Yes, he was in love with Olivia. She was...perfect for him in every way.

Passionate, intelligent, kind, funny—her company would be endlessly exciting, endlessly inspiring.

She makes me laugh, she makes me think, she makes me feel alive.

John felt his chest constrict.

She will challenge me to be more than I think I can be.

Olivia shifted beneath the blanket and made a small sound. Slipping a protective arm over her shoulder, John drew her close and brushed a light kiss to her tangled curls.

And what, he wondered, could he offer her in return?

Respect, equality, freedom to be exactly who she wished to be.

They were, he mused, not as great as her gifts to him. But perhaps his love would make up the difference.

As for Lady Serena...

Honor must come from the heart, John decided, not a rulebook. Olivia had taught him that one could take ideas and give them personal resonance. From now on, he would...not be bound by strict conventions.

Or corsets.

The thought was suddenly liberating, and he found himself smiling as he closed his eyes and felt the breeze on his face. It held a hint of warmth—dawn seemed to promise a cloudless day.

Oddly enough, he felt optimistic about the future when

he should be terrified. But somehow, whatever deities had been stirred by their pagan rituals, they seemed to be smiling down from the Heavens and whispering their blessings.

All will be well.

Casting a last look upward, he found the star Polaris—a guiding light in the constellations—and gave a mental salute.

"I will rescue Scottie," he whispered. "I will win Olivia's heart."

After all, I am the Perfect Hero.

Chapter Twenty-Four

*T*he servants are stirring to begin their morning chores." John shifted his position on the wooded knoll overlooking the inn and raised Davenport's special spyglass for another look. While still dark, they had left the cabriolet and horses in the meadow and made their way on foot back to the cluster of weathered buildings. Dawn was just lightening the gloom, its pale, pink-tinged glow rising up from the mist-shrouded hills.

A harbinger that all would be rosy in the coming day?

Olivia fisted her hands in the folds of her cloak. Omens were all very well, but there was no question of trusting in Fate or Chance. They would, she vowed, make their own luck.

"The shutters are open." John spun a few dials and rotated a latch on the telescope. "This instrument has an uncanny ability to magnify the low light. I can see a man giving orders to a charwoman. I think it a good bet that he is the proprietor." He shifted the lens. "And there is a stirring of activity in the stable. I see a light within."

"Then we should not waste any time in putting our plan into action," she said, turning to make her way down to the paddock area.

"Olivia..."

"We have been through this all, John. My role has little risk. It is you who will face whatever danger arises." And Prescott, of course, but that had no need to be said.

She heard him exhale sharply, but he said nothing as he fell in step beside her. They descended in silence through the trees, stepping lightly and keeping close to the shadows.

A brief pause by the storage sheds, where they had agreed to part paths...no last-minute review, just a fierce squeeze of her arm...a fleeting brush of his lips to her brow.

"Be careful," he growled, and then was gone.

Forcing herself to focus on the coming confrontation rather than the nebulous swirls of grays left in his wake, Olivia quickly loosened her hairpins and added another smudge of dirt to her cheeks. Sounding half-hysterical would require little dramatic talent, she thought wryly. Her nerves were stretched tighter than a drum.

Tha-thump, tha-thump. And her heart was pounding loud enough to wake the dead.

A last tug at her skirts, and then she set out at a stumbling run for the inn's entrance. Pounding a fist upon the heavy oak door, she raised her voice in a plaintive plea.

"Please, oh please, open up! There's been an accident...my carriage..." Olivia let her words trail off into incoherent sobs.

For several agonizing moments there was no response to her cries. But at last she heard shuffling steps approaching.

"Who's there?" came the gruff query.

"Lady Willis," she answered, choosing a name at random. "From Lincolnshire. My husband and I were on our way to Plymouth…snapped axle…deep ditch." Ratcheting her anxiety up another notch, she let out a loud moan. "Leg pinned…Frantic with worry…walking half the night."

The bolt slid back with a metallic rasp.

"Thank God!" A swooning lurch forced the man to catch her awkwardly around the waist.

"Steady now, madam," he growled, trying to control the wobbling of both her body and guttering candle in his other hand. "An accident, you say?"

"Yes, yes." Olivia kept a hard clutch on his coat. "We lost our way in the dark, I…" She let out another whimper. "F-forgive me. M-might I sit for a moment and perhaps have a sip of some restorative beverage? I fear my s-strength is nearly gone."

A grunt. "Ye had best come along to the private parlor and have a tipple of sherry while I fetch my wife from the kitchen."

That confirmed he was the proprietor.

"Bless you," she mumbled, hitching her weight against his hip to force him another step back from the door.

Heaving an exasperated sigh, the man shuffled a half-turn and lifted his light. "This way."

Pressing close to the age-blackened door frame, John listened to the retreating tread of their steps.

One, two…He counted to ten before slipping inside and following the wavering flame.

* * *

"Th-thank you, sir," stammered Olivia, accepting the glass of sherry with a trembling hand.

The innkeeper gave a curt grunt. "Rest here and regain your strength, madam. My ostler will take you to rescue your husband as soon we have finished helping our overnight guests to depart."

"But..." she said weakly, darting a quick look at the half-open parlor door. To her relief, there was a stirring in the shadows.

"It won't take long," said the man brusquely. "I've a duty to those who have paid for my services—"

A metallic *click* caused him to turn around abruptly.

"Actually, your guests will not be leaving quite so soon after all," said John softly. "You see, your friend Lumley and his cohorts have abducted my son. And I happen to know they have him captive in one of your rooms upstairs."

Olivia watched as he raised his pistol and let it hover a hair's breadth from the man's forehead. His voice, however, remained a mild murmur. "I repeat, they have *my son*. So naturally if anyone attempts to interfere in my rescue of the lad, I will not hesitate for an instant to squash him like a bug."

The innkeeper wet his lips. "N-naturally, milord."

"Then I am sure you are going to tell me exactly in which room he is being held, as well as every tiny detail of the upper floor's layout and where the other men are lodged."

The information spilled out in a babbled rush. "I assure you, sir," added the innkeeper, after blotting the beads of sweat from his upper lip, "I had no idea there was foul play involved—"

"Save your breath for praying that my son is un-harmed," snapped John as he drew a second pistol from his coat and checked the priming. "Else you will join your friends in hanging from the gibbet."

The man choked back a groan.

John looked at Olivia, his eyes glinting gunmetal gray in the low light. "Stay here and keep an eye on him." He pushed a heavy stoneware crock across the table. "If he so much as moves a muscle, break this over his head." With that, he slipped soundlessly from the parlor.

"I—I swear, I did not…" began the innkeeper.

"Quiet," ordered Olivia, listening for any sign of movement in the corridor.

The man cringed, fear pinching his mouth shut.

Deciding that he was too concerned with self-preservation to pose a threat, she moved to the door and cracked it open. There was, she recalled vaguely, a basic military adage about the importance of having a com-rade watch one's back. The crock, however, would be of little use…

A weapon—I need a weapon.

Olivia darted a look around the room, quickly dismiss-ing the candlestick and the pewter tankards aligned on the mantel. The poker, though lethally heavy, was too un-wieldy.

"Damnation," she whispered, clenching at her cloak in frustration. "Damn, damn, damn." Her fingers opened and then closed over something more solid than wool as they moved over the folds. Up on the knoll, John had handed her the telescope's felt bag to hold and she had shoved it in her pocket for safekeeping. It was only now that she re-alized it wasn't quite empty.

Davenport's ingenious little sling was still inside.

Giving silent thanks to the Devil for showing her how to work it, she pulled it free from the felt. With a twist and a *snick*, the metal parts unfolded and locked into place.

"Damn," she repeated, suddenly realizing she had nothing to serve as ammunition...

Well, not quite nothing.

At the very bottom of her pocket were two polished pieces of carnelian. She and John had played a cursory game of chess several nights ago with his new traveling set, and somehow she had overlooked returning a pair of captured pawns to the box.

In that instant, the words of her late father echoed in her ears. *Chess is war, poppet. And the art of war requires a soldier to improvise.*

Slotting one of the pawns into the sling's leather patch, Olivia ventured a step into the darkened corridor. The stairs leading up to the bedchambers were off to the right. Only the newel post was visible from her angle of view through the archway.

Pressing her back to the dark wood wainscoting, she inched forward.

Silence, save for the thumping of her heart.

How long had John been gone? It felt like an eternity.

Unsure how to proceed, Olivia hesitated, fearful a blunder on her part might put Prescott at risk.

Another step, just enough to allow a clear view of the stairs. Watching, waiting, she held herself very still.

The sound, when it came, was so furtive that she would have missed it had she not been listening very carefully. A faint scuff of leather on wood. Only someone up to no good would seek such stealth.

Drawing back the sling's band, Olivia held her breath. *Steady, steady.*

The snout of a pistol came into view, followed by a hand, an arm...a face, eyes intent on the shadowed landing above the planked treads.

Olivia had only seen Viscount Lumley from afar at several of the Season's entertainments. But there was no mistaking the thick jowls, the ginger sidewhiskers.

Taking dead aim, she let fly with the pawn.

The smooth carnelian stone caught him flush on the temple. With a wordless grunt he dropped to the floor.

Olivia raced to the spot and retrieved the pistol.

Then everything seemed to happen at once—*The sound of a door being kicked in. A shot. A scream.*

She bit her lip to keep from crying out.

A moment later, John appeared on the landing, the smoke from his spent weapon curling around Prescott's tousled blond curls.

"John!" she cried, her legs going limp with relief.

He halted halfway down the steps. "Er, might you aim that gun barrel at some spot other than my chest?"

"Sorry." Olivia dropped her hand. "My aim, however, was not half bad just a moment ago."

She gestured to the crumpled body at the foot of the stairs.

John let out a low whistle. "How the devil..."

"Davenport's sling," explained Olivia. "And one of your chess pieces. Alas, I fear you may have to purchase a new set. The dark pawn has likely gone to its Maker."

"A noble sacrifice, considering the circumstances." He hugged his son a little tighter. "I assumed Lumley had managed to escape. The man holding Scottie said he had gone out to have the coach to be brought around a half hour earlier than previously ordered."

"He was returning, and must have sensed something was amiss," she answered. "Thank God that the Devil's ingenious little weapon was so simple to wield."

"Amen to that," murmured John.

Prescott lifted his head from his father's shoulder and flashed a sleepy smile. "Look, Miss Sloane! I have an even bigger shiner to replace the one I got in the mail coach. Lucy will be awfully impressed."

"Indeed she will," agreed Olivia. "It's truly hideous."

"You think so?" asked Prescott hopefully.

"Couldn't be worse," she confirmed.

The lad grinned. "Oh, excellent!" He snuggled a little deeper into John's arms. "But I think I have had enough of adventures for a while. I'm ready to go home."

"I, too, am anxious to wash my hands of these miserable dastards and return to more edifying tasks." John kicked the taproom door shut behind him, anxious to shake off the prickle of disgust crawling over his flesh.

Thankfully, the task of settling accounts with his son's abductors had not taken long. The innkeeper had hurriedly patched up the wounded arm and bruised jaw of Lumley's two hired minions. Hearing that the earl was not going to summon the authorities and press charges, the pair had lost no time in scuttling off into the woods.

Like dung beetles seeking to burrow beneath a fresh pile of manure.

As for Lumley...

John cracked his knuckles, taking grim satisfaction in the sting of his scraped skin. The viscount's cracked head and pummeled face would likely heal by the time he arrived in Jamaica. But it would be a long and painful journey, and a permanently disfigured nose would serve to remind him of the perils of engaging in foul play.

As would a lengthy exile in the West Indies.

At first, Lumley had not been overjoyed at the prospect of leaving the comforts of England, but given the option of either embarking from Bristol on the next merchant ship bound for the Caribbean or facing off with pistols at twenty paces within the hour, the viscount had decided that a faraway tropical climate was preferable to a cold local grave.

A wise choice, thought John. *For I would have put a bullet through his miserable brain without batting an eye.*

Now it was time for a bath, in order to scrub the filth from his skin. He rubbed a hand over his bristled jaw. And pots of strong, scalding coffee to wash the foul taste from his mouth.

Olivia was already ensconced in one of the upper chambers, with the innkeeper's wife ministering to her needs. Fear of punishment for his part in Lumley's perfidy had made the man obsequiously anxious to please. Prescott was safely tucked in the private parlor, with a bountiful breakfast promised in short order.

All in all, John mused, things had ended satisfactorily. Some measure of justice had been served by the private punishment he had meted out. The Duke of Sommers was a powerful peer, and in any public prosecution, he could have used his influence to muddle the facts of the abduction, and ensure that Lumley got off lightly. And of course there was Olivia to consider—the chance of her part in the chase becoming known was too great a risk.

No, it was better this way...

A half hour later, freshly bathed and shaved, John was feeling in an even better frame of mind as he entered the parlor. The aroma of freshly baked bread, fried gammon, and steaming coffee filled the air, adding a sweet spice to his son's laughter.

Prescott was seated at the table chattering with Olivia in between bites of thick-sliced toast slathered with strawberry jam. Another boyish laugh, another animated gesture—which left a sticky streak of red on his chin.

John paused in the doorway, his heart lurching in a topsy-turvy spin from fear to joy.

Looking around, Olivia beckoned for him to come take a seat. "Your son has just been regaling me with an account of his journey, Wrexham. He is an intrepid traveler, and quite fearless in the face of danger. Perhaps, like Mungo Park, he will become a famous explorer of unknown continents."

"I didn't have to face hungry crocodiles," piped up Prescott.

"Perhaps after..." John hesitated, a tiny lump forming in his throat at the thought of what might have happened.

After I have kept him safe and had a chance to teach him all the things he needs to know as he grows into manhood.

"...Perhaps after he has spent a few more years studying geography," he finished.

"Mr. Taylor's lessons are boring, Father," said Prescott. "Miss Sloane's tales of traveling with her father, and the sort of studies he did, are ever so much more interesting."

"I would be happy to recommend some excellent scholars, if you wish," murmured Olivia softly. "Several of my father's former assistants are bright, capable young men who would be delighted to teach such an enthusiastic pupil as Master Prescott."

"Thank you. I will look into it when we return home."

"Huzzah!"

John watched his son punctuate his elation by wolfing down another huge bite of bread.

"Sorry," mumbled Prescott, his mouth full.

"He says he was only fed watery gruel, so no wonder he's very hungry," pointed out Olivia.

No stern looks, no prim discourse on etiquette—simply a smile of understanding.

"I think that for now," said John, "we may bend the rules concerning proper manners."

"When they are made of *steel* they won't be so flexible," intoned Prescott with a scrunched scowl.

Olivia choked back a chuckle.

"Scottie..." began John.

"I know, I know, I must swallow my true feelings and make the best of it." The lad licked a dribble of strawberries from his fingers, as if the jam could help sweeten the truth. "Even Lucy says that I must surrender to Fate."

"Lucy is very wise." Olivia was looking down at her plate, so John couldn't see her expression. Her voice gave nothing away.

"Scottie," repeated John. "Perhaps Fate is not quite so wicked as you think."

Prescott stopped chewing.

"I've come to the conclusion that you have a right to know a secret. However, like the rest of the details regarding this adventure, it must be guarded very carefully."

His son nodded solemnly. "Miss Sloane would be in

great trouble if it became known that she helped us, wouldn't she?"

"Yes. But that isn't the only secret you must keep. You asked me to meet Lady Loose Screw," continued John. "And I have."

Olivia went very still.

"It is Miss Sloane who wrote those letters. She is your unknown correspondent."

Silence. And then his son's mouth quirked up at the corners. "Oh, I've known that for ages, Father."

"But..." John straightened in surprise. "How?"

"Miss Caro—Miss Sloane's sister—told me," answered Prescott. "She explained that I must keep it a Very Private Secret, and be patient because there are always many daunting obstacles in the way of True Love." A pause. "So I didn't even tell Lucy."

"I think that I shall lock away my sister's books of romantic poetry," murmured Olivia. "And throw away the key."

"An excellent idea," said John. "There is a very deep lake at Wrexham Manor. With lots of thick, slimy mud at its bottom."

Prescott did not appear discouraged by the exchange. "Indeed, Miss Caro said her sister Anna, who is very knowledgeable about all things concerning romance, felt that the two of you were well suited and it was only a matter of time before you both came to realize it."

"Forget the key. Is your lake big enough for two bodies?" inquired Olivia under her breath.

"So." Prescott fixed them with a curious stare. "Have you found a path around the obstacles?"

John cleared his throat.

"It's not that simple," said Olivia very carefully.

"That's what Lucy said when I first wrote the advertisement," intoned his son. "She said marriage is very complicated for ladies and gentlemen of the aristocracy. They must marry for practical reasons and not for love." He made a face. "I'm not sure I want to be an earl when I grow up if it means I have to live with a lady who wears a steel corset."

"As I said, Lucy is a very wise little girl," said Olivia. "It is hard to explain but, well, things are not quite so black and white as she paints—"

Another cough, this one louder, cut her off.

"You need not worry about living within the strictures of a steel corset, Scottie," said John. "After long deliberation, I have come to the conclusion that it would be wrong of me to make an offer to Lady Serena. Lucy is only partly right. Ladies and gentlemen of the *ton* do indeed have a number of practical reasons to consider when thinking of marriage."

He looked at Olivia, trying to discern what spark of emotion might be hiding beneath the scrim of her lashes. "But that does not mean that the heart has no say in the matter. I do not love Lady Serena, and I don't believe that she loves me. Mutual respect may be enough for many couples. However, I have decided that I want to feel more than a lukewarm feeling for the lady I ask to be my bride."

Prescott expelled an audible *whoosh* of relief.

Olivia's reaction was impossible to gauge.

That, John decided, was an obstacle to hurdle at a later time. For now, it was probably best to simply deal with the immediate ruts in the road.

"Speaking of Wrexham Manor," he said, after taking a

long moment to pour himself another cup of coffee. "Unless the two of you are too exhausted to travel, I should like to leave for Shropshire within the hour."

The announcement drew an enthusiastic endorsement from his son. "That's a thumping good idea, Father! I want Lucy to see my eye before it fades to boring black."

"Yes, an excellent suggestion," agreed Olivia. "But won't logistics present a problem now that there are three of us?"

"I've arranged a way around that," answered John. "Lord Lumley will not be needing a wheeled vehicle for the next journey he will be taking." He quickly explained the reasoning behind his decision, feeling it important that his son understand why justice had to take a roundabout route.

"So we will make use of the viscount's coach to return to the Manor," he finished. "The innkeeper has agreed to lend us a stablehand to drive us, and I will send Wilkins back with him to retrieve the cabriolet."

"Ah." Olivia traced a pattern of small squares on the waxed wood tabletop. "It seems you are already thinking three moves ahead of me."

Strategy. John wished he felt confident about his plan of attack for the coming days. There were still too many pieces on the board to know how this particular chess game would play out.

Chapter Twenty-Five

*T*he trip back to Shropshire was a good deal more comfortable than the helter-pelter dash in pursuit of the villains, mused Olivia as she tucked the carriage blanket around her feet and snuggled back against the borrowed coach's plush leather squabs.

Padded seats, protection from the elements—and sleep, blessed sleep! Though pressing the pace, John was allowing them more than a few snatched hours of rest at night. To avoid scandal, he was still traveling as a mere "mister" rather than the Earl of Wrexham. But Lumley's innkeeper, ever anxious for whatever goodwill he could buy, had been happy to augment their dwindling purse, so the lodgings had been comfortable, even though they had deliberately avoided the fanciest establishments along the way.

"We should be home before dusk," said John, looking up from teaching Prescott the fundamentals of chess on his travel set. The carnelian pawn had been found lodged between the floorboards, undamaged save for a tiny chip on its rounded helmet.

A battle scar was a mark of valor, John had announced, dismissing the suggestion of purchasing a new set.

"I shall not be unhappy to see the last of the coach, comfortable as it is," she replied.

As to what would come next...

Olivia watched Prescott consider the board and then carefully move his knight. He appeared unmarked by his ordeal, she noted, offering up a silent prayer of thanks for the resilience of youth. Indeed, he had been more angry at having his London interlude with Lucy interrupted than frightened, for he had never doubted that his father would rescue him.

"Have a care, Scottie," murmured John, gesturing at the chessboard. "You must look carefully at the dangers, even when they are not staring you right in the face."

"Oh." The lad studied the positions of his father's forces and then nodded. "Your knight is poised to attack my rook."

"Precisely."

Prescott made a face. "Chess is complicated."

So is life, mused Olivia with an inward sigh. The earl's announcement of his intentions regarding Lady Serena Wells had occupied her thoughts for much of the journey.

John doesn't love the Steel Corset.

A flutter, soft as the beating of butterfly wings, started to rise from the depth of her rib cage. But a ruthless slap of reason sent it plummeting back down into the darkness. That the lady wasn't going to marry him was neither here nor there.

For neither am I.

Olivia recalled her response to his proposal with piercing clarity. Even now, the force with which she had uttered the word "NO" made her wince. What man in his right mind would ask again? John could rightfully feel that honor had been satisfied and turn his attention elsewhere.

Rejection, as she knew all too well, was painful.

She turned her gaze to the mullioned window, where a passing shower was pattering the glass with rain. *Rat-tat-tat*—the staccato sounds echoed her own unsettled mood.

Rejection. Yes, the past was a painful memory. For years, she had refused to admit just how much her erstwhile lover's abandonment had hurt. Devoting her passions to abstract ideas rather emotions seemed oh-so-much safer. She had been determined never to let love anywhere near her heart again...

"A penny for your thoughts," murmured John.

Looking around, she replied lightly, "They aren't worth a farthing."

He smiled, but a pinch of concern seemed to linger between his brows. "On the contrary, they are always of value to me."

Olivia watched a flicker of light from the carriage lamp dance along the sensuous curl of his mouth. What a fool she had been to blithely believe that the head was so much smarter than the heart. *Too late*—she had realized too late that she loved him.

Now it mattered naught.

"You've far more important things to occupy your mind. The parliamentary debate is only several days away." He would make it in time to give his speech, but only by the breadth of a hair.

That left no margin to moon about love, and her regrets for keeping it at arm's length.

"Whatever the ultimate outcome of the vote, your speech shall show that the voice of Reason and Right cannot be silenced by threats and intimidation. That in itself is a victory."

"I shall do my best to rise to the occasion," said John quietly. "I am very aware of being naught but the messenger. The message comes from..." He hesitated, darting a sidelong glance at his son. "...From a far more powerful force than me alone."

"Yes, there is an army of learned philosophers from both the past and the present whose ideas on justice have served as inspiration." The coach swerved sharply, and Olivia used the sudden play of shadows to shift her gaze back to the shades of drizzled gray outside the windowpanes.

John seemed just as willing to let the subject drop. Turning his attention back to Prescott and the chessboard, he placed the lad's rook back in its previous position.

"I shall allow you to replay your move, Scottie. Look carefully and see if you can spot the other dangers lurking close by..."

Yes, I must keep my eyes open, too, mused Olivia. Her own errant moves on the checkered tiles could not be reshuffled, so going forward, she must be extra vigilant about guarding her emotions.

"Thank God you are all safe!" Cecilia enfolded Prescott in a fierce hug as he clamored down from the coach. "I can't tell you what a relief it was to receive your note in yesterday's mail assuring me that all was well," she went on, looking up at John with a radiant smile. "Of course, I am now agog to hear what happened."

He descended the iron rung steps and turned to assist Olivia. "And so you shall. But let us do it over tea and sustenance, if you please. We've not been traveling quite as swiftly as the Royal Mail, but I daresay we are all feeling a bit tired and bruised from the rigors of the road."

"Of course—"

"Look, look! I've got another shiner, Aunt Cici," piped up Prescott. "And Miss Sloane assures me it's even more gruesome than the first one." He swiveled his chin to give her a better view of the mottled purples. "I can't wait to show it to Lucy."

"You look truly awful," agreed Cecilia. "And as for Lucy, her father and I thought it best that she remain here at the Manor until you arrived and assured us that the dangers were truly over. So you are in luck—"

"*Scottie!*" Lucy's excited shout interrupted the explanation. A moment later, she came bolting out of the manor's main entrance, trailed by the earl's huffing and puffing valet.

"Hold yer horses, Missy!" he bellowed. "That's no way te greet His Lordship—"

"At ease, Withers," called John, watching his son race to meet his best friend. "I think in this instance we may dispense with formalities."

"Yes, sir!" The burly former batman slid to a halt and snapped a smart salute.

"And Withers..." Prescott and Lucy's animated voices rose above the helter-pelter flapping of skirts and shirttails. "From now on, try to loosen up a little—there's no need to wear a steel corset."

"Corset?" The valet blinked. "Yes, sir!—Er, no, sir!"

Cecilia raised a brow but refrained from comment.

Turning away, she linked arms with Olivia. "Please come this way, Miss Sloane. We'll leave Scottie to regale Lucy with the tale of his adventure, but I'm sure you would welcome the chance to sit on a seat that isn't bouncing and partake of some refreshments."

"Thank you."

"You, too, John. For of course, I am dying to hear the full story of Scottie's rescue."

"Of course," he murmured, though there would be some judicious editing of the parts pertaining...to personal matters.

Once they were settled on the facing drawing room sofas, Cecilia went through the ritual of pouring tea and passing fresh-baked pastries as she listened to his report.

"Good heavens, how very brave and resourceful of you, Miss Sloane!" she exclaimed after he recounted the part about Olivia knocking Lumley unconscious with sling and stone. "I cannot thank you enough for all your help—without your courage and cleverness from the very beginning, Scottie might well still be in the clutches of those dastards."

"Anyone in my position would have done the same," murmured Olivia.

"Indeed they would not."

John picked up where he had left off, yet he couldn't help but note that a strange tension seemed to be tightening its grip on his sister. As she shifted against the sofa pillows, her expression turned more and more distracted. On her plate, the sultana muffin was now reduced to naught but a pile of buttery crumbs.

He paused in explaining his punishment of Lumley

and took a sip of his tea. "Before I go on, Cecilia, has something occurred here at the Manor that I ought to be aware of?"

"As a matter of fact, yes," answered his sister. "And as I was informed that the matter was urgent, I feel ought to tell you of it without further delay." With an audible sigh, she put aside her plate. "There is a letter for you in your study. It was delivered yesterday by one of Lord Seabury's servants."

Lady Serena's uncle. John felt his chest constrict.

Without a word, he rose. "Please excuse me."

The thud of his boots on the parquet floor of the hallway seemed to ring with a foreboding echo, and the rasp of the door hinges swinging open took on a sinister growl. Entering his study, he slowly crossed the carpet and took a seat at his desk.

Centered on the leather blotter sat the missive, stark white against the dark leather.

What the devil could it hold?

Had he been recognized on the road? Was malicious gossip already making the rounds about his traveling with Olivia? Was Seabury now demanding a formal declaration to quash any rumors that might tarnish his relative's sterling reputation?

John stared for a moment longer, then steeled his nerve. *No matter what is inside, I will stick to my guns*, he vowed. No cajoling, no threats would force him to alter his decision. His love for Olivia was all that mattered.

Taking up his letter opener, he slowly broke the wax wafer.

The paper crackled...there were actually two sealed messages inside the outer wrapping. One was addressed to him in a light feminine hand, the other in Seabury's bold scrawl.

"In for a penny, in for a pound," he muttered, making himself open Lady Serena's note first.

It was brief and took less than a minute to read.

After a small shake to clear his head, he read it again.

The words did not alter on the third time around. "Hell's holy bells." And with that, John let out a peal of laughter.

Cecilia waited until he was gone from the room to explain. "Lord Seabury is Lady Serena Wells's uncle. She is... well..."

"I know who she is," said Olivia, putting a quick end to Cecilia's embarrassment. "She is Wrexham's intended bride."

His sister made a face. "Apparently there is no formal agreement between them, but John seems to have some misplaced sense of honor about it. I do hope he comes to his senses, for it is clear to me that the lady in question would not make him happy."

"No?" Olivia felt it was not her place to respond with anything more. The earl had changed his mind once. Perhaps he might do so again.

"No indeed," said Cecilia decisively. "His show of steely reserve is naught but a suit of armor to protect..." She hesitated. "To protect a yearning that I don't think even he dares to admit."

Olivia longed to ask what yearning, but she swallowed the urge along with a sip of her now-tepid tea.

Cecilia rearranged the silverware next to the tea tray. Twice. "May I ask you a question, Miss Sloane?"

A reluctant nod.

"Do you love my brother?"

Yes or no?

"Yes," admitted Olivia, feeling that John's sister deserved nothing less than complete honesty. "But in truth it doesn't matter. He offered marriage, but as the circumstances were somewhat tenuous, I turned him down flat."

"My brother is too experienced a soldier to be daunted by a small setback," replied Cecilia thoughtfully. She drummed her fingertips together. "And if he is, then he doesn't deserve you."

"I . . ." *What to say?*

"Leave it to me," began Cecilia.

"Oh, you mustn't—"

"Ha, my brother is not the only one who possesses some skill in battlefield strategy." She winked. "And I have a feeling that he is more than willing to surrender."

Crouching low, Prescott peeked through the slivered crack. "Hurry," he mouthed, gesturing to Lucy to come join him in the shadows behind the half-open drawing room door.

Together, they inched a little closer to the decorative molding.

"That," whispered Prescott, "is Lady Loose Screw."

Lucy studied Olivia with a critical squint. "Hmmm. She doesn't look like her corset stays are made out of steel."

"No, no—she's as flexible as one of the acrobats at Astley's," assured Prescott.

"Hmmm." Lucy cocked an ear and listened for a long moment. "I like her laugh."

"So do I," said Prescott.

"She has mud on her boots—that's promising." A note of skepticism still shaded the little girl's voice. "Do you think she can toss a stone through the hoop hanging in the oak tree?"

"Ha! Better than that—she can knock a villain flat on his arse with a stone from a sling."

At that, Lucy looked duly impressed. "Well in that case, she sounds excellent."

"No, she's not merely excellent." Prescott grinned. "She's perfect."

After a cursory look at Lord Seabury's message, which offered abject apologies for his relative's shockingly scandalous behavior, John rose and returned to the drawing room.

"Lady Serena Wells," he announced, "has eloped with a captain from the Irish Guards. As I speak, they are on their way to Gretna Green, and from there they will sail to Dublin, where he is stationed with his regiment."

Cecilia's brows shot up in surprise.

"Apparently they have been in love for quite some time," explained John, "but as he is a man of modest birth and means, her family demanded that she make a more advantageous match. However, according to her..."

Looking down at the paper, he read aloud from the note, "*I have thought long and hard, Lord Wrexham, and I have decided that it would be most unfair of me to mislead you any more than I already have about my true self and true feelings. For far too long I have tried to pretend that I fit snugly into the rigid patterncard of propriety required by Society. But the truth is, I don't give a fig for the rules. I am tired of presenting a false face. There—I have said it! And by now you know that my actions speak even louder than my words.*"

John glanced up and caught Olivia's eyes for just an instant before going on.

"*You are a most admirable gentleman, but I do not love you and it would have been wrong of me to pretend otherwise. I apologize if these words cause you any pain. However, I sense that your feelings were never truly engaged. I wish you happiness in the future, and hope that you may find the same sort of perfect match that I have.*"

"It sounds as if her corset was crafted from something other than steel after all," observed Cecilia wryly. "Satin, perhaps. Woven of soft, silky, sensuous threads."

"There is a postscript." John chuckled. "*Allow me to offer a last bit of advice, sir—you had best warn any future object of your affection that your son is an Unholy Terror. She will have to be made of sterner stuff than I to win his affection. That, or she will have to have a few loose screws in her head to think of serving as a surrogate mother to such an Imp of Satan.*"

At that, Olivia's rigid features relaxed into something close to a grin. "She's quite right. It won't be an easy task, for it's not just Prescott whom any potential bride must impress. I have a feeling Lucy's opinion carries quite a bit of weight with your son."

"Of course it does," said Cecilia with an answering smile. "My nephew is quite a bright lad, so he's already figured out that women are far smarter than men in most every respect."

"Considering the present company..." John countered his sister's arch stare with an answering waggle of his

brow. "Only an utter fool would argue with that pro-
nouncement. And I consider myself to possess some
modicum of intelligence."

"That," said his sister in an irritating drawl, "remains
to be seen." She helped herself to one of the strawberry
tarts, and proceeded to pop a small morsel into her mouth.
"So it seems we must launch a new campaign to find you
a bride—"

"I am quite sure that His Lordship would prefer not
to be distracted from his upcoming speech by any further
thoughts of marriage," intervened Olivia hastily.

Was she blushing?

John glanced at Cecilia, noting her faintly smug expression. Knowing his sister's penchant for scheming, he
felt a small spark of hope flare to life inside his chest.

Perhaps Olivia's objections to matrimony were not as
impregnable as he had first feared.

"Really, Wrexham has had enough obstacles put in his
way as it is," Olivia went on in a rush. Turning to him, she
added, "When do you plan on leaving for London?"

"Tomorrow morning," he replied. "I must meet with
supporters of the bill for a final review of the proposed
measures."

"And I intend to travel to Town the following day
with Miss Sloane and the children," announced Cecilia.
"Scottie and Lucy are eager to resume their London
visit, for they still haven't seen all the promised sights.
And our return all together is necessary to ensure that
our alibi for Miss Sloane's absence holds water."

John nodded.

"And of course, Henry and I wouldn't dream of missing your speech," went on Cecilia. "We will be in the

spectator's alcove to cheer you on." She allowed a fraction of a pause. "Would you like to join us, Miss Sloane? I cannot help but feel you have been an integral part of this effort, so you ought to be there for my brother's triumph. That is, assuming you would care to."

"I would," answered Olivia. "Very much so."

"Excellent! Then it's settled." She sliced off another bit of the tart. "I shall also host a small gathering afterward at our townhouse, to toast what I am sure will be a resounding success."

"You have great confidence in me," murmured John.

Cecilia considered the statement for the space of a heartbeat before replying coyly, "I trust you won't disappoint me."

"A breakneck chase, a night spent on the moonlit moors, a daring rescue." Caro heaved a soulful sigh.

"Not to speak of a dashing hero," added Anna dryly, "who coolly shoots the pistol out of one villain's hand, then flattens the other with his fists."

"How frightfully romantic," exclaimed Caro.

"Ha! Don't wax poetic over the perils," chided Olivia. "We weren't exactly waltzing through the wilds. Unrelenting worry over Prescott, bone-jarring fatigue, and gnawing hunger were our constant companions. Not to speak of the danger that the earl's reputation might suffer if he were spotted with a lady."

"And yours?" asked Anna.

Olivia gave a dismissive wave. "Mine didn't matter. But Wrexham's effectiveness in Parliament could have been damaged by scandal." Suddenly aware of how selfish that sounded, she bit her lip. "I—I didn't mean that the way it come out. I am aware that my actions have an impact on you and Caro. Be assured that I—that is, we— were exceedingly careful."

"Caro and I aren't worried about ourselves, Livvie," replied Anna. "We are worried about you."

Her youngest sister added a loud assent.

"You set off on a very perilous adventure and though the way was fraught with dangers, you came through it unscathed," went on Anna. "I couldn't have written a more riveting plot... er, would you mind if I borrow the dancing-in-the-moonlight scene?"

"Feel free," said Olivia, giving silent thanks that the sisterly passion for the written word was diverting attention from further probing into her own private feelings. Luckily, she hadn't mentioned the fact that both she and the earl were bare-arsed at the time.

"However," mused Anna, "I might embellish it with bit of exotic spice. Readers tend to need outrageously exaggerated emotion to hold their interest." She pursed her mouth in thought. "Perhaps—"

"Oh, I have it! Your hero and heroine should be dancing naked in the silvery light of the full moon," chimed in Caro. "I could compose a song that they could sing to the stars."

"Because shimmying through the midnight shadows without a stitch of clothing on isn't outrageous enough?" asked Olivia.

"Literary creations require a flair for Drama," replied Caro loftily.

"Well, I would be quite happy to settle for a bit of mundane boredom in real life."

"Oh, pffft, what fun is that?" muttered Caro.

A sharp *tap, tap* cut short the exchange. Anna set down her pen and pressed her fingertips together. "Much as this discussion of literary inspiration is fascinating, let us not take a side turn from the path of my original point."

Olivia chuffed a martyred sigh.

"Which was?" queried Caro.

"The direction in which Olivia's life is headed," intoned Anna with a note of seriousness that did not bode well for what was coming.

"Actually, I'd rather not go down that road right now, if you don't mind," she responded quickly.

"Ha! I knew you would respond with a clever quip. Of the three of us, you are the sharpest, both with your brain and with your tongue."

"That's not entirely true—"

"Yes, it is," confirmed Caro.

"You are scathingly witty, and frightfully observant," went on Anna. "And you use your intellect to remain detached from passion."

"I care passionately about some things," she said in a small voice.

"Yes, abstractions and ideals."

"And what is wrong with that?" countered Olivia, though she couldn't quite muster any force to her challenge.

"Nothing," replied Anna. "Except for one thing—are you happy?"

Olivia looked down at her hands, which had somehow of their own accord knotted into fists. "Not all stories have a happily ever after."

"But they *should*."

Anna's voice was soft as a feather and yet her words settled heavily on Olivia's heart.

"You can write whatever ending you wish to, Livvie," insisted Anna, "if you would dare to pick up the proverbial pen and put it to paper."

She didn't answer, for all her clever *bons mots* seemed to have chosen that instant to desert her.

"Anna is right, you know," added Caro, eschewing her usual exuberance for a more subdued tone. "If you and Wrexham are in love, what is standing in your way?"

"*If.*" Olivia sighed. "For a very small word, it looms very large."

"You don't know if the earl is in love with you?"

"I—I don't," confessed Olivia.

"Well then…" A wicked twinkle lit in Caro's eye. "Why don't you ask him? I could write a sonnet containing the question."

"Carooooo," warned Anna.

"Oh, very well. Not a sonnet then." A pause. "Maybe just a rhyming couplet."

"Our sister has her own style," pointed out Anna. "She will decide for herself how to use it."

"*If,*" repeated Olivia. "*If* I decide to use it."

"I hope you do," replied Anna. "I have a feeling there are regrets hidden in the past that you've never shared with us. Whatever they are, don't let them cloud the future."

A breeze from the open window curled through the candlelight, stirring a sudden swirl of red-gold hues. "How did the two of you become so wise?" she asked, watching the colors melt away into the darkness.

Perhaps they are right—if there is a glimmer of a chance at love, why not reach out and try to grab it before it fades away to nothing?

Anna and Caro grinned at each other. "By listening to you, of course," they chorused.

"I'm not sure that's a very good idea. I seem to have made a hash of...of so many things."

"Take heart," said Anna, leaning across a stack of books to give her a hug. "You like the challenge of fixing things that aren't right."

"Exactly." Caro squeezed her hand. "May I at least write a poem for the wedding ceremony?"

A laugh welled up in Olivia's throat. "One thing is for sure, we are never at a loss for words in this family. Though at times I wonder whether it's a curse rather than a blessing." She blinked a tear from her lashes. "But one thing I never question is the fact that I am blessed with such wonderful sisters. What would I ever do without you two?"

"Get into even more trouble without our creative counseling," quipped Anna.

"Or find your life frightfully flat," suggested Caro. "You have to admit, between the three of us, life is never boring here in High Street."

"Boring, no," agreed Olivia. "Confusing, yes."

"You are very good at reasoning out conundrums," said Anna. "Indeed, you are very good at doing most anything you put your mind to."

"I wish that were so."

"Wishes are all very well," said Caro. "But sometimes you must take a risk to make them come true."

Chapter Twenty-Six

The buzz of anticipation was growing louder and louder, its low sound amplified by the arched ceilings and ornately carved stone. Olivia pinched at the pleats of her skirts, trying not to appear too nervous. A sidelong glance either way showed that the spectator alcove in which they were standing was filled.

"What a crush." Next to her, Cecilia's husband, Henry, blotted his brow with a handkerchief while his wife craned her neck to survey the peers assembled in the main gallery.

"Look, there is Sommers," whispered Cecilia, pointing out Lumley's coconspirator. The duke was conferring with several of his cronies, and Olivia was gratified to see he was looking grim-faced.

"The man has a nerve to show himself—"

A *shush* from Henry warned her to silence.

The conversation around them died, too, as John rose.

Olivia squeezed her eyes shut, sure that the thudding of her heart must sound as loud as cannonfire to the neighboring spectators. The tension was unbearable—in another instant, she feared that her lungs might explode from the force of her pent-up breath.

"Gentlemen, I stand before you today to speak about an issue of elemental justice." John's voice rose clear and confident above the lingering hum.

She felt herself able to exhale.

"Do we, as a nation, care for those who have fought so valiantly to preserve our freedoms…"

Edging forward, she dared to open her eyes.

"So we must rise up!"

Olivia felt a wave of emotion ripple through the packed crowd and knew as she watched the faces of the peers seated in their regal chairs that people were moved by his words.

Their words.

Clasping her hands together, she blinked back the sting of salt against her lids. *We did it—two as one, with the whole stronger than either of the separate parts.*

John spoke on, his voice alternating between soft and soaring. Just as rehearsed, he modulated his voice to lift the last lyrical passage to a heartfelt crescendo.

A thunderous applause broke out as he returned to his seat.

"By Jove, he did well," murmured Henry.

"Oh, exceedingly well," agreed Cecilia. "But then, I never doubted it for an instant."

"My wife is, of course, prejudiced," said Henry with a fond smile. "What is your opinion, Miss Sloane? Do you think Wrexham was good enough to win the votes needed to pass the bill?"

Olivia listened to the cheers echoing through the hall.

"I think he was more than good, sir. He was...he was perfect."

"A toast to your eloquence, Wrexham." Yet another of his fellow politicians clapped him on the back and raised a glass of champagne.

"Thank you, Sumner." John looked around Cecilia and Henry's drawing room, his gaze seeking Olivia as he quaffed a small sip. "However, the victory is not mine alone. There were a great many people who worked very hard to win passage of this bill."

"Yes, but you've proven yourself an able spokesman," said Sumner. "Let us meet sometime next week to discuss your future within our party. I think you have the makings of a very effective leader."

"Thank you," he repeated, grateful that Sumner nodded and then moved away to join several other colleagues who were seeking out his sister to take their leave.

A few more congratulations were offered, but to his relief, the room was beginning to empty. Only a few family friends lingered.

And Olivia.

She was there in the recessed corner of the display alcove, perusing some of Henry's collection of Elizabethan poetry books.

"Hail the conquering hero," she murmured, an enigmatic smile flitting along the dimly lit curl of her lips as he came to stand by her side.

John grimaced. "Oh, bosh—to the Devil with such drivel. I should hope you know me better than to think I let any of these undeserved accolades puff up my conceit."

Olivia kept her gaze on the gilt-stamped leather spines.

"You were wonderful." The slanting shadows made it impossible to read her eyes.

"We both know it was because of *us*, not *me*."

"You have more than proved your mettle in this field of battle, Wrexham."

The cool formality of his title caused his jaw to clench. He missed the intimacy of his given name spoken in her smoky whisper.

"From now on," she continued, withdrawing a step deeper into the muddle of grays, "you need no help in winning future victories."

There is only one victory that matters to me.

John touched her arm, the heat of her skin beneath the slubbed silk setting off a flare of longing. "Come, I've something I want to show you. It's in the library."

"But the guests," she protested.

"The guests are leaving, and Cecilia and Henry will keep those who linger entertained," he cut in. "This is more important than hearing more meaningless praise."

Olivia let him lead her through the side salon and into the corridor.

"What is it?" she asked.

"A surprise." The paneled door opened with a soft *snick* of the latch. Feeling a flutter of butterflies in his belly, John drew her past a pair of fluted bookshelves and into one of the side study nooks. Strange how facing off against an opposing force of French Grenadier Guards hadn't made him feel half so nervous as he felt now.

The light from the argand lamp cast a mellow glow over the work table. Centered on the polished oak was a chess set carved out of ivory and a deep, dark amber. In the flame's gentle undulation, the subtle hues of gold and fire-kissed honey seemed to come alive.

John heard her breath catch in an audible gasp. "It's—it's the Russian set from Mr. Tyler's shop!"

"I wanted to give you a...special token of thanks for all your help," he explained. "I thought you might like this set, and Mr. Tyler agreed." He found himself fiddling with the fob on his watchchain. "Sorry, it's not as exotic—or erotic—as the forces that first brought us together. But as soon as I touched the figures, it felt right."

"It's perfect," said Olivia.

"Nothing's perfect," he said wryly.

A wink of emerald flashed over the amber hues. "You are," she whispered.

The words were too muddled by the cracking coals in the hearth for him to be sure of what she had just said. Too cowardly to ask her to repeat them, John slipped into one of the facing chairs.

"Shall we give them a baptism of fire, so to speak?"

Olivia took the other seat. John had chosen to play the amber side, and as he squared the pawns into precise military alignment, she ran a fingertip along the contours of her ivory queen. *Black and white, dark and light.* And yet, like life, the essence of the game was rarely defined in such starkly simple terms.

Chess is so bloody complicated, Caro had once complained.

"Your move," murmured John.

Choosing a safe opening sortie, she nudged a pawn forward.

"What, no bold moves, no unexpected attacks?" he murmured.

The gentle teasing stirred the echo of Caro's admonition. *Sometimes you must take a risk to make a wish come true.* Did she dare play with her heart and not her head?

As John contemplated his response, Olivia watched his hands hovering over his pieces, the sun-bronzed fingers seeming to capture the sparks of light reflected up from the faceted amber. *Capable, caring*—now more than ever, she was aware of their strength, their grace, their gentleness.

Tears suddenly welled up against her lids. Oh, how she would miss his touch. The idea that she might never again feel him holding her was unbearably awful.

Ducking her head, Olivia drew in a steadying breath, feeling her courage flag, despite all the words of encouragement from her sisters. Perhaps it was better to feign indifference rather than risk outright rejection.

Or, even worse than rejection, she feared any hint that she was regretting her earlier refusal might result in an offer merely based on his sense of honorable obligation.

She didn't want his pity. She wanted his love.

There was a bond between them, to be sure. Camaraderie, perhaps, or something even deeper, twined in their shared passion for words—but he had never said "love" aloud.

Unsure of herself, Olivia maintained a stoic silence.

John shifted, and she sensed him watching her through the undulating flicker of the candle flame. The light danced over the opposing armies and his tapered fingers as he made his move.

She countered without uttering a word.

On they played, no sounds between them save for the faint *click* of the ivory and amber against the checkered tiles. One by one, the soldiers surrendered to the subtle play of attack and counterattack until there were only a few pieces left on the board.

"It appears we have a stalemate," said John finally, after surveying the positions.

"So it does." She reached out to shift her king back to its staring square but all of a sudden his fingers encircled her wrist.

"A moment, Olivia."

"W-we must not indulge in such intimacies as given names anymore, Wrexham."

"Why not?" he pressed.

Because. The warmth of him against her skin sent a shuddering pulse of need spiraling to the most intimate spot of all. "Because."

"Because isn't an answer," said John. "It is a shield."

Then why do I feel so achingly vulnerable?

"You've allowed me to share your passions—your words, your ideas, your sensuality," he pressed. "But as to your true feelings, those you keep well guarded."

Olivia found her tongue too tied in knots to answer.

"What is it you fear? The chance that you might be hurt again by love?"

"I wasn't in love." Somehow, she managed to maintain some semblance of steadiness to her voice. "I was infatuated. There is a big difference."

"True," agreed John. He released his grip, and the sudden curl of chill air against her skin stirred a pebbling of gooseflesh. "Are you in love now?"

"I—I thought the game of thrust and parry was over."

John leaned in, a glitter she had never seen before lightening his brown eyes to swirling shades of molten amber. Olivia felt a little like one of the primordial flies that could often be seen, trapped for eternity, within the ancient resin.

"There are still a few moves left to be played." His palm slowly slid up her forearm.

"That's cheating," she rasped. "None of the chess pieces are allowed to move in such a way."

His laugh was low and husky. "I've made up a new variation. In this match, the goal is to checkmate the queen. And the pawns"—he tickled his fingers over the crook of her elbow and up to her shoulder—"are allowed to move in a less regimented direction than straight or diagonal lines."

"Wrexham—"

"John," he corrected. His hand was now lightly twined in her hair. "You didn't answer my question."

"No wonder you have a sackful of medals for prowess on the battlefield," said Olivia, trying not to inhale the spicy essence of his scent. "You are utterly relentless—and ruthless—in your attack."

"Am I?" Rising, he pulled her up out of her chair and drew her close. So close that she could feel the beat of his heart stir the hair's breadth of air between them. "In this particular campaign, I feel I've been utterly inept."

"You," she whispered, "could never be called inept."

"Yet I've done nothing but trip over my boots in my attempt to cut through the opposing army and capture my queen."

The tickle of his warm breath on her cheek stirred a lick

of need between her legs. "I'm not a queen. I'm an idiot." A rueful grimace tugged at her mouth. "A cretin, a—"

His lips silenced the litany.

She held herself very still, all thoughts giving way to simply savoring his taste, his feel, his scent.

John.

JOHN.

His essence had her dizzy with longing—had she said his name aloud? She was only dimly aware of a sound slipping free as she opened herself to his kiss.

An answering growl reverberated in his throat as their tongues touched and twined in a dancing, delving lover's embrace. There was nothing gentlemanly about John's response—the rumble of raw, masculine need sent shivers skating up and down her spine.

"Marry me, Olivia." It wasn't a request, it was a demand.

Olivia felt as if every bone in her body had suddenly puddled into a pool of liquid desire. Clutching at the broad slope of his shoulders, she leaned in against his length, acutely aware of solid, chiseled muscle and aroused male.

His mouth broke free and was now tracing a hot, wet trail along the line of her jaw. "Marry me," he repeated.

"But…" *But I hardly dare hope for such joy.* "…But I'll never be a conventional countess," she cautioned.

"Which makes you the perfect countess for me." John slowly slid his hands up to frame her face, the touch of his palms deliciously warm against her skin. "I've no intention of being an indolent earl who fritters away my existence in frivolous pleasures and drunken debaucheries. I want to use what talents I have to serve a higher good."

Good. At heart, he was such a *good* man.

"Admit it, Olivia, we match up well," he went on. "Like chess, our life together will play out in infinitely intriguing variations of two equals challenging each other, inspiring each other." He pressed a light kiss to the tip of her nose. "I love your intelligence, I love your passions." For an instant, his eyes darkened with a swirl of primal lust. "And I love your body."

That look make her hot all over. "I won't temper my tongue, you know."

"Did I neglect to mention that I love your tongue?"

"Even if I shock you at some times?" she asked, thinking back to their first smoke-shrouded encounter.

"I should be greatly disappointed if you didn't." His smile turned a little crooked. "One should never become complacent, and you shall..." His mouth quirked. "...How did Cecilia phrase it?—rattle my cage enough to keep me from becoming too self-satisfied."

Olivia felt her throat tighten. It was oh-so tempting. But despite all his eloquence, she still hadn't heard the one sentiment she yearned for.

"It seems that a number of my physical and mental attributes meet with your approval. But..."

"Ah." John's eyes took on a more intense glitter. "But the sum of the parts does not quite equal your expectations?"

"I'm not overly interested in mathematics," she mumbled.

"No, of course not. Language is your field of expertise. And you wish to hear me express my feelings in proper English."

"That would be nice," responded Olivia.

"Nice?" One of his divinely deft hands closed over her right breast, and through the layers of silk and cotton, his thumb found the sensitive nubbin and began slow, sensual stroking.

"More than nice," she gasped as the air slowly leached from her lungs.

"Ah. Does that mean if I do this"—her left breast was suddenly afire—"it would be twice as nice?"

"You do have a way with words," she replied, arching into his touch.

"I've a good deal more to say on the subject," he murmured, his voice growing a little ragged, as if he had imbibed a bottle of brandy in one gulp. "However, I think for now I shall keep it short and simple."

No, no, no. She wanted it to go on forever.

"I love you, Olivia," said John.

She met his gaze and in that instant, she knew it was true. His dark eyes were alight with molten fire.

Joy swelled inside her until she feared she might burst apart into a thousand little pieces.

"Have I rendered The Beacon speechless?"

"I'm not The Beacon with you," she said. "No fancy rhetoric, no fiery monikers—I am just Olivia."

"Who is, my love, wondrous beyond words."

Olivia let out a squeak, but only because he suddenly spun her around and thrust her up against one of the carved bookshelves lining the alcove.

"I don't think—" she began.

"That's right. Don't think." He nudged his knee between her legs. "Just feel."

She gasped as John propped a booted foot on the acanthus leaf rail, lifting her off the parquet floor in a frothing of skirts. She was now sitting astride his thigh, with the heat of him pressing against her most feminine spot. His hard possessive kiss rocked her back. Her own eager response slid her forward.

Oh. Oh. Oh. The sensations pulsing through her body were unbearably wonderful.

He laughed, a low, rough-edged rumble redolent of smoke and shared secrets. A wicked gleam danced in his eyes.

Looking down, Olivia saw her skirts were now ruched up over her knees.

"We shouldn't—we mustn't—be doing this," she protested feebly. "It's against every rule of civilized behavior."

"To the Devil with rules. From the very beginning there has been nothing remotely conventional about our relationship. Why change now?"

Why, indeed?

John's kisses now seemed to be everywhere at once—on her jaw, on her throat, on the "V" of flesh dipping down between her breasts. "There is something to be said for giving in to primal urges from time to time."

Hitching closer, she found the fastenings of his shirt and slipped her hand inside, her fingers slowly tickling through the course curls peppering his chest. She heard his breath catch in his throat and smiled. That she could bring such a look of desire to his face was as heady as drinking a goblet of the finest champagne.

Excitement bubbled through her blood.

He nipped her earlobe. "You make me want to cast caution and common sense to the wind. It's . . ."

"Exquisitely exciting," she murmured. "Enticingly

erotic." She paused for breath reveling in the male textures of his body. "But that may be because I'm not thinking very clearly."

"Yes, I'm finding it hard to think, too. Especially when I am touching you here." A rustle of silk. "And here."

Olivia was finding it difficult too. Pleasure was pulsing through her veins, tingling over her skin, hazing her brain. "This," she heard herself say, "is really very naughty of us." Her lips found his again. "Your sister would be shocked if she knew."

A whisper of mirth quivered against her mouth. "I have an inkling my sister knows exactly what is going on in here. And heartily approves. So…" A delicious warmth was now sliding up the inside of her thighs. "…Don't stop what you are doing."

"Oh, well, in that case…" Emboldened by the note of need in John's voice, Olivia let her hands rove from the slabbed planes of his chest down over his ribs and around to the long, lean line of muscles surrounding his spine. She wanted to know every fiber and sinew, every subtle shape and contour of his beautiful body and how they responded to her.

"I love touching you," she confided.

Love. Strange how love could transcend mere words. Never, ever had she dreamed of finding a man with whom she felt so elementally entangled in mind, in body, in spirit.

"And I you." John's demonstration snapped her out of her reveries. "Which reminds me—you haven't said yes yet."

"Haven't I?"

"Definitely not. I would remember it."

She traced a fingertip along his jaw. "How do you spell 'yes'?"

"You don't spell it," he growled. "You feel it. Here, and here."

She let out a little purr.

"And here."

The sound was now more of a moan. "That's *very* wicked." And very wonderful. "I—I think you had better stop, before our tentative tiptoeing down the Road to Perdition turns into a runaway gallop."

"Then say it," demanded John.

Deciding that her teasing had gone on long enough, Olivia hitched closer and leaned her head on his shoulder. "Yes."

"Louder."

"Ye gods, if you are going to revert to being the Perfect Military Officer and bellow orders at me, I may have to reconsider."

"It wasn't precisely an order." He smiled. "It was more of a request."

"Well, in that case..." A resounding "yes" filled the alcove, its echo mellowed by the carved wood and leather bindings.

"Excellent. That means we—"

A much louder sound suddenly intruded on their intimate interlude.

Rap, rap. It came again. "John? John? That's enough chess for one evening. It's time to return to the drawing room. Henry has brought up a special bottle of port from the cellar."

John let out a martyred sigh. "You know, much as I

adore my sister, she has an unfortunate habit of interrupting us just when things are getting interesting."

"And Scottie and Lucy are eager to join in the celebration," added Cecilia. "Cook has made them a pitcher of festive fruit punch."

He eased Olivia down off his knee and helped her fluff her skirts back into place. "But I suppose in this case we had better bow to convention and put off our wild urges until later."

The loss of his big, warm body drew an exhale from Olivia as well. "True. I imagine that by this time Cecilia and Henry are wondering what sort of game we are playing in here."

He chuckled. "No they're not."

She straightened his collar and retied his cravat. "I hope they won't mind having the Hellion of High Street as part of their family."

"I think they are nearly as happy as I am." He blew out another breath. "Speaking of which, three weeks of reading the banns of marriage is a deucedly long time to wait before we can become man and wife. However, much as I would prefer to obtain a special license and have the ceremony tomorrow, it's probably best to be patient, so as not to stir any whispers of scandal in Society."

"My sisters would find it highly romantic if we were to do something shockingly scandalous," said Olivia dryly. "However, my mother would not. And seeing as she's suffered enough worry on my account, I ought to allow her to enjoy the moment she thought would never come."

Flashing a roguish grin, John drew a slim book out from one of the bookshelves. "I shall present her with this gift when I pay her a formal engagement visit." He angled the gilt-stamped title into the candlelight.

All's Well That Ends Well.

A spark of joy, sweeter than summer sunlight, lit inside her. She still had her secrets, but the shadows were gone. "I couldn't have penned a better summation myself."

"And now, my love, let us go announce our betrothal."

Chapter Twenty-Seven

*H*uzzah!" exclaimed Prescott on hearing the happy news. His voice rose in excitement, along with his glass of punch. "Huzzah! Huzzah! Huzzah!"

John refrained from remarking on the berry-red slosh of liquid that was now dribbling down his son's shirtfront. Olivia wouldn't bat an eye at strawberry jam in the hair or a frog in the pocket. The thought made him smile.

"Yes, huzzah," added Lucy after a tiny hesitation. "I admit that you were right, Scottie, and I was wrong. Writing the letter was an excellent idea."

"Thank you, Lucy," murmured Olivia.

"You are welcome, Miss Sloane," replied the little girl with equal formality. "Will you show me how to shoot with a sling?"

"We had to return Lord Davenport's weapon, but I daresay we can contrive to make something similar on our own. And the back lawns of Wrexham Manor offer all sorts of interesting objects for target practice."

"Huzzah!" chorused Lucy.

"I told you that taking pen in hand was worth the risk of getting a birching from Wilkins the Wasp," said Prescott rather smugly.

"A knack for putting words on paper seems to run in the family," said John quickly before Lucy could retort. He winked at Olivia. "It seems we owe a debt of gratitude to Mr. Hurley's newspaper for bringing us together. I shall be sure to send him a case of champagne from Berry Brothers."

She waggled a brow in warning.

Yes, some secrets we will keep just to ourselves, he thought to himself. That Olivia and he would have a lifetime together of sharing not only secrets but passions and friendship was far more intoxicating than the rare wine gracing his crystal goblet.

"Speaking of which," murmured Cecilia, "I just received a note from Lucy's father saying that sacks of letters in response to the advertisement are still arriving at the inn."

"You may assure Simmonds that the matter will be taken care of," replied John.

"I propose another toast," chimed in Henry with a lop-sided grin. "To Hurley, to Simmonds, to the Royal Mail coach!"

"I think perhaps we've all imbibed enough spirits for the night," said Cecilia, slanting a look at her husband's cheerfully flushed face. "And the children have already been up long past their bedtime." She rose, ignoring the grumbled protest from Prescott. "Come along, you two. We have a very full day scheduled for tomorrow. First we must stop and pay our respects to the Sloane family. And then we shall finally finish our tour of the Tower menagerie."

"And if some villain tries to snatch Scottie again," said Lucy, "I shall knock him on his bum and feed him to the lion."

"No villain would dare challenge such a highly decorated warrior," said John. He had awarded the little girl one of his medals for valor, and she had worn it proudly pinned to her dress ever since. "However, the danger is over. You two are safe."

Lucy's chest puffed out with pride, but she didn't look quite convinced. "Maybe Scottie and I could take boxing lessons at Gentleman Jackson's saloon, just to be sure."

"Oh, what a corking good idea." Olivia cracked her knuckles. "I have always wanted to learn how to throw a right cross."

John repressed a bark of laughter. The legendary pugilist would probably fall into a dead faint if a female tried to set foot in his exclusive establishment. "I've a better idea. I shall hire one of Jackson's assistants to come give you all private lessons at the Manor."

This time it was Olivia leading the shouts of "Huzzah!"

"The Manor is going to be lots more fun to visit, Scottie, now that Miss Sloane will be there," confided Lucy in an overloud whisper.

So it is, thought John, offering up a silent prayer of thanks for pens, papers, and a newspaper editor who knew a good story when he saw it.

"You are supposed to be sleeping." Closing the bedchamber door behind her, Lucy padded toward the desk, where a single candle was burning brightly.

"So are you," answered Prescott, not looking up.

"I heard a scratching noise, so I thought I had better

come investigate." She craned her neck to look over his shoulder.

"What are you writing?"

"A letter."

Lucy gurgled a warning sound deep in her throat. "My father says there is an old adage about pressing your luck…" She angled a step closer. "It's not another advertisement, is it?"

"Yes." Prescott carefully dipped his pen in the inkwell and resumed his efforts.

"For what?" pressed Lucy, unable to contain her curiosity.

"A brother," replied Prescott. "Or a sister," he added hastily. "Girls are not so bad."

"Oh, no," said Lucy decisively. "No."

He looked up with a scowl. "Why not? It worked like a charm last time. Even you admitted tonight that it was a good idea."

"Yes, but…" Lucy took a perch on the corner of the desk. "Do you know where brothers and sisters come from?"

"Of course I do, you goose," he replied. "From storks, who drop them down the chimney."

Lucy fiddled with the end of her braid.

"There are an awful lot of stork nests in London," went on Prescott. "Surely someone who reads the *Morning Gazette* knows of one that contains what I'm looking for." After adding a last line, Prescott picked up the letter and handed it to her. "Here, read it over. I think it's rather better than the first one, if I say so myself."

She skimmed over the scribbling and shook her head. "Brothers and sisters do *not* come from storks."

"They don't?"

"Most definitely not."

His eyes narrowed. "Since you are so smart, I suppose you are going to tell me where they really come from."

"Well, as to that, I overheard Jem discussing babies with Sarah the barmaid, and…" She made a face. "I didn't exactly follow all they were saying, but trust me, it did *not* involve storks. I think perhaps this is something you should leave to your father and Miss Sloane."

"You really think so?"

Wadding the paper into a ball, Lucy tossed it into the still glowing coals of the fireplace. "Yes."

"But—" began Prescott.

"Trust me on this, Scottie." She reached for a fresh sheet of paper and slid it over to him. "If you want to write to Mr. Hurley again, why not simply thank him for the advertisement's resounding success."

An insistent *thump-thumping* interrupted a most delightful dream. "Go away," muttered Olivia, pulling the bed quilt over her head in hopes of recapturing the image of John's supremely sensual mouth and all the lovely sensations it had been stirring along the arch of her neck.

"Wake up, Livvie." The bedchamber door burst open, admitting her sisters.

"Look, look! We have something amusing to show you," said Caro.

"Mmmph." Olivia opened one eye just long enough to catch a flutter of newsprint and then shut it again. "Whatever it is, can't it wait until a more civilized hour?"

"It's nearly noon," exclaimed Caro. "You never sleep so late in the morning."

"Perhaps she's practicing to be an indolent idler of a countess," said Anna dryly. "Would Your Ladyship like a pot of chocolate served to her in bed?"

Uttering a very unladylike word, Olivia sat up and threw a pillow at her younger sister's head.

"Does that mean you would prefer *café au lait*?"

"Arggh. Please don't mention any sort of liquid libations." When Olivia had shared the momentous news with her sisters on returning to High Street, Anna and Caro had evinced not even a tiny bit of surprise—or none that she could remember. But then again, after a rather late and boisterous evening of festivities with John's family and a nip of celebratory sherry with her siblings, the details of the entire night were a trifle fuzzy.

"Remind me not to drink port again," she mumbled, wincing as a blade of sunlight cut through the window draperies.

"Because only the finest champagne is fit for a countess," announced Anna. "Ha, ha, ha."

"Oh, please, put a cork in it," retorted Olivia, and then took her head in her hands. "Ugh."

But despite the touch of queasiness in her stomach, she felt a delicious warmth spreading through the rest of her body as she recalled John's arms around her during the carriage ride home, and the intimate endearments he had whispered in her ear.

Love. Of all the words she had ever penned, that was perhaps the most powerful one of all…

Paper crackled as Caro once again waved the *Morning Gazette*. "Will you two stop your quibbling long enough for me to read this aloud?"

"Oh, go ahead." Olivia expelled a sigh. "It's likely the only way I'll get rid of you."

Caro rolled her eyes. "Ha! What would you do without us?"

"Go back to enjoying a peaceful sleep and sweet dreams," she replied dryly. Her smile, however, belied the teasing tone.

"Dreams of dark eyes and a shining suit of armor," chortled Anna. "And don't try to deny it. For all your avowals to the contrary, at heart you're as much of a romantic as we are."

"I am," admitted Olivia. "Truly. Madly. Deeply."

Caro rapped her knuckles on the bedpost. "Well, speaking of romance, there is a notice in this morning's newspaper on just that subject. It says—and I quote—*The editor of this newspaper requests the ladies of Mayfair to cease sending letters in response to our recent advertisement for a wife. The position has been filled. No other candidates need apply.*"

She looked up thoughtfully. "You know, Anna, have you considered that a newspaper advertisement could add a very interesting plot twist to your new work-in-progress—"

"Don't you dare," warned Olivia.

Anna's expression was impossible to read. "Never mind my novel," she murmured. "Do you think if *I* put an advertisement in the *Morning Gazette*, I would find a Perfect Hero for myself?"

Caro took a seat on the end of the bed and drew her knees up to her chest. "It seems to me that Perfect Heroes are rarer than hen's teeth. But you never know where you might find one…"

Anna Sloane delights in writing tales of romantic adventure and heated passion. But when she meets the gorgeous Marquess of Davenport, he shows her that reality can be even better than her wildest imaginings...

Please see the next page for a preview of

Sinfully Yours.

Chapter One

Alessandro twisted free and fell back against the rough stones just as a dagger thrust straight at his heart. Steel sliced through linen with a lethal whisper, but the blade cut naught but a dark curl of hair from his muscled chest.

"Tsk, tsk—you're losing your edge, Malatesta," he called, flashing a mocking smile. "In the past, your strike was quick as a cobra. But now..." He waggled an airy wave. "You're sluggish as a garden snake."

"You're a spawn of Satan, Crispini!" Another slash. "And I intend to cut off your cods and send you back to Hell where you belong."

"Oh, no doubt I shall eventually find my testicolos roasting over the Devil's own coals. But it won't be a slow-witted, slow-footed oaf who sticks them on a spit."

With a roar of rage, Alessandro's adversary spun into a new attack.

Whoosh, whoosh—*moonlight winked wildly off the flailing weapon, setting off a ghostly flutter of silvery sparks.*

As he danced away from the danger, Alessandro darted a quick glance over the tower's parapet. The water below was dark as midnight and looked colder than a witch's—

"Crispini—watch out!" The warning shout had an all-too-familiar ring. "Le Chaze is behind you!"

"Damn!" muttered Alessandro. He had told—no, no, he had ordered—the young lady to flee while she had the chance. But no, the headstrong hellion was as stubborn as an—

"Damn!" muttered Miss Anna Sloane, echoing the oath of Count Crispini, the dashingly handsome Italian Lothario whose sexual exploits put those of the legendary Casanova to blush. Throwing down her pen, she took her head between her hands. Several hairpins fell to the ink-spattered paper, punctuating a heavy sigh. "That's not only drivel—it's *boring* drivel."

Her younger sister, Caro, looked up from the book of Byron's poetry she was reading. "What did you say?"

"Drivel," repeated Anna darkly.

Caro rose and came over to peer over Anna's shoulder. "Hmmm." After a quick skim of the page she added, "Actually, I think it's not half bad."

"I used a knife fight to liven things up in the last chapter," said Anna.

"What about those clever little turn-off pocket pistols we saw in Mr. Manton's shop last week?" suggested Caro.

"Chapter Three," came the morose reply.

"Explosives?"

Anna shook her head. "I need to save that for when they hijack the pirate ship." She made a face. *Hijacking*— even that sounded awfully trite to her ears. "I don't know what's wrong with me. I seem to be running short of inspiration these days."

Caro clucked in sympathy. Like their older sister Olivia, the two younger Sloane sisters shared a secret passion for writing. "You've been working awfully hard these past six months. Maybe the Muse needs a holiday."

"Yes, well, the Muse may want to luxuriate in the spa waters of Baden-Baden, but Mr. Brooke expects me to turn in this manuscript in six weeks and I'm way behind schedule." Anna was much admired by London's *beau monde* for her faultless manners, amiable charm, and ethereal beauty. Little did they know that beneath the demure silks she wore a second skin—that of Sir Sharpe Quill, author of the wildly popular racy romance novels featuring the adventures of the intrepid English orphan Emmalina Smythe and the cavalier Count Alessandro Crispini.

"Perhaps you can bribe Her with champagne and lobster patties," quipped Caro, whose writing passion was poetry. "We are attending Lord and Lady Dearborne's soirée tonight, and they are known for the excellence of their refreshments."

Anna uttered a very unladylike word. In Italian.

"You would rather wrestle with an ill-tempered Word Goddess than waltz across the polished parquet in the arms of Lord Andover?"

"Andover is a bore," grumbled Anna. "As are all the other fancy fops who will likely be dancing attendance on us."

Caro lifted a brow. "Lud, you *are* in a foul mood. I thought you liked Andover." When no response came, she went on, "I know you'll think me silly, but I confess that I'm still a little dazzled by the evening entertainments here in London. Colorful silks, diamond-bright lights, handsome men—you may feel that the splendors of Mayfair's ballrooms have lost their glitter, but for me they are still very exciting."

A twinge of guilt pinched off the caustic quip about to slip from Anna's lips. Her sister had only recently turned the magical age of eighteen, which freed her from the schoolroom and allowed her entrée into the adult world. And for a budding poet who craved Worldly Experience, the effervescence of the social swirl was still as intoxicating as champagne.

"Sorry," apologized Anna. "I don't mean to cloud your pleasure with my own dark humor." She shuffled the stack of manuscript pages into a neat pile and shoved it to the side of her desk. "I supposed we had better go dress for the occasion." Knowing Caro's fondness for fashion, she forced a smile. "Which of your new gowns do you plan to wear? The pale green sarcenet or the peach-colored watered silk?" Her own choice she planned to leave in the hands of her new lady's maid. The girl was French and had already displayed a flair for choosing flattering cuts and colors.

"I haven't decided," replied Caro with a dreamy smile. "What do you think would look best?"

"You are asking *me*?"

"Only because I am hoping you'll ask Josette to come with you and give her opinion."

Anna laughed.

"Not that you don't have a good eye for fashion," said her sister. "You just refuse to be bothered with it."

"True," she conceded. "I find other things more compelling."

Caro cocked her head. "Such as?"

"Such as..." *A restless longing for something too vague to put a name to.*

Anna had carefully cultivated the outward appearance of a quiet, even-tempered young lady who wouldn't dream of breaking any of the myriad rules governing female behavior. Up until recently it had been an amusing game, like creating the complex character of Emmalina. But oddly enough, a very different person had begun to whisper inside her head.

The saint dueling with the sinner? As of yet, it was unclear who was winning the clash of wills.

"Such as finishing my manuscript by the due date," she replied slowly.

"Well, seeing as you are so concerned about being tardy," said Caro dryly, "perhaps we ought to start off this new resolve of good intentions by heading upstairs now."

Much as she wished to beg off and spend a quiet evening in the library, hunting through her late father's history books for some adventurous exploit that might spark an idea for her current chapter, Anna hadn't the heart to dampen her sister's enthusiasm. She dutifully rose.

"Oh, come now, don't look so glum," said Caro. "After all, inspiration often strikes when you least expect it."

* * *

Slipping behind a screen of potted palms, Anna exhaled sharply and made herself count to ten. The air hung heavy with the cloying scents of lush flowers and expensive perfumes, its sticky sweetness clogging her nostrils and making it difficult to breathe. Through the dark fronds, she watched the couples spin across the dance floor in a kaleidoscope of jeweltone colors and glittering gems. Laughter and loud music twined through the glittering fire of the chandeliers, the crystalline shards of light punctuated by the clink of wine glasses.

Steady, steady—I mustn't let myself crack.

"Ah, there you are Miss Sloane." Mr. Naughton, second son of the Earl of Greenfield and a very pleasant young man, approached and immediately began to spout a profuse apology. "Forgive me for being late in seeking your hand for this set. I've been looking for you everywhere."

Forcing a smile, Anna made no effort to accept his outstretched hand. "No apologies necessary, sir. The blame is mine. I—I was feeling a trifle overwarm and thought a moment in the shadows might serve as a restorative."

His face pinched in concern. "Allow me to fetch you a glass of ratafia punch."

"No, no." She waved off the suggestion. "Please don't trouble yourself. I think I shall just pay a visit to the ladies' withdrawing room"—a place to which no gentleman would dare ask to escort her—"and ask the maid for a cold compress for my brow."

Naughton shuffled his feet. "You are sure?"

"Quite." Suddenly she couldn't bear his solicitous

smile or the oppressive gaiety a moment longer. Lifting her skirts, she turned before he could say another word and hurried down one of the side corridors.

Her steps quickened as she passed by the room reserved for the ladies and ducked around a darkened corner. From a previous visit to the townhouse, Anna knew that a set of French doors in the library led out to a raised terrace overlooking the back gardens. It was, of course, against the rules for an unchaperoned young lady to venture outdoors on her own. But she had chosen the secluded spot with great care—the chances of being spotted were virtually nil.

The night air felt blessed cool on her overheated cheeks. "Thank God," she murmured, tilting her face to the black velvet sky.

"Thank God," echoed a far deeper voice.

A pale plume of smoke floated overhead, its curl momentarily obscuring the sparkle of the stars.

"It was getting devilishly dull out here with only my own thoughts for company."

Speak of the Devil!

Anna whirled around. "That's not surprising, sir, when one's mind is filled with nothing but thoughts of drinking, wenching, and gaming. Titillating as those pursuits might be, I would assume they grow tiresome with constant repetition."

"A dangerous assumption, Miss Sloane." Devlin Greville, the Marquess of Davenport—better known as The Devil Davenport—tossed down his cheroot and ground out the glowing tip beneath his heel. Sparks flared for an instant, red-gold against the slate tiles, before fading away to darkness. "I thought you a more sensible creature than to venture an opinion on things about which you know nothing."

Anna watched warily as he took one...two...three sauntering steps closer. Quelling the urge to retreat, she stood her ground. The Devil might be a dissolute rake, a rapacious rogue, but she would not give him the satisfaction of seeing her flinch.

"Sense has nothing to do with it," she countered coolly. "Given the rather detailed—and lurid—gossip that fills the drawing rooms of Mayfair each morning, I know a great deal about your exploits."

"Another dangerous assumption." His voice was low and a little rough, like the purr of a stalking panther.

Anna felt the tiny hairs on the nape of her neck stand on end.

He laughed, and the sound turned even softer. "I thought you a more sensible creature than to listen to wild speculation."

"Indeed?" Feigning nonchalance, she slid sideways and leaned back against the stone railing. Which was, she realized, a tactical mistake. The marquess mirrored her movements, leaving her no way to escape.

"I—I don't know why you would think that," she went on. "You know absolutely nothing about me."

"On the contrary. I, too, listen to the whispers that circulate through the *ton*."

"Don't be absurd." She steadied her voice. "I am quite positive that there's not an ill word spoken about me. I am exceedingly careful that not a whiff of impropriety sullies my reputation."

"Which in itself says a great deal," drawled Devlin.

"You're an idiot."

"Am I?" He came closer, close enough that her nostrils were suddenly filled with a swirl of masculine scents. *Bay rum cologne. Spiced smoke. French brandy. A hint of male musk.*

Her pulse began to pound, her breath began to quicken.

Good Lord, it's me *who is an idiot. I'm acting like Emmalina!*

Shaking off the horrid novel histrionics, Anna scowled. "You're not only an idiot, Lord Davenport, you are an *annoying* idiot. I'm well aware that you take perverse pleasure in trying to…"

Cocking his head, he waited.

"To annoy me," she finished lamely.

Another laugh. "Clearly I am having some success, so I can't be all that bumbling."

To give the Devil his due, he had a quick wit. Biting back an involuntary smile, Anna turned her head to look out over the shadowed gardens. Flames from the torchieres on the main terrace danced in the breeze, their glow gilding the silvery moonlight as it dappled over the thick ivy vines that covered the perimeter walls.

She shouldn't find him amusing. And yet like a moth drawn to an open fire…

"What? No clever retort?" said Devlin.

Anna willed herself not to respond.

"I see." Somehow he found a way to inch even closer. His trousers were now touching her skirts. "You mean to ignore me."

"If you were a gentleman, you would go away and spare me the effort."

"Allow me to point out two things, Miss Sloane. Number one—I was here first."

The marquess had a point.

"And number two..." His hand touched her cheek. He wasn't wearing gloves and the heat of his bare fingers seemed to scorch her skin. "We both know I'm no gentleman."

Devlin saw her eyes widen as the light pressure on her jaw turned her face to his. It wasn't shock, he decided, but something infinitely more interesting. Miss Anna Sloane was no spun-sugar miss, a cloying confection of sweetness and air that would make a man's molars stick together at first bite. He sensed an intriguing hint of steel beneath the demure gowns and dutiful smiles.

If I had to guess, I would say that she's not averse to the little game we have been playing.

She inhaled with a sharp hiss.

Or maybe I am simply in a state of drunken delusion.

It was entirely possible. Of late he had been imbibing far more brandy than was good for him. Only one way to find out.

He would give her a heartbeat to protest, to pull away. Yes, he was dissolute, but not depraved. A man had to draw the line somewhere.

She made a small sound in her throat.

Too late.

The tiny throb of her pulse beneath his fingertips had signaled her time was up. Devlin leaned in and felt their bodies graze, their lips touch.

A mere touch, and yet it sent a jolt of fire through him.

He froze. The distant laughter, the faint trilling of the violins, the rustling leaves all gave way to a strange thrumming sound in his ears.

Anna shifted and Devlin shook off the sensation. It *must* be the brandy, he decided. He had just come from his club, where he had been sampling a potent vintage brought up from the wine cellar. Women had no such effect on him.

A kiss was a distraction, nothing more. A way to keep boredom at bay.

"Go to Hell." Anna's whisper teased against his mouth as she jerked back.

"Eventually," growled Devlin. "But first..." He kissed her again. A harder, deeper, possessive embrace.

Her lips tremored uncertainly.

Seizing the moment, he slipped his tongue through the tiny gap and tasted a beguiling mix of warmth and spice. Impossible to describe.

He needed to taste more.

More.

Clasping his arms around her waist, Devlin pushed her back a little roughly, pinning her body to the unyielding stone. She tensed and twisted...

I am Satan's spawn.

...and then went still.

Time seemed to stop, hang suspended within the shifting shadows of the fluttering leaves. A myriad sensations seemed to skate over his skin. *Fire. Ice. The slow softening of her resistance.*

Anna made another sound. No words, just a soft feline purr that drifted off into the darkness. She moved, tilting forward in a tentative tasting of her own. Entwined, they swayed, weightless in the cool caress of the night.

Somewhere close by, a door opened and shut.

The echo broke the strange spell. With a shudder,

Anna wrenched free of his hold, a gasp fluttering through her gloved fingertips as she touched her lips.

Disgust? Disbelief?

Devlin blinked, not quite certain of his own feelings.

For a fleeting moment it looked as though she was going to speak, but instead, she shoved him aside and walked off without a word.

Walked with her head held high, her spine ramrod straight, he noted, rather than pelter off in a torrent of tears and sobs.

Hard and soft—no question Anna Sloane was a contradiction.

Which made her a conundrum.

But Devlin liked puzzles. They kept his own inner demons at bay.

Fall in Love with Forever Romance

A HOPE REMEMBERED
by Stacy Henrie

The final book in Stacy Henrie's sweeping Of Love and War trilogy brings to life the drama of WWI England with emotion and romance. As the Great War comes to a close, American Nora Lewis finds herself starting over on an English estate. But it's the battle-scarred British pilot Colin Ashby she meets there who might just be able to convince her to believe in love again.

SCANDALOUSLY YOURS
by Cara Elliott

Secret passions are wont to lead a lady into trouble... Meet the rebellious Sloane sisters in the first book of the Hellions of High Street series from bestselling author Cara Elliott.

Fall in Love with Forever Romance

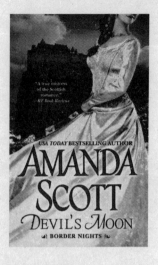

DEVIL'S MOON
by Amanda Scott

In a flawless blend of history and romance, *USA Today* bestselling author Amanda Scott transports readers again to the Scottish Borders with the second book in her Border Nights series.

THE SCANDALOUS SECRET OF ABIGAIL MacGREGOR
by Paula Quinn

Abigail MacGregor has a secret: her mother is the true heir to the English crown. But if the wrong people find out, it will mean war for her beloved Scotland. There's only one way to keep the peace—journey to London, escorted by her enemy, the wickedly handsome Captain Daniel Marlow. Fans of Karen Hawkins and Monica McCarty will love this book!

Fall in Love with Forever Romance

A KISS TO BUILD
A DREAM ON
by Kim Amos

Spoiled and headstrong, Willa
Masterson left her hometown—
and her first love, Burk
Olmstead—in the rearview
twelve years ago. But the woman
who returns is determined to re-
build: first her family house, then
her relationships with everyone
in town...starting with a certain
tall, dark, and sexy contractor.
Fans of Kristan Higgins, Jill
Shalvis, and Lori Wilde will flip
for Kim Amos's Forever debut!

IT'S ALWAYS BEEN YOU
by Jessica Scott

Captain Ben Teague is mad as
hell when his trusted mentor is
brought up on charges that can't
possibly be true. And the lawyer
leading the charge, Major Olivia
Hale, drives him crazy. But
something is simmering beneath
her icy reserve—and Ben can't
resist turning up the heat! Fans
of Robyn Carr and JoAnn Ross
will love this poignant and emotional military romance.

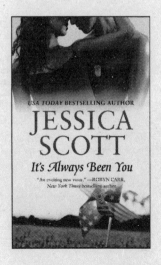

Fall in Love with Forever Romance

TOTAL SURRENDER
by Rebecca Zanetti

Piper Oliver knows she can't trust tall, dark, and sexy black-ops soldier Jory Dean. All she has to do, though, is save his life and he'll be gone for good. But something isn't adding up...and she won't rest until she uncovers the truth—even if it's buried in his dangerous kiss. Fans of Maya Banks and Lora Leigh will love this last book in Rebecca Zanetti's Sin Brothers series!